# ____Thin Men of Haddam____

C. W. SMITH

# _Thin Men of Haddam_

Grossman Publishers–New York 1973

First published in 1973 by Grossman Publishers
625 Madison Avenue, New York, New York 10022
Published simultaneously in Canada by
Fitzhenry and Whiteside, Ltd.
SBN 670-70039-8
Library of Congress Catalogue Card Number: 73-7187
Printed in U.S.A.

*ACKNOWLEDGMENT*

Alfred A. Knopf, Inc.:   From "Thirteen Ways of Looking
at a Blackbird" from *The Collected Poems of Wallace Stevens*, Copyright © 1947, 1954 by Wallace Stevens. Re-
printed by permission of Alfred A. Knopf, Inc.

*To Gay*

*O thin men of Haddam*
*Why do you imagine golden birds?*
*Do you not see how the blackbird*
*Walks around the feet*
*Of the women about you?*

*WALLACE STEVENS*
*"Thirteen Ways of Looking at a Blackbird"*

# Sal si Puedes

# One

Bond asks how far Méndez thinks it is. He stretches an arm across the back of the driver's seat; Méndez sights along the barrel of his finger to just below the horizon where a slushpit burns, pitching smoke the color of wrought iron into the sky. The level sweep of the countryside below normally joggles his perspective; too, he must squint against a midday sun arcing like welder's light above the plain. From where he and Bond sit in the jeep atop the mesa the smoke uncurls like a sooty finger from a cube of firework gunpowder. Noting these conditions Méndez gauges cautiously, offers his measure.

"Two and a half miles."

Bond leans into the back seat, guffaws. "Nope, four and seven-tenths. Drove her last Saturday." Then, bobbing forward, draping a hand brown as oil-stained cowhide on the back of the empty seat, he relents. "Would of thought so too, though."

Before the riddle, Méndez was brooding, but about what he can't remember; he skims the smoke but finds no clue there. Sunlight flickering on the land pricks his eyes; he swings them left to the top strand of the barbed-wire fence, where a coyote hangs from his front paws, eyes like dried mulberries, tufts of loose fur dangling down his coat: the carcass looks like a bag of fur and bones patched together with sinew by a blind Indian bent on parodying creation. The wind gusts, blowing sand, and the stiff body bangs against the wire, tail whipping in circles: he's trying to climb the fence before he's shot. The image agitates Méndez—he imagines it distracts his memory.

"Must be ten years since I been hunting," Bond says. "Last time I went I bloed the end of my boot off, missed my big toe by a half a red hair."

"Jesus, you windy old fart, why don't you let a man alone?"

Bond laughs. "When a man claims he wants quiet all he wants is to churn hisself up. Listen to an old man mutter, takes your mind off things."

"But I don't *want* my mind off things."

"We was down in south Texas and I had my nephew's walleyed, moonstruck coon dogs—"

"You know I've heard this story must be at least a hundred times," Méndez mutters.

Bond swings forward. "Listen, you smart-ass pepperbelly," he drawls, then, because it will vex Méndez, over the back of the seat he extends an arm with an empty, white-cotton work glove pinned to the cuff of the sleeve (he lost the hand in a drilling-rig accident), then slaps the glove against the dusty cushion. "I can tell you this much—YOU AIN'T NEVER UNDERSTOOD IT!" His audience reproven, he lowers the glove: "They was bluetic coon dogs with eyes yella as a July sun. They wasn't just half-crazed, why they was plumb, plumb—" he falters, waiting for an adjective, then his maniacal, brick-colored face dances to the edge of Méndez's vision—"plumb *newrotic*," he declares, slyly dealing out a word from his listener's vocabulary.

"So after we had done set up camp," Bond continues, but Méndez's attention dissolves downward, caught by the sluggish dip and bow of the pumping units in the basin below him—icons of what he calls the Awl Cult. The idol of the cult—the pumping unit —is a large, metallic object constructed in the image of an animal (a more ordinary but perhaps more accurate analogy could be drawn between the unit and a monolithic grasshopper): from its midsection protrude two legs attached at the bottom to wheel-shaped weights which rotate, slowly, over and over, giving the entire structure the air of a two-legged horse trotting wearily in place. Méndez imagines himself to be a cultural anthropologist, snaps a photograph of the unit, adds a gloss: "Shown above is the fetish of the Awl Cult, a primitive religion of numerous adherents. Detailed study of the idol as a synthesis of modes of transportation has led many observers to conclude that, spurred apparently by a regeneration of primitive technology, the Cult deified motion on the premise that changes in spatial location are consequential to alterations in spiritual status. Some have noted that such a belief leads to the dangerous acceptance of the illusion of freedom without the substance of it, as the motion of the Image—that of a two-legged horse trotting wearily in place—so ironically gives witness to."

"Oil!" Méndez snorts.

"Chasing after those high-wared dogs—they was havaleeners around somewheres and pretty soon they come up on this here thicket and like a damn fool I started in to crawling—"

"Javelina? Last time I heard this story it was mountain lion."

"Well, God-da-mity! Sometimes I'd swear you didn't have the sense God give a golf-ball: havaleener, alley-cat, jack rabbit, stepant, cow paddy, or just a place to bleed our lizards, it don't matter! So there I was, crawling on all fours like a wart hog through this thicket," he goes on, but Méndez ignores him. He brushes a film of caliche fine and white as chalk dust from the knuckles of his left hand; the powder grinds farther down his pores. He shifts his brushing fingers to the juncture of his thumb and index finger, poises them over a faded tattoo, a small blue cross with two minute dots above the transverse bar—the sign of the *pachuco*, the *cholo*, etched with sewing needle and india ink twelve years ago, when he entered high school. While his thumbnail furrows the upright of the cross, as if he were thinking either of the process required to remove it or of making the line more visible by gouging it out, a hawk circles high above them hunting quarry, his outstretched primary feathers wavering at the ends of his wingspread like fingers drummed languidly on a translucent surface, gliding in a slow, drooping arc, foot by foot descending in a spiral whose counterclockwise bearing disconcerts Méndez, puzzles him (yet he can't explain his perplexity, doesn't know his sense of order assumes that things which descend in spirals [screws, bolts, bottlecaps, perhaps even history] descend clockwise; thus, the hawk's langorous, counterclockwise helix appears as unnatural as a contradiction whose fallacy he senses but can't articulate), then the hawk banks its curves, drops, and, a quarter-mile away, hidden behind a thicket of mesquite, an enormous flapping of wings as something is eaten. Slowly, with gathering momentum, images superimpose in a tumbling, disjointed montage—face of another *pachuco*, a member of his old *palomilla*, called the Snake, classroom desk, a pickup, pearl buttons on a western shirt, pack of Luckies, greasy overalls, patio outside their bungalow an Italian villa a word a lecturer used doubleteam? no doublegang no *doppelgänger* five children and someone returned from California—and tugging images apart to date them he recalls a college classroom and anecdotes from the life of a poet, then recently driving Houston's pickup into town on a Saturday, getting a haircut that day?, buying a new shirt, gassing up the truck at Colby's while burrowed safe, snug behind the wheel of the air-conditioned Ford, an upright, ice-cold Coke between his thighs, thinking of the patio he was planning?, and as a dark red rag swiped at the windshield he was retucking the new shirt into his belt, feeling watched as he admired the pearl buttons on the breast pockets, sipped from the Coke, replacing the bottle carefully, and peeled the strip of red tape from the pack of Luckies—and the rag had halted as if stuck to the windshield—what poet saw his *doppelgänger* one evening on the patio of his Italian villa?—saw a face bearing a two-inch knife scar above the right eyebrow with eyes the color and shape of minute ball bearings peering at him so coldly that for a moment he felt paralyzed, delicately pinching the tape from the cigarette package between the thumb and index finger of his right hand, framed in the gaze of the former Snake, who he had thought would remain in California forever, returned with five children to wear greasy overalls at a filling station, the corners of his mouth beginning a slow curl like burning paper: *Ay, ese! Cómo está El Vendido?* he said, accusing Méndez of some betrayal whose nature was all too clear; Méndez replied with a hint of irony that he was the same man still.

As Méndez sifts through these images, the tailings of which will reveal Manuelo, his cousin, Bond raves on like an actor rehearsing a violent role before a mirror, his handless left arm whipping the glove in the air like a lariat: "Just when I'd almost reached thuther side of the thicket I seen a movement up ahead and I thought God-da-mity now I'm in for it, here I am on my hands and knees about to be eye to eye with one of them ugly bastards—" (*Manuelo!* Méndez thinks.) Bond's arm drops to his side. "But I might better back up long enough to talk about the feller who dreamed up the notion that a dog can smell fear on a man because I mean to tell you that old boy's due for a first class ass-kicking."

Now that Méndez has unearthed Manuelo, the discovery seems more a transfiguration of anticlimax than a revelation.

And Bond won't leave him alone. "Now you listen up," he admonishes, jabbing Méndez's shoulder with a stick-hard finger of his one good hand. "This here's important. Sometimes I could swear this feller was pure-dee son-of-a-bitch, because when you come to think of what he could of said and put it upside what he offered up, then you can see what I mean. I'll give you a fer instance—suppose he said that a dog could *see* fear on a man, why then that wouldn't be no problem: the biggest, meanest, ugliest caynine in twenty-six counties wouldn't pay you no mind because it ain't no trouble to *act* like you don't feel something you feel. And I don't doubt but what this here very idea didn't cross this old boy's mind and he probably throed it out just because it wasn't mean enough. More in likely this old boy's out hunting with some dogs and he seen one of his buddies who he knoed was nervous about dogs trying to *act* like he wasn't afraid so the dogs wouldn't *see* his fear, and so he probly sidled up to this buddy of his and whispered real serious and sly in his ear, 'You know . . . a dog can *smell* fear on a man.' And when he said that this other old boy probly thought he'd piss his pants. I ain't saying the idea ain't true, because it might be, but they's some ideas just don't do no good to know whether they's true or not, especially them there ones like this here one you can't put out of your head. Now you look here how mixed up it gets—" He stops to recall Méndez's attention with a second jab. "If you fear a dog and you think this here idea is true, then the first thang happens when a hunnerd pound German *sheep*-herden dog starts growling is you think of ways to outsmart him, you say to yourself, 'I'll act like I ain't afraid of him and maybe that'll change my smell,' but you ain't so sure you can change your *smell* by acting different, and when he's growling louder and louder and getting closer and closer the idea comes to your mind that if he's so good at smelling that he can smell fear, then he can damn sure smell the smell of a man trying to change his smell by acting like he's not afraid—I mean there ain't no limit; he can smell outright, undercover, sideways, double-back and upside-down fear. So then you start thinking maybe you can fool the dog by fooling yourself, that if you can talk yourself into *thinking* that you ain't afraid, then surely the dog can't smell something on you that you think you ain't got, but the first time you come face to face with the dog again, you get the feeling that he can smell bettern you can *think*, that all you're doing is smelling like a man who talked hisself into thinking he ain't afraid. Or even if by chance you ain't afraid and up comes this here dog and you give him a pat or two on the head, all the time congradulating yourself, it won't be five seconds until you start worrying how long it'll last, and the more you start worrying about how long it'll last, the more you start being afraid of being afraid, and the more you start being afraid of being afraid, the afraider you'll get until finally you know that if he can't smell *ordinary* fear on you, he can smell the fear of being afraid you'll be afraid. Hellfire, for all I know, a dog can even smell the fear of being afraid you'll be afraid of being afraid. This here notion got started and to this day there ain't no way of knowing whether it's true or not, but it's only people's fear keeps it alive; least, I never heard of it working to anybody's advantage."

Bond pauses, resettles himself in the rear seat, and begins to roll a cigarette with his one good hand, an intriguing process worth close observation of its extraordinary detail, but Méndez cannot part from his preoccupation long enough to note it: he thinks of Manuelo, who is presently hitching a ride on the rear of a sprung-framed '49 Indian motorcycle whose driver is part Mescalero-Apache and an Airman 2nd Class AWOL from his post at Lackland AFB. Méndez concentrates on Manuelo, who straddles the saddle's back rim, skin of his face pulled taut by drag, eyes blearing near the end of their ride. He might have caved the

Indian's head in with a rock and stolen the cycle had the Indian been other than exile, like himself, but the Indian emits the acrid smell of pariah, has offered Manuelo small kindness—the penultimate Camel from an aging pack carried in his pants pocket—and has thus removed himself from the range of Manuelo's volcanic frustration. In return Manuelo has offered him a taco at Gómez's.

Bond's production of the One-Handed Cigarette Roll has passed unattended—Méndez refuses to acknowledge the one-handedness simply to thwart Bond, whose cigarette rolling he believes to originate more from histrionic impulse than economic necessity.

"But I never gave no thought to none of this before the day I'm telling you about," Bond says, then bedecks the cigarette with a crowning lick along its gummed line (he had molded the paper in a crease in the lap of his Levis, sprinkled it with tobacco, then rolled it in the crack between his first and second fingers with his thumb). "Never had no fear of dogs, never gave it no thought. You take like August, when nothing stirring starts preying on people's minds and first thing you know somebody's seen himself a monster in a pasture somewheres. *Never* fails. Onct years ago in Arkansaw" (Méndez hears but wonders why he listens; he *wants* to think about Manuelo—that is, feels he *should*, thus *should want*—but Manuelo's features keep dissolving one by one like those of a cinema ghost, then reappearing as he strains to reconstruct his image) "around the Fina station one night with four five other old boys, paring our fingernails with penknives and making bets on whose Coca-Cola come the farthest away, when up drives this old boy who claims somebody done seen him a weird-looking thing up by the reservoir road, says that somebody else who saw the old boy who seen it said it looked like a ape, ran like a horse. Twict as big as a man. Hair all over its body and fangs long as your fingers. Said it was carrying a live shoat under its arm, tearing chunks of meat off it and eating them raw. We laughed, somebody said it must be one of them wowzers, somebody else thought it might be a buck nigger run off from the *in*sane asylum, and Billy Bob, man who run the station, said that he wisht they'd bring it to him when they caught it because he needed somebody that mean to rassle truck tires. Ever damn one of them acted like they didn't believe a word of it, but believe me they was aching for an excuse to think it was true. Old boy who come up with the news said he wasn't saying it was true, he was just saying what they was saying, but he knoed of cases where they'd had to kill something like that, in fact his daddy hisself had hept hunt one. Billy Bob went inside to answer the phone, come back out in a minute and ast if anybody'd seen Crabtree's kid, R.B., been missing since noon. Everybody was real silent for a minute, then they started putting two and two together and come up with twenty-six: that thing took Crabtree's kid, and inside half an hour they was thirty-one men and half a dozen cars gathered around that filling station. They had them twelve shotguns, six deer rifles, a brace of twenty-twos, an armload of pistols, a stack of tire tools, and two coon dogs, one named Riley and the other Squirrel. Somebody even brung one-half a pair of walkie-talkies, about as useful as tits on a boar hog. They was champing at the bit to get at that thing, they had hopped theirselves up into a frenzy over what it had done to that kid, yelling and carrying on, then they got organized and broke into five teams of six apiece. They was all chose up, except for this one old boy who was left over, and nobody wanted him because of who he was. Now *he*—"

Anticipating still another detour in an already circuitous narrative, Méndez ignores the exposition relevant to the thirty-first person, a welder of East European extraction named Clement Limnick, who was tolerated in the community only because he had married a local girl and because his arthritic hold on things American left their own touch more secure—he could never seem to remember that the local high school football team was labeled by the same word used to describe an indigenous species of wasp, so that when asked in a crowded barbershop what he thought of the Yellow-jackets that year he would invariably answer that they seemed thick and very frightening—and who, according to Bond, was afflicted both with periodic seizures of epilepsy and the persistent illusion that the community of man was composed of equally portioned and inextricably interlocking segments whose total could only correspond with the sum of the community's individual members. Méndez shifts slightly in his seat, tightening his jaw, a line jutting up suddenly from his memory—"Had somewhere to get and sailed calmly on." He thinks of Manuelo, who now asks Gómez to feed the Indian at his cafe; while they wait for tacos Manuelo stretches himself on the back of a chair, head slack, bowed. Gómez, at his grill: "So what happened?" Manuelo doesn't stir, doesn't want his anger dissipated in talk. Gómez shifts his weight from his right foot to his left, then back again, nervous, as though he fears Manuelo's anger might be aimed at him. "No work at the employment office, eh?" While he dunks a taco shell in the deep-fry cage, Gómez watches Manuelo over his shoulder. Then, as Méndez might guess he would, he tries to assure them both that he is faultless: "I told you I'd give you a job." Manuelo, whose toes have been tapping out a deliberate, martial cadence on the linoleum, claps both heels against the floor and glances up at Gómez: "Look, mahn, you know you can't do it. Forget it." Gómez appears to consider Manuelo's response, waits cautiously before answering: *Sí.* A sigh—hard truth to face. But Méndez would think Gómez feels secretly relieved.

"So when they got out by the reservoir and divvied themselves up again, this old boy was left by hisself, and since nobody had come up with a track to spoor with, Riley and Squirrel was jumping at anything that moved—"

And Méndez would also guess that as Gómez watches Manuelo he feels thankful that his own son, a sergeant with the Special Forces in Viet Nam, always gets three squares a day, or, as Gómez put it yesterday: *He gets clothes on his back, food in his belly, his children go to school.* Sure, what else? Gómez is the proprietor of a small cafe, a cafe which—yesterday—had the distinct air of a business without much business. Méndez and Bond had gone into town to pick up supplies for the ranch, and while Bond got a haircut Méndez wandered over to Fat Man's Cafe. He had anticipated a quiet half hour alone with a cup of coffee so that he could brood—with that peculiar pleasure/pain of scab-picking—about the radically unstable shifts in fortune (Fortune) the events of the previous two weeks had brought him.

Fat Man's brought him still another turn. As he entered and seated himself at the counter, Gómez rose from his lawn-chair perch behind the register to pour him coffee, the motions of his limbs weighted, plodding, like those of an old man on a damp morning.

"What's happening?"

Gómez leaned against the counter, mute, one hand gripped around the handle of the coffee urn, the other spaded in his hip pocket. His head twisted to one side as though something in the street had captured his attention. Recalling that Gómez sometimes remained incommunicative until he had sold a week-old piece of manufactured pie, Méndez dug into his pocket for change.

"Got any pie?"

"What kind you want?"

Méndez shrugged, then snapped a quarter against the counter-top with a touch of annoyance; Gómez slid a plate of apple pie toward him, scooped up the quarter and flipped it into the cash drawer after punching the No Sale button, palmed the drawer shut—his motions not brisk but perhaps hurried, as though the transfer of money were a clandestine activity—then he pressed the folds of his rotund belly against the drawer, crossed his chubby arms over the chromium ledge, and let his chin down onto the cushion of his wrists. His eyes shifted in their sockets like weary game birds resting in a temporary shelter.

Méndez nibbled at the pie, then shoved it aside.

"So what's happening in town?"

Gómez hesitated, his gaze floating over the empty tables beyond the counter.

"Rich get richer, poor get poorer."

"I know who's getting richer—who gets poorer besides me?"

"Manuelo for one—you remember him, no? Your cousin? I loaned him fifty dollars since July. García pays his doctor."

Méndez drew a long swallow of tepid coffee to still his irritation at Gómez's sarcasm, then grimaced.

"How come?"

Gómez raised his head from his forearm and turned toward the front window. "Why you think, mahn? You don't have to ask; it's the same as always—no job, sick wife, a houseful of kids, and nothing to eat but Gravy Train."

"I thought he was working construction."

"Got laid off a month ago."

Gómez's scrutiny converted Méndez's ignorance into guilt.

"I been busy. Since the old man died out there, everything's been up for grabs."

"*Órale.*" His okay is curt, skeptical. Méndez let it pass.

"Has he tried the employment bureau?"

"I think tomorrow. But you know those people. . . ."

Méndez nodded.

"Maybe out at the ranch—" Gómez gestured vaguely.

Méndez faltered. "Yeah, sure. I could ask. . . ." he replied lamely after a moment. Gómez allowed a wry smile to curl the corner of his lip as he swiped at the counter with a rag. He eased himself down into his aluminum lawn chair behind the counter, then retrieved a G.I. Joe comic book from the window ledge and walled off his face with it. Méndez fumed in silence—how many times had he run up against this myth about his control over the affairs at the ranch? Even before the elder Houston had died he was nothing more than a glorified flunkey, "foreman" in charge of only Bond and Carlos, who lived in town and only worked now and then. He could ask about a job for Manuelo, but he knew full well that there was nothing for him, unless he should replace himself. Or Bond. Perhaps in the future . . .

"You think I don't want to help?"

Gómez grunted.

"Did you think I wouldn't?" Agitated, Méndez shuffled his feet, then lifted his right buttock to ease his wallet from his pocket. "Did you think that? Here." He pointed a twenty-dollar bill at Gómez. "All I've got. *Dáselo.*"

Gómez refused to look at the bill. "Give it to him yourself."

"Mother of Christ! What's it matter? Come on, mahn, I've got things to do."

Gómez let the comic drop to his lap. "You're a busy man, eh? Maybe you'll be President someday, eh?" He glared at Méndez a moment, then raised the comic book to his face, his accusing eyes transformed by its cover into the raging features of Sergeant Kelly, gook-killer *extra-ordinaire* whom the cover artist had frozen in the act of ripping the pin of a hand grenade out with his teeth. Méndez burned a moment, then Gómez's accusation, coupled with the irony of his hypocrisy, drove him to attack.

"All right—how come you come off so clean? You tell me that? You sat around here on your butt for six months browbeating your boy into joing the army and going to Viet Nam just to—" he hesitated, aware that his anger was pushing him beyond the bounds of tact, "to be a . . . goddamn mercenary." He finished nervously, haltingly, sorry he had said it.

*"Hombre!"* Gómez roared, slapping the comic to his lap. *"Nada mas!"*

Méndez watched while a film of tears shimmered over the pupils of Gómez's eyes and welled along their lower rims; tremors pulsed upward from his gut and lodged themselves in his fleshy cheeks, and Méndez had the perplexing sense that it wasn't anger Gómez felt; for a long moment he locked his gaze on line with Gómez's, trying in bewilderment to read the nature of the other man's emotion, then Gómez dropped his eyes, embarrassed. It was as though he had suddenly been stricken by a heart attack and had been ashamed to ask for aid.

"*Mire, hombre.*" Méndez began softly to apologize, but Gómez waved him quiet.

"My boy . . ." He peered out the front window. "My boy, he's been wounded twice now, he can't be so lucky third." His voice was strangled, phlegmy.

"*And what good, amigo?*" Méndez countered gently.

Like a turret, Gómez's head rotated slowly to level gleaming eyes at Méndez: *He gets clothes on his back, food in his belly, his children go to school.*

*El Puto!* he could have answered but didn't. Instead, he rose and left the cafe with the sour consideration that for Gómez to encourage his son to become a mercenary and still make pretenses to morality was blatant hypocrisy. And the sacrifice would be for nothing. The words of Aguilar's letter of some two weeks past still rang in his ear: despite the blood shed by *la raza,* nothing would change at home.

And now, seated in the jeep, his vision idly framing the dashboard instruments, he thinks that the worst whore is the one who won't admit to prostitution. His hearing is dead to Bond's tale:

"While this one bunch was coming up through the woods on the east side of the reservoir they heard this sound like the bray of a donkey with a heavy case of asthma. Something was thrashing around in the woods, so they spread out and this one old boy laid hisself down behind a log and started sweating as this thing crashed around in the undergrowth, getting closer and closer and louder and louder, and then he spied this shadowy figger up ahead and he got scared and started in to squeezing the trigger on his shotgun and just before it went off he *knoed* the thing he was shooting at wasn't no monster and that there never had been no monster to begin with, he had knowed it all along just like the others had knoed it but there wasn't a one of them wanted to think there wasn't no monster—and just as this old boy jerked the trigger he seen that he had shot the foreign feller in the midst of a fit." Limbs askew, Bond sprawls limply in the rear seat like a scarecrow pummeled and gutted by dogs. Apparently Méndez isn't listening, so he continues, much softer: "Everybody told him not to worry. Coroner called it accidental death." He pauses, exhaling heavily, and stares at Méndez's unconscious back. "But you know he never knoed what that meant and the more he thought about them two words the more they started to seem like a nonsense noise like hogs rooting—it didn't have no connection with him—and he started getting this feeling that he was living in a foreign country and that he had done something that was against his own law but it wasn't against theirs and they had give him this here piece of paper that had these foreign words on it which they thought was supposed to tell not to worry; in fact, seemed like that paper said that it was good he did what he did because everybody seemed more worried about him than about the feller he shot." Spent, Bond pauses. Then: "And he, he," Bond breathes, but his voice uncoils to a limp strand inert on the air. Silence.

Méndez slowly grows aware of treble saw and ratchet of crickets, hiss of wind in the tall, dry grass, but nothing more, no voice.

Bond has fallen mute in the rising action of his tale; now, at least, Méndez can't remember having heard an ending. Bond's silence distracts him; he twists his head to peer into the rear seat, where Bond gazes out across the pastures, preoccupied, his pupils narrowed against the light. "So?" Méndez asks, not to be accused of inattention. Bond's pupils flick right, throb slightly, then recede to focus on Méndez's face. "So?" Bond returns the question.

"So you were hunting with some dogs."

"Yeah," he answers, his voice flat. Then adds, brightly, "So I was." He rustles in the seat, bends forward. "So I was crawling on my hands and knees through this here thicket I was too lazy to walk around and they was this thrashing and carrying on in front of me and I thought I'd done had it for sure, that one of them ugly havaleeners was going to be poking his face right into mine, that sharp little horn gouging at my eyes. I heard a dog growling and something tearing through the brush at me and I couldn't stand up and I couldn't even get up on my knees to shoot at it, and all of a sudden one of them mad coon dogs busted through the brush, snarling and rolling those red and yeller eyes and baring fangs long as rake teeth. For a minute I was real relieved, then the idea jumped into my mind that that dog didn't know who I was, that he thought *I* was the havaleener, so I said *'It's me, boy, it's me,'* but my voice just whipped him into a purple frenzy—he took to pawing at the ground and barking in my face and he was so close I couldn't get the rifle between us, and he commenced to back me out of that thicket, his face so close that I could see his gums and streams of spit drooling down his fangs and chops. So I backed up little by little, trying to remind him who I was, but I'd done forgot *his* name, so there wasn't no way I could make myself familiar to him. About that time all them other dogs had up and decided that the othern had cornered something big so they come leaping up behind him and they couldn't see me very well because he was in the way but they was going to take his word for it. And *they* commenced to howl and bark and snap their jaws and tried to work their way around him to get to me, and all sorts of crazy ideas leaped into my head—I got to thinking that, what with how good a dog can smell, they *knoed* who I was all along and they was pretending not to know so that they could just go right ahead and tear me limb for limb and everybody would just say, 'why them poor devils thought he was a havaleener,' and *then* I got to thinking that they knoed that I knoed it and they got a special pleasure from knowing that I knoed that they knoed who I was and couldn't prove that they knoed, almost like they was saying to me, 'You go right ahead and shoot then go tell your nephew that you shot us because you knoed that we knoed who you was and let on we didn't and you knoed there wasn't no way of really knowing it was true or not so you shot us—and you know damn good and well your nephew'll have you in a straight jacket in two seconds—you just go ahead and tell him that you shot his dogs because they knoed who you was.' " Bond pauses to catch his breath, "The whole thang reminded me of a dream I had about a flying saucer."

Méndez has heard the saucer story countless times too, including yesterday while going to Manuelo's, he remembers. He had left Fat Man's and stood outside on the walk trembling with the afterburn of the argument with Gómez, and as he was replacing the twenty-dollar bill into his wallet, Bond appeared, ruffling his copper-colored hair with his one good hand.

"God-da-mity! He shore sheared me! Must of

gouged my scalp a dozen times—and to think I paid a dollar-fifty for it. Be cheaper and less painful in the long run to get some dog tags and a rabies shot!"

Ignoring the complaint, Méndez clambered across the cutaway panel of the jeep, slid in behind the wheel, and beckoned curtly with his right hand.

Bond nodded wearily. "Hurry, hurry. Getting too old for it."

Méndez alligator-clipped the ignition wires together, jammed his instep on the starter plunger, swearing when the engine failed to catch.

Bond chuckled. "Man, somebody shore lit a bonfire under *you!*"

Méndez frowned, then when the engine finally fired he jerked the jeep in gear and it reared back from the curb.

"Damn if I didn't fall asleep in that barber chair and have me the weirdest dream I ever had," Bond chirped as the jeep left Fat Man's to the rear. He seemed oblivious to Méndez's state of mind. "Dream about a flying saucer."

Méndez dropped his jaw an inch to prepare for comment, hesitated, then reset his teeth together. Bond watched him, waiting.

"I was staying in my uncle's cabin. You remember, the one up on Bull Shoals?" Ordinarily the question would have been rhetorical, but Bond let it hang, demanding a reply. "You remember me telling you about it?"

Méndez responded against his will. "You've told me this story half a dozen times."

"Naw, I meant the cabin. I just now had the dream."

"Oh bullshit, mahn!"

"I've been known to speak with a forked tongue, but

I ain't lying about this here dream," Bond insisted. "You mean you don't believe it?"

Tired of bantering, Méndez gave in. "All right. All right. But Jesus, try to remember what comes out of your mouth from one day to the next."

"Well, I can't help how much I remember and I can't help how much I dream. My granddaddy used to say I was born dreaming and never woke up. Now ain't that the truth?"

"Yeah." Méndez thought of Manuelo. "Some people dream their lives away while others suffer."

"That ain't the whole truth, because sometimes, you know, the dreamers do a bit of suffering and the sufferers do a bit of dreaming." Annoyed, Méndez listened as an oral vestige of Bond's former life as a shirt-sleeves preacher slid beneath the surface of his voice—a tone of wearied melancholy used to express sentimentalisms whose content Méndez found as irritating as the form.

He eyed Bond. "Just don't *preach* to me, mahn, I got things on my mind."

He braked the jeep sharply to avoid a dog scurrying across the street, then drove on, slower. Bond had taken his outburst in silence, and now his eyes remained on the street before him. Méndez sensed he had hurt Bond's feelings, and after a moment he felt the flat edge of guilt nudging against his chest.

"Sorry," he muttered at last. "You were talking about a dream?"

"Flying saucer," Bond offered brightly, but Méndez lapsed into sour inattention, feeling cheated to discover that Bond's obliviousness to his indignation had turned his rage toward all Anglos toward Bond, and because he felt guilty at centering his anger on the aging, one-handed buffoon, his anger evaporated into disgust, then depression—the most useless, he felt, of all emotions. He felt a momentary flash of self-loathing that Bond could—whether intentionally or not (worse yet if it were unintentional)—manipulate his emotions so easily. At a stop light he watched as a family of *pochos*, native-born migrant workers, crossed in the walk lane, the bronze, almost beardless face of the father scrubbed and weathered, his short frame erect in cardboard-stiff new Levi pants and jacket, his head a pedestal for a pristine-tan straw hat. Beside him walked his wife, her trunk encased in a dull grey *rebozo*, while their four children rushed ahead, then behind, gamboling around a parental maypole. All were decked out in new garments whose purchase no doubt explained their chattering and their elation: the mother laughed once and stooped to retrieve a ribbon fallen from a daughter's hair, and the two largest boys broke momentarily from the circle to pitch and return a large parcel wrapped in brown paper. Méndez felt the throb of a headache as he watched them regather at the curb. Maybe they had been working the irrigated grain sorghum fields east of town—they were a little early for cotton—then perhaps they would move north to the Colorado beet fields, to be followed by throngs of *braceros* and *mojados*, the legal and illegal Mexican nationals who surged into town every fall to pick and chop the cotton. Bad news for everybody, he fumed. For the Manuelos it meant less work to go around. The poor preying off the poor. Méndez watched the father break off from the family at the curb, heading, he guessed, for a *cantina* in the Mexican *barrio*.

"Huge silver thang looked like a big cigar right down there in the draw by the crick and me all by myself, not a soul in ten miles. I started worrying about what to do, not knowing whether to go out and inspect it or what, but I finely grabbed my over-n-under and started creeping out toward it, but it come to me that if they was so advanced that they could *get* here, then they more in likely had a good idea of what was on my mind, so I put the rifle down and started thinking real loud—*I come in peace, I come in peace*—because the idea hit me of being the first human being to talk to them people from outer space and I sure didn't want them to think we was *hos*-tile. But the closer I got the more afraid I got because I thought they could read my mind but I couldn't read theirs and they was going to know that I was afraid of them and couldn't trust them and that *would* make me *hos*-tile—like somebody once said, you don't have to be afraid of nobody except somebody who's afraid of you—and that sure wasn't no way to come in peace. And I thought they kneed that —I could see them sitting out there in that machine hearing that one thought vibrating off the top of my head—*I come in peace*—but hearing all the rattling and squeaking that was going on beneath it too, and thinking how puny and weak and hypocritical and false these creatures was. They had the wrong man—they oughta go talk to them Schweitzer and Einstein fellers, they could set them straight about what kind of people we was. But then I got to thinking that was just a crock of bull, that maybe I ought to protect myself and that I was acting like some damn fool out of a TV movie —you know, the feller in the white coat and spectacles that breaks through the *po*-lice lines and says, 'But we *must* try to talk to them,' and the general in charge says, 'Get back you crazy loon, don't go near that thing,' but the damn fool does it anyway and gets his head bloed off. And then I thought that they could hear my mind saying all this and they was just sitting back in that saucer laughing to beat all hell because they had got this here idiot earth-man so balled up in his head he didn't know whether to shit or go blind. Hellfire, they didn't *need* no fancy weapons, all they had to do was just sit there and them earth-men'd just lose their minds and run off babbling. Finely, I got so tired of *thinking* that I said to hell with it and stepped out into the pasture right next to the thing and thought as loud as I could—*Awright, if you fellers can read my mind there ain't no use in me summarizing it for you— I'm stupid and afraid and probably just curious as a cat and don't know nothing about nothing and you probably even know that I'm thinking this about myself so you won't attack me, but by God, I come in peace! Don't pay no attention to anything else you hear in my head because I'm trying like hell not to think it. I'll tell you all I know, the President's name and where he lives and how to grab a frog or whatever, but if you want some real high-powered information you'll have to go somewheres else to get it.* And I'll be go to hell if this here door in the side of the saucer didn't come open—blam!—just like that and this big booming voice came into my head —*Enter*—it said. So I took a big breath and walked up to the doorway. I took one last look around me, smelling the spring breeze, listening to them country whip-poorwills, looking at the moon and the stars, then I stepped inside. There was a big room with shiny silver walls bare as a baby's bottom, nothing but walls, floor, and a ceiling with kind of weird-looking bumps that put out a lot of light. So where are you, I thought. Naturally I'd give up the idea of talking—just a waste of breath. You can't see us, this voice said. Well, I thought to myself, they ain't geniuses, anyway, but then I had to apologize real quick. We're in your head, this one voice said, we don't have no form. I chewed on this for a minute then I thought, what do you want from me? 'Don't be afraid, we just want to ask you a few questions.' So shoot, I thought, I'll do all I can, do my best. They was four five different voices in my head and they commenced to ask me questions, real simple ones, really surprised me—I thought they'd want to know about our missles and thangs—but this one voice ast me who Red Grange was and another wanted to know about Clerasil. This went on for a while until I begun to feel a little weird talking to voices in my head, so I ast them if they wouldn't mind turning themselves into something I could look at while we talked, because it was like listening to the TV without the picture. They said, sure, they'd do her for me but they could only take the form of the thing they was nearest to. It took a minute for this to sink in, but I finely decided to try it. Okay, I thought, it's stywainer to me, and pop! there was six of me standing in that room! Really give me a start for a minute! It was real strange, talking to six of me, with all of me standing around in a circle like we was at intermission at the movies, me asking myself silly questions that I already knoed the answers to.

"Hey, where we started?" Bond saw that they had turned off the main drag onto an unpaved street toward Manuelo's house. Méndez ignored the question. "Hell, I guess it don't matter to me none. Nice day and lots of time." Bond glanced appreciatively into the clear, wind-swept sky.

"We're taking a trip down to 'Sal si Puedes.' You're going to see how the other half lives." He smiled wryly at the double-edged irony with which the people of the *barrio* had nicknamed their neighborhood—Get Out If You Can.

Bond dropped his eyes. "Man, somebody sure rattled your chain today. There ain't nobody in nineteen counties don't already know how poor your people are."

*His people*—despite his desire to feel pride Méndez felt a twinge of resentment at the inclusion, then some of his earlier indignation returned at the implications of Bond's comment—his people, not Bond's: thus Bond absolved himself of responsibility. A tirade sprouted suddenly in the back of his brain but he cropped it short—maybe forcing Bond to see this squalor would suffice to move him.

"Sure, they all know, but they don't *do* anything."

Bond's empty glove flapped limply in the wind. "Aw, I wouldn't say that. Church I used to preach at every Christmas sent around—"

"Oh man! Don't give me that Christmas basket nonsense with all those fine Christian folk with their annual pittance of two dollars worth of canned goods, those constipated mealy-mouths congratulating themselves with a sack of two-bit candy and complaining of the lack of gratitude and that there was a beer or two in the refrigerator and somebody was smoking a cigarette—as if everyone should forgo some petty pleasure for an entire year to make themselves worthy of whatever little dropping might issue from those uptight pucker strings!"

Bond averted his face, his eyes following the reddish ruts of sand banked along the street. Méndez equated his silence with defeat, so he drove on without further comment, his gaze skimming the weathered, rotting remains of frame houses once occupied by Anglos, noting—as though collecting a list of grievances to be presented later to the world at large—sagging porches, missing pillars, roofs with half their shingles missing, broken stands of picket fence: the obvious exterior details of *barrio* housing. He watched Bond stare at a shack of greasy tar paper and galvanized roofing tin, its yard a depository for rusting buckets and hunks of several rusting autos, and pity for Bond (who sometimes reminded him of a puppy who must be forgiven after discipline) made him pluck two cigarettes from his shirt pocket and pass one on to Bond, who took it with an abject nod of thanks. From the rear of the shack they heard the swift, upward clatter of a Spanish curse hurled outward toward the street, a voluminous rejoinder from within, then the sudden explosion of *ranchero* music from a radio. Above them the diseased, half-defoliated arms of elm trees dropped splotches of shade onto their faces.

Beneath a large cottonwood ahead, Méndez saw three men gathered in various postures of counsel and appraisal around the open hood of a '56 Ford while a fourth, his head hidden by the bill of a baseball cap, bent far into the engine compartment to perform some operation, his arms plunged deep into the crevice.

As he eased the jeep beside them, braking, two of the men turned in unison to give him vague, indifferent glances of inquiry, then rejoined the others to scrutinize the fourth man's work. Méndez waited a minute, then unclipped the jeep's ignition wires, killing the engine. In the silence that followed, the man grunted as he strained beneath the hood, then the silken shuffle of shoes in sand and the soft clink of wrench on metal in the motor housing rose to Méndez's ears.

An oily bolt was handed up from the depths of the engine housing to a stocky, mustachioed man with a cataract on one eye. He studied the head of the bolt, then ran his thumbnail along the threads.

After a pause, a tattered gasket followed the bolt: the man with the cataract took it, flipped it over in the palm of his hand, then tossed it with irritation into the sand. Three bolts later Méndez felt free to state his business.

"Anyone seen Manuelo?"

The man under the hood froze his movement and turned his head slightly to the side in a stagy gesture of disgust that conversation should intrude upon his work. The three men watching over his shoulder backed off slightly. A hand rose up to readjust the bill of the cap, then disappeared again. Méndez heard a *clunk*, then the staccato clicks from the ratchet of a socket wrench.

The man with the cataract squinted curiously. *"Manuelo who?"*

Stung, Méndez realized they hadn't recognized him.

*"Manuelo Méndez. My cousin."*

There was a huge clatter as the man beneath the hood dropped his tools and craned his head up suddenly, grinning, the scar above his eye cut short by the cap.

"Well, kiss my ass if it ain't ole Tío Taco. You down here selling life insurance or did the finance company send you?" He winked at the others.

Méndez searched the gilded mouth for ambiguity and found in the taut corners of the lips such a perfect balance of malicious and benign intent that he was amazed at the Snake's capacity to emit at once two polar opposites of feeling: the other man's eyes, unmoving, their dull glint suggesting the cool study of a biologist severing flesh, struck off a memory of another confrontation with them two weeks earlier at the filling station. The Snake blinked once, his mouth still fixed in ambivalence. Méndez could play it either way he wanted.

Méndez returned the grin in the same spirit. "Actually I just came down to foreclose a few dozen mortgages."

The Snake chortled, the crescent wrench gripped in gesturing hand.

"*Huáchale*, mahn, doahn get all uptight." He lapsed into Los Angelese. The open mouth of the wrench pointed at Méndez's throat. "Jew do thaht mahn ahn somethin baahd hoppen to you."

Incredible—a twenty-seven year old *chuco*. Although the Snake (Jesús Gutiérrez, Jesse to his teachers) had added twenty pounds of flesh, had married and fathered five children since Méndez knew him in high school, the momentum of his mind had been arrested somewhere in his teens by, by what? Méndez could never be sure; he only knew that he himself had gone through so many Méndezes since that time that he felt there was absolutely no similarity between the image of himself in the Snake's mind and the Méndez who was staring back at him. The realization that he had changed and the Snake had not momentarily freed him from a complex of interlocking fears that the other man's presence seemed to construct in him: that he might have become something he might once have vowed never to become, and that he might have once been something he no longer approved of.

"Well, have you seen Manuelo?" He aimed the question at the Snake but let his eyes include the others. It surprised him that the Snake answered indifferently that Manuelo was probably at home, then turned back to his work, the wrench disappearing into the bowels of the motor.

Burning from the Snake's second insult to his *machismo* within the space of two weeks, he drove the remaining block and a half to Manuelo's slowly, trying to shake off the sharp agitation his former *amigo de confianza* had produced in him, first by edging the other's barbs into some convenient corner of *envidia*, the envy of his fortunate lot, but they slipped aside to shame him and he was forced into a comparison instead —what was Jesse doing for Manuelo, anyway?

At Manuelo's Méndez sat a moment surveying the junk in the yard: rusting u-joints, bottom third of an oil drum, license plates, motor-oil cans, roller bearings from a railroad car, the shards and hunks of auto motors long since oxidized and functionless, jack handle, gas cap, an enamel pail, its bottom patterned with ragged bullet holes. Méndez gazed, perplexed. Taken piece by piece, maybe these things will lead to Manuelo himself, like the pigiron blazes dropped by a mechanical bird, leading to its nest in the Garden of Wrecked Machinery. If not a means to an end perhaps a meaning in itself—but that required a common denominator. One had to begin with particulars: near the house he spied an army-surplus entrenching tool jabbed upright in the sand—had someone tried to start a garden? Near the street a Pontiac hubcap, the apex of its dome adorned by an intaglio, a red (but plastic) Chieftain. (At last, something interpretable, a last monument to *that* conquered people, a transmogrification of nobility and integrity into synthetic substance. The Chieftain's profile tumbles dizzily, centered on the wheels of history.) And in the center of the yard, nailed atop a three-foot

two-by-four, the hubcap's mate served as a bird bath.
. . . But these things, these scraps—maybe they are
religious symbols? Sympathetic magic: icons to entice
the well-oiled god of progress? Does Manuelo get the
feel of Western Civilization by touching rusty bearings? As children he and Manuelo played in a limp-
winged B–25 at the end of a deserted runway, pretending they and it were airborne. A rusty bearing staves off
death, the illusory permanence reassures him.

Nonsense. He had stared into Manuelo's yard until
the mechanical etcetera no longer radiated supernatu-
ral significance; with the life shrunk from it, it was only
a heap of junk to be pawned off to a scrap-iron dealer.

Although Manuelo's house lacked paint, someone
had decorated the window frames by nailing bottle tops
along them in rows. A license plate with three of its six
numerals scratched out—leaving the house number
showing—had been tacked atop the front door frame.
Reluctantly Méndez lifted his left leg over the cutaway
panel and eased himself out of the seat.

"If it's okay with you I think I'll go in too," Bond
said. "Hadn't seen old Manwello in a good while."

A vision of the juxtaposition of Bond with Manuelo
and the ensuing chaos of strained emotions made
Méndez hesitate. As it faded, he reminded himself that
the visit might be good for Bond.

"Sure." He hid a smile behind his hand. "I'm sure
old Manwello'll be real glad to see you."

As they stepped along the crumbling concrete walk,
the heavy, sweet-and-sour smell of garbage reached
Méndez's nostrils. He kept his head lowered, watching
the spots of paint and oil on the walk pass beneath his
feet. Absurdly, grass grew between the cracks in the
walk but not in the yard.

On the porch he stood before the warped and sagging screen door, momentarily searching for a stable place to knock. The door wobbled on its hinges and the frame bounced off his knuckles, sounding like a muted punching bag.

After a moment the inner door was yanked abruptly open by a young girl clad in cut-down military fatigues. A single rope of black hair—bound by a rubber band —looped around her neck and down the collar of the shirt, exposing delicate, rose-like ears with tiny golden bobs in their pierced lobes. She frowned in adolescent impatience.

Méndez tipped back the brim of his hat.

*"Está Manuelo?"*

*"Momentito,"* she mumbled, vanishing into the dimness. Through the open door came a violent, urgent creak and rumble of a rocking chair on wooden floors, the sound madly accelerated as though a restless child were testing the limits of the chair's endurance. Bond cleared his throat.

The girl reappeared, still frowning.

*"Quién es?"*

Méndez removed his hat, grinning. *"You don't remember me?"*

Puzzled, the girl hesitated, then laughed. *"Es mi primo Raphael!"* She hastily palmed the door full open, an ochre flush spotting her cheeks. "Gee, I'm sorry. It was the hat. I wasn't thinking."

"Well, you too," Méndez admitted. "You've grown so much."

As the girl shifted aside to let them enter, her dusty bare feet stepped into a splash of sunlight, their painted nails flashing like red minnows in the pool of yellow rays. Méndez's gaze rose up the vertical plane of her body as he tried to guess her age, but except for the small, nubile mounds at the shirt pockets, her slender figure was lost beneath the bags and angles of the fatigues. The identification tape had been ripped from above the left breast pocket, leaving a dark green strip of material, and on her right sleeve he glimpsed the silhouette of corporal's stripes. Obviously she needed a new dress. He would talk to Juanita about it.

Inside, the girl shut the door behind them to keep out heat and dust, then padded out of the shade-drawn dimness, murmuring something Méndez could not hear. The frantic, pendulating rumble of the rocker leapt at them from a far corner; squinting he discerned that the chair's wildly swaying occupant was an old woman—her hands were clamped vise-tight around the chair arms and her features were rutted like an ancient raisin into a grimace, as though the rocker were propelled by someone else at a pace beyond her safety, a rider of a runaway horse. He suddenly remembered her: she was his aunt's grandmother. She had halted him outside the hardware store one day with a darting, upraised palm, begging in querulous lamentation—*Un veinte, señor, un veinte, un veinte, un veinte, un veinte* —and he had literally fled from her. His most vivid recollection of the old woman was that she kept preserved in a Mason jar the cataract that had been removed from her eye by surgery.

Politeness dictated that he greet her, but she was oblivious to their presence. Beside him Bond skimmed his eyes across the room, his gaze lighting upon every object but the old woman, his face set carefully in a mask of good cheer. His hat was crammed into the pit of his handless arm, and with his right hand he stroked his thin, wiry hair. Méndez did not recognize these as preparatory gestures until Bond stepped away from him.

"Bway-nos-*dee*-ass scene-*yore*-ay." Bond stood beside the rocker, his head jerking like a spectator at a ping-pong match. "Ko-mo *es*-ta *oo*stead?"

Méndez strode to Bond's side and tugged gently at his elbow.

"It's okay. Forget it." A touch of vertigo settled in his stomach as the old woman arced dizzily in the corners of his eyes. "She doesn't know who we are."

"Naw, it's okay." He turned back to the woman. "Yo *es*-toy Ro-ber-to Bond."

The old woman's jaw wrenched open, liberating a gravelly *Ahhhhhhhhhh* whose volume throbbed with the rocker's pitch. After a moment the monosyllable waned and disintegrated into unintelligible mutterings.

"Ko-mo?" Bond asked her.

As Méndez urged Bond to let the woman be, her moronic cry rose again into a squall that reverberated in the room until Méndez felt his head would burst, then gradually, like a siren fading into the distance, her voice descended in a phlegmy glissando to a stop. With it died the motion of the rocker.

"What'd you say?"

In the silence Méndez heard the purl of Spanish from somewhere in the rear of the house, then the rustle of clothing and the shuffle of feet in the hallway.

"I said—"

"He's in the back." The girl was standing in the entry to the hallway, a chubby baby straddling her hip. Above her, fastened to the header of the doorframe, a plastic crucifix gave off a dim, luminous glow.

Bond patted the old woman's forearm in parting, then left her side to inspect the baby.

"Wal, looky here." As he awkwardly chucked the baby's chin, it crouped twice, hoarsely, then buried its mouth in the girl's sleeve. "Es-tar mooey hair-mo-so."

The girl beamed. *"Gracias."*

*"Es tuyo?"* Méndez asked flatly.

The girl faltered, stroking the child's nap of sable hair.

*"No. He is of a friend."*

While she playfully wove the long coil of her own hair around the child's neck and shoulders, Méndez grimly weighed the ambiguity of her answer. A lecture would be pointless—if she didn't understand the economics of child-bearing by now, nothing he could say would help. He leaned into the baby's face, watching as it mechanically registered his presence with a slight flicker of its pupils. On a sudden impulse, he turned to the girl and kissed her lightly on the brow.

*"You have my blessing."*

The corners of her lips arched quickly in gratitude, and before he could straighten up she leaned upward and straining on the tips of her toes brushed his cheek with a girlish kiss; then, embarrassed, she pivoted on bare, callused heels and led them down the hall, the thick cord of hair swaying lightly across her back with her stride. Behind her, feeling the cool, damp kiss on his cheek, he had a foreboding that he was about to experience one of those periodic epiphanies which led from pride to humility: *she* blessed *him*; with an open, uncomplicated kiss of gratitude she had blessed this emotional miser with his patronizing superiority and his paltry, tortured, and neurotic convolutions of an adult heart. Down the hall the bedroom door swung open, shunting a cube of hazy yellow light filled with darting motes into the passageway. Her name, which he had been struggling to remember since she met them at the door, flipped like a flash card into his mind: Candelaria. Candelaria, which—typically—the Anglos bastardized to Candy. The myriad implications of that single linguistic twist momentarily infuriated him— Candelaria, the light and essence diminished, transmogrified into some minor pleasure of the palate. They took the dignity, the spirit, and left a minuscule hunk of artificial sweetener in return. Manhattan Island for a palmful of mirror shards. Napalm bombs and Tootsie Rolls.

Hesitating at the threshold, Méndez saw that most of the family had gathered in the room. In the far corner diagonal to the door, a small boy had barricaded himself behind cardboard boxes. He immediately recognized him as Roberto: the boy's mouth was disfigured and twisted, the flesh of his upper and lower lips fused by scar tissue halfway across the labial opening where he had bitten into an electric cord as a baby. Although not a mute, the boy seldom talked—he expressed himself with numerous (interchangeable) combinations of grunts, signs, and signals whose dearth of nuance left the impression he was retarded. Unless, Méndez considered, you studied the hostile, glittering black pupils of his eyes—that bitterness meant intelligence.

Apparently their entry had interrupted a game of war, for the boy glanced up at them in annoyance, then resumed aiming a wooden rubber-band gun at some unseen but squealing human target beneath the bed to his left, his eyes fixed coldly, as if for all his heart he wished his weapon were lethal.

Candelaria eased herself tentatively onto the edge of the bed, gently tugged the baby's grip loose from her shirt sleeve, then with her hands supporting his back centered him in the sag of the moldy, naked mattress and began to unpin his diaper. She halted in the middle of the process to look inquiringly at Manuelo, who lay supine and motionless atop another unmade bed next to the window, his head reclining in a plane of sunlight. His right arm hung over the edge of the bed, trailing his fingers along the dusty floor, and his left arm was draped across his eyes, leaving only the lower half of his face visible.

"Papa?"

Méndez thought Manuelo might be asleep, for he showed no sign of having heard the girl. It seemed his cue to enter, so he stepped into the stuffy, overheated room, the acrid smell of urine burning in his nostrils. After a brief survey for an appealing place to sit, he settled on leaning in an awkward stance of casual relaxation with one palm against a wall whose surface was plastered with newspapers and perforated with random, fist-sized holes. Bond shuffled in behind him, nodding at the children.

"*Qué has hecho?*" He watched the figure on the bed for signs of consciousness. Shirtless, Manuelo's rib-lean trunk resembled the pale underside of a beetle, brittle somehow, thin-shelled. The cavity of his chest narrowed to a vulnerable, concave stomach which disappeared beneath beltless, faded jeans. The fingers of his left hand fisted together once, then released.

"Look aroun, mahn." His eyes remained hidden under the cover of his arm, and his voice, soft, evenly modulated, almost flat, gave Méndez no hint of his state of mind.

"*One sees only the children of God,*" Méndez joked.

After a pause, the faint beginnings of a sneer seeped into Manuelo's lips.

"*Perhaps somebody should remind God of that. It*

*makes thirteen years now that he has not made child-support payments."*

Méndez chuckled and picked up the banter with relief.

*"God has many children and his ways are mysterious and very slow. Maybe one should appeal to this man who calls himself Saint Claus: his gifts aren't too large but they come with greater regularity."*

*"What color's his skin?"*

*"God or this Claus person?"*

"Duh-duh-duh-duh-duh!" Spewing imitation gun-fire through the deformed aperture of his mouth, Roberto whirled and jabbed the barrel of his gun against the temple of his adversary, who was trying to squirm out from under the bed. "Duh-duh-duh-duh-duh!" The boy winced and grabbed his head in pain. Roberto started to fire again but held himself in check when Candelaria slung him a sharp glance of disapproval.

*"The man called Claus."* Manuelo clenched his teeth, and his voice convulsed upward. *"The other has shown us his."* Candelaria looked over at him anxiously and for the first time Méndez sensed the intensity of his despair: a minute tremor passed along his lower lip, then faded as his cheek muscles sagged, pulling his lips downward in a fix of grim exhaustion. Lax and totally without energy, his slender body seemed to recede deeper and deeper into the stained mattress, buoyed above its surface only by his shallow, irregular breathing. The spirit of play vaporized instantly; Méndez wondered whether to continue the game.

*"The skin of this hombre called Claus appears to be red."*

Manuelo scoffed weakly. *"An Indian."*

Between them, the impetus for banter unwound to a deadening halt. What next? Méndez self-consciously fingered his chin and glanced cautiously at Bond, who leaned hat in hand against the doorframe, his face a mask of mild and obsequious bewilderment, as though he couldn't decide whether to pay polite attention to a conversation he couldn't understand or pretend not to listen. In either case, he was searching for a way to participate, and Méndez regretted having brought him. Above them a wasp buzzed in angry spurts against the intersection of wall and ceiling, ceasing periodically to hobble, as though one-legged, in fitful ellipses around an imagined point of exit. Manuelo began to flick the nails of his fingers one by one against the floor, tapping like a drummer at an execution.

"Méndez," he said, as though pronouncing the name of someone not present. "Always joking."

Apparently Bond had been waiting for an opening, for he chuckled—much too loudly—in agreement. Startled, Manuelo jerked his arm back from his forehead and glared at Méndez, the area around his eyes the dull black of coal fragments. Obviously he had not slept for some time.

"*Quién es?*" he demanded.

Méndez grabbed frantically for an answer that would include an explanation, but Bond stepped forward, taking his cue. "I bet you don't even remember me," he challenged nervously in hearty good fellowship, waving his empty glove. Manuelo stared at him incredulously, as though he were a personification of an absurd *non sequitur*. Bond hesitated, then scribed a waist-high arc in the air with the glove. "I knoed you when you was just a little feller." Méndez immediately saw with a curious mixture of one part relief and two parts discomfort that Bond was caught in the obligation to take his turn and make some contribution lest some silent, nameless antagonism descended on them like a net. Manuelo continued to gaze at him in a kind of angry puzzlement, as though he had been shaken roughly awake by a total stranger to be jabbered at in a language he didn't understand.

"Course you might not remember me." His indirect plea for a response failed to penetrate Manuelo's consciousness, so he turned to Méndez, who quickly averted his eyes. Temporizing, Bond licked his lips.

Another sentence, like the line of a poem recited before an audience by a child who barely knows it by rote, dropped forth: "Usta work right longside yore daddy picking cotton." Some of the amazement slipped from Manuelo's features, replaced by a peculiar, clouded expression of curiosity that did not seem to be directed toward the content of Bond's statement.

"You know, he couldn't speak a word of English and I couldn't speak a word of long-knife then." He gazed suddenly upward at the ceiling as though he expected a memory to be filmed there. "Yeah, we worked right longside trading lunches and what not, and I had me this old Model T a fella give me because he got so mad at it he couldn't stand to look at it and me and yore daddy worked like niggers to get that thing runnin." He nodded belligerently to no one in particular for emphasis. "Yeah, yore daddy was as good a Messkin as you'll ever find." Horrified, Méndez felt his relief turn to embarrassment. The old man's nervousness seemed to be passing; he was, in fact, warming up, having somewhere in his preceding narrative burst neared his unusually low threshold of self-consciousness. Although it seemed an aspect of the old man's character he deliberately tried to shed as superfluous, Méndez recognized from his face that enough remained to bring him to that peculiar stage in his monologue where the self-conscious choose to say too much rather than stand pat, like amateur discus throwers who by fluke come within a foot of the world's record, then struggle with increasing unsuccess to beat their own mark. If there is a God in Heaven, Méndez thought, he won't allow the old man to go on. But he knew better.

"God dog! We had us a time one night in that thang, both of us drunk as skunks on bath-tub gin, hunting jackrabbits with a spotlight, and we come roaring across a cotton patch and turned that old T over on its back right in the middle of it, fruit jars, flashlights, and shoulder weapons raining down on us like hail. Both of us crawled out laughing so hard I thought I was going to bust my appendix. We sat there in the middle of a furrow seeing who could howl the loudest at the moon." He caught himself up suddenly, as though aware that he was babbling, then went on more somberly. "We was the best of friends and they wasn't either one of us could speak the other's lingo." Manuelo flung his arm back across his eyes, his mouth turned painfully up in something that approximated a grimace. Méndez could not bring himself to look directly at either one of them: he studied the marble-sized balls of lint beneath the bed Manuelo lay on. He could hear Bond's feet shifting hesitantly.

"Yessir,"he trailed off. Was it tag or prelude? Sweet Mary let it be a tag. "Yessir, some of my best friends—" Méndez gritted his teeth, but the predicate remained unvoiced. He glanced furtively at Manuelo, who was clenching and unclenching the dangling fingers of his left hand. Apparently, something of the atmosphere in the room reasserted itself on Bond, for he drew himself up slightly as if in retreat.

"Times change, I guess," he added finally. Méndez sensed an oblique reproach in the platitude. Bond gazed at them a moment, then moved to the bed where the child lay in clean diapers and began to chatter softly with the girl, his lowered voice a signal that he would no longer intrude on their colloquy.

The full flower of a sneer blossomed on Manuelo's lips.

*"Maybe you are a guide?"*

*"Maybe."* Méndez appraised the condition of his fingernails.

Manuelo eased his arm upward, uncovering his right eye.

*"Or maybe you are selling him my daughter."*

*"Don't be stupid, man."*

*"It was a joke."*

*"The humor of it escapes me."*

Manuelo chuckled, then levered himself up on one elbow with a ragged burst of animation. His lips worked into an odd grin as his eyes flicked toward Bond, then returned to light on Méndez's face.

*"Get me his job."*

He watched, amused, as Méndez's features quivered their way through a series of contradictory twinges, his eyes flitting along the far wall as if to connect the dots of one fist-sized hole to another. Before Méndez could answer that it wasn't possible, Manuelo jerked the prop of his elbow from under his body and flopped back down on the mattress, masking his eyes with his forearm.

*"That was another joke."*

Méndez resented the obvious test of his loyalty.

*"There are only three of us, he and I and Carlos. And he has been there—"*

*"Are you not,"* Manuelo paused, then wrenched the last word out sarcastically, *"el jefe?"* he snickered. *"Papacito?"*

*"Yes and no."* He felt his palms grow damp. *"Maybe, I don't know. It could be that in another week I too will be without work."* That it might be him lying exhausted and hopeless on the bed made him shudder. *"The old man died. His son is there now, and he doesn't know me."* Houston's unexpected offer three days ago to possibly make Méndez a kind of partner in the ranch coupled with his own suddenly burgeoning plans for a co-op or a commune which Aguilar's letter had inspired rose with an insistence to be spoken, but he held it back —it was all too tentative.

Manuelo still peered at him suspiciously.

*"If you've seen the younger man, then you know what he is,"* Méndez challenged.

Apparently the point scored; a sigh of concession escaped Manuelo's lips.

*"I do not know his plans, but I will ask about you."*

*"Gracias,"* Manuelo muttered.

Manuelo looked momentarily placated, so Méndez slackened his knot-taut muscles and slid down the wall into a crouch; with his arm arched over one knee, he doodled in the sand filming the floor, surreptitiously eyeing first Bond, then Manuelo; the real issue, he saw, had been adroitly side-stepped, the *deus ex machina* of the old man's death had partially resolved the question for him. But no matter: ultimately he would have seen to it that Manuelo got Bond's job, for Bond had no immediate family. And what, some speculating inquisitor in his brain pondered, if Bond too had six children?

A co-op, a commune of sorts, seemed their only hope.

*"You have been to the gasolineras?"*

Manuelo nodded curtly.

*"And to the place called ManPower?"*

A snort of reproach. "Mahn, you know what happens there—work one day a week cleaning somebody's garage."

Depressed, Méndez trailed a finger through the grime, etching out a wobbly "&c." He had so little to help Manuelo with—all his leads were nothing more than the ordinary channels of employment that, even if they led to jobs, the jobs themselves were only stopgaps. Pointless to mention welfare; in their terminology Manuelo was "employable"—sound mind and body. All he had left was a crumpled slip of hope scurrying on the wind of rumor.

"Everybody says that because of the war there's a lot of work in the oil fields." He was so unconvinced himself that his statement sounded like the lead line of an interviewer who expects his subject to deny it categorically.

Manuelo rocked up on one elbow. "Mahn, you don't believe that shit, do you? You don't think that just because some fat-assed gringo says they need people in the oil fields that they take *me? Chingao!*" He whacked the mattress with his fist, then swung his legs over the edge of the bed, clumping bare heels against the floor. "Lemme tell you something, mahn, I mean this thing is the way it is." A rage in Manuelo's eyes—did he feel accused of not trying to find work? He was straining forward, bent-waisted and tense as a prizefighter, his outstretched fingers kneading and gripping the air. "I went to this place because a guy says that because of the wahr there was nobody to work, so I went and give my name in this office, and it was real ahrly, mahn, about six-thirty in the mornin, and they sent me to a room where there was benches and about twenty guys seating aroun. They had lonches in sacks and gloves and were smoking cigarettes and drinking coffee from Thermos bottles, but me, I didn't have nothing, mahn, nothin. In about an hour, some other guys come in and pick out the guys they want to work for them, and then some more guys come in and this went on until about ten o'clock and there wasn't nobody left but me and this steenking wino." He vaulted from the bed and strode about the room, flinging his arms as though trying to halt traffic. Bond, the girl, and the two boys craned their heads in unison, startled. "This goddamn old wino was seating there so goddamn dronk he couldn't even hold his head up. He kept falling asleep, then he'd wake up and drop cigarettes all over the floor and try to get this goddamn bottle of wine out of his pocket, tryin to get up and falling all over me, this steenking dirty wino—all he wanted was to work and get some more wine. And then this ather guy, this ather sonabeetch," he hesitated near the wall, fuming, shaking a fist the size and density of a baseball at waist level, "this ather sonabeetch come in and look aroun and I'm thinking, *yeah, mahn, les go to work, show me that goddamn work*— His entire frame was quivering like a snake's rattle—"me seating there without a penny and he come in and TOOK THAT GODDAMN WINO OFF TO WORK!"

Exploding, hair flying as he whirled, he spun and slammed his fist through the wall, ripping a hole the size of a cannon shell in the sheetrock. Bond stood rigid in horror by the bedstead, straining on the balls of his feet, while Candelaria quickly poised herself over the squalling baby. Tearing out from behind the boxes, Roberto dashed from the room, an odd, mutant giggle spurting from his mouth. *"Blah-dah-dah-dah-dah-dah-dah-dah-dah!"* they heard him spray the hallway with elongated, maniacal bursts of gunfire. Manuelo rather absently examined his knuckles, then plopped down on the edge of the mattress, casually, as though he had only intended to dramatize an exclamation point.

"He took that goddamn wino." He stared at the floor, nodding sadly as if in disbelief. "So I got so mad that I got up and went to the office where I give my name and told this guy I give my name to what happened and he got up and went somewhere to tell somebody about it, then he came back out and told me to tell this ather guy what happened so I told his ather guy what happened and he got up and went somewhere else to tell this *ather* guy what happened and came back and told me to tell this ather guy. I was tired of *tellin,* but I went to the ather guy. He wasn't there." Exhausted, he lay back as though faint, the sweat on his brow gleaming in the slant of light.

"He never is."

Manuelo rubbed his eyes with his knuckles, then exhaled a long breath from his expanded cheeks. *"I tell you one day I will cut out their cojones and carve my initials in their faces."*

*"They have none."*

*"Sí. Like ghosts. They are not there."* He revolved his head to nod toward Candelaria. *"Should I be a woman like her mother? Should I let the whole world rape me?"* He looked at Méndez. "No more, mahn. Tomorrow I'm going to Sangre de Christo, and if nothin happens there—" He rolled over onto his left side, facing the window. "I just don't know, mahn, I just don't know."

They sat for a few moments in silence. Roberto's victim watched with a flat, impassive face as void of expression as a war orphan's; Manuelo's head drooped gradually below the window sill and he feigned sleep, his body drained, sweating. Bond shifted weight from foot to foot and looked inquiringly at Méndez. The heat in the room had grown intolerable, steaming the smell of fouled diapers and sweaty socks; the child on the bed coughed wetly, then broke into a choked whine. Méndez struggled to his feet, rubbing his sleep-deadened thighs.

"Well, something may turn up. I'll look around and ask Houston."

Manuelo shrugged apathetically.

At the front door, Méndez handed the girl a bill whose value had somehow slipped to rock bottom during his conversation with Manuelo. "Not much, but maybe it'll do some good?" He gestured helplessly.

Candelaria broke into a broad grin. *"Gracias, Muchísimas gracias."* Her grateful voice probed his eardrums like a scalpel.

# _Two_

The wind has picked up some: in the basin swirls of sand float capriciously over the pastures; the occasional gusts tug at Méndez's hat as he turns to peer behind the jeep, steering it in reverse down the two-rut road, the engine whining when the wheels engage deep sand. He had spied the herd of cattle slowly making its way toward the tank battery where an oil spill glitters in the sunlight.

Bond is laughing gleefully. "You got to pay a little better mind to what I'm telling you or yore going to miss the best part. Now you don't even know it, but this here tale is a test of yore powers of concentration: hellfire, it ain't nothing to listen to somebody tell a story right from the beginning to the end, why any damn fool moron can stick right in there, but it takes a mighty powerful mind to foller a story like the one I'm telling."

"Yes, indeed."

"Awww, you can do bettern that—any fool can claim he can't foller because the story's dull. Looky here—what do you think about this here study a rocks that come up out a the ground?"

Méndez smiles indulgently. "Are you referring to geology or archeology?"

"Why gee-ol-o-gee, you damned idiot, them other people dig up things that ancient people left in the ground."

Méndez concedes, not wanting to quibble.

"Well?"

He has forgotten the query. "Well what?"

Bond wails, exasperated. "Can't you even answer a simple question? What do you think a—"

"It bores me."

"Ah-hah!" Bond pounces, then dips his head, triumphant. "Just what I thought."

Méndez senses the advance guard of a monumental headache ascending in the back of his brain as the jeep bounces down the rocky incline of the mesa. "You're so damned predictable—if you think I'm going to ask why or how you knew that all along you're out of your rabbit-assed mind." Scanning ahead, he has already anticipated Bond's conclusion. "Why can't you ever just make a point by *stating* it in a simple, ordinary declarative sentence? Why do we always have to wade through some gooey miasma of questions and answers?"

"How else are you going to learn?"

"Learn *what*, for Christ's sake?"

Bond slaps him on the shoulder, chortling. "How to think with yore head instead of yore ass."

The Platonic dialectic as practiced by a redneck

jester and a wetback dropout—the idea momentarily amuses him, but not enough to see it continued.

"Okay." He twists again in the driver's seat to look at Bond in the rear of the jeep, defeated by the tedium of the conversation. "What's the point?"

"Well, now they's *some* fellers go plumb ape-shit over these here rocks that come up out a the ground, right?"

Méndez threatens him with a pointed finger. "If you have something to say, I'll listen, by God, I'll listen even though I already know what it is, but I'll be damned if I'm going to play stooge."

Bond nods agreement. "Now, you suppose they's something in them rocks that draws them fellers like a magnet?" Before Mendez can protest the use of the rhetorical question, Bond waves him off. "Have you ever busted a rock open and found a little hunk a interest in it?"

"Look," Méndez says with mock gentleness. "You needn't apologize to me because your stories have no inherent interest in them: some people have it and others don't, it's just that simple."

"Why you marble-headed, chili-eating wetback, what do you think I'm trying to tell you? It's like a sack lunch—you've got to *bring it with you!*

Méndez seems to have left this metaphorical lunch at home today. Or at Manuelo's yesterday. He must ask Houston about Manuelo, but how to do it? Should he begin a long series of sly manipulations whose object is to edge Manuelo into Bond's job? He sidles his gaze up to the rearview mirror, letting his covert glance coldly measure Bond's features while he chatters gaily about some experience he had in the hardware store. No use —he can't work himself into hating Bond; the truth is he's fond of the old man, like it or not. But his feelings are irrelevant when it comes to making this decision—Manuelo *must* have work, not only because he is Manuelo with six children but because the centers of power must break and redistribute: value judgments aside, change is inescapable, inexorable—the center cannot hold. But why Bond? If it were anyone else, there'd be no problem.

"Here's the way it was—now you listen up," Bond continues. "When I come out of that thicket bass-ackards and lit out for the camp, my legs a churning like a locomotive, I hadn't gone ten feet before I tripped and that goddamn rifle went off—kablooey!—and bloed a hole right in the tip of my boot. Them dogs screeched to a halt, sliding on their hineys, and my mouth hung open for a minute while I just stood there gawking at that hole. Godamity damn! I thought—I done went and shot my goddamn toe off! And then I commenced to hoop and holler and howl and leaped fifteen feet straight up and *that* liked to of turned them hounds plumb inside out—why they was one come out a his crouch like a tranchewler and sprung high as a hayloft pawing the air, growling, biting, a howling and baying: his mind had done exploded from the strain; why, if he'd a been put up in a cage by hisself right then he'd a gobbled hisself up, tail-first!

"By the time I made it back to camp them dogs had ripped off both my hip pockets and the cuffs of my pants and we tore up through the camp, scattering the fire, with me hollering and the dogs yapping. I yanked up a stick and stood in the doorway a Billy Bob's tent trying to beat hem back but two of them crawled under the flaps in the back, so I just ripped the side of the tent open with my bare hands and scrambled for

the pickup because I figgered they couldn't get me
there unless they knoed how to operate a can opener
and I wouldna been surprised to see they did—"

What can Méndez do for Manuelo? Brood about
him. Imagine how things went this morning at the
employment agency, conjure images of his reporting
back to Gómez, where he is now, using Gómez to repay
the Indian's kindness, but for Gómez it is the least he
can do—he busy-works at his grill: he can't sit and read
his comics without fear of offending Manuelo, but he
can't talk to Manuelo, either, for Manuelo slumps in
the chromium and vinyl chair, sullen and incommunicative. So Gómez is forced to play the mourner at
the funeral of a very distant relative, sympathizing
without sympathy, for he feels imposed upon: Manuelo's problems have jarred the gentle, natural rhythms of
what had been a fine day. (Or so Méndez would think.)
In truth, Gómez is glancing surreptitiously over his
shoulder, watching as Manuelo ignites wooden matches with his thumbnail and lifts them to his eyes,
studying the flame with the fastidious intensity of a
child pulling wings from a beetle. He allows the flame
to creep towards his fingertips, where he lets it linger
a burning second longer before he blows it out. Another match. The Indian, langorously digesting his free
tacos, his chin propped up on his fists, focuses likewise
on the flame, his gaze less attentive, as though he were
watching some flaccid after-dinner entertainment.
Then still another match. Manuelo is intent on scorch-
ing the flesh of his brain with the memory of what
occurred at the employment agency in Sangre de
Christo: he will not allow himself to betray himself by
gradually forgetting his humiliation and letting time
gloss it over—he wants this hurt to hurt forever. Never,

he vows, will he be lulled into feeling anything but black, despairing hatred for them, for that gives him the true vision of how they are. All else is wishful thinking. *Cabrones! Pendejos!* Telling him he had too many children, sitting there telling what he already knew, an arm laid across the desk showing a shiny gold watch. If he wrapped the watch around his fist like brass knuckles the sharp corners would score the flesh in the pink man's face. Tiny red veins like spiders's legs in a limp nose, fragile squares of glass for eyes, hair gone from thinking too much about the wrong things, fingers weak like strips of foam-rubber—no man, a *maricón*, some *thing* they put before him with malicious delight to watch him seethe when it said no and he couldn't argue. Where was the *real* thing, the thing behind this paper bag of words? How much did they pay this thing to tell other people what they already knew, that they couldn't work? How many tons of groceries could he buy with meatless words, explanations of policy, accusations—if meaningless noises were the currency of the country, he'd have to learn to babble like the thing they put before him: I'mhardlyresponibleforregulationspassedbythelegislaturewhichrequireyoutobeemployedafullsixmonthsbeforeyouareeligibleforunemployment. *Chingao!* If that was all it took to make enough money to wear a fine suit and a gold watch he'd start to work on it right away—the secret was to make the words seem like they came from somewhere else more important and make them scramble in the ears. It was possible, though, that only gringos could do it, maybe they were born with it. Or maybe they learned it in college. Shit. He waited three and a half hours just to hear some flour-faced *gavacho maricón* babble at him, all the time wanting to rip that watch off the man's wrist, wrap it around his own knuckles and gouge the strips of flesh from the face, crunch those little square pieces of glass under his heel and stab his eyes. What right did that *thing* have to tell how he had too many children? Goddamn them, goddamn them, goddamn them!

Méndez could have anticipated even the minutest details of Manuelo's trip to Sangre de Christo, knew even when he heard Manuelo tell him he was going there that the trip could not possibly be other than futile, for he knows the characters—*de facto* Mexican office boy, the half dozen lethargic, aloof, and unhelpful secretaries, and the two principals—a man named Thomas who, when not buried in a sports-car magazine, could be counted on at least to apologize for their inefficiency (apologize, that is, to those he felt deserved it), and a Simpson, the man Manuelo talked to. Méndez has talked to Simpson once before, three or four years ago, just after he married Juanita and had returned to the ranch but was thinking of leaving it for the umpteenth time. Protected by seniority and civil service regulations, Simpson personified for him the principle that in a bureaucracy everyone rises to his own level of mediocrity, and Simpson found his level quickly: embittered, somehow carrying the air of a man who was sitting in for his vacationing subordinate (he had been there ten years), he seemed to feel that the material given him to work with was to blame for his own incapacity to function. He had a penchant for patronizing and an idiosyncratic habit of prying into an applicant's personal affairs irrelevant to the position applied for: on learning that Méndez was newly married, he leaned forward confidentially and said that doctors claimed that ill-matched pubic arches were the cause of nine out of ten divorces, then proceeded to give a digital demonstration of the proper and improper fit of pubic arches. It was something to think about. He kept staring at Méndez as if to elicit a response (did he want a detailed description of Juanita's genital anatomy, or did he just forever rue the day he married low-arch?), but Méndez simply told him he wasn't interested in the pube-inspection trade—he was looking for something a bit more challenging. Simpson handed him another form to complete.

Manuelo had no pencil. A young Latin dressed meticulously in an olive two-button suit had sauntered down the line of applicants waiting on the wooden benches and passed out application forms. Manuelo told him he had already done that once before, but the other answered in English that it wasn't his department and tossed the paper into Manuelo's lap. Prissy little *maricón.* Up the line the half-dozen other applicants—Anglos clad in various work garb—fell to filling out the forms, but Manuelo sat motionless, listening to his stomach growl. It was 8:45. He left the house at six after tossing down a half-cup of tepid coffee, his daily ration, then trotted out to the Sangre de Christo highway and shivered in the crisp haze of morning, thumbing a ride. He rode for forty minutes in the back of a pickup, bare arms and neck exposed to the chilly blast, back draft swirling bits of straw and dirt from the bed into his eyes. By the time he reached the employment office he was exhausted from shivering, dirty—grit caking the corners of his eyes—and hungry. Very hungry. He tried not to think about it, and when the office opened (he hunkered before the double glass doors for half an hour, listlessly pitching pebbles into the parking lot) he immediately sought out the fountain and gulped down almost a quart of tooth-piercing, refrigerated water to still his stomach, but it only muffled the growling. When he moved on the bench, it set up a quavering lap and slosh of its own within the hollow confines of the cavity. Maybe filling out the form would get his mind off his stomach.

He scanned the double row of benches, one against each wall of the wide, elongated hallway in which they sat, searching breast pockets for an extra pencil. Across from him sat a burly Anglo in faded overalls and work boots, with a steel hat cocked back on his head. In that slender pencil pocket on the bib of his overalls a pencil, big yellow one, new eraser. The man crossed his legs and bent at the waist, his jaws working a wad of tobacco as he worried over the form. Shit, it was useless to ask that big redneck hunk of crap for anything—he knew the type, the beefy-handed bohunk whose very bones went cold at the thought of Messkins or niggers. Manuelo shifted on the bench, the glob of stomached water jiggling; the more he assessed the other man's features, the more he grew convinced he wouldn't part with the pencil.

"Hey, mahn," he threw out testily, "Why don't you lemme use your other pencil?"

Squinting, the burly man looked up, annoyed.

"Because I need it in case my othern breaks."

Just like he knew, he should have kept his mouth shut; what was happening to his pride? He drew up his legs beneath him, rose from the bench and marched down the hallway toward the inner office—if they wanted the goddamn form filled out they could give him a pencil. As he passed up the row, out of the corner of his eye he saw two other Anglos struggling mutually to understand the form, mouthing the headings to each other.

He paused in the doorway of the inner office, standing at the edge of a corral-like structure beyond which lay desks for the secretaries and the two male heads of the organization, neither of whom was present. Directly before him, just on the other side of the railing, two girls with bouffant hairdos perched upon swivel, back-brace office chairs, giggling to each other. Salivating, he watched as one lifted a large pastry the color and shape of a sun-bleached patty of cow dung to her lips and tugged delicately at its edge with her incisors, holding a palm beneath the bottom to catch the crumbs. On her desk coffee steamed in a styrofoam cup; wisps of dissipating vapor curled above it lazily like hickory smoke, permeating his nostrils.

"You got a pencil?"

Breaking from her colloquy, she glanced at him distastefully—her eyes moving to the waist of his beltless Levis, then skimming the wrinkled front of his half-buttoned shirt. Leaning forward, she rescued her cup of coffee, moving it beside her typewriter, then turned —her skirt hem riding almost thigh-high with her movement—and rummaged in the bottom drawer of her desk. His groin flashed hotly with a flitting fantasy of violation, then she caught his eye and jerked upright, her mouth screwed down sourly.

"Bring it back." She handed him the pencil with a gesture that suggested she was a victim of her own boundless generosity. He was so offended by her manner that as he plucked the pencil from her grasp he focused on her crotch and let his tongue flick out once across his lips. *Puta!*

Reseated at the bench, he began the dreaded task of completing the blanks of the form, never certain he understood what was required of what blank or whether it went above or below the line. He could barely write.

He brooded over the first few blanks a while, then, vising the pencil between thumb and middle finger—tightly, as though it might be given to fits of violence—he printed his name, age, and address. Squinting, he tried to envision his social security card, which he had left at home in his billfold (no point in carrying a wallet without money), but only the first three digits were clear. These he drew carefully into the space, then made up six others to follow them, craftily making certain that no two digits were repeated. Below these lines a large section was blocked out on the sheet for, he finally surmised, information pertaining to his education. Relieved, he passed it by: since he had only attended three years in a school whose name he could never remember, he felt justified in leaving the entire space a clean, pristine white. Perhaps they would appreciate his neatness. New space: "Yrs. tech. or voc. trng."? Health history? Shit, it was impossible. Why couldn't he just *tell* them all this? He swung his head up, searching for someone who might help him, but saw no one. Nothing left to do but guess: his head and voice were whole, so he scratched "OK" above the line. He had no idea what the abbreviations meant. The outside doors burst open and the young Latin entered, balancing on his fingertips a plastic tray supporting two ceramic mugs of coffee. Monogrammed. For *los patrones*. Goddamn flunky thinking he's so big. As he passed, Manuelo rose and flagged him down by flapping the form before his eyes. Coffee jiggled onto the tray. Sweet revenge.

"What's this mean, mahn?"

The boy glared at him, then sent his gaze to the end

of the directing finger. "Years of vocational training," he said briskly, then stepped forward, but Manuelo grasped his sleeve.

"What the hell they want to know *that* for?"

The boy demonstrated the famous *quién sabe?* shrug, parted his sleeve from Manuelo's pincers, and scurried down the hallway. What was vocational training?

After a few moments of bewildered study, he understood that the next section required a history of his previous employment. Okay, but how to spell those things? One word with numerous qualifying adjectives will do, Méndez could say bitterly: "one who is present"; "one who attends another to render a service." *Attendant* comma gas-station comma parking-lot comma men's-room comma car-wash comma model 3499BX. Farm worker and cotton-picker at ten, and once at fourteen lucked into a job in the produce department of a supermarket, shucking onions, rotating tomatoes and oranges, peeling the rotted leaves of lettuce heads, stacking lemons. Cool and fresh the air that oozed up from beneath the produce counter, fine spray that misted stacks of green beans: up and down the counter he strolled working ceaselessly on a display— a cherry slightly out of kilter, a pyramid of apples with a minor cant, smoothing here, poking there, that tomato begged a quarter-turning. *Chingao!* Those idiots in the back dumped an entire crate of cabbage carelessly in the bin and he forgot himself because he had forgotten himself, had over a short week's time totally lost his sense of being a stupid greaser kid and had cultivated an inappropriate sense of proprietorship in that artificial garden; not that it was *his* produce, but that it was—since Safeway & Co. had accepted *him*—

his to protect for Safeway, even from the grapefruit-bruising hands of picky housewives. And this hopelessly incongruous feeling of Safeway Defender made him storm into the back room, yelling at the produce manager: "Look what them goddamn people done to that produce, mahn! They put that whole crate a cab-basch on top a the ather and I worked my ass off to make that display right." He expected the produce manager, as his superior and therefore as Greater Defender of Safeway & Co., to be as filled as he with rage over the injustice done to the company by its Enemies.

The produce manager was carving slabs of avocado and sliding them into his mouth, the ball of one foot resting on a sack of potatoes. The two violators of Manuelo's display huddled across the room muttering conspiratorially. The manager's gray eyes gleamed oddly.

"This here artist says yall done screwed up his masterpiece."

One of the other two glared at Manuelo, then stabbed at a lettuce crate with a case knife. "Who the hell's he think he is, Pie-cuss-o?" His accomplice chortled mightily, adding: "Or old Snakeshit." He struck a mock, poet-at-a-picnic pose. "Between yore thighs yore pussy lies. It makes my peter rise. Snakeshit."

The manager turned to Manuelo, laughing. "I'm real sorry about that. Naturally we can't expect a artist a yore caliber to work under these here conditions." He nodded playfully toward the other two. "So I'd guess best thang'd be to find a place where you don't have to put up with cruds like them hasn't got no appreciation."

"Yeah," Snakeshit called out boldly, having sensed which way the winds of management were blowing, "Some place like greaser-town."

The hammer Manuelo flung at his head missed and caromed off the wall; frightened, the boy dashed for the front of the store, but Manuelo's diving tackle brought him down just inside the double swinging doors. A moment's scuffle later Manuelo was straddling the older, heavier boy, pounding his face with his fists, but the produce manager yanked him off and slung him against the concrete wall, walloping the breath from his chest. Stunned, he lay limp in a pool of ice water draining from the freezer locker, while the manager turned to fiddle with some invoices and the other two boys kicked him repeatedly in the head and rib-cage, then pushed him into the alley where he leaned against the brick wall, vomiting. When he regained his breath, he tore into the garbage cans, scattering the trash up and down the rear of the store.

Dishwasher, gardener, mechanic, construction worker: all these had to be spelled out, complete—he decided after deliberation—with dates of employment and salary. He rested for a moment, his head tilted against the wall, eyes closed, feeling his stomach coil and crawl upon itself like a waking viper. Only one more day of that, though: as his stomach shrunk the hunger bothered him less. They had made the mistake of gorging themselves on Méndez's twenty dollars, although he knew it should have been saved and parceled out in daily allotments. They took flowers to Elena in the hospital, who looked worried until he lied and said Méndez had brought a hundred. And candy. Cactus candy. Pink and lime and rose. Pleased, she nibbled on the chunks, dabbing the sugary surface with a darting tip of wet tongue. When the children trailed off down the hall together to find the bathrooms, he leaned across her bed, licked the tiny crumbs of candy from her lips and gently plucked her nipples until she began to sweat and her legs spread open slowly, like blooming petals of a flower. Something in her back, she said. Her doctor said, she told him giggling, that she was trying to grow a tail at the base of her spine. Ball of hair. The doctor had cornered him later and blew at him for ten minutes on how she should have been brought in earlier and Manuelo had endured the humiliation of the harrangue only by reminding himself again and again of how ignorant the doctor was of what he had to go through just to get her there—her *mamá grande* and the other older women in her family had sat around jabbering for three days while Elena ached, arguing about whether her ailment was *mal natural* or *mal puesto*—and finally those siding with sorcery lost out and the others cooked up *medicinas caseras*, the last of which was a lotion composed of gasoline, alcohol, garlic, pepper, camphor, and energine which they applied directly to the small of her back. When she didn't get any better, he got angry and made her come to the doctor. Those old women even still believed in *ojo!* And here this doctor was acting like he had been negligent in getting her there.

Then there was the money involved—did he think they had money enough to come running to his office each time something went wrong? Ball of hair! He scoffed—how much would he owe the hospital and the doctor for that?

The paper had slipped from his weary fingers and fallen to the floor; he retrieved it from the grit and dusted it off. His head ached: the air in the anteroom was clogged with smoke and the temperature had risen with the morning until they all were sweating. He peered into the main office and saw the secretaries parading through a door to the rear of the room, chattering spiritedly as they disappeared for their first coffee break.

For the next fifteen minutes he struggled with spelling the words he needed to fill the spaces, listening to the word in his mind, then echoing it aloud and transcribing it phonetically to the form, which he pressed against his knee. When he finished the section, he stretched, then leaned forward, propping his chin between his palms, his inattentive gaze lighting on the hair-oil smudges on the wall opposite his bench. Then, again, but altogether unintentionally, he found himself staring at the girl's crotch. She was posturing before him like a sullen, impatient teacher collecting an examination from a back-row troublemaker, her hand extended for the form.

"I'm not through yet," he snapped. She shrugged and passed on down the line.

He turned back to the form, skipped over a question he failed to understand, and discovered happily that the remaining blanks only required the names and ages of his dependents, which he listed proudly, one by one, like a man revealing a straight flush card by card at showdown. After rolling the form into a tight cylinder, he inserted his middle finger into an open end, then, when the girl returned, he held his hand out palm up and extended the finger with the form still wrapped around it. Blushing furiously, she snatched the form off his finger and handed him a card bearing the number 16.

"Have you ever been convicted of a felony?" Manuelo had failed to answer the question, but had he done so he would have described a chain of events culminating in a monumental absurdity, Méndez might think. *The Pepsi-Cola Bottling Co., Inc., & Safe-*

*way Food Stores et al. vs. Manuelo Méndez.* Not that it ever got that far. Their own prejudice saved Manuelo. And the TV cameras. Pepsi saw a chance to doctor up its image. Joan Crawford and Manuelo Méndez—you scratch my back. . . . Surely Manuelo couldn't have been shrewd enough to premeditate the outcome; pure native wit coupled with a lucky impulse got him off. Trembling, dumb, confused Messkin— "But I thought it was for everybody!" *Har har har Messkin's so dumb . . . ass . . . hole in ground.* Even made the papers. Human Interest. Touch of Humor to Liven Up a Dreary Day: *Loser Winner in No-Contest Contest.* Pepsi probably didn't like the headline but the story gave them nationwide publicity. When Méndez first read it, reclining on the bed sipping cold beer, he laughed steadily, helplessly, his diaphram stuck to his spinal column, until he broke into a croup, choking on the beer. Juanita strode in from the kitchen, grinning in anticipation. Shaking, he passed her the paper; she skimmed the article, and her amusement held a brief skirmish with her compassion. *Probrecito, probrecito,* she murmured, then her voice fluttered out in playful spurts of guilty laughter.

Counterpointed ironies: peeping out from behind the story's final paragraph was the information that the legal winners, a Mr. and Mrs. Clyde Redfearn, had, after Pepsi turned them loose for ten minutes to ransack the store, returned to the checkout stand with $7.86 worth of groceries. (Hence the PR man's anxiousness to transform Manuelo's obvious thievery into an act of Pepsi generosity.) Chuckling, he flopped back on the bed. The Redfearns drove a '49 Packard, faded green. Had a truck farm west of town. Pepsi–Cola Bottling Co., Inc., *et al.*, promotes a contest exploiting greed—winner gets ten minutes of legalized looting while a crowd of vicarious plunderers cheers them on. Oh, he knew exactly what happened, he could envision it, Official Stop-Watch, Countdown, and all. Saturday morning shoppers milling behind the ropes, craning necks, *boy if it was me*, and the Redfearns, he wearing patched brown khaki pants and shirt, scuffed hightops with a cowboy heel, she stolid, squat in a baggy dress whose fist-sized floral pattern had faded into weak blobs of watered color, like pools of lilac light, both in their seventies, grasping the handle of the pushcart, leaning on it like a walker. Oblivious to the crowd's urging, she killed a precious minute digging into her purse for a grocery list, then they trekked across the frontier into the Land of the Free Canned Goods. No mad sweeping of shelves, her list said "plums" and nothing more than plums. Hmmmm, two brands, sizes, prices—she guesstimated the cheapest (years of doing this), old eyes warily reading the label for the weight of the contents. On to Meat—did Mama want a chuck roast? No, it looked too grainy, but that there fryer sits there plump and plucked, planned to get one anyway. To the Garden (the very same from which Manuelo was ousted years ago)—clacking dentures they passed up apples but picked up pears, half a dozen (for preserves!), and a clump of turnips. She inspected potatoes, brushing buds from their eyes with her thumb, then sacked a dozen and weighed them. Slow, so slow, and old they crept around the store, for a while beyond the sight of the sweating PR man. Over in Detergents, then Housewares, it was almost time—there they came around the bend. Clyde paused before the tobacco stand and fingered several cans of snuff, but he didn't see his brand. Before they reached the cameras, the PR man intercepted them and shoved two cartons of Pepsi into their cart. (Clyde hasn't drunk Pepsi since the late forties: he still remembers "Pepsi-Cola hits the spot, twelve full ounces made from snot.")

*ANNOUNCER:*

(Standing before man-high stack of Pepsi-Cola) "Here they come folks, our big winners with their cart just loaded down with goodies. Let's see what they have." (As Clyde and Melba move toward checkout stand, Announcer manuevers to the basket.) "Well, sure enough they picked up some of that wonderful Pepsi." (Clyde frowns. Announcer begins holding up items from the cart, one by one. Housewives strain against the ropes, trying to see the individual items, comparing what Melba took to what they would have taken.) "We've got a chicken, plums, a five-pound sack of flour, a spatula. . . ."

As he named each item, Melba felt somehow naked and ashamed, as though they were rummaging through her chest of drawers.

*ANNOUNCER:*

"Well, while the checker adds up the winnings we'll ask our winners how they feel. Clyde, how's it feel to be a winner in the Pepsi-Raid-A-Supermarket Contest? Did you have any idea when you walked in here today that you were going to walk away a winner? Did you make any plans on how to make the most out of your ten minutes? What do you plan to do with all those groceries, Clyde? I guess with all you've got, you're real glad Pepsi's going to foot *this* bill! Tell me, what was your first reaction when they told you you were a winner?

*CLYDE:*

(Nervous, imagines the questions require responses.) "Just fine nope not much just what we came to get eat em most likely nope I hope we didn't put em out none." (Méndez wished he were in Clyde's place: for ten years he has wanted to answer a "How does it feel . . . ?" with "Like a dream, a wet dream.")

*ANNOUNCER:*

"Well, we have our grand total now." (Checker, dumpy, peroxide blond, turns left profile to camera, hands announcer check slip.) "The checker's just handed me the check slip. And what is it? Our winners have walked away with a Grand Total of Seven Dollars and Eighty-Six Cents Worth of Groceries!" (Muttering among the crowd: *I* would have . . .)

Then, as Méndez pieced the story together later: scurrying out the "in" side of the automatic doors with a bulging sack of foodstuffs, Manuelo crashed headlong into the assistant manager, who had gone out for coffee. He had entered the store a half-hour earlier with the sixteen-pound sack folded neatly and tucked beneath his belt, saw the cameras and the more-than-ordinary commotion at the checkout stand, and remembered the contest. Two ways to look at it—it was either the wrong time or the right time to cop a bag of groceries. He had done it once before without a single problem—you push the cart and get the groceries, bag them near the front but out of sight, then standby the door, Waiting for a Cab.

This time he had strolled the aisles for twenty minutes, rich in the affluent shadows of brightly packaged goods stacked almost as high as Christmas trees, whistling along with Muzak in the refrigerated air. His only limitations were logistic; decisions had to be made judiciously—a box of Wheaties, for example, displaced an area equal to three plastic bags of beans. Like working a mechanical puzzle or fitting odd-shaped blocks together, he found it pleasurable to exercise the capacity for projecting dimensions and imagining weights, and he enjoyed himself thoroughly, plucking each item from the shelf, appraising its suitability and checking it through an elimination process. Although his method was relatively rational and based on a priority of need, his choices were sometimes affected by an intuitive and creative inspiration of the moment, by chance tumbling suddenly into pattern and order. A can of Hi-C caught his eye, and when he rolled the bulky cylinder slowly through his palms, he realized that almost a hundred packages of Kool-Aid could fill the same space. He congratulated himself. Absolutely no reason why he should bother to take *water* from the store, and this insight in turn lead him into a series of brilliant, dehydrated selections which included bouillon cubes, powdered milk, chocolate (a luxury, but genius deserved a bonus), potatoes, and eggs. Concur-

rent with the inspiration he experienced a mild disappointment that they would never know to what heights
of soaring creativity, order, and finesse thievery might
be raised. On he went, humming the airy zing and plip
of Muzak, until the manager broke in to announce that
the contest would be under way. Would the customers
please clear the aisles? This, Manuelo saw, would create
something of a problem. For some reason he had assumed the contest would be centered at the checkout
stand and thus the management would be doubly occupied. Therefore, he had reasoned, the moment was
as *right* as a nail driven flush in two straight blows. He
simply hadn't counted on their clearing the aisles. But
no need for anxiety, for he had artfully cracked open
the carapace of logistics and left the meat intact—the
problem of the getaway could be solved. (Over the span
of twenty minutes the feeling of Cat Burglar Jewel
Thief had stolen over him like the delayed pulse of a
double shot of tequila. He suspected that some kind of
strategy was necessary but tossed the suspicion into the
junkyard of his amateurish past: professionals like himself preferred to wing it, darting from tactic to tactic,
and hang on the existential heights of improvisation.
Clear summer nights he led the family across a moonlit
pasture and through a loose board in the back wall of
a drive-in movie, where—on the terrace in front of the
refreshment stand—they sat in metal lawn chairs and
munched bags of popcorn brought from home. In two
or three movies in particular he had noted what he felt
were useful approaches to thievery, devices in every
thief's stash of gimmicks: imposture [with or without
costume], bluff, confusion, and a certain discreet
manipulation of the laws of improbability. Not a thief
by nature [although the gringos say so, Méndez would

think: *them Messkins'll rob a man blind;* but then so would Billy Sol Estes], he considered it a last resort, and even in his one or two successful attempts the total stolen amounted to less than what the average white, middle-class teenager shoplifted weekly from the drug or dime store. He was convinced the methodology of the movies was sound, although the logic that brought him to that conclusion was not.)

Despite his attempts to reason with the problem of the getaway, an impulse to dash out the back door kept quivering upward in his spine like mercury in a thermometer, but he chilled it with the reminder that he had to keep his head. He guessed immediately that he would need a place to hide. (That it did not occur to him to assume the role of legitimate customer—something that even the most inexperienced of third-rate con men would have considered—and stand with the rest of them near the front, attested to not only a life-long sense of alienation that no filmed fantasy of well-oiled gears of clever robbery could ever negate but also to a subjectivity, an incapacity for detachment. Méndez would conclude that successful crime required a thorough understanding of what it was to *not* be a criminal, required that the criminal crawl inside a set of responses totally unfamiliar to those who had never known the status of citizen.) But where? He waited until the last stragglers—a jabbering clutch of four women, followed by the butcher and his helper—had vacated the area around the meat counter, then he slipped behind it, tugging the cart behind him. He bagged the groceries swiftly, his nervous haste canceling the care with which he had culled the items, then he crouched behind the counter, shrewdly leaving the bag a full twenty-five feet away from where he squatted.

A few moments later he watched the reflection of the Redfearns float in the chromium trim of the meat cutter as they passed before the counter. The keen and liberating winds of uncertainty had shifted to the north —not only did he not know what to do next, but hunkering behind the counter like a fugitive had stripped him of his faith in his own professionalism: that protective cloak was missing and he found himself shivering noticeably in the chilly air.

He saw the butcher, his apron splashed with the scarlet imprints of entrails, break from the huddle of employees on the fringe of the crowd and start down an aisle for the meat department just as the Redfearns were rolling near the checkout stand. Manuelo dragged the sack of groceries to the end of the counter, past the sight lines of the spectators, cradled it in his arm, and stepped out along the aisle nearest the wall. It was empty, but the far end opened onto a portion of the perimeter of customers circling the Redfearns and the TV announcer—if he could manuever behind them without being seen, he might pass safely out the door behind their backs: their attention was centered on the contest.

But his steps grew more hurried with each long yard he covered; his fingerpads left damp spots on the bag, and when he glanced down to readjust the load he saw with horror that the sack was branded on the side with a foot-high emblem of the 7–11 food chain. Fumbling, he struggled to rotate the sack so that the label pressed against his chest. A few customers standing in the outmost circle of spectators—those who had been forced to peer over taller heads—began to lose interest once the Redfearns's tally was made and turned back to the store proper to resume shopping. His heart thundered in the cave of his breastbone as a huge female, amorphous somehow, like a monolithic amoeba, parted from the circle with the inevitability of cytokinesis and shunted her loaded cart down the aisle toward him. Her ponderous, Amazoid flanks—bound up in toreador pants—protruded from both sides of the cart, suggesting greater boundaries of territorial requirements than her own flesh actually displaced, like a negative electromagnetic field. Floundering he went left, but so did she, then they both veered right. She smiled embarrassed amusement at the cliché, but he was cursing under his breath—their maneuvering had brought her cart diagonally across the aisle. Averting his eyes, he jerked the front of her cart aside and hurried around her bovine form, squinting, on the verge of exploding into tears of frustration. He had been trapped, events had conspired against him, some malign force he hadn't even been aware of had given him the idea of coming on this particular morning and had fooled him into thinking the time was right. He was *wrong,* wrong as a man who imagines he is having a pleasant conversation with a *bollío* only to discover that the pleasantries lead only to gross provocations.

While he faltered at the door, eyes whipping back and forth between "in" and "out" signs, "in" swung open and, like an exhausted and hysterical swimmer flailing the last ten feet to safety, he plunged through the doorway and collided with the assistant manager.

They (the sheriff, the manager, his assistant, and, later, the Pepsi PR man and a newspaper reporter) had not wanted to dignify the theft by making an arrest, Méndez guessed. But they did not arrive at such unanimity through an executive meeting—the alternative to arrest arose quite naturally as the hybrid shoot of their various motives. Hearing Manuelo's unthink-

ing protest, his completely spontaneous outburst—
"But I thought it was for everybody!"—the reporter
envisioned his entire article: it was the very log from
which human interest stories were hacked (national
wire services rejected ordinary petty robberies without
a gimmick), and somewhere in the back of the PR
man's mind a feeler quivered in harmony with the
reporter's notions. Too, the PR man most likely anticipated that to juxtapose ten minutes of legalized
looting against an arrest for petty theft might appear
obscene to certain ordinary minds unenlightened by
the realities of higher salesmanship. Their conference
would have been amusing to observe. The sheriff usually wore a soft gray Stetson, immaculate, and stared
into other people's eyes with the ingenuous attention
of a child or a pig. His mode of dress—a dark, pinstripe
suit below the cuffs of which shimmered the burnished
surfaces of black Wellingtons—suggested an inten-
tional blending of the old and new worlds. From his
predecessors he retained the hat and boots (although
the form of the latter had undergone a transformation:
his immediate predecessor had worn stovepipe cowboy
boots, but equipped them with walking heels—*his* contribution to the inevitable march of history), for, except
for the suit, which gave him something of the appearance of a manikin advertising appropriate dress for
plainclothes detectives, his hat and boots and eyes
differentiated him as a lawman in much the same manner as an earthworm is characterized by its annelid
setae. The suit he had adopted from the chronicles that
presaged the new—Dragnet, M-Squad, and 77 Sunset
Strip—along with the shoulder harness: he had fore-
gone exercising his ancient perogative of the hip holster
in favor of the inconspicuous bulge.

Like those of many provincials, the sheriff's attitudes

toward other regions constituted a bundle of positive and negative impulses whose indeterminate direction tended to frustrate him, and he was not a man to revel in the ambiguity of reality. On late-night talk shows glamorous people—movers of the nation—chatted incessantly of the east and west coasts, leaving the impression that the United States consisted of two narrow bands of fertile terra divided by an uninhabitable void which could be traversed only by non-stop jet. The sheriff did not know he resented this, but tourists with out-of-region license plates discovered it when they overparked. Not that he was overbearing—these people were, after all, part of that great milieu that produced senators, movie stars, and industrialists—he simply felt it his duty to remind them that, stagnant backwater of history or no, law and order still reigned over chaos in these regions. In short, the sheriff oscillated between contempt, envy, and admiration for outsiders and was not aware that all three emotions were inextricably related.

The PR man hailed from White Plains, New York. He was a Jew, but the sheriff didn't know it. He had never to his knowledge seen a Jew, for—except for one or two trips to Dallas and a hitch in the air force, which he spent mostly at Amarillo—he had never been out of the county. Had the PR man invited him to his son's *bar mitzvah* he would have happily accepted with the assumption that the other man's son had just opened a tavern. That a real Jew might actually materialize within his legal jurisdiction was beyond his imagination: Jews were all much too occupied in New York with their International Conspiracy to spread their subterfuge where it would not profit them. They were dark and squat, with long noses and bald heads which they mopped frequently with handkerchiefs. They talked funny and consumed what leisure time that remained from conspiring by counting money or playing violins. Their names all ended with Stein or Berg.

The PR man's name was Allan Ross. He was as tall as the sheriff, but he had more hair. He dressed quite smartly in an expensive cocoa suit, and the sheriff could only criticize his rather odd, perhaps sissified (Italian) shoes and his foreign-looking (Tyrolean) hat. Jovial and ebullient but efficient of motion and manner, Ross had completely charmed the sheriff by asking him a few rhetorical questions and nodding gratefully at the sheriff's answers. That a man who made his living traveling around the country at the expense of Pepsi-Cola, Inc., should seek the counsel of those who really knew the local terrain gave the sheriff the sense of being part of a vast and highly intelligent army whose officers had horse sense enough to know that native scouts were indispensable.

It was only when the PR man suggested an alternative to the Mexican's arrest that the sheriff balked: he didn't try to tell this Ross how to run his business and it seemed pushy for Ross to interfere with his. But this Ross put it persuasively (sensing the sheriff bristle, he shifted his approach: taking the sheriff aside and laying an arm across his shoulder, he rephrased the suggestion into terms of favor, pleading Pepsi's image), and the sheriff understood, wallowing deliciously in the feeling that Pepsi's reputation depended on his decision, just as Ross had known he would. For the sheriff—who had not experienced such a feeling since he stopped a state representative for drunken driving—it was a question of his own ambivalence: he was caught between demonstrating that law enforcement in these regions was not nervous-nellied and weak-kneed like its urban counterpart and exhibiting a breadth of vision which included the possibility that minor infractions could be overlooked in favor of a greater benefit to the nation-at-large. (Fortunately it never occurred to Ross to make an appeal for mercy for Manuelo: he prefaced his suggestion with the comment that he knew the sheriff had his duty to perform, that he himself would—*in any other situation*—never presume to interfere with justice.) Having already been included on the Pepsi team, in the end the sheriff's uneasy but transcendental patriotism overcame his ethnocentrism. "All right," he said, "if Pepsi wants to pay for them groceries it's all right with me, but that Messkin don't deserve it." He proceeded to lecture Manuelo on Pepsi's generosity. Ross took care not to congratulate him for doing the right thing. He had played the sheriff like a pinball machine whose point of tilt he had long ago discovered.

So they chose to humilitate Manuelo rather than arrest him, a choice determined partly—Manuelo understood later—by his own prideless and disgusting outcry on being caught. (Seated beside the dozing Indian at Fat Man's with still another humiliation imprinted on his brain like scar tissue from a burn, he sees —or wishes—that he could have fought them instead of yelling like some dumb *campesino*. Fear drove him into cowardice, into betraying himself. He holds them at bay with a loaded pistol: *you have this thing and you let somebody take what they want and you don't even know if they need it and I take it because I need it and you'd put me in jail. Cabrones! There's no justice in you. Chingan sus madres!*) The crowd converged, surging, laughing, violent bows of their carts bearing full upon him. Helplessly, his eyes swept faces as indistinguishable as blank clots of pizza dough, then his gaze hung upon the face of the elephantine woman with whom he had jockeyed in the aisle. She swelled in the front rank, an oddly symmetrical pattern of three wrinkles on her forehead like the stamp of a giant chicken foot giving her an air of intense concentration and suspense, as though she might be waiting for the final, break-tie play in a pro-football game. Manuelo was smothering to death, the air around him suddenly stripped of its oxygen. While he gasped, head bowed, cheeks flushing, the sheriff marked each item taken from the bag with the label of his humor: *well looky here at this here Quik. Perty good, but looks to me like it ain't quite quick enough.* It did not seem peculiar to Manuelo that the volume of laughter was wholly unproportionate to the quality of the sheriff's humor. Nor did it to the sheriff: cast suddenly by the grace of his cleverness into the limelight, he carried on in this vein for some minutes until his self-imposed thematic restrictions—Messkin as thief—proved too rigorous for his imagination, at which time—while the contents of Manuelo's bag were handed down a chorus line of official persons desiring roles in such rollicking comedy—the announcer stepped forward to save the show. How did it feel to be a winner? Did he have any idea when he came in here today that he was going to walk away with a load of free groceries? (Loud laughter.) After the PR man paid the bill, they released him and he carried the sack of groceries halfway home, pausing at the midpoint atop an overpass to sling the sack over the railing. Below, on the pavement, it exploded on impact into a frenzy of color, killing them all.

Sniggers on the street, mostly from his own people. Some—admirers, apparently—repeated his own sentence to his face in a way that suggested they admired his ingenuity. He was not among them; he bloodied the nose of a friend who used his own words as a *mosca*, a jibe.

At Fat Man's the Indian rises to feed Gómez's quarter into the jukebox. He plays two by the Beatles and one by a mariachi band called Los Tres to cheer Manuelo up. Although he does not care for the melody, he enjoys translating the lyrics. Once or twice he verges on asking Manuelo for help but is discouraged by the other man's glum, trance-like focus fixed on the glut of blackened match-sticks in the ashtray. "I am as the bird whom the winds have flung so far from home, over the mountains and out to sea. I cannot return to you for my heart is filled with sadness and my lips are chapped beyond repair." Was that right? he wondered.

Long after the tone arm has lifted, a residue of the tune's melancholy ambience lingers in the objects of the room, as though their molecular structure had broken loose enough to admit the frequencies of lamentation; eventually the keen predominance of grief in the atmosphere chips away the shell of the Indian's serenity. He pushes back from the table and prepares to leave, gathering himself up like a listless housewife picking up after children. He talks Gómez out of a pack of cigarettes, waves good-by to Manuelo, who stirs long enough to return the wave and watch the Indian roar off on his cycle, a complex of reflections between mutually opposing plate-glass windows on either side of the street giving the impression that the Indian is vanishing in two opposite directions at once.

Manuelo's glimmering pupils flick rhythmically with the rise and fall of the fat man's arm, following the arc of the swatter as Gómez hacks at the counter-top, feeling the dull ache of a cut coagulating on his right calf. Pink *maricón* face. Each dead fly a bit of flesh and blood. He had to wait a full hour for them to call his number, bench boards torturing his lanky hams. The tobacco smoke had condensed into a fog-like cloud the temperature, it felt, of steam, invading his lungs like gas and turning the lining of his stomach a litmus red. He tried unsuccessfully to doze with his face cupped in his hands but a slow ache burrowed its way into his head. Finally he stretched restlessly and walked around the corner to get a drink of water to redampen his stomach's growling, but the cooler eeked out a pencil-sized squirt of water so cold it bit his teeth and so feeble he had to slurp it like a dog.

As he returned to the bench, the secretary advanced to the mouth of the passageway and called out number 17. The burly Anglo, whom he had approached about the pencil, lumbered up from the bench. "Yo," he answered and followed the secretary into the inner office. As if on reflex Manuelo drew his feet beneath him, sprang upright and stalked after them into the corral, where the secretary waved the Anglo off to the left and had just reseated herself at the typewriter when he accosted her, leaning over the front of her desk, towering. "Hey mahn!" he snapped. Her mouth tightened like an invaded sphincter. "How come this ather guy come before me? I got 16." Mute with irritation, she took the card and examined it to let him know she wasn't going to take his word for it, then rose and padded across the carpet to a desk where a balding, flush-joweled man sat brushing lint from his coat.

Simpson, Méndez would groan. Although Manuelo failed to percieve it, Simpson was in foul humor, his mouth draped across his face like spoiled meat. Last night he read a provoking article in *Reader's Digest* entitled "Get It Off Your Chest," and he thought it sage advice. However, he did not get it off his chest when he discovered that his wife had neglected to retrieve his other suit from the cleaners (although his daughter found herself grounded for unclear reasons). He failed likewise when the bank phoned this morning to report an overdraft (because, he was certain, they had overlooked a deposit), and his awareness of his failure to practice the principle expressed in the article has given him one more reason to affect it. So, Méndez would guess, not only is his ill humor the outgrowth of his sense of his own humanity (we're all imperfect), it has become—for the time—a virtue, like courage or honesty. To these conditions add that the boundaries of Simpson's oddly shaped tract of propriety have always, as Méndez has seen in the pubic-arch exchange, enclosed commentaries on the intimate aspects of an applicant's life; add that Simpson has for some ten or fifteen years stored a volatile mixture of prejudice and misgiving about the poor and their conditions, a mixture which only lacks the catalyst of overt hostility to activate it.

Simpson approached Manuelo's problems with the grace of an elephant in armor. *Well, seems as if you omitted a matter of minor importance here,* Simpson began with a sardonic smile. *U.S. Citizen?* Much skepticism, poising a pencil over the blank. *Yeah,* Manuelo replied with a glare, daring him to ask for proof. Simpson hesitated then filled in the blank with a tight little smile as though whatever he wrote there might be a secret little joke between the two of them that he was willing to share, for the moment, like the patronizing conspiracy of a football coach padding the grade of an aspiring quarterback. *Too early for the cotton harvest so there's not much chance there.* Manuelo kept mute—he knew that or he wouldn't have been there. The blob sucked air through tiny nostrils, its insect appendages scratching at his form. It sat in a swivel chair; wrapped around one of its delicate limbs was a white-gold watch which it checked frequently, frowning as it looked over Manuelo's form. Cufflinks. On the desk accouterments of power: ballpoint pens with glittering, tubular cases, a rack of rubber stamps, monogrammed coffee mug, a stand of six pipes, two books, a newspaper, a stack of letters, a pair of fingernail clippers that reminded him of a silver minnow—all these objects he viewed from the oblique perspective of a chair a good three inches lower than the man's.

Finally it appeared to him that the inspection might be nearing completion—the man had turned the form over and was shaking his head sadly to himself, a prelude, Manuelo thought, to speech. He grew nervous and agitated, worried that his inability to complete the form correctly might prove him inferior to whatever job the man might secure for him.

"I been here since seven-thirty," he blurted out. "You got a job or what?"

Simpson refused to answer, but shot Manuelo a glance intended to reaffirm his own authority. It was accompanied by a disgusted turn of lip, as though he had inadvertently bitten off the head of a worm. Finally, he dropped his eyes back to the form, bowing his head over it, the palm of one hand pressing against his forehead. His other hand held a pencil which he tapped periodically against the paper as if to test its reflexes. Manuelo recovered his silence, but fell to cracking his knuckles one by one then all together in a steady, quintuplicate pattern of pops. *Chingao!* Why couldn't this silly bastard forget the form and talk to *him*—the form didn't need the job. He was here in flesh, blood, and bones (and nerve ends which rattled and vibrated like the miniature tin players in an electric football game). The way the man just sat there reading the form, furrowing his brow, sighing, ducking his head, rubbing his nose, tapping the application with his pencil made Manuelo feel as though he was under surveillance by an unseen observer. His spinal column suddenly became a conduit for ice-cold, coursing water as he realized the man was about to speak: he looked up from the paper. How long had Manuelo worked the construction job that ended a month ago? Encouraged, Manuelo told him that he only worked the job three months. The faint scent of hope had ridden on the breeze of the question—maybe there was some provision that covered those who couldn't work long enough to support their families? But no, he had forgotten about gringo logic. He did not fully comprehend the first time the man explained it; that is, he understood the words, the meaning, but not the logic. According to this man, he could get money if he had worked longer, but as it was he couldn't get it. Rules said he had to have been in the service of his employer for six months to be eligible for unemployment insurance. What went on in their minds? If he *had* worked longer, then he wouldn't *need* the money so much. Was this *his* rule? What kind of stupidity was it that led a man to make up a rule that says that you can get money if you don't need it, but you can't if you're desperate for it? Did *he* make that up?

Well, he was *hardly* responsible for regulations

passed by the state legislature. His smile infuriated Manuelo, who didn't want to drop the subject so readily—Look, he worked as long as they let him but construction stopped. No matter: with the war on in Viet Nam it was hard for builders to get loans. Goddamnit, that wasn't *his* fault—then they should take the money from the people who wanted the war, he didn't *know* anything about it, didn't *care* anything about it—he just wanted to work. The man was sorry, but there was simply nothing they could do for him.

Sputtering, Manuelo exploded into discordant chunks of anger like a piano dropped ten stories to the pavement. He spurted from the chair and clutched at the edge of the desk with one hand while the other flailed at the air. What did he wear that fancy suit for and smoke six pipes and write letters and sign papers and wear a gold watch for if it wasn't to find people work? He glared murderously at the man. Was he going to do his job or not?

Simpson's cheeks turned the brownish red of overripe peaches. He had had just about enough of his loudmouthed bellyaching. Did he think a job would solve his problems? Is *that* what he thought? Here. He spun the form around and shoved it toward Manuelo, tapping a manicured nail against a blank. What did this say? Fuming, Manuelo assumed his literacy was in question. Okay, so he didn't fill it out right—he didn't read English too well. No, no, no. The man might *hope* that Manuelo didn't fill that part out correctly, but he feared he did. It said Manuelo had six children. Manuelo nodded dumbly. And he was only twenty-nine? Yeah. (What was this leading to?) The man's mouth expressed disgust, and Manuelo momentarily regretted his own surliness, sensing that had somehow provoked a response that might interfere with his opportunities. But it looked hopeless, anyway. As he spoke he felt tears welling in his eyes. "I didn't sit here all morning just to hear you remind me how many kids I got. I need a goddamn job."

The man bent toward him. "Now *you* look," he hissed. "We don't work miracles around here. I'm going to tell you something that might be of more benefit than some piddling job I might scrape up for you, I'm going to let you in on a little secret. The real problem isn't our lack of positions—it's your need for work. Why do you think you need a job so badly? Because you've got too many children, that's why. You people have just got to learn that you can't just go on having children and expect us to worry about what happens to them. You've got to learn to control yourselves."

Manuelo felt as though he had just placed the final piece in an extremely intricate puzzle. He had hitchhiked and frozen his balls off, hungry, tired, waited all that time, got treated like a hunk of crap, and it ends like *this*. Somehow it all made sense.

"Sonofabeetch!" Although he was enraged, his epithet took on the flat finality of an objective statement of fact.

"Just calm down," Simpson admonished evenly, his meager wad of anger spent. "We'll try to find you a job."

He did not calm down, but he did keep quiet. Still, he didn't get a job. The man said that although it was time for lunch he would make one call for Manuelo. He phoned a service station. Was she ready? He carried on an extended conversation with the other party concerning the relative ease with which his present automobile could be serviced as compared with his wife's, during which time Manuelo began to snatch the watch off his wrist, loop the band around his own fist and strike him repeatedly in the face, the sharp projections on the band-clasp scoring his flesh, gouging long strips down his cheeks. When Simpson seemed to be terminating this part of the conversation and shifted into his query, Manuelo hopefully lifted his animosity. Did his place, by the way, need another hand? He waited, nodding this way and that as he listened to the other party. The other man seemed to be asking a question, for Simpson's eyes arched upward at Manuelo automatically and almost unconsciously as if to verify something, and when he did Manuelo knew it was all over. "Yes," Simpson answered, and Manuelo stomped out of the office.

He hitchhiked back from Sangre de Christo carrying a rock the size of a baseball whose purpose was unclear to him until three teenagers in a grill-less '57 Chevy with primer-spotted fenders braked as if to pick him up, then swerved onto the shoulder, the hippo-mouth grill-hole yawing down on him, wheels spewing gravel: in the wake of the exhaust he chunked the rock and saw it bounce off the rear deck of the Chevy. They did a highway patrol backup and spun out after him to take another pass but he vaulted a barbed-wire fence, cutting his leg, and hid in a gulley until he heard the car squeal off again. Five minutes later the Indian appeared.

Gómez would like to relieve himself of the burden of this man who sits like a murderous presence, his body coiled upon itself, at his counter in a cafe empty but for them. Although it is still the middle of the afternoon, he considers closing up, and he rehearses its progressive stages, imagining himself moving about the room mopping tables, snapping off lights in the back, thinking that at some point these motions might penetrate Manuelo's trance and speak for Gómez's need to leave, penetrate it where his words have not. But even were he to put these acts in motion, he could not bring himself to clear the cash drawer with Manuelo seated just beside the register, no matter how painfully empty it is. Gómez is greedy but not cruel, selfish but not insensitive.

Thus he is caught between his responsibility and his sense of impotence to help. He eases into his lawn chair and sighs, elaborately, histrionically, with a heavy suggestion of finality. Manuelo blinks, but his pupils remain fixed to the blackened sticks in the ashtray.

*"I wish something . . ."* Gómez offers vaguely, helplessly.

Still no sign, only a faint tremble along the slender ridge of flesh below his jaw-line as his fingers test the tensile strength of a plastic spoon which Gómez hopes he does not break.

*"Look—you come home with me and have some cabrito, eh?"*

The silence contains the tension of the interval between the unpinning of a grenade and its explosion; Gómez, though normally unflappable, feels himself tighten up, grow just a little angry at the guilt this victim produces in him. Gómez won his naturalization in the service in World War II; he survived the Bataan Death March and scraped together enough cash with the G. I Bill to start his business; he's paid his dues, and the campaign ribbons displayed under glass on the back wall prove it.

"All right then, mahn," he says, piqued. "You tell *me* what you're going to do."

The spoon snaps; Manuelo lifts his head to fix conscious eyes on Gómez as though Gómez's words were the unexpected appearance of a wall at the end of a tunnel; he does not answer Gómez, nor does he need to, for Gómez watches fear-struck himself as Manuelo's features pass from desperation to a gigantic swell of rage, his body gathering like the coiled-taut sinew behind the rattler's bite.

# Méndez

# One

"You know a cow's damn near the dumbest thing on earth? You know a cow don't even know its own shadder? Cows is so ignert that you can't even call one to you; if you want one to get somewhere you got to be anywhere but there and then he'll go. It just plain hurts my pride to work for something that hadn't got no more sense than to drink something that'd kill it."

Bond stands with a bootheel resting on the rim of his shovel blade, the handle tucked into his armpit. Beside the jeep, one foot hiked up on the fender-step, Méndez scribbles on a pad balanced atop his upthrust knee.

"You think we ought to let them drink it?" He smiles, dipping his head toward a knot of Herefords near a patch of mesquite a stone's throw from the tank battery. Bond confronts them; they return his stare, their long, white faces clumped in apprehension, like unwilling witnesses to an accident that isn't over yet.

"Git!" Bond brandishes his shovel—the cattle bolt and bump each other, mill a moment, then trot twenty yards beyond the mesquite and collect again.

"No," he snorts. "But I never did aspire to operate no idiot stick; I don't figger this here's really *our* line a work."

Méndez arches his brows quizzically, then continues writing—*fourth time this month you've let the tanks run over. Cattle are up close and we don't have time to wait for your crew to get here. We'll cover and bill you.* Next time though, he vows, that lazy bastard will have to explain a letter to the supervisor.

He folds the note, then studies the problem, tracing the pool of oil back to its source beyond the barbed-wire fence enclosing the battery yard, his eyes working their way against the rivulet of pitch-brown crude oil trickling through the red sand in the yard after oozing, like a great stain of molasses, down the silver belly of the nearest tank.

While Bond leans on his shovel, Méndez steps off the perimeter of the pool, hands on hips, making the foreman's ritual survey of the task like a dog circling a spot before he lies down on it, then returns to the jeep and rummages beneath the driver's seat for his gloves.

"They wouldn't get here in time."

Bond shrugs. "They got insurance."

The pipes above the tanks grumble, then give off a muted gush. Bond sighs, jabs the spade of his shovel into the sandy earth, grunts, then lifts a heaping shovel-ful of loose sand and slings it out into the middle of the pool where it humps for a moment, then seethes and disappears, absorbed by the oil.

"Look at that, will yew? We'll be here all night."

He glances toward Méndez, who nods to assure him his complaint has been registered, then he plunges into a steady rhythm with the shovel—dip, jab, lift, and sling: the way his one arm coils about the shovel gives Méndez the impression that Bond himself is just a fulcrum for the tool.

"You're real good at that," he jibes as he stands beside the gate stuffing the note into a fruit jar whose lid is nailed to the gatepost.

"I don't know what they got in mind, anyway," Bond mumbles behind him. "They oughta have better sense than to send a fossilized old cripple and a lazy wetback pepper-belly out to do a job that ain't even necessary."

"Ours is not to reason why."

Bond protests, but the wind darts between them, bringing the *chugga pop chugga chugga pop* of the one-lung engine running the nearest pumping unit; Méndez strides toward the catwalk, then takes its metal stairs three at a time with his palms on his knees. Atop the horizontal ramp that spans the distance between the two tanks, he holds his breath to keep the crude oil fumes from asphyxiating him, reaches over the railing, glances quickly to the east where the unit bobs, busily pumping oil into the battery, then wrenches the handle of a valve to divert the flow into the empty tank.

Spewing out his pent-up breath, he whirls away from the tanks to face the wind, then stands leaning against the railing, his chest heaving. He likes to look out across the pastures from this height; it reminds him of standing at the railing of an ocean-going tanker. Gusty all day, with long, dry strands of buffalo grass weaving violently in waves across the plains between the battery and the mesa, which stands like an island without a lighthouse. Bond is saying something—Méndez can see his lips moving—but he's not looking up. Talking to himself. From up on the catwalk the old man looks older, more as though his spine might begin to curl upon itself, like an old dog sleeping, any day now. Slowly scooping sand from the perimeter and heaving it into the pool. Should help him. Shouldn't let that old one-armed man shovel by himself.

But his eyes move west and his heart jumps when he spies a cloud of red dust billowing out behind a tiny, yellow machine in the distance—the Cat's in Dillard's pasture again! When he first spotted it there, just three days ago, he went limp in dismay, then jerked his twenty-two out of the jeep and picked off a clutch of beer cans half-hidden by the sand in the bottom of the bar ditch. He shot up an entire box of ammunition before returning to the jeep where he slumped in disgust, watching through the binoculars as a man with a white shirt and tie and trouser cuffs tucked into the tops of his cowboy boots walked around planting stakes with red streamers tied to them.

While the Cat skinner graded off the field. They had no right to grade off that field, no right to build anything on it. He fumed, but after a half hour it appeared as though they weren't going to take but a quarter of the field and he felt some relief to think that his place stood in the virgin three-quarters. Because it was an auspicious beginning which smacked so much of the origin of storybook revolutionaries, he used to joke at college to his Anglo friends that he was born in a cotton field, although his aunt had not been too clear about the precise location and her later senility made her memory suspect. Dillard's field had been the most likely place; before Lemuel sold it to Dillard he had grown cotton on it himself and, aside from a smaller plot on the northern border which didn't match his aunt's descriptions, it was the only acreage used for that. He amused himself by studying their envy as he conjured up images: sprung from humble beginnings, from a furrow his father had ploughed (maybe). When the day came, or so he lied, she bent over, stooping from the weight of the cotton sack, felt the pangs; later he came screaming into the world while the midday sun throbbed against the earth and the others cheered and clapped. He didn't tell them what he privately believed—that he was born not in the middle of the field under a throbbing sun, but rather in the center of a mesquite thicket bordering the field. While hunting with a slingshot when he was nine, he chased a covey of quail into one of the many thickets skirting the field and stumbled into a clearing with a freshly dug prairie-dog hole in its center. He'd knelt and peered into it. The hole smelled rich and damp and he sat awhile kneading the clay earth diggings which formed a parapet at the mouth of the hole, then, later, he rose and found a stone the size and shape of a grapefruit with a flat bottom and scratched his initials and birthdate onto the underside with his knife and laid the stone in the clearing. Every birthday from then until he was thirteen he made a pilgrimage to the clearing and leaned against the stone a bouquet of gladiolas stolen from the housekeeper's flower bed. After he was eleven and had learned to shoot a twenty-two, Lemuel or one of the hands would take him rabbit hunting; if whoever accompanied him was heading for the field where the stone was enshrined in the center of the thicket, he'd strike out toward the mesa and yell back that he'd spotted a coyote. Once he almost had to resort to shooting into the thicket to scare one of the hands out. He shudders to recall that he might have shot the man, a wiry old cowboy called Buckwheat who taught him how to make a little gun out of clothespins that shot beans or the heads of matches and another kind of a gun, a long pistol cut from a slab of wood, with a clothespin mounted on the handle, that shot large rings of rubber scissored from an old inner tube. Although he doesn't like to remind himself, he liked to hunt rabbits.

Lemuel always said to eat what they killed, but Buckwheat claimed the rabbits gave people the "bluebonnet" plague, so he lied to Lemuel when asked what they had shot. Lemuel sometimes talked about the conservation of Mother Earth, a phrase which made the hands smile. The first time Méndez heard it, it hung in his mind and he whispered it to himself like an invocation: *Mother Earth, Mother Earth, Mother Earth.* He'd go walking in the pasture and repeat it as he stepped along, one word for the left foot, the other for the right, like a cadence. She stopped, he thought, where Lemuel's fences stopped; somehow her body was circumscribed by the same fences that marked off the property. That was before Lemuel sold the forty-acre field to Dillard, when he was eleven, and he went out to watch as Lemuel and Buckwheat drove metal stakes into the ground with a sledge hammer, then fastened five strands of barbed wire to the posts; the lowest came to his shins and the highest struck him across the eyes. He stood beside the fence feeling the prongs with his fingertips and imagined how the barbs might tear the hide of cattle hung on them and how they might puncture his own flesh if they caught him. The following year when he was twelve he crept gingerly through the fence to perform his annual rite, but the year after that he stopped.

Lemuel's fences, Lemuel's land. Now the land of his son Robert, whom Méndez remembers mostly as a boy some two years older, twenty pounds heavier, and two inches taller, a difference—to Méndez's childhood perspective at least—that had made him seem gigantic. Bobby resented any attention his mother gave Méndez (or so Méndez feels, did feel) and generally either bullied him or sulked and refused to notice him. Occasionally when he was bored, though, he would lure Méndez into some game in which he never failed to cast himself as the victimizer and Méndez as the victim. One day Bobby was standing out by the corral trying unsuccessfully to shoot sparrows off the electrical line which ran from the house to the barn. Méndez leaned against a cornerpost of the corral fence at a respectful distance, observing in silent triumph as Bobby, cocking the BB gun against his knee, missed again and again. Bobby finally paused as though aware of his observation.

"Want to shoot it?"

"Sure," Méndez answered warily. As he sidled slowly along the fence struggling to appear as though he were not coming forward solely to shoot the gun, Bobby began plinking at the sparrows from the hip; they remained in place, unruffled.

"I can hit them."

"No you can't." Bobby shot again, close enough to scatter the birds from the line.

"You didn't hit them."

"I hit one. Here, you can try it now." But as Méndez reached out to grab the barrel, Bobby drew it back. "You can shoot it if you'll tell me where your mother's grave is."

"No," Méndez whined. "I can't. I promised." The fiction of his mother's grave was a standing argument between them ever since her departure for a strange place called "Los Angeles" a year earlier, and the confusion in his mind of the city's name with "angels" had prompted the conclusion that she had died; too, there was a sharply-etched memory of his mother, Teresa, bawling *I must go, I must, I must,* in the rear of his Aunt Lucinda's people's house while he stood sick and confused by the screen door with his belongings in a cardboard box waiting for Frances to pick him up in her car, and the grief, the lamentation only further encouraged the logic of her death.

Bobby scoffed, cocked the gun and aimed it at a new line of sparrows that had settled on the wire. "She ain't dead, you jerk."

Before he could pull the trigger, Méndez spun away, screaming, "It hit me! It hit me!" He clutched his side and knelt in the dust beside the fence. Frances came dashing out of the house with alarm. Squealing, he told her that Bobby had shot at the barn and it had bounced off and struck him in the side.

"He's lying," Bobby snarled. "I wasn't even shooting, you little bastard!"

"Bobby!" Frances tried to raise Méndez's shirt to look at the place on his side he was clutching with both hands.

"Here, let me see it."

He hoped by some miracle there would be a mark there.

"Where did it get you, honey?"

When she tried to pull his hand away, he grew belligerent. She turned to Bobby. "I've told you to be careful with that thing!"

"But he's lying. It wasn't even cocked!"

Frances's brows knitted inward. "Raphael, are you sure?" Her lack of committment to his wound made him angry. "Let's all go inside and have some cookies," she suggested after a moment.

"I don't want any," Bobby yelled, then slung the BB gun over the corral fence and whirled toward Méndez. "Why don't you go find your own mother and leave mine alone?" he spat out, then ran out of sight around the corner of the house. Helplessly, Frances watched him vanish.

"Don't pay any attention to him."

"But my mother's dead."

"No, she's only in another *city*," Frances replied wearily.

"But *why?*"

Frances gestured listlessly with her left hand, the stone of her wedding ring flashing in the light. "She probably had her reasons—you'll see. Now come on inside and I'll put something on it."

Her vague defense was no defense at all and he was troubled by it for years until he understood in his later teens—long after Frances had left the ranch—by quizzing his Aunt how he had come to be separated from his parents and from the scattering of relatives still living in town. And then he saw that her vagueness had subtly worked to cast doubt on his parents and to mask her own motives. Had she told him the whole story he might have been able to judge her role in the events in a way which would give discredit where discredit was due, but as it was at that time he could do nothing but ache from the disparity between the lack of explanation and his need to know. A year later he was finally told that Teresa had gone to be with his father, Alfredo, who had gotten a job in Los Angeles and that they would send for him or return. This, too, was from his Aunt Lucinda's people; Frances persisted in turning his questions aside with half-hearted assurances which contained no information at all. But he was not told until years later that his father, Alfredo, had been critically injured and that a friend, a co-worker, had written that Teresa should come to Los Angeles. Shortly after her arrival there, Alfredo died. Heart-sick over his death, stranded in Los Angeles without family or money, she wound up marrying the friend, a widower with two children, and soon she was pregnant by him. Although her new husband discouraged it, Teresa had letters written through a *notario* about Méndez, wanting him to be sent to her, but Frances apparently balked at length, arguing that the boy was about to begin school and that she knew Teresa and her new groom would soon be off on the migratory circuit, so couldn't he stay with his *madrina*, where he would be near relatives and would receive good care? Teresa let things slide by until at last—so Méndez assumed—even the desire vanished and Frances's argument became her own. But there was more to the mystery—why couldn't Frances have told him more? (That Teresa had not told him more he was willing to ascribe to his age and her distraught condition, plus the fact that in her mind at least, any separation had been intended only as a temporary condition, and guilt would explain her inability to offer anything later.)

Frances never openly demonstrated affection for either when both were present, but in his mind's eye Méndez saw her squandering her love on Bobby with profligate inebriation in his absence, alternately cooing and humming the half-forgotten snatches of Mother

Goose rhymes, her throat vibrating against the back of Bobby's neck, ruffling then smoothing his hair or trailing her bony fingers lightly across his cheeks. She let Méndez sleep in the main house on the living-room couch when he was sick; she got up during the night to drape the inside of her long, cool hand across his forehead, set a pill on his extended tongue, or, if he asked, bring him a warm Dr. Pepper in a coffee mug. He couldn't help but wonder on those occasions if Bobby didn't receive this treatment on a whim.

Perched upon a chromium-legged stool with the heels of her loafers hooked on a cross-rung, Frances helped Bobby with his second-grade reader. She held the book in her left hand, her thumb laid precisely along the crease, much too close to his face, and he stared at it as though it were something he had done wrong. While she nodded patiently, coaxing him to concentrate, Méndez would try to chin himself on the back of Bobby's chair or, if reprimanded, would back away and imitate a bomber, spreading his arms and buzzing with his lips as loudly as he dared. Despite his attempts to create a subliminal disruption, Frances kept her gaze on Bobby, bobbing her head as he cautiously, almost grimly, placed each word singly in the air like a chess player who wouldn't be allowed to retract his piece once it was committed. When she urged him to read faster Bobby edged around her by storing up blocks of words while his hands gripped the edge of the cushion he sat on and his legs and his heels thumped against the rungs of the chair; he'd discharge chunks of the phrases in staccato bursts and fall silent in retreat to link another train together. Méndez sought to exploit these pauses by tapping the metal panels of the gas heater with his toe or by asking

Frances to tie his shoe or by venturing a few mumbled lines of "Jesus Wants Me for a Sunbeam," which Frances had taught him to sing. Attributing his persistent intrusions to intellectual curiosity, she made him her second pupil; afternoons when Bobby was away in school she'd put him on her lap to read. Where his own mother had been wide, Frances was long, thin, even fragile—would she blow away? He could feel her jawbone just beneath the surface of her skin when she laid his head against her cheek, and he knew he could have imagined her whole skull stripped of flesh, but he didn't. The book stood on the table propped against the sugar bowl; Frances wrapped her tubular arms around his waist, and when he looked down he could see freckles on her left forearm and her long fingers curled loosely in his lap like fleshy sepals of a sea anemone. Her cheek felt warm; she smelled of powder, and as they spoke in undulating unison of Puff's running, and coming, her breath floated against his cheek. If he did especially well, she laughed with delight, the sudden exhalation patting his forehead, the hum in her throat vibrating against his shoulder. Her delight made him try harder, and by the time he entered school six months later, he was up with, if not beyond, his Anglo classmates, whose north-side school contained no brown face but his—his cousins went to the "Mexican" school. Frances praised him by calling him a good example, a bit as though poor ones were all too readily available.

After Bobby discovered what went on when he was away at school, he claimed Frances for himself on Saturday afternoon. It was spring; Méndez could hear them reading through the open dining room window, their voices tranquil, unhurried, so after edging through the kitchen door he crept into the room and poised himself behind them with an excess of silence. But when they failed to interrupt their reading to acknowledge the restraint with which he avoided interrupting them, he began pacing restlessly behind the chair, stealing glances over Bobby's shoulder at the open page in an effort to skim it before Bobby could recite it. Bobby twisted in his seat to glare at him with an animosity whose intensity originated not so much in the present interruption as in an earlier incident. During the morning they had argued over a quarter Méndez had found on the floor of the machine shed, which Bobby claimed to have lost there and which he won possession of after a brief struggle. *Bastante!* Méndez had muttered beneath his breath: he knew nothing infuriated the other boy more than for him to mumble in Spanish. "What'd you call me?" Bobby grunted, shoving him up against the workbench. Despite his fear, Méndez thought it funny that Bobby should react so violently to such an innocent word, but he didn't dare laugh. "Nothing," he said. Bobby released him. "I called you a *bastante*," he sang out clearly after he was free of Bobby's grasp, then dashed out of the shed with Bobby sprinting behind him. Even though Bobby had wind enough to chase him into the pasture in front of the house, Méndez was lighter and faster and after he had squeezed through the barbed-wire fence just ahead of Bobby and had charged through the field dodging the clumps of buffalo grass for a hundred yards or so, he looked back over his shoulder, then fell off running. Bobby was leaning against a cedar post at the fence line, panting with exhaustion. In a moment he pushed away from the post, leaned forward, and braced the top of his body by locking his elbows and palming his knees. Méndez wondered if he was about to vomit. *"Bastante!!"* he yelled gleefully. *"Bastante!!"* Bobby lurched forward, snatched up a hardened clod of sand and hurled it at him, but it burst like a half-damp Roman candle into a reddish spray before it reached him.

Frances was pursing her lips in disapproval. "Don't bother Bobby when he's trying to read." she snapped. Her sharpness wounded him, but he thought he detected beneath the command some special plea for the handicapped. Sensing victory, he kept quiet while Bobby arduously traced, with constipated precision, Columbus's trail to America. He faltered on "conqueror," mispronounced it twice until Frances corrected him.

"What is it?" he asked.

"I know, I know!" Méndez blurted, even though he wasn't certain.

"Hush!" Frances hissed. He was glad she didn't call his bluff.

"It's a man," Bobby announced after a moment. "You can tell by the 'or' "

"Good," Frances bubbled.

Méndez could guess the rest. "A man who conquers," he put in mincingly.

"Shut your trap! Mother, I was going to say that!"

"One more word and you're going outside," Frances said hotly to Méndez, a sudden flush alighting on her cheek as though a red lamp had been switched on in the room; he knew she meant business, so he nodded and slipped back into retreat along the windows, where he disconsolately picked at the loose chunks of putty along the edges of the panes with his thumbnail.

A few moments later, after Bobby had finished his

required lesson, Frances sought to mend feelings by having them all three read from a comic book together, each taking a different part. Both he and Bobby wanted to play Scrooge McDuck; they argued.

"We'll read it twice."

"Me first!" Bobby wailed.

"That's not nice," Frances said.

Méndez got the part. Bobby read Donald with testy and sullen indifference, not even bothering to imitate the half-quacking articulation he knew from the animated cartoons, but Méndez wallowed in the part of Scrooge, gesticulating broadly for special, interpretative emphasis as he read. In his joyful haste, he misread "paunch" for "pouch."

Bobby jumped, howling with laughter. "Paunch!" he cackled. "God, you're dumb! Paunch! You dumb greaser!"

Frances sprang from the stool, jerked Bobby up by the arm and flailed at his buttocks with her free hand. "Don't you ever say that again!" she screeched, while Bobby ran in dizzy circles around her, attached to the pivot point of her body by her wrenching grip on his bicep. "You hear me? You hear?" She swatted at him clumsily; Méndez stared at them with frozen horror at the violent intensity of her anger. "That's not nice, *do you hear me?*" she chanted obsessively, maniacally, bordering for one small moment on hysteria, and although Méndez was relieved that Bobby was her target, some sense of a thin-skinned thing expanding beyond its capacity made him hold his breath to watch them spinning. She yanked Bobby to a stop, whirled him around to face her and jabbed her finger in his face. "It's not a bit nice," she scolded, calmer. "He's every bit as smart as you are."

Outraged, Bobby jerked himself free of her grasp. "Only because you help him! That's the only reason!"

Shocked, Méndez stared at them in revelation: he saw that they both believed it. Mulling over these vignettes years later he could piece together the murky puzzle of her unconscious premises and rationalized intentions. In her own fashion she had been determined to disprove her own buried assumption that he was genetically inferior, that by her missionary efforts she could elevate him to the level of her own son, that he would be better off raised by her than by Teresa. Only this could explain her anger at Bobby, whose role was like that of some uncontrollable ventriloquist's dummy of her own subconscious. Only this could explain her insistence that Méndez be left behind when Teresa was preparing to go to Los Angeles to be with Alfredo. After all, she might have coaxed, it's only temporary: you'll bring Alfredo back and the boy will be an added burden. It was a good argument, considering that at the time he and his mother were living in town with Lucinda's people, with whom she did not get along, and she must have been half-afraid that the boy would be neglected.

The dim awareness that he and Frances and Bobby were participating in some experiment of Frances's making, however half-realized on her part, made him study harder on his own. Lemuel gave him an old mildewed dictionary which had been serving as a doorstop and with it Méndez began wading through a knee-high stack of western adventure magazines left in the closet of the cottage by the transient hands who were addicted to them. By age nine he was by far the most articulately bilingual inhabitant of the ranch, speaking far more English than most of Lemuel's occasional *braceros.* Neither Lemuel nor his Anglo workers spoke any Spanish beyond those basic abortions they had appropriated for their own use—"stywainer" *(está bueno),* "nodder" *(nada),* "deenairo" *(dinero),* "cahser" *(casa),* "senior-eater" *(señorita),* and the names of a dozen or so foods. Frances, however, made a greater effort both to learn the language and to pronounce the words as Spanish-speaking persons might, which only confirmed everyone's nascent suspicion that the proper pronounciation of foreign words was a distinctly feminine, if not schoolmarmish, virtue, an appropriate activity for preachers and the mothers of pale and listless sons, but hardly suitable for men who sweat and made their living with their hands. Before he and Méndez's father left for El Paso four years earlier, Méndez's Uncle Paco, Mauelo's father, had served as a translator, during the year he worked on the ranch, but since then none had been needed, for Lemuel's work force was small and mostly Anglo. After he became aware that the boy could understand basic concepts and directions and could express them accurately in either language, the elder Houston came to rely on him more and more as an interpreter and took on more *braceros* and *mojados* who worked for lower wages than their domestic counterparts.

Translating, interpreting—ways, he found, to repay old debts. The fee slips carted home from school like some ponderous burden of old sins, the lunch tickets: at last he could think of what he got from them as the principal of a loan and not outright charity. The first time Lemuel availed himself of his services as an interpreter occurred one evening shortly after supper when three of *la gente* appeared at the back stoop without visible means of transportation, carrying blanket rolls.

Houston talked at them through the screen door; they stood in a ragged semicircle in the sand, the porch-light weak, almost watery against their drawn and dusty faces. From time to time a hand would sweep across the air before a head to clear the gnats away. One, the spokesman, shifted uneasily from one foot to the other and clutched his hat in his hand. "Wark," he said, pointing to himself and his two companions, then bowing his head obsequiously toward Houston, who towered above them inside the doorway. From his vantage point in the kitchen just behind Lemuel, Méndez watched the spokesman play the part of *péon* to the hilt.

"You greenbacks or wetbacks?" Houston joked wryly. He was toying with them, making a complicated pun they would not have understood even if he had spoken in Spanish. The gist of it was that he wanted to know if they were "green-carders," *braceros* officially under contract by agreement between the American and Mexican governments, or illegal immigrants, in which case he would not be subject to Farm Security Administration regulations regarding either their pay or their boarding. Doubtless they recognized the word "wetbacks" but it was a double-edged question for them. Méndez watched them flounder a moment, exchanging glances with one another, trying to decide if Houston was like most ranchers and growers who preferred wetbacks because they were cheaper and less trouble, or whether he was the occasional crank who abided by the letter of the law.

"You speak any English?" Houston grunted finally when they failed to reply.

"No, Señor."

"Raphael, get yore hiney out here and talk to these boys."

Méndez slid off the kitchen stool, eased past Houston in the doorway and stood on the stoop.

"*Niño,*" the spokesman asked, "*will El Señor report us to la migra?*" Some appeal in the man's tone, some assumption that Méndez would naturally be on their side and that the question was asked of one member of *la raza* to another made Méndez want to be certain.

"*I don't think so,*" he said finally.

"*Bueno. Tiene trabajo, El Señor?*"

"What do they want?" Houston asked him.

"They want to know if there's work."

Méndez knew that because of the wartime demand for cotton Houston was planning to till some of his pasture land within the next week and plant it, and as he watched Houston rub his chin thoughtfully he waited anxiously, hoping to be the bearer of good news.

"Well, I could use one good steady worker, but I'm afraid I hadn't got no use for all of them."

"*El Señor dijo que hay trabajo duradero para un hombre pero no para todo.*"

"*Uh!*" the spokesman grunted. "*Vamos de paso.*"

"*Y estamos bruja,*" a second, an older man with a cataract on one eye, put in suddenly.

Houston looked at Méndez expectantly. "They're just passing through. And they're broke."

"Best I can do is a place to sleep—take them out to the cottage with you." Méndez relayed the message and they accepted Houston's offer with what Méndez thought to be unnecessary scraping and bowing. And just as they were all turning to go to the cottage, Houston said to Frances in a lusty burst of unaccountable pride, "You know, I'll be go to hell if that boy ain't just as smart as his Daddy and his Uncle Paco." They wouldn't need a lantern to cross the yard, Méndez thought, because surely he must be glowing like one of those electric eels they read about in school.

Perched on the brink of his narrow, army-surplus bunk with his knees chocked beneath his chin and his arms hugging his shins, Méndez watched warily as the trio invaded his room without ceremony. Bare of furniture except for the metal bed and an unpainted, three-drawer dresser, the room was home for him, its defects long since transformed into virtues through familiarity —on the unvarnished wooden floor lay large blotches of motor oil left there by leaky machinery when the cottage had been pressed into service as a tool shed, and always there lingered in the air some persistent but untraceable odor which reminded him of old mayonnaise jars. He looked at the spokesman, whom the other two called Emilio. *"There is another room,"* he said, pointing through the archway into the kitchen to indicate the room used by the extra roundup help. The other two hesitated, looking uncertainly toward Emilio, but Emilio only shrugged, his features impassive, stoic. He dropped his blanket roll onto the floor under the front windows. *"No difference,"* he said: no point in worrying about comfort when things were always temporary—one slept where one found oneself. That Emilio apparently did not covet the luxury of Méndez's downy mattress shamed the boy—he should learn to be so hard.

He watched Emilio kneel beneath the windows to pluck at the knot in the twine which held his blanket in a roll. In a moment he gave the roll a push and it uncoiled, revealing a deck of cards, a little cloth sack of what Méndez took to be tobacco, a Prince Albert can which turned out to contain matches, the head from a safety razor with the stub of a pencil jammed in its end for a handle, and a small bundle he guessed to be a change of clothes, which Emilio placed together at one end of the blanket, then, yawning, he fell to stroking and smoothing the blanket out with large sweeps of his hand, almost absently, languidly. Finally he tugged off his boots, after a good deal of grimacing and grunting, seated himself cross-legged on the blanket, and began to roll a cigarette. After he lighted it, he took a deep drag and exhaled wearily with both exhaustion and relief. *"Here,"* the older man with the cataract called out from where he lay in the center of the floor. Méndez could see a long, curving scar on his cheek when he turned to speak. Emilio tossed him the papers and tobacco.

After the other had returned them to him, Emilio turned to Méndez.

*"You smoke, niño?"* he teased with a wan smile.

The direct address startled Méndez; he shifted uneasily on his bunk until his legs were beneath him in imitation of Emilio's Indian posture and tried to return the man's smile. *"No, gracias, señor,"* he replied after faltering a moment.

The third man chuckled inexplicably. *"Let it rain,"* he said. He had laid his blanket along the wall to Méndez's left and was now staring oddly at the unpainted sections of quarter-inch plywood which served as a ceiling in the cottage. Emilio laughed. *"A roof brings back old memories, eh?"* the man with the cataract joked with the third. Nodding, the third sighed with elaborate irony.

*"Once when I picked peas in the state of Illinois we stayed in houses that had water and lights,* Emilio put in. *"There was even a separate house with toilets and showers and wash basins."*

*"No kidding?"* the man with the cataract exclaimed. *"Let's go there, then."*

*"However,"* Emilio continued, smiling, *"they charged you for it; another time we slept in tents and still another we slept on the ground and the children got sick because it rained all the time and there were no toilets."*

They lapsed into silence, Emilio and the man with the cataract both reclining moodily on their elbows to pull at their cigarettes, their free hands propping up their heads. In a moment Emilio stirred, retrieved the deck of cards from the pile of articles. *"What do I owe you now, Uncle?"* Emilio asked the man with the cataract as he shuffled the cards. Although the man looked older than Emilio, an ironic waver in the younger man's tone, almost like a grace note, made Méndez think they weren't actually related by blood.

"Uncle" grunted. *"Two million pesos."*

Emilio clucked his tongue in mock concern, then began to deal three-handed poker; Méndez traced the lines of his bony profile, wondering if his father looked anything like that—wiry but underweight, the flesh on his face only padding the ridges of bone like a tight cloth covering; when he craned his head to deal, the cords in his neck pulsed then ebbed, and when he smiled the light caught an L-shaped glint of gold along two edges of his left front tooth.

*"You gamble, niño?* Emilio looked up suddenly at Méndez and winked. Caught staring, Méndez flushed and hesitated, trying to find a way to return the banter, but could only manage to mumble *"No, señor"* before the other turned back to his cards. After they had completed another hand, he breathed deeply, then spoke up. *"I could learn."* Emilio glanced up in momentary puzzlement before recognition flickered in his

pupils. *"Ah!"* he said. *"Of course. Come on over here and help me out."* Méndez scrambled off the bed and bounded across the room to scoot in between Emilio and the man who lay on his stomach. Emilio's coarse woolen blanket gave off the dry and airy smell of heavy dust.

Emilio gathered up a new hand Uncle had dealt him and peered at cards one by one as though to increase the suspense for himself. *"El Señor is your father?"* he inquired almost idly, his gaze still fixed on his cards.

Méndez nodded vigorously. *"Oh no, señor. He is in California, working in a shipyard. He helps a welder. El Señor is my padrino."*

Emilio cocked his head and winked at the others as if to say that Méndez's father was a shrewd one to make his *patrón* his son's godfather. The implication that his father had somehow pulled a fast one on Houston distressed the boy.

Emilio scrutinized the final card, a four of hearts, with the air of one whose most ominous prophecies have been fulfilled. *"And your mother?"* he asked, squinting.

*"She too, señor."* He felt some need to explain, but before he could, Emilio yawned widely, then sighed.

*"Everybody says there's much work there. But I heard on the radio that the sailors are beating up la gente in the streets, so I don't know."* He tipped his head, giving Méndez a sidelong glance. *"And you, niño, how come you're not there?"*

*"They're going to send for me,"* he told them brightly. He could feel his cheeks tingle. Uncle and the third man exchanged a fleeting glance.

*"How long have they been there?"* Uncle asked.

*"Not long,"* he lied.

*"I still think we should go there,"* Uncle said to Emilio insistently.

Méndez was startled by the possibility. *"Oh!"* he blurted out. *"Take me with you if you go, please!"* He hardly knew he had spoken.

*"Too far,"* Emilio said to Uncle.

*"I speak good English and we could pretend I was your son and I could tell anyone who asked that you lost your cards,"* he went on, breathlessly, afraid to stop.

*"See there, hombre,"* Uncle said to Emilio, impressed by the boy's reasoning.

Shaking his head sadly, Emilio turned to Méndez.

*"What if they didn't believe you? What do you think would happen to you?"*

*"But I'm a U.S. citizen,"* Méndez insisted.

*"Can you prove it?"*

*"There are papers in the house."* In the den somewhere, maybe. But where? He knew he had a birth certificate, his parents had been careful about that.

*"Perhaps they wouldn't believe them,"* Emilio continued gently. *"And then you'd be sent to Mexico* · *·th us. No, niño, it's a good idea, but it's too tricky.* ⅃e swung his gaze back to Uncle. *"Too far,"* he repeated.

*"How far is it?"* the third asked.

*"Too far,"* Emilio snapped.

Méndez recognized that he had unwittingly reopened an old wound between them; he listened in embarrassment as they began arguing about going to California, but before the issue was settled a knock on the front door of the cottage broke off the discussion.

Méndez opened the door; Frances was standing on the stoop holding an old blue enamel pot by its wire handle with one hand and a sack half-full of bread in the other. Wisps of steam bearing the aroma of vegetables and beef eeked from beneath the lid and rose to his nostrils. When she stepped beyond him into the room, Emilio and the other two got quickly to their feet.

"I brought you some soup," she announced, rather brusquely it seemed to Méndez. She extended the pot toward Emilio almost impatiently, as though the handle might be too hot, and her features expressed some odd attitude he didn't altogether understand. She eyed Emilio impersonally, distantly, as though she were responsible only for delivering the items and not for the impulse behind them, even though Méndez knew it must have been her idea.

*"Gracias, señora, gracias,"* Emilio murmured, ducking his head in little motions, then he gingerly took the pot and the sack of bread from her hands, carefully maintaining his distance from her as though they were passing things to one another across a chasm.

"You'll have to leave in the morning," she said to him. "Leave," she repeated. *"Salir. Mañana."*

*"Gracias, señora,"* Emilio went on, smiling. The other two mumbled in support.

"Tell them," Frances said to Méndez.

*"La señora wants you to leave in the morning,"* he spoke bluntly and petulantly to Emilio. Her rudeness hurt him.

*"Oh sí, sí,"* Emilio assured her with the same bobbing motion of his head with which he had emphasized his gratitude for the food. It was as though he didn't fully understand what she had meant, although Méndez knew he had.

"Come out here a minute," she said to Méndez, indicating the exterior of the cottage with a minute jerk of her head, then, turning to the other three, she smiled wearily. *"Buenas noches,"* she said to them. They returned her valediction in a ragged unison.

Outside she told him he would have to sleep in the main house on the sofa; despite his protests she remained firm and even sent him back to retrieve a blanket from his bed. When he went in she followed and stood just inside the door, causing Emilio and the others to scramble awkwardly up from where they had just reseated themselves in the center of the floor and had taken the lid off the pot of soup which steamed at their feet. As he crossed the room behind Emilio's back he tried to think of some signal to let them know that if they decided to go to California he wanted to go with them, but he couldn't imagine a way that would escape Frances's detection short of expressing the wish openly in Spanish and he wasn't certain that she wouldn't understand it. He dawdled at his cot, tugging sluggishly and moodily at the tucked corners of his olive-drab blanket, feeling their impatient presence behind him—they were all itching for him to finish, Frances so she could leave and the other three so that they could return to what was doubtless their first hot food in some time. The bottom corner of the blanket next to the wall hung on a spring, then tore loose when he gave it a jerk of annoyance; he recrossed the room and stood by Frances, the torn corner of the blanket gripped in his fist, watching as Emilio's gaze lingered obsequiously in the vicinity of Frances's person, not really alighting or focusing with any sharpness on any part of her anatomy —he looked as though he might break into another chant of *gracias, señora, gracias,* but was holding back lest she interpret it as an attempt to rush her out the door. Méndez couldn't catch his eye.

"Why can't I stay out there?" he whined as she

smoothed out a sheet on the sofa. "Because, that's why," she replied firmly but gently. He didn't understand; during roundup there were always at least three other men who regularly bedded down in the cottage. He presumed this fact had slipped her mind and sought to bring it to her attention.

"But during roundup—"

"I don't want to hear any more about it."

She pecked his forehead with dry lips then vanished, leaving the kitchen light on so he could find his way to the bathroom. Annoyed, he plopped down on the sofa and removed his shoes the way he had been told not to, by digging at the heel of one with the toe of the other, not bothering to unlace the strings. Light leaked from under the doorways to the kitchen and to the hall leading to the bedrooms, vaguely outlining the dim shapes of the furniture in the room. It was still early, he guessed; Frances would stay awake probably for another hour or so reading, and he'd have to wait for still another hour after that to make certain she and Lemuel were sound asleep: the prospect of such a long wait discouraged him. Maybe he should get up and try to find his birth certificate in the den—but what if they caught him? Well, it wasn't stealing, the paper wasn't theirs, it was *his*, he had a right to it. Nevertheless, he knew that if they caught him they'd keep him from running away.

The ponderous old Kelvinator in the kitchen lumbered up, startling him. He listened a moment as it labored, groaning and straining, like a tired swimmer treading water. It occurred to him that he could sneak out during an "on" cycle and the noise of the refrigerator would cover any sound he made. How long did a cycle last? He tried to count the seconds, lipping the numbers mutely, taking care to insert "and" between each, but after a few moments he found his mind ebbing away from the task like a dinghy tied too loosely to a dock—he lost count somewhere between two hundred fifty and three hundred. No matter, time enough to get out under cover of the rumble, anyway. Plan ahead while he waited. California was a montage of beaches, an ocean he had seen only in pictures, and hearsay visions of orange groves, grapes, lettuce—the harvest crops of the migratory laborer's stoop-and-unstoop-labor railway. He knew from his Aunt Lucinda that many of *la gente* lived together in a place like a *barrio* in the city of Los Angeles, so all he had to do was to get there. But how many people lived there? He had heard the city was huge; how could he find his real father and mother? To remember his father was to think of trains and lizards—of trains because when he was three Alfredo and Paco worked track on the Texas & Pacific and they had all lived in a boxcar on a siding and because, even though Alfredo was thin, the taut, precise way he moved suggested the concentrated energy of a locomotive. At times, though, he seemed less strong, his flesh mortal, reptilian: working without a shirt he revealed a concave, hardened belly a little paler than his arms and face lined with muscles which looked like long, thin ridges of ribs or elongated tendons—not soft certainly, but sunk inward upon itself as if gathering together some last defense; the veins on the backs of his hands pulsed and bulged with blood as though the vessel walls could barely contain such pressure. . . . His father whistled . . . oddly, though—only from the middles of tunes. It was as though the tune had been whistling itself inside his father's head and a portion of it leaked out suddenly through his lips when he

didn't seal them tightly enough. . . . They stood together in a field a few yards from where he sat on the
edge of a pickup bed. His mother had dark, curly hair
with occasional strands of wiry gray stiff as tiny pieces
of platinum wire; when the upper half of her body was
wrapped in a *rebozo*, she looked stout, almost bovine,
but unwrapped she was softer, the separate, bulbous
parts of her anatomy hanging together as if by amiable
agreement. A confetti breeze nudged the hem of her
long cotton skirt. . . . His father said something he
couldn't hear, his mother giggled. . . . Her back was to
him. . . . She spoke. . . . His father smiled and jabbed
at the dry earth before him with the toe of one boot,
sending up a puff of dust that drifted away on the
moving air, growing like a smoke ring, larger, larger,
dissipating and expanding, dreamily, until it was indis-
cernable in the distance.

He awoke just before dawn when the refrigerator,
ending an "on" cycle, shuddered to a halt. He cursed
himself for falling asleep; now he'd have to wait until
it went on again to leave. Holding his breath, he
clenched his fists and drew himself upright on the
couch with a careless motion calculated to sound as
though he were only turning over in his sleep, then sat
stock-still, listening to the crickets in the flower beds
just outside the window give off their ratchety purr.
Above them he could hear—high overhead—the
muffled, half-audible wash of an airplane, but he heard
no stirring from the other rooms. In a few moments the
refrigerator heaved itself back into operation and he
rose, wrapping his blanket around him, and crept nervously through the door and into the lighted kitchen,
hurrying to ease the back door open as quietly as possible before the compressor kicked off again. Outside, he

nudged the door back into the frame behind him so that it would stick shut without clicking the latch.

Although a good twenty minutes remained before the sun would rise above the ridges across the highway to the front of the house, a deep haze of violet, pre-dawn light filtered into the yard and made him visible as he darted from the stoop to the barn, trying to avoid detection. He went around behind the corral to get to the cottage, and when he reached the front door he released his breath with a sigh. He eased the cottage door open and stuck his head inside; it was empty. Dazed, he stepped into the room and squinted in the half-light for some sign of them, some thing they had forgotten which might tell him they hadn't completely gone, but he found nothing. Stumbling about in the dimness he reached his bed. In the mattress was the long, deep imprint of a man's body—he pitched forward into it and cried.

# Two

Méndez knows that had he not expected to see Houston there, he might not have recognized him to be the adult version of the blonde-haired antagonist of his childhood as the man and his wife stepped from their coral Thunderbird at the cemetery, late for the service. The woman in the passenger's seat didn't wait for Houston to help her; even though the angle at which the car was perched upon the incline made it difficult for her to do so, she bumped the door open with her shoulder and swung her legs out, awkwardly, then hoisted herself upright by pressing one hand against the back of the seat and by clutching the doorframe with the other. Her clumsy, halting motion gave Méndez the fleeting impression she was crippled, an impression only partly dispelled when, a moment later, she stepped away from the car, teetering on high heels as she made her way up the spongy grass on the incline, her eyes locked onto the ground as though she might have been trying to walk a rail. Coattails flapping in the September gusts, Houston appeared behind her and moved up to take her elbow; as they walked he jerked his head to the side to keep the wind from lifting his shocks of blonde hair.

At the grave-site, he traded solemn expressions and a meaningful handshake with the minister, then stood in an attitude of respectful concentration with his hands entwined behind his back, as though at parade rest. Méndez was surprised to note that his face contained nothing of the beefy air of smug satisfaction he had expected to find encouched there like some well-fed, hibernating beast, nothing of the weakness and malice Méndez had put into it in the fantasy he had constructed on the way to the cemetery: Robert and spouse were not present at the mortuary and Méndez had imagined searching for Robert before the service began, finding him in a motel room, lying on the floor with his fist clutching the neck of a whiskey bottle, babbling and giggling. Méndez jerked him upright, slung him into the shower, slapped his face from side to side, then carried, tugged, carted, and pulled him to the funeral which (in the fantasy but not in reality) was an open-casket service, then dragged him staggering but half-sober and moaning up to the casket where he began to whimper, then his knees gave way and he vomited on himself and into the open casket.

Basically a long rectangle, Houston's face had the angular features—the jutting brows and prominent chin—of a male fashion model, but any suggestions of *savoir-faire* or fastidious grooming were altogether missing: his face was the color of day-old white bread.

The flesh beneath his eyes and under his jaw puffed like the meat of a bloated mushroom. Méndez thought it the face of a loser. Or, if he hadn't actually lost the war with whatever he'd been battling, his forces were streaming back from the front in rag-tag, broken fashion. Grief? Somehow that itself didn't account for Houston's beleagured appearance; grief alone might have lent some dignity to his features, but the ashy, swollen flesh beneath the eyes failed to provoke any analogies with Greek masks: whatever his suffering, it wasn't the stuff of tragedy, Méndez thought.

He took an immediate dislike to Houston's wife. She wore her copper-tinted hair cropped close to her skull in thick ringlets the circumference of golfballs, and, like her husband's, her own features expressed a lack of spirit, exhibiting in place of some genuine sense of life that brittle sensuality frozen by decorum and orderliness so commonly demonstrated by sorority girls. Although her eyes seemed too small, Méndez recognized that she had the well-defined, even graceful features that everyone might publicly label "pretty" but wouldn't expect to remember. She kept her eyes lowered, skirting the casket, and not once during the service did she raise them above the level of her in-laws' torsos, but retained her grip on Houston's elbow as though he were a buoy standing in the halfway mark of a long swim. He guessed they were both embarrassed by their tardiness. Too, he considered generously, she probably felt awkwardly conspicuous in the tweedy but somber dark-brown suit, the hemline of which hung a bit too low to be altogether stylish in Evanston but which nevertheless revealed far too much thigh at a graveside service for a Texas rancher whose female relatives included sun bonnets in their casual wardrobes and who were now all clad in below-the-knee length, heavy-bosomed dresses of cheap, bruise-blue wool or black jersey. Méndez guessed that the skirt she wore was the longest she owned. Like the hemline, her makeup and accessories reflected an unsuccessful struggle to compromise between mourning and chic sophistication. Aside from the barely perceptible presence of eye-liner, she wore no makeup other than a thin coat of frosty pearl lipstick she had brushed onto her mouth, but on her earlobes she had clipped, in some unfortunate lapse of the imagination, earrings the size, color, and shape of slices cut from the butt end of a carrot.

After the minister had folded the leather cover of his Bible over, he nodded to four workmen dressed in khaki who had hunkered silently about the trunk of a large elm during the service; they rose and drifted uncertainly past him and up to the grave to lower the casket. Houston and his wife, standing beside one of the A-frame stanchions which held the coffin suspended in the air above the grave, shifted around the end of the grave and over to Méndez's side of it, thus blocking his view, and when the workmen began to lower the casket on thick, brown ropes, he couldn't see it until it reached ground level and then he watched through the arch formed by the Houston woman's calves and the hem of her skirt as it dropped in steady jerks into the damp-earth grave.

That afternoon he tried to shake his sense of suspended animation by going about his chores as usual. When he returned home he found that Houston's wife had come to visit.

"She's very talkative," Juanita told him as he sat at the kitchen table sipping a beer while she ironed. "That's why I didn't get anything done."

"What'd she talk about?" He was anxious to add information to the dossier he had begun on the woman at the funeral.

"Herself mostly, I guess. In a roundabout way. And Lemuel's son—he's called Bob."

"I know." It occurred to him that he had never told Juanita about knowing Lemuel's son as a boy. He had mentioned Frances but not Robert. "We grew up together in a way," he added uncertainly to dispel from his mind whatever embarrassing reason had kept him from telling her that earlier.

"Oh!"

Her exclamation irritated him. "You might say we didn't graduate in the same class, though."

"Was he here long?"

"Born here. They left when he was . . . oh . . ." He paused to add in his head but was distracted by the image of Frances and the boy departing in her '38 Ford together. He had hidden in the hayloft while they packed the car, watching through a crack in the bleached oak siding. Frances came looking for him, presumably to say good-by, but he wouldn't answer her call. "Twelve," he said finally. "Twelve, I'd guess."

Juanita looked pleased. "This must be a homecoming for him, then."

"I doubt it's really home to him," he cut in icily, as though in ignorance she had defended him against some just accusation. "Most of the time he and Frances were away somewhere. He probably thinks home is there, not here. But you were talking about her—"

"She's lonely. I like her, I think."

"What did she say?"

"Nothing really definite. This and that about how much he was away from home, his work, their life." She turned one leg of a child's denim overalls over to be pressed. "It sounds . . ." she hesitated, dabbing absently at a seam with the point of the iron. "Stimulating. Oh, but in a very bourgeois way, of course," she added hurriedly.

"Lonely, huh?"

"Yes." She hooked her thumbs under the shoulder-straps of the overalls and held them up before her for inspection. "Why are you gloating?"

"I'm not," he insisted. "What else did she say?"

"She asked a lot about Jimmy."

"She wants children?"

"Yes."

"She say so?"

"No."

"But you got that idea."

"Yes."

He nodded, then watched in silence as she turned her back to dig another garment from the basket of articles rolled into damp cylinders. His portrait of the Houston woman was emerging like a photo under developer; gradually the details would crystallize into some coherent image, but at present the sketch was vague and even somewhat contradictory—a lonely but dissatisfied woman who leads a *stimulating* life but who wants children?

"Would anything about her surprise me?"

"You can find out for yourself if you want—they invited us to dinner tomorrow night."

He pressed the bottle to his lips like a trumpet mouthpiece and let the beer into his mouth in tiny spurts while he ruminated over this new development.

"Huh!" he said finally. "Are we going to eat in the kitchen or in the dining room, I wonder."

Juanita clucked her tongue in disapproval.

"Really," he went on. "Is it just a gesture to show us how liberal they are?"

He could see a muscle throb along her jaw as she flared, her eyes locked to the iron. "Maybe you'd prefer they did something nasty just to prove how bigoted they are?"

He would have preferred to be left alone, of course, but instead found himself on Tuesday evening sampling a martini its maker said was "as dry as the Rio Grande in the summertime," an effect achieved, Houston claimed with a chuckle, by passing the cork of the vermouth bottle over the martini glass. Méndez had made the mistake of admitting he had never tasted a martini (a deficiency of experience he privately thought a virtue), and had thus stumbled onto a veritable treasure-house of conversational material dear to Houston's heart. Apparently in his circle the martini was something of an idol around which an entire lore had arisen, flourishing like the dogma of a religious sect: anecdote, lecture, demonstration and mock debate all cohered loosely into a liturgy which Houston intoned through the course of three martinis while Méndez felt a stupid grin rising from the recesses of his overheated brain, a grin he struggled to check by pressing his lower lip against the chilly rim of his cocktail glass.

"Let me freshen your drink," Houston offered to Juanita. She was seated on the couch and had responded to Houston's running commentary on drinks and drinkers with what Méndez thought was immoderate and girlish laughter. Although she had carefully nursed only one martini along throughout his discourse, she was an amateur drinker; the flush along her olive cheeks and the brightness in her pupils told him she was a bit tipsy already, unconscious in the pleasures of enjoying herself—Being Out, Having a Drink. A long, thick strand of her glossy hair had fallen in front of one eye in the style of a forties starlet whose name he could never remember; she left it there to dangle and arc across her left cheek. Was she being coy? Houston was waiting with his arm outstretched to take her almost-empty glass. She passed a covert glance through the scrim of her hair over to Méndez.

"Oh no thanks," she laughed. "I guess I better go help Jane while I can still walk."

Houston chuckled with the pleasure of a host who gauges his own success by the intoxication of his guests, but he didn't press her to take more. Alternately giggling and struggling to check herself, she rose unsteadily and teetered a moment in the narrow space between the coffee table and the couch, then made her way more soberly toward the kitchen.

"Attractive woman," Houston murmured, his gaze lingering along the undulant lines of her buttocks as she disappeared through the archway into the kitchen. She did look ravishing in the new dress—something she had purchased especially for this evening. Méndez hadn't noticed it until they were crossing the yard from the cottage to the main house, and he was irritated to think that she had bought the dress at a time when the future was so uncertain. Made from some unidentifiable fabric the color of lime sherbet, it fell against the lines of her body like satin and napped in her folds and recesses. "Slinky" and "clingy" came to his mind. It made him nervous. Although the hem was a respectable mid-thigh length and while the neckline couldn't have been called either "plunging" or "daring," the way the material seemed to fall softly away from the rises of her body, emphasizing her pear-shaped breasts, had made him itch with desire for her, and so he had been caught between pursuing that desire with a compliment and complaining about the purchase. Fixed between those two poles, he had done nothing except trudge miserably and silently beside her on the way, uncomfortably chafed by the starch in his shirt.

"Did you meet at school?" Houston was asking.

Méndez nodded, stroking his tie and rearranging it along the front of his shirt.

"So did we," Houston muttered half-aloud. Méndez thought he heard an overtone of regret; he looked at Houston, who had turned his gaze downward into his drink as though to discern the outlines of some minuscule object floating in it. It was a melodramatic gesture which smacked of world-weariness, and Méndez realized that Houston had been at the martini shaker long before they arrived—he knew a case of weltschmerz when he saw one. How many had he drunk? Who the hell was this man, anyway? He kept looking into Houston's puffy, furrowed features for some sign of the boyhood bully he had known.

Houston looked up suddenly as though remembering Méndez's presence, then readjusted his features.

"Mind if I ask you something personal?"

Méndez wondered a moment if his question was related to Juanita.

"Probably," he joked nervously. He had always hated that preface. "I'm only kidding," he relented, smiling. "But I reserve the right to be offended."

"You're not like a lot of your people, right?" Houston barged onward as though unaware of Méndez's resistance.

"How do you mean?"

Houston shrugged. "To begin with, you've got an education."

Méndez nodded warily. Was he going to be asked to defend "his own people" from the charge of laziness? "But I have a fortunate turn of circumstance to thank for that," he said, hoping to forestall the comment he anticipated from Houston. "Besides, I didn't graduate."

The precise nature of the question grew steadily more obscure to Méndez.

"What is it you want to know, anyway?"

"I guess I was wondering why you hadn't done more with it."

Méndez felt his ears burn; Houston himself seemed to see that the comment carried more implicit criticism than he had intended. "I didn't mean, of course, well . . . I'm sure there's something here that means a great deal to you," he rushed in. "You've obviously found some kind of peace here, you've found what a lot of people who are running around like madmen in the cities haven't found, and I wondered what it was." He finished with a wide, drunken flourish of his arm. Such gross flattery ordinarily would have made Méndez squirm had it been sincere, but he was dead certain it wasn't, if only because Houston had absolutely no way of knowing if this mythical "peace within" was what held him at the ranch. What was Houston driving at?

"I don't know," he returned lamely. "I imagine there's no one particular thing that holds me here. A texture of things, maybe. The same things that tie anybody to a place." Such as a job, he thought with horror, seeing suddenly that Houston was apparently trying to sidle into the subject of the future of the ranch. "Why do you ask?"

"No real reason, I guess. I just wanted to know your plans, if you had any. I know you must be wondering what's going to happen now that my father's gone."

"It had crossed my mind a few times," Méndez put in more dryly than he had intended.

Houston smiled. "I wish I could tell you something definite, but it's so soon and all. The whole place . . ." He let his arm arc before his body to encompass all his vast holdings, holdings which included, Méndez realized with uneasiness, himself. "Too much to think about at once. Not to keep you on tenterhooks, of course."

"Oh, I've got a few irons in the fire," Méndez lied artfully. "No need to worry on my account."

Houston smiled broadly to show his heartfelt sympathy for those with uncertain job futures. "I can say this —Jane isn't cut out to be the wife of a cowhand, so . . . well, I just don't know yet, you see. I'd appreciate it if you'd stick around a couple of weeks just so I can think, stick around and run things like you always have. I'll double what you make now if you'll hang on for a couple weeks."

"Sold," Méndez said, too eagerly. "I haven't made any *definite* commitments yet."

"This place has a lot of memories. To tell the truth, I'd like to spend some time just walking over the land. Smell some things I haven't smelled in years. It seems like . . . oh . . . well." He looked away. "I guess it happens to everyone." Hearing Houston's phrases fall out in little chunks like rabbit droppings, Mendez was reminded of the boy he had known. "That . . . well, it doesn't matter, I guess." He gazed off toward the kitchen. "It all comes out in the end," he lamented with sudden bitterness. "The same I mean. You know?" He turned to appeal to Méndez. "You know?"

Nodding, Méndez gave his vague assent even though he had no idea what Houston was talking about. Houston mused in silence a moment, then sighed and rose to refill his glass from the martini shaker standing atop the stereo cabinet beneath the windows. To disrupt the silence, Méndez asked about his job with the State of Illinois, and Houston—gesturing and pointing with the index finger of the hand that held his drink—began a monologue explaining his duties: he advised the Department of Welfare on legal intricacies with welfare cases, reviewing and passing judgment on specific problems in interpreting what he termed a "horrendously circumlocuted" and "unnecessarily obtuse" manual of regulations. Reading beneath that, Méndez guessed that his real job was to decide if the state stood to be legally or politically embarrassed by withholding funds in certain cases. He claimed to find the work "interesting" but missed "not working with people." He spent most of his time "cooped up" in his office with stacks of papers.

"Let me tell you something, Méndez," he charged as though Méndez were about to deny the truth of what he said. "When I first went into this work I had a very quixotic idea about my own role in righting wrongs done to individuals by bureaucracies, but little by little I came to see myself as an arbiter between agency and individual. And then finally I guess you might say that I came to see myself as a guardian of the state's money." He offered the final stage of his metamorphosis with a trailing hint of apology, which Méndez noted but did not allow to influence his own private interpretation of information—namely, that Houston had expended a feeble effort at idealism and had then reverted to type. "I got sick of greed," Houston continued. "Sick of seeing person after person try to milk the state just because it was a government agency. I saw case after case of fraud so blatant that it was obviously perpetrated in the spirit of . . . well, *play*. Like cheating on income tax. It's disgusting. And you can't imagine the flimsy rationalizations people use to try to excuse themselves for screwing their government." As Houston went on to illustrate his thesis by citing case histories, it was obvious to Méndez that Houston only came in contact with those cases on appeal by tireless individuals, and that for every fraud perpetrated by an individual aggressive enough to try it, there were doubtless thousands of legitimate suits never pursued by the poor, who were fatalistic about the responsiveness of the governments to their needs. He began to hate himself for listening so tolerantly to Houston describe with such tragic overtones his transformation from misguided idealist to realist. Why was it, Méndez wondered, that all the self-professed "realists" he had met also turned out to be experts on things like the chemical composition and classification of martinis?

"You're a rare bird," Houston was saying. "A man who has what he wants, knows what it is, and doesn't ask for more. I think they used to call that wisdom." Although Méndez acknowledged the compliment by murmuring, he was perplexed and confused by such outright flattery based on such flimsy grounds. How could Houston pretend to know that much about him? Did he really believe what he was saying?

At dinner, Houston worked himself into a talking jag, his face overheated, his hands nervous, excited, constantly in the midst of gesticulation. He hardly ate.

As he continued his confessions, Méndez listened absently while plucking at the breast of his Cornish hen and scanning his memory to decide if the label on the white wine was one he had heard of before. He guessed that Houston was feeling some of that peculiar openness that allows people to bare their souls to complete strangers; Houston seemed to view his own speech as a series of parables all illustrating the same moral that altruism and idealism were but childish illusions that dissipate with experience. Méndez thought it strange that he was so insistent on this point.

"This is a great age for self-acceptance," Houston announced while he lifted a forkful of wild rice from his plate, held it momentarily, dropped it, then raised it once again, as if to estimate its weight. When he paused, he peered, squint-eyed, into the flame of the candles on the centerpiece, striking a melodramatic pose of pensive introspection. "Don't you think? I mean, why not? I got tired of feeling as though I was doing something heroic only to find out I was only being stupid, that I was left holding somebody else's bag. I went into the Army when I could have gotten out of it. I wouldn't go now. It set my career back three years, I had just passed my bar so after I got out of OCS they sent us to Fort Buchanan where they put me in the provost marshal's office. I didn't know anything about military justice, so the CO put me in charge of preparing *defense* briefs for enlisted men who had gone AWOL or had broken into bubblegum machines. A military version of the public defender."

"Some of them were real criminals," Jane piped in.

"Let me tell this," Houston snapped, then smiled in apology. "It was all there, everything they say about military justice: double jeopardy, no presumption of innocence. At first I thought I was supposed to *defend* these people. I thought that between myself and the prosecution we could arrive at the truth about some guy's guilt or innocence." He wagged his head sadly, then lapsed into silence and sipped at his wine.

"And what did you discover?" Juanita asked. Her eagerness annoyed Méndez.

"What do you expect? Our purpose wasn't to determine guilt or innocence, it was to define the nature of guilt and set a punishment for it. Guilty if charged. I was horrified at first." His mouth arced slowly into a smile designed to mock himself. "Just like I was once horrified to think there was no God, just as I was horrified to think that husbands and wives didn't stay faithful to one another." He chuckled, downed the remainder of his wine, and began to pour himself another glass.

"They're not the same things at all," Jane said stiffly. "Why should you have hated yourself for doing your job? If you had felt better about it, you might have been a captain by the time you got out."

"And you might have been a captain's wife."

"Well . . ."

"And there'd still have been all those majors' wives to contend with."

The tension between them embarrassed Méndez; he set his eyes on his plate while Juanita chirped and chuckled at their banter as though it were all in good fun.

"Anyway, that's beside the point," Houston said when Jane didn't answer. "What I'm trying to say is that I knew at first I was only the proverbial cog in the wheel, but I had respect for that, because I was out to set the world on fire and I felt like what I did made a difference. I may only be a cog, I thought, but without me the wheel can't turn. At first I was worried because by civilian standards the punishment of crimes in the military was severely out of proportion to the seriousness of the crime. AWOL cases by the hundreds, mostly always boys under twenty with rank of Pfc. or less. I wanted to see justice done—that was my job— and at first I likened AWOL to desertion under fire. Well, like the army I thought that a crime, any crime, occurred out of context of the criminal's life—because we're concerned with the *crime*, we forgot that the *crime* which is so important to us is only another act in a series of acts in a man's life. I mean that men don't go AWOL out of the blue—their *crime* comes to us out of the blue because that's the only aspect of their life we're interested in. Don't you think? Well, so after soldier after soldier showed up in the stockade after being caught or after having turned himself in I saw a pattern of predictable crisis situations in the boy's life that, to him anyway, seemed to demand his presence elsewhere than in the army. There was nothing but the *law* to hold him in the army, nothing but fear of reprisal, because not a one of them could be said to be holding down creative positions of high salary and responsibility." Houston paused to chuckle at himself. "No *motivation* to stay there other than fear. Most of the cases occurred not when someone would leave the post without a pass; it happened almost always that someone who had a pass or a furlough would fail to return at the appointed time. He went home and his new life in the army was remote for him and his old life reasserted itself with its priorities—time after time it was a matter of a girlfriend on the verge of being lost to a rival who was present to press his case or a sick

parent who needed tending to. It usually never occurred to the boy to tend to the latter case through
legal channels—they're semi-literate, anyway. Sometimes they got off with restricted privileges but mostly
they were given stockade time. What a waste, I
thought. In either case, their commanding officers were
not usually interested in the motivation as much as they
were interested in the effect the punishment might
have on other members of the company. Deterrence.
But not *too* much." He sipped from his wine glass,
then held it histrionically between his fingertips near
his mouth. "What I'm getting at is that I tried to care
about those semi-literate hillbillies and small-town de-
linquents and ghetto street characters that the army
fills its lower ranks with." His lids half-closed. "But in
the end they just *bored* me." He opened his eyes to
study the effect of his words, but Méndez finished
eating. Why did Houston want him to think he was so
decadent? That he had said what he did to shock
Méndez suggested that if he really had been bored by
them, it was a boredom about which he felt deeply
uneasy.

"You weren't easy to live with then," Jane com-
mented as she rose to clear the table. Houston had
hardly touched his food, and when Jane grasped the
edge of the plate, then looked at him in hesitation, he
shrugged and motioned for her to remove it.

"I wasn't docile I suppose you mean. Maybe I was
worried about what was happening to me; in the end
I didn't care whether the boy or the army got justice.
To be frank, I had begun to think that there were more
important things for me to do than worry about
whether born losers got fair treatment from an inflexi-
ble and indifferent institution. It all looked *hopeless,*"

Houston sighed with what Méndez thought was genuine discouragement.

"The Famous Coffee House Raid," Jane said sweetly. "Why don't we go into the living room and you can tell them about *that?*"

"Did you think I wouldn't?" He smiled, his head weaving slightly. Méndez guessed he must be a veteran drinker, for despite the four martinis and two glasses of wine that Méndez had seen him drink, he showed few signs of drunkenness. "Of course you did." As he stood beside her he chucked her beneath the chin, pinching her flesh in a steady grip between his thumb and forefinger until she winced. He smirked at her, then turned and strode into the living room.

"I'll bring the coffee," she said in an odd, almost apologetic tone to his back.

"The coffee house raid," Houston began when they were seated again. "It was a microcosm of the Viet Nam war right on your doorstep. It was near the end of my hitch, I had, oh well, I think I had maybe three or four months left. Getting short and getting itchy about it. The provost marshal had been an old colonel ready for retirement all that time and his twenty years were up in March, and this was September. A lieutenant colonel, not overly bright but not ambitious either, he was just biding his time like the rest of us, and he spent about half his time at the pool or the golf course; he knew we didn't give a damn and didn't care. Well, hell, we had one of those classic army situations—a *loose* outfit. Ripe for the classic turnover. Barrett, the old CO, retired in March and we gave him a nice party and waited with apprehension—which turned out to be justified—for his replacement. Colonel Slinger. Really. Young bird colonel just back from Nam and he was RA

all the way. So for six months I had given up riding the
fence I'd been riding because the situation, with Barrett, had been the kind that called for that kind of
response. We tightened up in a hurry, but a couple of
the other short-timers like myself resented having to
get hyped up just to finish out the remaining couple of
months. We all wanted to get out easy, just kind of
*slide* down those remaining days half-drunk and well-
fed. Slinger changed all those plans we had had. He
wanted to prosecute and he didn't care whom or for
what. We all sensed that we could find ourselves facing
dereliction of duty charges if we didn't play things by
the book. Which we did. But he didn't. Well, I mean
he had his own book. There was a coffee house which
opened up off the post just before he came and he was
hot to shut it down but he wasn't really sure how he
could do it *legally*, and by legally he didn't mean according to law, he meant without fear of legal reprisal;
how he could do it *free*, that was his problem. It was
an average, run-of-the-mill coffee house complete with
tables made from telephone cable reels, wine bottles
with candles in their mouths, peanut shells on the floor,
fish net draped from the ceiling, posters on the walls,
the hangout of misguided but well-intentioned young
Catholic priests, frizzy-haired and smelly would-be po-
ets who had dropped out of this or that junior college
because their genius had either been cramped or ignored and who were now Reading from their Work or
Talking About Art when they weren't sleeping or taking dope, and bad guitar players, dozens of them. Well,
a perfectly innocuous place really, with no more power
to move a man's spirit or to form his convictions than
a High Church Episcopalian reading Norman Vincent
Peale to a troop of aborigines." Despite the pain of

intense disagreement, Méndez laughed. "Yeah," Houston chuckled, encouraged. "The bland leading the bland. But there was one hitch—soldiers went there. Mostly to find girls, although why anyone would want any of the scrawny, buck-toothed refugees from Little Abner I saw reading poetry there the couple of times I investigated is beyond me. But when the soldiers *went* there, somebody would start working on them about the war, oh not *hard*, you know, because they were shrewd enough to see that only special personalities could be shamed or browbeaten into fighting against the military establishment, so they were cool, wary. Ask questions, suggest books, talk about the issue when a soldier was present, but not directly *to* him or accusingly. We sent a couple of people down there to find out what the pitch was. On Slinger's request. Slinger had found himself an A-one problem, a challenge really to his legal resourcefulness. If the problem had been strictly *military* he could have solved it readily by canning whoever he wanted. This was harder. He could manage to do something about soldiers who frequented it, but he couldn't touch the *place* or the civilians who ran it and that drove him up the wall. He could have it declared off limits, and that's what he resorted to at first, of course. The owner complained to the commanding general that there weren't sufficient grounds, that such a move hadn't been made to protect soldiers from any kind of menace to their hygiene, either physical or spiritual. Nor was the place a 'nuisance,' in the ordinary sense of the word. I mean, they *knew* what was going on. It wasn't the first time someone had complained publicly that their business could no longer be patronized by GIs, but it was, to local memory at any rate, the first bona fide case of political repression.

And no one cared, which doesn't surprise me now, but it did then. I think I expected a huge uproar, citizens in arms over it, because even *I* knew that when you looked at the question objectively from an legal standpoint, their civil rights *had* been violated, and by implication the act threatened every business establishment in the area. But they didn't care," he chuckled, wagging his head, "not only did they not care, they were *proud* of us. Because they thought the coffee house was *evil*, because they associated it with an entire strain of the culture they found repulsive, many of them wouldn't have been disturbed if we had carried out a search-and-destroy mission on the place. Slinger, if he thought about it at all, would think that the end justified the means, that here right outside the immediate confines of the post was a enemy outpost, a real enemy, as real as the Viet Cong, and he was *accustomed* to *killing* people he disagreed violently with, or trying to kill them, or seeing to it that they were killed, so he was inclined to be impatient about arguments that he wasn't acting *ethically*. He recognized that this guy had a legal right to run his coffee house, but he didn't think those legal rights were as important as the fact that they had no *moral* right to exist at all, anywhere, anytime." Houston smiled wryly. "Well, the fleas on the dog. That's what I finally understood. The townsmen were the fleas and the post was the dog. If a flea itches, the dog scratches and kills it and the others aren't going to bother complaining. Any notions of altruism here are purely illusory and I began to see that the *idea* of law was perfectly laughable."

"It must have been a dark night of the soul," Méndez cracked.

Houston smiled wearily, without offense. "It might

have been had any of this happened two years earlier, but as I said, I wanted out, that's all. I saw what was happening, understood it in my own detached perse-pective, but none of it meant much to me at the time. Like any other experience, I was too busy being in it to analyze its ultimate effect on me or even predict anything. Well, hell, I didn't even know it was an *experience*, it was just something I did, something we were all doing between seven-thirty and four-thirty weekdays and then forgetting about when we went home.

"Meanwhile, all the coffee-house people were work-ing on their own little drama in which we were the villains who were *plotting* ceaselessly, tirelessly, at all hours of the night to rob them of their political man-hood. Naturally when Slinger had the place declared off limits then it *did* become politically potent—GIs who before had been only mildly interested in the dissident viewpoint *saw* proof of what those in the coffee house had been saying, that the army was repressive. All the off-limits orders did was to segregate those GIs who had gone there into more pliable and workable groups—where before the soldiers who went there had been motivated by different things, now only those who were politically motivated went. Few soldiers wanted to risk a court martial just for a few minutes dreary talk and a five-minute feel in the back of a cab. So the off-limits order applied only to those the army had no need to worry about anyway, and the ones left who came and went furtively became a group unto themselves, began to know that precious solidarity of the minority op-pressed—I'm not making fun of it, you understand—" he waved toward Méndez. "So when these GIs went there they cast themselves in the role of the persecuted among fellow victims: now they had a cause. Looking on, I wanted to throw up my hands. Slinger couldn't have handled the whole thing more stupidly. If he wanted to *destroy* them, he should have offered them a corner in the enlisted man's club and given them a big budget they could come to depend on and send some USO ladies to run their mimeograph machines. That's what I meant about a Viet Nam war right on our doorstep. Slinger no more understood how to cope with these people than most of our commanders in Nam knew how to cope with a guerrilla force. In terms of military tactics, their counterthrust cost him more than his thrust had gained, but he didn't even know it.

"Their presses got hot. They had had a little newsletter that they distributed to anyone who came around, but before the off-limits order they hadn't bothered to circulate it around town or on the post. It was full of bad poetry, semi-literate reviews of occult books and a few pieces from the underground syndicate. Their renewed enthusiasm was demonstrated first of all in the newsletter, which went from two pages to eight and seemed dedicated to personal testaments, many of them apocryphal I imagine, of injustices suffered at the hands of *local* military authorities. Where these victims had been hiding themselves until this point I don't know. They printed up about a thousand where before they put out about two hundred, and got one of the GIs to distribute it clandestinely on the post. The moment this was discovered, the commanding general and Slinger got together and decided to confiscate every one they could find, but they could never know if they had found them all, so they issued a general order that any found by any troops on any part of the base were to be collected by the company officers. Uh-huh!" he said, noting Méndez's smile. "You guessed it. Within twenty-four hours there were people *looking* for a copy to read, people who had never even *heard* of this coffee house and who wouldn't have given the newsletter a single glance if it had been handed to them on a street corner. Classic result of forbidding people to read something.

"So Slinger lost the second battle. Then he recruited a double agent, a chaplain's assistant named Bryant who at first didn't appear to be very bright, but later we found out that he was a triple agent—he was a short-timer with a grudge against the military, but he managed to convince Slinger that his little sister had been turned into a dope fiend by a hippy and that his brother had been killed in Viet Nam and so he wanted revenge. Both items turned out to be true, but he had rather shrewdly led Slinger to believe that he wanted revenge on the hippy subculture when he actually wanted revenge on the military establishment who he thought responsible for both the death of his brother and the destruction of his sister because the 'hippy' was discovered to be an FBI *agent provocateur* in a commune on the West Coast. I'm not kidding, he really was. Anyway, this had happened since he joined the service. He was a clever con man, but cold and ruthless, dedicated. A maniac, really, but a persuasive one. Bryant discovered that as a result of their new notoriety, the coffee house was receiving funds from like establishments across the country. Things were looking bleak for Slinger, and I imagine he grew more and more frustrated that with every tactic his enemy seemed to counter and jockey into a more advantageous position, and I suspect he chalked up their capacity for success to the legal restrictions against his wiping them clean by ordering an air strike—if he could deal with them on his terms, then by God watch him go! But he couldn't. If he could have really faced that fact, then he might have allowed himself to consider alternatives that might have led to the successful completion of the mission, but he was hung up on that one little *if* and couldn't seem to think beyond it. I had no interest in dissuading him—not that I wanted *them* to win; I had nothing at stake in the outcome, and I just looked back nostalgically to the old days with Barrett, when the coffee house posed no threat to our national security and it was best to pretend it didn't exist. Anyway, Slinger's plan of attack contained a long chain of ill-conceived moves: first, he decided to harass them by holding frequent raids on the place to apprehend GIs who were going there on the sly in civvies. He loved to lead these raids personally, because it gave him an opportunity to wear his forty-five in public, but every time they'd sweep the place there'd be no one there but civilians because Bryant had given them warning, but he kept telling Slinger that the place was full of people from the base and even gave Slinger some names. He was shrewd enough to let Slinger catch one, a scroungy little Pole named Bryznick, a ten percenter from the word go whose political sensibilities were grounded in a civics course he slept through in a high school he dropped out of and whose interest in social justice reached no further than a bitterness because he had been drafted instead of receiving a hardship deferment because his father was allegedly unable to work because of a whiplash injury. Bryant saw to it that Bryznick was captured, for he must have assumed that Bryznick would do them more harm than good at the coffee house. That was *Bryant's* mistake; he didn't understand who he was working for. I imagine it—is this boring you?" He looked inquiringly at Méndez and Juanita. "Here I am going on and on about something what happened to me some time ago."

"Oh no," Juanita protested. "Go on."

"Bryant's mistake," Houston continued. "The theme of this tale is *The best laid plans of mice and men.* Because Bryznick was the kind of person who turned everybody off and because Bryant apparently didn't like him, Bryant must have thought that he could get rid of him easily by letting Slinger capture him, then they could go on without him at the coffee house and his disagreeable personality wouldn't interfere with their recruiting. Bryznick was slovenly, illkempt, sullen, ignorant, and bellicose—he had B.O., bad breath—the works. He was *rank,* I tell you, rank. A perfect capture for Slinger, almost a symbol of everything Slinger hated, a prototype for what Slinger thought of all those people who hung around the place —he couldn't have been more perfect than if you had constructed him out of Slinger's imagination.

"Slinger made six or seven fruitless raids on the place before Bryant gave him Bryznick. Bryznick didn't go quietly; he yelled and Slinger cuffed him around a bit, which stirred the others up. That's what I meant about Bryant's mistake. I think Bryant may have been bothered that his side harbored such unsavory persons and he had figured on making Bryznick a sacrifice for Slinger. Of course that's what happened—Bryznick became the sacrificial lamb toward whom everyone now bent their tenderest regard because they hadn't liked him before, and now felt guilty because they hadn't liked him so he became their martyr, their representative even. It must have disheartened Bryant to see his

_148_

plans go to hell. He probably had only meant to disappear somebody he thought disagreeable. Slinger was overjoyed at his catch and having Bryznick in the stockage gave him great encouragement. Well, it gave *everybody* great encouragement, now everybody had a *focus*. Bryant was embarrassed because if he had thought about it enough he would have preferred for the military establishment to have incarcerated not some moronic and smelly Pole but another Gandhi, for apparently he didn't understand that Bryznick could be more disagreeable to more people where he was than at the coffee house, and Bryant wanted to recruit the masses of soldiers to rise up against their leaders—he was in the right *place* to do it, Bryznick was, in the stockade there, among the disaffiliated, but he had no leadership qualities; to the contrary, he had a negative charisma, people found themselves attracted *away* from him. The priests and the owner and the kids who ran the newsletter probably found him embarrassing too, but they weren't going to admit it to themselves because they felt too guilty about not liking someone to whom an unjustice had been done. Now Bryant was trying to work his way around to luring Slinger into committing himself to some act that might have nationally embarrassing repercussions for Slinger and the army. Oh, I really don't mean to suggest that Bryant was really planning anything, I think he was just playing things by ear, he wasn't a *designer* or a strategist; like Slinger he was only a tactician with only the vaguest kind of objective, following the inclinations of temperament. What I mean is that Bryant would have liked to have found some way for events to work themselves out so that he could capitalize on some mistake of Slinger's." As Houston stopped to unwrap and light a cigar,

Méndez wondered how much of his story was purely conjectural—how, he asked himself, could Houston pretend to be so knowledgeable about other people's motives?

"So to the Big Raid," Houston continued. "The whole business was getting messy, it was getting to be a great big pain in the butt—if the ladies will pardon me—because Slinger grew more frustrated daily and had us all working overtime 'investigating' the people involved in the coffee house, looking for something to get them with, all this under the guise of reconsidering the off-limits order. Then Bryznick escaped from the stockade, and this nearly tore Slinger apart in two separate directions—his catch had escaped, but that meant that he could enjoy hunting him down again, and this time the charge would be more serious—escape, desertion, and striking an officer, so of course as Bryznick became a bigger and bigger criminal, then Slinger's role became more important too. Bryant found out that the local coffee-house people were hiding him in the area, incredibly enough—stupid, don't you think?—but he didn't know where. I think he may have been suspect to them at that point in the sense that they didn't know for sure that he was working with them against the army. He had a week left to go in the army. He went to Slinger and to the local police chief and suggested a drug plant together with a raid on the place, arrest a few of them and charge them with drug possession, then bargain with them to dismiss charges in return for Bryznick, who meanwhile was playing the role of revolutionary in exile to the hilt—he wrote an entire issue of the newsletter, if you can call his execrable prose writing—relating how he was tortured for hours on end at the stockade under the explicit orders of Slinger. It may have been true, but I doubt it. Since some of the people who were present when Slinger made his capture and had seen him manhandle Bryznick a bit, they had no difficulty believing Bryznick's story. It was Bryant's idea that as soon as he left the army, he'd blow the whistle on the whole deal, he'd tell the press how Slinger and the local chief faked an arrest and planted evidence all in order to squelch dissent. On Bryant's suggestion, Slinger picked a Wednesday night, because on that evening the place was used for a meeting of the local chapter of the SDS and most of the people there were all active in the movement, whereas on a weekend there were a lot of other people there who were for the most part apolitical, and we, Slinger I mean, didn't want to round up somebody who wouldn't know where Bryznick was. What Bryant didn't know was that Bryznick was hiding in the attic of the coffee house because he thought it would be a very original and clever place to hide—well, considering Slinger's level of sophistication, I suppose it really was. Really, there were too many things coming to bear on the same event for the event to contain them—Bryant had apparently never told any of those people that he was an agent for them; I think he rather liked the idea that he could manipulate opposing forces to his own advantage without either of them being aware of it.

"At any rate, the night of the big raid, Slinger wanted all of his junior staff to come along for the assist, and for the show of force. Now this had been coming but I had blocked it out. I wanted desperately not to go on that raid. I didn't mind participating in Slinger's schemes as long as I could do them within the confines of my office during duty hours—to take them out into the world was to act them out, I suppose and

_151_

as long as it was always a matter of a written report, a telephone call, a conversation in the hall, it seemed more like the stuff of fantasy, it seemed harmless. Maybe there was a bit of shame involved too, who knows? Anyway, I didn't want to go, but I didn't see any way I could duck out, so I went."

"Now Robert," Jane chided, "you're going to give yourself the black hat again." She turned to Méndez and Juanita. "He's leaving something out."

Houston sighed elaborately. "Now how can we start out again if you persist in thinking that your interpretation of reality is more accurate than mine?" He was smiling at her, mechanically.

"Well, you always sell yourself short," she objected. "You're not mentioning how much you agonized over going and how much you were worried because you knew about the deal between Colonel Slinger and the police chief." Méndez understood by her tone that this information was supposed to make Houston seem more noble than his own words had, but he failed to see how they functioned that way. He suspected that ultimately they had the precise effect that she intended.

"I didn't *agonize* over going," Houston returned heatedly. "I didn't care enough about any of it to *agonize* about anything. And as far as the fake arrests and planted evidence were concerned, I had no way of knowing then whether my suspicions were true or not, and even if they were, nothing had actually taken place yet." He turned back to Méndez. "Anyway, the coffee house was in an old frame one-story structure that used to house a Pentecostal church, and it sat next to a vacant lot and an automobile scrapyard near the outskirts of town. Slinger's plan was unnecessarily elaborate—as many raids as he had held on the place, all he would need to do would be to drive up in front of it and walk in with the chief of police and some of his forces and that'd be it. But Slinger wanted us to *converge* on the place—it was right out of the movies—from four different directions, four different forces composed half of MP's and half of local civilian police, twenty of us in all. We were all supposed to keep in radio contact so that as we all approached the building from four different directions, we'd all wind up there the same instant. I know Slinger had an image of a dragnet in his mind, a map with pins progressively closing on the target. It was utterly ridiculous, and the two civilian police who were in my jeep were muttering about the whole affair because it had been their night off and they'd been called in especially for this assignment and weren't inclined to be very zealous about catching the army's offenders anyway. My radioman and the driver got confused about where we were, thought we were falling behind, so they speeded up and sure enough we got there first. We were supposed to deploy from the vehicle—Slinger's words—and advance on the place from the west side, along the edge of the junkyard. Whoever was supposed to cover the rear had had a flat, we discovered as we parked and 'dismounted,' but it couldn't be called off because we had already arrived. Slinger was really mad and cussed me out over the radio because we had gotten there ahead of everybody else. The order had been for us to form a line along the west side and walk toward the building with pistols drawn —Slinger had insisted on that because of the shock value I guess, but the civilian police couldn't do it on such little pretext. I wasn't going to do it, but then I thought what the hell—everything is screwed up anyway and the whole business was so disgusting and absurd that I didn't much care what I did. Somebody spotted us through a window on the west side of the building. That must have seemed weird to them, to see four men—the radioman stayed in the jeep—lined up against the junkyard fence walking in a skirmish line toward the coffee house, with no reinforcements. There was a stir inside, faces kept bobbing back and forth peeking between the curtains. What happened was that they thought their cover had blown and that we knew Bryznick was in the attic, so in their panic they were going to try to get him out of the building before we had it surrounded. As we got closer to the building, Slinger barreled up in front and they all hopped out and he, two MPs, and a civilian rookie didn't even knock on the door, they busted it down— well, if I had bothered to keep track of the legal violations of rights and procedures that night I could have gotten Slinger hung—so there was a good deal of panic inside I guess, because I heard a shot, then Slinger came running back out the door and yelled at me *'Cover the back, goddammit,'* so I trotted over toward the back door, and then it burst open and out ran Bryznick right past me, terrified—he looked about as much like a hard-core revolutionary at that moment as my grandmother might have—and he took off running toward the back of the junkyard away from me. *'Shoot, goddammit, shoot!'* Slinger was hollering from the front of the building. *'Shoot that sonofabitch!'* I raised my gun and yelled at Bryznick to halt. The civilian police had their hands on their pistols but kept them in the holsters, looking at me expectantly. Slinger screamed at the front of the building with his pistol out, raving like a madman because I stood in his line of fire. *'Shoot that bastard, shoot him, shoot him!'* and

I looked back at Bryznick who was just about to disappear over the fence, leveled the pistol at him, and pulled the trigger. God!" Houston spat with a sudden anguished vehemence which startled Méndez. "Would you believe I meant to miss him? I honestly did!"

"But you didn't?" Juanita blurted out.

"No, he didn't," Jane answered before Houston could reply.

"No, I meant to miss, I really did. The shot hit him in the calf. Broke his leg." He sighed, nodding his head from side to side, sadly. "Knocked him off the fence," he added after a pause, then glowered moodily at the ash on the end of his cigar.

"They killed him," Jane informed Juanita.

"Who?"

"Colonel Slinger did."

Méndez watched Houston glare with barely suppressed anger at Jane, then turn away to refill his glass. The silence tensed into a chill and in a rare moment of compassion for Houston Méndez wanted to see him off the hook.

"What came of it all?" he asked Houston.

"Bryant got out and went to the press," Houston began sourly and without enthusiasm as though reciting by rote a speech whose words no longer had an meaning for him. "He didn't have much of a story because Slinger got Bryznick without making any false arrests." He fell quiet a moment. "Nobody won. The coffee house is still there no doubt and probably still off limits. Oh well . . ." He trailed off, deflated, as though he was no longer interested in the subject.

"Jane and I are doing what they call 'starting out again,' " he broke his own silence to announce abruptly, looking at her with a smirk.

"I really wish you wouldn't tell people that." Her smile was strained.

Houston winked broadly at the Méndezes and jerked his thumb toward Jane. "My wife thinks that if you don't tell, it never happened."

"And *he* thinks that if something happens, you have to tell people about it," she said to Juanita. Méndez squirmed on the couch—apparently he and Juanita were to be the sounding posts for one of those uncommunicating couples who are forced to air their marital tensions before observers. Much to his irritation, Juanita giggled.

"Let me tell you what she did," Houston chuckled mirthlessly. He leaned forward as if to confide in the Méndezes something which he wished to keep Jane, who sat on the far end of the couch with her arms crossed over her breasts and her gaze riveted on the end of her shoe, from hearing. "We were on our second honeymoon, see . . ." he spoke in a stage whisper and paused, glancing over as if to invite her objection.

"We never had a first," she said, playing Maggie to his Jiggs as if on cue. "Unless you call two days in a Holiday Inn beside a freeway to St. Louis a honeymoon."

"How far do you need to go?"

"Farther than from the bed to the bar and back."

Houston threw up his hands with a mock Jewish gesture.

"So who left the bed already?"

"Oh, you're a real hot one, you are!"

"I don't ever hear you complaining," Houston shot back tensely, his smile artificial, grim.

She watched him for a moment as if planning a retort, then her mouth drew up slowly in victory. The glitter in her eyes chilled Méndez.

"You think I'd complain to *you?*" she returned with leisurely malice.

They glared at each other in furious silence for a long moment; Méndez tried to signal to Juanita his desire to leave and let them fight it out themselves, but Juanita refused to acknowledge his glance.

"Raphael—" she faltered, speaking to the Houstons, who slowly and reluctantly broke away from their standoff to turn toward her. Méndez groaned inwardly —she obviously intended to relate some wifely anecdote calculated to set them all at ease by dissipating the Houstons' particular tension into something more general, into Husbands vs. Wives. He could feel her dark eyes sweep toward him mutely asking permission to use him this way, but he perversely ignored her gaze.

"The night we were married," she went on, "Raphael took me to see *By Love Possessed* at the drive-in, and when we got home he studied for a final."

"Christ, Juanita," Méndez muttered in disgust, shaking his head.

"Aha!" Houston pounced, winking at him. "The truth will out."

"Not really," Méndez protested weakly, then withdrew. Bitterly, he thought that the truth rarely outed; he and Juanita had already been living together for a full six months before they were married and she was two months pregnant at the time; she had gone to bed that night with a head full of curlers knowing how much he detested them; lastly, his grade in the Economic History of Twentieth Century America was vital to him—if he was to lead his people out of the wilderness, shouldn't he be prepared? He and Juanita could make love at any time, but the final exam was given only once. He could offer this information in his own defense to take the sting out of her attack on his manhood, but maybe too his silence would shame her. He looked up to see Jane eyeing him curiously.

"The Great Deflowering had long since taken place," he blurted out despite himself. He sent Juanita a glance that told her not to pursue the subject unless she wanted the details made public. "Or don't you remember?"

She blushed. "Yes."

"Of course she does," Jane charged. "Only a man would forget something like that."

Houston chuckled and leaned toward Méndez like a fellow conspirator. "Jane thinks history is a thing apart from people's memories, she thinks it's a thing you can point to that lies outside somebody's awareness of it."

"Oh, you're so intellectual. You should be rich you're so smart."

"Another one of your curious little assumptions."

They glared at each other. Sensing that a silence was about to descend, Méndez rose quickly and tugged at Juanita's arm.

"Guess we'd better go. Tomorrow and so forth."

"But the night's young," Houston laughed, "and we've just begun to get acquainted. Jane and I enjoy the murmur of quiet conversation, the clink of glasses . . ." he shrugged ironically. He was perceptibly drunk. Suddenly he smiled and leaned over to pat Jane on the thigh. "You should stick around for the good part, where we start getting physical."

Jane tittered and gave him a broad, counterfeit look of seduction—Méndez saw that suddenly they were friends again. The ease with which their animosity appeared to have vanished amazed him.

"You want them to watch?" Jane laughed, coyly.

Juanita giggled and pressed close to Méndez, taking

his hand in hers. Houston squinted, looking at her with what Méndez recognized to be a purely libidinous interest.

"Why not?" Houston asked.

Méndez felt as though he were suffocating.

Outside, the night air was crisp and clear and the sky stretched into a infinity of stars. He inhaled deeply as they walked, clearing his head.

"I wonder why they've never had children," Juanita mused, leaning against him. She was pressing her cheek against his right arm and her words rushed out in a blur —she was a bit drunk.

"I don't know," he offered wanly. He still resented what she had done.

"That's what's wrong with her, I think."

"It's probably not that simple."

She halted and when he turned she pulled his head down to her and kissed him openmouthed; her legs parted and she straddled his thigh, moving against him playfully.

"That's a good martini," he joked when they parted.

She giggled. "It tastes divine that way. Raphael, I love you and I'm sorry for what I said."

He kissed her for a reply. She got tight easily but not frequently and when she did she was always more responsive. With his right hand in the small of her back he pulled her up against his knee and she gave a gutteral moan from the back of her throat. They were standing in the middle of the clearing between the main house and their cottage.

"Must be quite a show we're putting on."

"Better than theirs," she murmured. He kissed her again and they walked arm in arm to their cottage.

They decided to have some wine and a snack. They

both wanted each other so badly that there was absolutely no urgency about it; going to bed was something they might put off for a few more minutes just to prolong the anticipation of it. She left the kitchen light off; he sat at the table with his elbows propped upon its surface while she rummaged in the refrigerator, bent over, the hem of her skirt cocked up over the top of her stockings—she had lovely legs, really, and he stared at the backs of her thighs and calves with pleasurable longing while she looked for the cheese and chatted about her impression of the Houstons. The first time they made love—the first day after their engagement —she was wearing a pleated riding skirt, fawn-colored, calf-hugging boots, and a light blue blouse. He was surprised that she matched their surroundings so well, that her skin, the skirt, her blouse, and boots reflected the tones of the dunes and sky that afternoon of late spring. It gave her an aura of earthy naturalness that he attributed to the effect of his presence—he had a romantic notion that his influence on her life had already begun to reach into things as subtle as her unconscious choice of the colors of her clothing, that where before she had met him she had been artificial and plastic, now his influence had eased its way into that intuitive part of her touch on life until gradually she had finally begun to live from that more essential part of herself. They stood together on the highest peak looking off across a sea of undulating sand dunes the color of hide. Beyond the perimeter of the dunes lay a grassy plain, and beyond that rose a pastel sky streaked with wisps of cirrus cloud. He liked to think his presence gave her the extraordinary sense of something stretching across space and time, that he turned things lyrical by merely juxtaposing his presence with them. He wanted her to feel that the wind that moved across her cheek and ears, humming and lowing as though across the mouth of a giant bottle, was like an onshore breeze recently come from an ancient dynasty halfway around the world; he wanted her to feel as though history itself were a sunlit courtyard he had led them suddenly into.

A wooing: he had been careful to select what he thought were items which would reflect his poetic originality—a bottle of dry red wine (expensive—$1.49 a fifth; he was accustomed to drinking Gallo's Paisano which was a dollar a gallon), three red Delicious apples which he plucked after turning over half the stock in the supermarket bin, searching for those whose pulp was plump and firm enough to make a kind of popping crunch when bitten into, leaving a crater the color of bleached young moss—a bit green but sweet. He took three rather than two or four so that they might be forced to take communion with the third. He also bought some Gouda cheese because he liked the way it could be cut into little wedges and the red plastic covering stayed with each individual piece like a wraparound piecrust. All these items he had packed into an old rucksack purchased especially for the occasion at an army surplus store. "Cheesus," Juanita said when he carved her a chunk. "This is good-a." "Ummm," he agreed. "Dairy good-a."

He had spent the entire day working on his image. He owned three pairs of Levis, one pair so new that the leather brand in back had not yet begun to shrivel from washing, one pair in medium service, and one pair faded and spotted with dabs of paint and motor oil. Near the cuff of the right leg of this pair was a triangular rent where he had caught the cuff climbing through a barbed-wire fence. Wearing the first pair was out of the question, the second might work, but the third looked the most appropriate—except for the oil spots. The dabs of paint were perfect, but the oil was too much. The idea of taking the second pair and bleaching them out then somehow managing to get a bit of paint on them crossed his mind, but it seemed too elaborate a preparation, so he took the third pair and scrubbed the spots of oil with gasoline, then washed the trousers at the laundromat. They came out perfect. Clean but wrinkled. Respectable but not bourgeois. The trousers of a poet, artisan, and revolutionary, the trousers of a man whose intense feelings and passionate thought flowered forth in the works of his hands. From his roommate he borrowed a long-sleeved flannel shirt with a brown and green plaid pattern—green and brown for earthiness, fecundity. This he carefully rumpled before donning, then rolled the sleeves up to his elbows and was careful to let it blouse out around his waist a bit to suggest a carelessness of dress, as though he were occupied with much more important matters—life, death, the origins of consciousness and the cosmos. A tree-feller, rail-splitter, wood-cutter, rose-and-tomato-grower who could be found down beside the river working tirelessly, slowly, and diligently on a body of verse that was destined to stand as the primordial and eternal glimmer of a hard, gem-like flame. Verses chiseled from stone, smelling of damp clay and tender shoots. Juanita was the rich and carefree beauty who was to meet for the first time in her life a man of real substance and values, of strong moral conviction and immense intellectual powers, a man who would alter the basic pattern of her life: she might find herself at his side through countless years of poverty while he created the formula for curing muscular dystrophy in children;

he was the antithesis of her world, she was a glamorous child amongst vacuous debutantes in high places, and he was the genius ignored during his lifetime. He was her opportunity to become the fully vibrant human on the outside that only he knew her to be on the inside. Later on he saw that he was simply a paragon of maladjustment and that he had created a role for her to play in some psychodrama of his own construction. It was image-making at first sight.

She was neither rich nor carefree nor glamorous. He had assumed she had money because she was attending college, and at the time he suffered from an exaggerated sense of his own importance and individuality and suffering, as though only he could be an underdog in a world of prodigal riches. He assumed she was rich because to him her clothes were stylish. He assumed she was carefree because she had a penchant for badinage that kept him straining to be clever, and he assumed she was glamorous because when he first met her she was seated at a table in the student union with a clutch of the jabbering daughters of Texas new rich. She stopped him as he passed with a tray loaded with soup bowls (he was working as a busboy in the cafeteria) to ask if he had done his biology assignment yet—she was the lab partner of the girl who sat beside him in lecture, and she had missed the last session. He looked down at her, then across to her companions, who were ignoring his presence with an indifference he felt equated contempt. For a moment he wallowed in the teeming bundle of injustices that he collected on the spot: where they were callous, he was sensitive; where they were stupid, he was intelligent; where they were unfeeling, he was compassionate. They were the dull majority, he was the resourceful minority; they the oppressors, he the oppressed; they the decadent and impotent status quo, he the budding young revolutionary. And he was infuriated that they had the time to chatter about their social life while he had to cart dishes, then ask him about an assignment that they (she) should have gotten—baby, he thought, I'm going to show you what *real* life is like. "Meet me by the fountain in twenty minutes and I'll tell you," he said.

She was to be his first convert. Yet what he discovered later was that like himself she was attending college only because she had saved money for it since she was in the eighth grade; in addition to this money she had only what her father, an elevator operator in a San Antonio hotel, and her mother, a worker in a pecan shelling and packing factory, could send her. Her brother and two sisters, all younger, sent her little bills in the mail for frills. Her family were all hoping that she'd become a teacher; she was the first member of her family to complete high school. She had cultivated the habits of a working girl with middle-class aspirations who waits for the fashions to filter down to the discount houses, where she then shops and selects prudently, considering function and versatility first, stylishness second. He had ignorantly assumed that a certain style meant a certain income; the subtle nuances of appearing more affluent than one is were alien to him. Later he discovered that her only connection with the sorority girls at the table was that one of them, a rushee, was her roommate.

He also recognized later that she didn't mind giving the false impression of affluence, gaiety, and glamour —she was after all as susceptible as any other girl to the influence of American pop-cult dictums directing every woman to be the one men find most desirable. The day they went to the dunes, she had spent the morning changing skirts, ironing blouses, bathing too early— leaving her convinced she needed a second bath before he picked her up. She has confessed to him that she made her face up to get the "natural" look, then scrubbed her make-up off to get that "fresh-scrubbed" look but succeeded only in looking like someone who'd scrubbed her face to get that fresh-scrubbed look. Hair up, down, curled, uncurled, ratted and teased, brushed out—after an hour of this she was ready to cry. Some deeply embedded sense of her own unworthiness eventually made her suspect that none of her own clothes would make the right impression, so from her rushee roommate she borrowed the knee-line, pleated riding skirt and suede boots. She wore one of her own blouses simply because she didn't feel she could afford to be more indebted to her Anglo roommate—she felt inferior enough.

Meanwhile, across the campus Méndez slipped his feet into his weathered Wellingtons and borrowed his roommate's lightweight nylon jacket which he intended not to wear but to toss casually over his left shoulder with his thumb crooked into the hanging strap just inside the collar. He had paid special attention to the condition of his underwear.

They spent the early afternoon hunting arrowheads. She talked about her family in response to his questions, and as it slowly dawned on him that she wasn't rich, that she was not indeed from one of the old aristocratic families in San Antonio, and he felt vaguely disappointed: if she hadn't grown up in the lap of luxury and materialistic values, then she was no longer a *project* and if she was no longer a project, he wasn't sure he wanted to seduce her—mere seduction was for fraternity boys, and he wanted to give a woman a Total Experience, to turn her psyche inside out and shock her to the depths of her self where she might erupt into light and freedom. They strolled hand in hand in the hardened hollows of the dunes, looking in the wind-blown bottoms for chips of obsidian or flint and shards of pottery. She kicked over a fire-blackened stone and they kneeled to brush away the sand and found a shard with a wavy black and red pattern painted on it. Bluffing, he tried to date it about the sixteenth century, having once spent an hour or so with a book on Indian artifacts. He tried to discuss it casually, without lecturing, struggling to strike that apologetic note of self-irony which suggested that he knew his deeper interest in arcane matters might not exactly enthrall his listeners. Then historian became historiographer and meta-physician: he half-turned into the wind and looked off toward the horizon, squinting, letting the wind toss his hair, letting her look at him while he mused about the disparity between their sense of the present and the evidence of the ageless continuity of human life. Oh, he had depth. When he glanced at her, he thought he spotted a trace of bemusement in her eyes.

In a hollow of a group of dunes they drank the wine and ate the cheese and apples, dividing the third as he planned, the blade of his pocketknife slicing the halves like soft white pine. They were seated on a blanket, cross-legged, facing each other, and her skirt was draped over her thighs just behind her knees; she had laid a napkin in her lap, and in the hollow between her legs atop the napkin sat her half of the apple and a small hunk of cheese. Sipping from the wine bottle, he watched her nibble on the cheese, replace it carefully into her lap, then he passed her the bottle; she raised it to her lips and her eyes half-closed—he watched her, knowing that she was being watched and enjoying it. She tossed her hair away from her shoulders, revealing the small circles of gold in the pierced lobes of her ears, and as she turned aside he studied the delicate, rosy flesh of her ear. She lowered the bottle and dabbed at a dribble of wine running down her full flushed lips with a corner of her tongue. She smiled at him, then pointed into her lap. You may eat that if you wish, she said. He had the startling sensation that she wasn't referring to the cheese. Their knees were almost touching, and his eyes traced a line to the warm, wet center of her body, the single fruit of her tree, and he suddenly wished he had a dozen appendages, a dozen fleshy projections and she a dozen matching cups. He imagined the tips of his fingers in her ears, her mouth, her sex, then his tongue and then his root. While he worked out variations on this theme, she struggled to her feet to brush the crumbs out of her lap and stood above him looking down, smiling. She knew he could see up her dress; he had the distressing sensation that he was being toyed with. He checked an impulse to lean forward and bury his face in the V beneath her skirt. After a moment, she reassumed her cross-legged position before him. Their knees touched.

"You know," she said, smiling, "you're much nicer than you think you are."

He considered her comment to be a challenge to his manhood, so he returned her smile, leaned forward, toppled her over backward and fell between her legs. As he remembers it, her thighs eased open like the two halves of the apple he divided; her skirt rode up around her waist, he pressed his belly into her crotch. He nibbled playfully on her lower lip, then slid his open mouth onto hers and when he sucked the breath from her lungs and forced it back into them, the thrust of his wind deep inside her chest seemed to overwhelm her; for a moment she went limp, the vibrations of her soft moan reverberating against her breasts, echoing in them as she pressed against him. He slid his mouth along her cheek to her ear and tongued the damp, tea-colored flesh; her hips rose slowly and forcefully, pressing against his belly like a single hand kneading bread.

"What do you want to eat?" she was asking, her head still stuck into the refrigerator, only her buttocks and legs visible to him. He laughed.

"Anything."

He grew moony over the sweet, plump curve of her buttocks protruding from the half-opened refrigerator door. Give the old gal a toss in the hay—like old wine or sages she grew better with the years; in bed she mellowed like irascible queens grown old, and her body emitted the scent of the western coast as blown from ashore to home-bound sailors—not of virgin-sprung flowers exploding into bloom, but of pastry in the oven, coffee on the stove, and a hickory log glowing in the hearth. Where on that afternoon in the dunes they had acted a good deal like two amateurs struggling to give each other the impression that each was a professional, aping the techniques, the mask, the postures of skilled lovers, they now made love a good deal like two professionals struggling to give the impression of amateurs: two hustlers out to con each other. It had taken on that bittersweet mixture which allowed for the grace and ease of hearty laughter, the healthy injection of bawdy folly into a balloon of romantic illusion.

"You're a good-looking woman," he said idly.

She giggled. She must have known how much of her was visible. As she bent lower to check the hydrator for vegetables he rose from the table and stood behind her, the seed of a fantasy sprouting in his head: lift dress, take her panties down to her knees and probe her depths while she has her head in the refrigerator. He immediately killed the fantasy, feeling vaguely guilty about its implications—that he wanted to dehumanize her, plunge her like a bitch while she had her head in cold storage. Still, he ached to do it. He pressed against her; her hands ceased rummaging and she leaned slightly backward into him. He slid his hands beneath her dress and ran his fingers along the furrow he felt there.

"Ohh," she shivered. "You're not going to get anything to eat."

"Think not?"

"I don't care. Ummm, that feels good."

"*Quieres mas?*"

"*Sí, mucho mas, muchísimo mas.*"

"*Como este?*"

"Sí, or any way. I don't care. Oh, yes, do *that*, just keep doing *that.*"

"You like to be touched *here*, like *this?*"

"*Oh, tú sabes que me gusta mucho!*"

"You like to be kissed here?"

"Uuuuh."

"*Tú quieres coger, muchacha?*"

"*Sí!*"

They made it to the bedroom floor and he closed the door to with his foot; he knew she would insist on it no matter how urgently they needed each other: she didn't want Jimmy bursting in to find his parents humping away on the kitchen table while the vitamin bottles and salt and pepper shakers and water glasses went crashing to the floor; it might damage his little psyche to find his mother stretched out on the kitchen table moaning while his father stood beside it on a stack of newspapers pumping away for all glory while the dishes jumped and the toaster rattled its way off the far end of the table —no, that wouldn't do, so he carried her just past the bedroom door, stopped to kiss her; she went almost limp and they fell to the floor where they coupled on the throw rug amidst loose shoes and books and a broom, hairpins and a pile of dirty socks; he turned his head sideways to face a shoe the size of Mother Hubbard's, and beneath him Juanita clasped his flesh in hers and milked it.

"She's got the hots for you, you know," she said later as they lay drowsily in bed. She was kneading his feet with hers.

"How do you know?"

"I just do," she answered mysteriously. He shrugged.

"You'll stay away from her, won't you?"

He snorted. "Now how can I do that?"

"You can *try.*"

He grunted reluctant assent.

"What did you two talk about in the kitchen?"

"She wanted me to talk about you."

"How do you know?"

"She kept telling me things about him and then looking at me as though I was supposed to trade stories with her."

"Did you?" It didn't displease him to think that Houston's wife had some juicy nugget of information about him to turn over in her mind.

"No."

"Good. Why not?"

"Are you disappointed?"

He scoffed. "Of course not. Look," he turned toward her. "There's nothing attractive about her; she's a bitchy and brittle piece of plastic womanhood, and she hasn't even got a good body."

"You've looked, have you?"

"Come on," he said, exasperated. "She's the personification of everything I hate."

"That's what I'm afraid of," Juanita said simply, rolling away from him. "That's what I meant."

He never knew she understood him so well. And far into the night before he finally dropped fitfully off to sleep he was troubled by the sense of something ominous having intruded into the carefully constructed order of his life, as though he had stepped aboard a child's merry-go-round only to discover a homocidal maniac at the controls.

# _____ Three _____

"Hey!" Bond yells.

Méndez knocks his fist lightly against the railing, looks away from the pasture where the Cat raises a dust cloud many times its size, then he stalks the length of the catwalk and vaults down the stairs. At the jeep he rummages under the driver's seat for his gloves and pulls another shovel from the rear seat.

"What're they doing over there?" He nods toward Dillard's field.

"Don't know for sure." Bond peers, shading his eyes with his hand. "Gas station, I'd say."

"Gas station! Now we really need another goddamn gas station. It ought to have a hamburger stand beside it to uglify it up a little." He flings a shovelful of sand into the pool, violently. "Another goddamn gas station. Architectural wet dream of a . . ."

"Man oh man," Bond laughs. "Somebody sure rattled yore chain today. What do you care what they put up there? Even if they gouge out a snake pit and slap a board fence up around it, it ain't no skin off yore nose."

Méndez looks up from his shoveling. "Let's say I have a sentimental interest in that cotton field."

"I never did see anybody in my whole life who had such a mind full of things," Bond chuckles. "That cotton patch is just a cotton patch and that's all. You get things all bloed up in your head, just like my Uncle Delbert did when he got to thinking that he could beat Las Vegas playing solitare."

"Hold it!" Méndez cocks his shovel back to throw a load of sand but checks the motion; when Bond remains silent, he tosses it into the pool. "I been listening to you all afternoon and now you're going to listen while I tell you a story. You had your chance, you wandered around in that tale about your nephew's dogs for an hour and a half and never *did* end it. You interrupted yourself a dozen times, now this time I'm going to do it."

"But I wasn't done yet," Bond wails.

"Tough."

"Let me say . . ."

"No."

"Just one . . ."

"No."

"Thang. Okay?"

"You can't do it."

"What?"

"Say just one 'thang.' "

"Yes I can."

"No you can't."

"I'll listen to yore story, but you got to let me say this here one thang before you even begin," Bond interjects hurriedly. Méndez watches his eyes, his sly grin.

"All right. What is it?"

"You think you know the end to my story. You think all that stuff about monsters and flying saucers and hardware stores don't have nothing to do with the story about my nephew's dogs."

"That's right."

"No, it ain't. I never told you the ending of that story."

"You locked yourself up in the pickup."

"That's just the end of that chapter. That ain't the whole end, the final end, the *end's* end. You ain't even heard the important part." When Méndez falters, Bond rushes in to cinch his lead. "Course I can't get *through* the end of my story without getting *to* it, and I'll have to stop off at my Uncle Delbert's to do that."

Méndez grits his teeth and continues to shovel.

"So go on and tell yore story," Bond admonishes.

"Without interruption?"

"No more than what's necessary to keep you honest."

"Okay." Méndez straightens up from scooping the sand and jabs his shovel upright in the earth like a flag in unclaimed territory. "This is a story about Friar Marcos."

"Who?"

"Just listen up." He pauses to pluck a cigarette from his shirt pocket and light it, struggling to remember the exact phrases he has written in his notebook, which were prompted by Aguilar's letter and the invasion of the Houstons. "We're always conscious of the land, of fences and their meaning."

"Cost you a ready-made," Bond interrupts, nodding to the cigarette package bulging in Méndez's shirt pocket. "If I'm going to have to listen to a whole lot of . . ."

"Okay. Here—"

"Thanks."

"Fences and their importance," Méndez exhales. "And history. We can't do anything to it. Take that pumping unit for instance. Made in the image of—"

"You won't mind if I just go ahead and just keep chucking sand into this here pond, will you?"

Méndez waves him on. "The image of huge green brutes who ate each other in the jungles that were here before the sea washed in. They had territorial imperatives, but when the sea crushed those bellowing forests beneath granite and shale and sandstone and caliche the boundaries they had sensed, those markers of their greed, were buried with them. It's odd that we should be trying to contain their world. This oil—" he nods toward the pool, "was once a solid marker of that territory. Let that brute find his territory now . . ."

"If he looks anything like a cow he won't be having a hard time, no quicker'n we're getting this here pond covered," Bond grumbles.

"After the seas receded, the land slept, dried out, took seed, and gave birth and only God knows how much later Indians wandered into this basin to scratch a meager living on these mesas. But they only laid claim to what they could catch or grow. And if a single Indian possessed no land himself, as a member of the tribe he held the deed to all he saw—sun, star, rock, and tree. We think it's strange, yet we assume that one man may actually have a right to a certain geographical location, and that a collection of his fellows can award it to him as they see fit, and that they can collectively decide that he may do with what's on it, under it, or above it as he sees fit. What's even stranger to me is the notion that a man ten to twelve thousand miles from a place could tell another man that if that location did exist, then the man could 'claim' it as territory belonging to God—who by implication didn't already have it—and the Holy Roman Emperor, and himself, the conquistador. Imagine Coronado's mind, or the mind of any of them for that matter. They came looking for the Seven Cities of Cibola. They had heard wild tales about islands of black women who could screw a man to death. Well, Montezuma's Mexico did exist and it had been fabulously wealthy, the entire continent north of it had been unexplored, so in some way it's understandable that they actually believed that there were Seven Cities, though they should have been suspicious from the legendary number alone. But they carried a strange contagion, a disease that led them to assume that even if there *did* exist an entire continent of horny black women and a civilization whose streets were paved with gold then they necessarily had a right to it. Well, that contagion led Friar Marcos to go forth and take possession of all the land he saw and convert the natives. 'Here, I'll give you a deed to the whole shooting match,' Mendoza might have said. 'I'll just make it blank and you can fill in the inconsequentials like boundaries later, just as long as they include the Seven Cities with just a little on the other side of the city limits for good measure.' Maybe Marcos had good intentions. He set out for the Seven Cities but let a black man scout ahead. Named Stephen, I think. One of the four survivors of the Navarez expedition. Stephen kept ahead of Marcos a few steps, leading the way to Cibola, which turned out to be a Zuni pueblo with total assets of probably not more than ten to twenty dollars, but they killed Stephen; Marcos was afraid to walk into his Cibola and claim it so he peered at it from the top of a distant hill, from where it looked a lot larger and richer than it actually was. He imagined it to be a new Mexico, another Peru. He erected a cross, a couple of sticks bound together and propped up by stones, and laid claim to the city and the territory beyond in the honor of Don Antonio de Mendoza, first viceroy of New Spain." Méndez broke off suddenly with a bitter chuckle. "It's absurd—here is this insignificant little friar adventurer hiding on top this distant hill laying claim by means of this 'small and slender cross,' as he called it, to all the vast territories beyond the city which he had heard about but which he was not going to explore because he wanted to return and report the first one. It's like a peeping Tom laying claim to the object of his voyeurism. I guess the ultimate irony is that even though neither Marcos nor Padilla nor Coronado nor Cardenez ever found what they had hoped for, they were able to get what they did find from the Indians, although some of them died trying. And all of them died." Méndez flips his cigarette butt down into the sand at his feet. "Then the Merkins."

"The *who?*"

"Merkins," Méndez laughs. "Your ancestors. Or more to the point old Lemuel's grandfather—the settlers. Like the green brutes and the mad friars, they had their territorial imperatives too and they put up thousands of miles of barbed wire like metallic extensions of their nervous systems and felt they owned anything or any*body* who happened to fall within those boundaries, and when they found something underneath, the

Okies and the Arkies came to uncap those cavities. The myth is they grew rich overnight, but the truth is closer to maybe one in ten thousand, and most broke their backs working twelve-hour days on the slippery, junk-strewn floors of drilling rigs, drank, slept in boom-town tents or boarded flophouse shacks. Gradually it ate them piecemeal." He nods toward Bond. "A finger here under the casing rack, an eye taken by a cat chain, toes beneath the tubing. Or it took them all at once: a chunk of metal the size of a man's head slipped quietly out of the crow's nest, dropped ninety feet and drove him through the flooring of the substructure. Or he caught fire and jumped off the floor, like a thin-skinned comet. And by the time a decade, four children, and twenty-five thousand work hours had slipped past he had forgotton about his own dream of the Seven Cities, and that dream was superseded by another: one of these days he'd have enough money just to get shut of this country."

Méndez straightens up from the fender, takes his shovel and moves to the edge of the pool.

"Well, that was quite a mouthful. It was a mighty perty speech, but when I come out here from Arkansas I wasn't looking for no Seven Cities or even a million dollars—I just wanted me a job a work."

"So?"

"So I didn't have no dream othern a pot to piss in, a warm bed, beef stew, and a woman now and then. And you talk about me rattling off and wandering here and there in a tale—why hellfire boy, you done covered a billion years, a hunnerd and seventy-six thousand people, and twenty-eleven governments in that little speech. I know what's wrong with you—you ain't happy unless you ball everything up in your mind, and that's what I was trying to tell you about my uncle Delbert Sills."

"No, I was making a point about ownership, and about using the land."

Bond looks up slowly, squints with gradual recognition. "Now looky here, son," he says seriously. "I know and *you* know that man has a lot a cockeyed plans, and I know and *you* know that we both know ever inch a this here property and how to stay alive on it and that he don't even hardly know where it starts and stops. But you got to keep it in yore head that *he's* got the deed to it."

"Well, you tell me what you think of a man who—"

"I done told you it don't matter what I think a his plans." Bond cracked a grin. "He's got *his* head all balled up like my Uncle Delbert, too." He paused to extort permission to begin his tale.

"All right—go on."

"Well, thanks a heap, don't mind if I do. Course now Delbert's problem was a little different. He got into hot water because he's a real scientific-minded man." Bond stood up straight and hitched his pants up by a belt loop as though in preparation for a hundred-yard dash. "Delbert had a terrible hankering after *organization*. He always kept the top half of his gas tank full, never let it get below the middle line; he said it was just as easy to keep the top half full as it was the bottom half. That's the kind of man he was. He could even refold a road map the right way. He kept little notebooks full of numbers that told him how much tax he paid last year and the year before that, what his odometer said the last time he rotated his tires, how many miles between quarts of oil, and what all his credit card numbers was, and he'd memorized his credit card numbers in case he lost the book and he had the book in case he might forget the numbers. He could tell you right off the bat his social security number, driver's license number, license tag number, military service number, plus all the telephone numbers he'd ever had. I wondered lots a times why all the sharp corners of all them numbers didn't pierce his brain. Might have, maybe that's what was wrong with him.

"He swore he was going to die on his seventy-second birthday because that's the average life span. I know that sounds crazy, but that's what he believed. I used to tell him over and over that maybe he wasn't average. 'Yeah,' he'd say. 'I guess it could be a lot sooner.' I looked at him and he looked at me and I never did ask again. I guess it give him some kind of comfort to make it definite." Bond pauses a moment to wipe the sweat from his eyebrows with the sleeve of his right forearm. "But about the solitaire—he liked to play against Las Vegas: you know, where you pay a dollar apiece for ever card in the deck, then you get five back for ever one you put out front. Most of the time he lost money on it a course, but ever now and then he'd run the whole deck out there and it'd perk him up a bit. I tried to tell him that he was playing a losing game to begin with, that it wasn't called Las Vegas solitaire for nothing, and if there was one chance in a hunnerd that a man could *win* at it, then they sure wouldn't play it there no more, but Uncle Delbert didn't pay no attention because he had something else at stake. Las Vegas was . . . well I don't know rightly what. Maybe it was whatever it was that he was guarding against by writing all those numbers down in that little notebook. When something wasn't going right with him, he'd lock hisself up down in the basement and play until he'd beat it. He was like

a drunkard. Aunt Mildred'd beat on the door to tell
him supper was ready, and he'd just holler back, 'Be
there in a minute—I'm just gonna play until I win a
little something.' Then, after about twenty minutes
and supper was stone cold, she'd holler again and he'd
say, 'Be there in a second—I'm just gonna play till I
quit winning' and then a half hour later she'd yell again
and he'd answer that he'd be up in a jiffy, soon's he quit
losing. At first I tried to help him, but I could just as
well have kept my mouth shut because eventually he
started *perdicting* and that's why he went crazy. You
listening?"

"Yeah." But he isn't. He considers telling Bond
about the offer Houston has made him, but he is
plagued by the dilemma of it, too engrossed in the
conflicts it presents to discuss it openly. Houston has
become a benefactor, and a benefactor whom the
beneficiary resents with all the contempt the subject
has for the tyrant, no matter how benevolent he might
be. Cockeyed plans, he thinks. He could supply adjectives for those plans which might better describe the
seriousness of their misdirection, the utter extrava-
gently wasteful frivolousness of them, the contemptible
motivation of them. Had Lemuel known what would
follow his death, he might have disowned his son,
Méndez likes to think.

" 'You oughta drive over to Odessa and goatha public liberry and get a book on this thang,' I told him.
'They's probly one on card games and you can probly
find out what the odds is for winning and losing.' I had
a good notion of what they was, but I didn't tell him
—I thought if he discovered it hisself, then he'd give
her up. 'It don't matter,' he told me, 'because even if
the book said I only had a chance in a hunnerd of

winning, what the book don't know is that one win is worth ninety-nine losses.' Then he took out a big thick notebook. 'Besides,' he said, I done figgered them myself,' and he commenced to haul out sheets of paper with scribbling all over them where he'd been charting his games. 'I found out they's a curve to all this,' he explained. He showed me a graph where he'd started the evening losing a little, then gradually more and more, but then he started back on the upswing until he was winning more than he was losing. 'Trouble is,' he said, 'sometimes it takes me three four hours to get her back up there.' Well, I could see I wasn't going to be much help, so I left him alone. I went back early one evening about a week later. He come up from the basement, grinning. 'You win?' I ast. 'Got her beat all the way.' He sat down at the table and started writing something. 'Who you writing?' Mildred ast. 'Las Vegas,' he said, whistling. 'I'm sending them a bill for two hunnerd and seventy dollars.' Mildred and I just looked at each other. What he'd done figgered out, he told us later after he got out of the hospital, was that the key to the whole thang lay in getting over the losing hump and staying on the winning streak. He started noticing patterns that come up early in the game, so he got to seeing if he could predict the outcome of the game by the time he reached the thirty-eighth card and he found out he could do her, or come within two three cards of it. So when it looked like on the thirty-eighth card he was going to lose, he'd just write the score down that he'd done perdicted then move on to another game, and when he reached a winner he'd play it out all the way to stay on his streak—he'd play half games until he got hot, then he'd stretch them out. Then he got the notion that if he could get even faster, then he could reach his winning streak sooner and maybe even get more money because he knoed that in the past sometimes he'd play until he was about ready to drop off to sleep and it'd be right in the middle of a hot run and he'd quit and a course the next day the cards would of cooled off. So he took to perdicting along about the twentieth-fifth card, got good at it, went along that way for awhile, then a week later moved down to the eighteenth card, got good at it, went along that way awhile, then a week later went down to the tenth, got good at it, then finely one day he got the notion in his head that he could perdict the outcome of the game from the first card and he started whooping and hollering down in the basement.

"The *next* day he figgered out that the didn't need that first card and the day after he discovered he didn't even need the deck at all—he could play five hours of nonstop solitaire just sitting in an easy chair, mumbling to hisself. That's when we started worrying about him. He'd sit there in the parlor with his eyes glazed over, muttering like he was talking in his sleep—'Aw' or 'Uh' —or he'd start chuckling when he finally reached a hot streak and lean forward and jerk his head in little jerks as he laid down ever card in a hot game in his mind. He played them all out to keep her going. At the end of ever night he'd get up and go over to the kitchen table and write Las Vegas a bill for whatever he won that night, if he won. You still listening?"

"Ummm," Méndez nods.

"Listen up because this here's the most important part. This went on for a month and Mildred was about to lose her mind over it, so she talked to people about what to do, and somebody told her to put a pillowcase over his feet when he was asleep and put his head in

the moonlight coming in the window and that'd draw
the crazy blood out a his head and down into his feet
and then he could just walk it out. She tried that but
it didn't seem to work, and, anyways, Delbert had hit
on a new plan—he saw that if he could perdict the
outcome of each individual game before he ever begun,
then there wasn't no reason why he couldn't do her
faster and faster until he could perdict the outcome of
an entire night of play in two, three minutes. But that
left him four hours with no playing to do, so he spent
the other three hours and fifty-seven minutes working
on the next day and the day after that. Oh, I tell you
he was getting into that game *deep*, and finely two
weeks later, when he done worked hisself up to his
seventy-second birthday and found out he still owed
Las Vegas a dollar fifty, he busted out crying and babbling and we had to send him off. When I saw him later
I tried to cheer him up. 'You mighta lived to be a day
moren seventy-two,' I said. 'Why, if you coulda hung
on one more day you mighta won it all back again.' He
just turned two eyes toward me that looked like two
pissholes in a board fence and you woulda thought by
the look on his face that he was sick to his stomach and
I'd just offered him a bowl a pickled hog brains to settle
it down."

"You think that might happen to Houston?"
Méndez smiles.

"Haw!" Bond cackles. "Him and some others I
know."

"You were the one crying about having to paint the
house and the fence."

"Sure! But I ain't doing no plotting and a planning
and a worrying on my *own* account." He heaves a load
of sand into the pool. "Now where was I? Oh yeah!

_184_

Now, if you can keep thether marry-archie music out a yore ears long enough to hang on, you might see in the end how it all fits together. If I remember right, when I left off before the dogs had done chased me through the campfire and the tents and into the cab of the pickup. I was shivering from the shakes, and I rolled up the glasses in the truck as quick as I could but them dogs'd leap up in the air and I'd see their faces level with mine and their slobber'd fly out and hit the glass and I was trying to get my boot off to see if I had bloed my toe clean off. . . ."

Free to plot, plan, and worry on his own account, Méndez tunes Bond out. Deciphering the code of Houston's intentions had been vital to him; in the week following Houston's arrival Méndez had tried to sec-ond-guess the other man out of fear—so many possible acts could leave Méndez homeless, jobless, futureless. It didn't help that he disliked Houston on what he considered to be objective grounds; the story Houston had told left Méndez with the chilling, uneasy sense that Houston—even though he was more complicated and intelligent than Méndez remembered him to be—had become a kind of amoral drifter, disconnected and alienated. Nothing of his father had been passed on to him.

So Méndez was left to hope—if not blindly, at least with the myopia of those seduced by their wishes—that Houston would simply go away. He watched for com-plaints about muscle aches or sand and heat, or hunger and thirst. When they went out in the jeep, Méndez always parked in the sun; he "forgot" to fill the water can. But Houston never complained, and he wasn't to be driven away from the ranch by mere discomfort. Too, he even seemed enthusiastic to learn: he watched attentively as Méndez and Bond and Carlos tattooed the Hereford calves and sprayed the herd with a chloro-dane solution, then he ostentatiously inspected the tat-too-pliers when they were finished and once even slipped the tail of his shirt into the jaws to try the tool, branding his shirt with the Rolling "J" and a numeral. Méndez noted, though, that most of his questions focused on the cost of things. Did he intend to run the place himself? Méndez had wondered. Or did he only intend to be an absentee owner and wants to know if it would turn a profit? Itchy about his own status, he had come close to initiating a discussion about the future but never did. That Houston didn't seek his counsel annoyed and depressed him.

He was heartened, though, to see that Houston quickly grew bored with all the tedious mechanical tasks that were required to keep the ranch functioning.

On Saturday morning, he and Bond were splicing fence wire just west of the scrub-cedar hollows; tired of watching, Houston strolled along the fence away from them with large, even strides.

"What's he measuring?" Méndez asked Bond as they watched Houston's back disappear over the sandy ridge before them.

Bond spat. "Hisself."

"Reckon there'll be enough?"

"Naw. But he won't know it until it runs out."

Maybe that would be reason enough to wait things out, Méndez thought.

Houston made an allusion or two to "guest houses," a reference Méndez didn't understand until he went into the den at Houston's request to retrieve a govern-ment manual on stock ponds and spied on his desk an artist's pad opened to a penciled set of plans. The sketch appeared to be an aerial view of the main house, the machine shed, the barn, the bunkhouse, Méndez's cottage, and the horse shed. Each building was labeled and he could recognize each from the exterior shape and relative position, but what he didn't recognize were their altered interiors—each building had been remodeled to serve as a dwelling, their open interior spaces partitioned off into bedrooms, living rooms, baths, kitchens, and closets. Méndez was puzzled. At the bottom of the sketch were doodles and figures which might have represented the sum required to make such a transformation: "$80,000." Below that figure he saw "pool?" with "$3500" beside it. Looking back at the sketch, he could discern a dimly penciled oval in the quadrangle between the main house and the outbuildings. Pool? He was slow to take it in; the concept was foreign to him. Had Houston come across some harebrained scheme for treating cattle? A pool of what? Cesspool? Was he groping ignorantly on his own with the perennial problem of the sluggish laterals of the septic tank? If so, Méndez could certainly take care of the problem cheaper than the $3500 that someone had apparently quoted him. But why all the houses?

Finally it hit him: a dude ranch. Houston had no right to do that—as a cattle ranch, it turned a profit every year with a lot of hard work and careful planning, and Houston had no right to convert it. It was productive, and if Méndez had learned anything from Houston's father it was that if something produces, you don't stop it from producing; life was the eternal struggle to make the unproductive produce and the productive ever-producing.

And despite his earlier plea to Méndez of ignorance about how to run a ranch and his request for help, no more than three days had passed before Méndez found himself no longer in charge. Thursday morning as he strode out of the tool shed carrying a fence stretcher, Houston had intercepted him.

"Morning," Houston said. Then spat. Méndez noted that although the trajectory of the globule had a distinctly amateurish arc about it, it was nevertheless a hearty imitation of the gesture of prelude in the ranching country. He would have laughed had he not been so concerned as to what Houston's authoritative manner portended. "Where you off to?"

"I thought we'd fix a little fence, then go up to Northrup ridge and replace that joint of leaky pipe at the stock tank—the water's running out onto the ground when the mill pumps." He spoke lightly, as though offering a suggestion.

Houston grunted, frowning.

"How many does it take?"

Méndez smiled. "How many what?"

"Men," Houston replied crossly.

"Oh . . ." Méndez paused and appeared to be estimating: if Houston didn't know the answer to that question, he could never run a ranch. "One can do it," he said finally.

"Good. I've got something else in mind for that old one-armed fellow and that Torrez lad."

"Well kiss old rusty!" Bond groaned when Méndez found him in the bunkhouse shaving. "What color?"

"He didn't say."

"Uh-huh! Fence, too, I bet you a dollar to a dough-nut."

"Yes, but he wants you to finish the house first."

"He's just pissing against the wind to put a nickel down for something like that. Painting the house!"

Bond stamped his feet. "Yew tell him about getting them calves to the auction in Odessa?"

Wearily, Méndez eased himself down on the edge of the old man's unmade bunk. "I didn't say anything about it."

"Well, God-da-*mity!*" Bond snorted, letting his straight razor arc cleanly across his weathered cheek in a single motion. Dully, Méndez recognized he was showing off.

"He's in charge now," Méndez answered after a moment. He sounded sullen and resentful, even to himself. "He didn't ask me and he won't. He's too proud."

"He'll proud hisself right outa bizness."

Méndez shrugged.

"And then where'll *we* be?" Bond persisted.

Méndez mused in silence about a new plan of approach, then glanced up to catch Bond's gaze in the mirror.

"What've yew got in mind?"

"Well," Méndez began uneasily, searching for a way to make what he had to say sound benign. "We could just watch out for things behind his back but not too well. I mean we could let him go on his own long enough to let him screw up so he could see how ignorant he is."

Bond chuckled.

"What's so funny?"

"You reckon we might *help* him screw up a little?"

Méndez winced at the idea of deliberate sabotage. Bond was watching him quizzically; he couldn't tell if the old man was serious or was just testing him.

"No, I really wasn't thinking of that." He considered a moment. "Only by omission. Calculated neglect."

"Do what he says and nothing else?"

Méndez nodded.

"Sounds all right to me." Bond raised his knee and wiped the razor clean on the leg of his Levis. "Except that if what he wants us to do today's an example, I'd just as soon tell him what oughta be done—it'll be a lot less work in the long run."

Méndez grinned. "We all have sacrifices to make."

"What's yours?"

"Having to take orders from him."

Bond laughed, loudly.

For the next three days Méndez kept careful account of Houston's mistakes in his spiral notebooks, comparing the other man's decisions with his own and projecting the probable consequences of each. As well as he could tell, Houston seemed concerned only with the appearance of the ranch—after Bond and Carlos had painted the house a particularly unattractive shade of luteous yellow the approximate color of old piano keys, they were instructed to coat the board fence which surrounded the "yard"—a large area which took in the house and all the outbuildings—the same color, a task which inspired Bond to take his frustration out by dreaming up descriptive phrases for the color, the most lively of which was "monkey-pus yeller." Houston had a sign made of wrought-iron which said "Rolling J Ranch Bob Houston Prop." in mock-rope script; this he directed Méndez and the other two to hang from a large arc made from pipe over the entrance to the ranch. They spent the entire day at it. "The Rolling Jackass Ranch," Bond said over and over as they struggled to raise it aloft from the bed of the pickup while Carlos straddled the pipe high above them and tried to connect the sign. Houston then took a dislike to the old cattle guard at the entrance beneath the new sign; it was bent out of shape and was constructed of two-inch pipe. He had another made from railroad rails at a welding shop in Odessa, sent Méndez all the way there to pick it up, and they wasted an entire afternoon lifting the old one out with a rented winch truck and planting the new one.

Houston had the half-mile entrance to the main house regraded and graveled.

Then the lake. At first Bond thought that the lake was to be a stock pond. The pasture between the house and the highway lay in a three-to-four-acre depression, and in the spring the rains gathered there but soaked in shortly for the summer; this pasture gave the ranch one of its best feeding crops of Johnson grass, and Houston decided to submerge it.

"We'll extend the side fence out over to the high ridge," Houston explained, letting his arm sweep out to conjure up the new fence. Méndez could tell he liked the feeling of imagining new structures spring to life at the command of his most casual gesture.

"If we do that the cattle can't get from the other pasture into the pond, though," Bond put in easily.

Méndez smiled.

"That's the idea," Houston countered gruffly. Although he still tolerated suggestions from Méndez, any comment from Bond, whom he thought a drifter, a transient cowboy, rankled him.

"Huh?"

"I don't want the cows in there. I'm making a lake."

"A lake?" Bond gasped.

Houston tapped the top of his thigh with a rolled-up sketch of his plans. "Yep." He grinned. "A five-acre lake. And every bit of land you see between here and there that's not under water will be part of a three-hole golf course."

Bond whistled softly. "I'll be damned." He exchanged a look with Méndez.

"Right there's a feller that better put his hat on when he goes out in the sun," Bond said later when they returned to the bunkhouse. "Ten acres of the best permanent pasture on this place and he's gonna put it under water or make a golf course out of it." He nodded in disbelief.

Méndez had been thinking about it for two days: he had already seen the plans. "Don't you see what's happening? He knows he'll never be in charge as long as this is a ranch like his father had. He'll make it into something he knows something about, so he'll—well, so he'll know something about it."

Bond slumped in silence for a long moment as if digesting Méndez's explanation. "Hellfire," he grunted. "Maybe I oughta start studying up on how to be one of them people that carries them golf-bags around."

"A caddy?"

"Yeah."

Méndez looked out of the corner of his eye at Bond's profile—he was rubbing his one hand thoughtfully across his cheek—and Méndez felt a tremendous pang of anger and frustration to see that the old man was seriously contemplating the possibility.

"I guess you really can't blame the man," Bond went on slowly, struggling to be fair. "Something really ain't yours until you put your mark on it."

"But it's not *his* in the first place!" Méndez exploded. "It's mine. Ours. Anybody's but his. If he wants to build a goddamn carnival or whatever the hell it is he has in mind let him go buy up some goddamn sand farm outside of Lubbock and stay the hell away from here. He doesn't have any *right* to do what he wants to do." Fuming, he plopped down on a metal folding chair beside the foot locker that held all of Bond's worldly goods.

Bond waited patiently until Méndez calmed down. "Yew better watch out," he said softly, "or you're going to get yourself fooled."

Then, Tuesday, eight days after the Houstons' arrival, things fell in place for him. When he returned to their cottage in the early afternoon from completing the last section of fence to be painted, he could hear Jane talking in the kitchen; he let himself in quietly through the screen door to the living room and stood awhile listening to the disembodied voices floating into the room from the kitchen. Jane's grated in his ears, shrill and nasal; the throaty alto with which she had been addressing him all week long in their brief skirmishes had vanished.

"He won't admit it though," she was saying. 'He's the funniest man about things like that. He couldn't wait to have our friends down for a visit. He's *so* proud of this place," she chirped. "Have you noticed how *Western* he's been lately?"

Inwardly, he groaned. That explained the paint job and the other changes. Appearances. He was disgusted —he and Bond and Carlos had spent three or four days of valuable time painting a backdrop for some little drama Houston had in mind for the visitors. Vanity. No doubt he'd buy some new boots with riding heels and a tooled belt with a pearl buckle and a Western shirt. And hat. Spurs? God!

Jane went on. "It should be fun, but I'm worried sick

_193_

about what to feed them, because I want to do something different—" she paused and Méndez suddenly understood what she was driving toward. Did Juanita? "Something appropriate," she continued. "Could you give me your recipes for enchiladas and that chicken stuff?" *Mole*, Méndez grimaced to himself. *Mole*, you idiot.

"*Mole?*" Juanita asked.

"That's it!"

"Sure."

"I'd appreciate it."

"Why don't I just make it all up for you? There's nothing to it. Tell me how many people, and we'll go get the stuff and I'll make it up for you."

Méndez groaned inaudibly.

"Oh, I couldn't ask you to do that," Jane gushed, signaling that Juanita had her permission to do it.

"I wouldn't mind at all. No trouble."

"Oh no."

"It's okay," Juanita insisted. "You've been so nice to me and Jimmy, it's the least I can do."

"Well, I hate for you to." But you'll let her, Méndez thought.

"I'd enjoy it," Juanita said.

"Oh *would* you? With all the guests coming I've just got *so* much to do—" Méndez tried to imagine what she needed to do but couldn't. "The house is such a mess," she added lamely.

"Could I help?"

Before Jane could manipulate still more work from Juanita, Méndez clomped his boots on the living-room floor and coughed.

"Hi!" Jane greeted him brightly as he appeared in the doorway. Her eyes emitted the glint of intrigue, sending a mute appeal for him to acknowledge the possibility.

He nodded, smiling coolly. "How's tricks?"

"Fine," she answered with some bewilderment. "I was just telling Juanita—" she nodded to Juanita as if to identify her for him—"that we're having guests this week. From Chicago." She faltered, unsure of whether to continue. "Friends," she added, almost stammering. She was seated at the kitchen table with her back to him and had half-twisted awkwardly to see him, her eyes blinking uneasily.

For a moment, he reveled in her discomfort, then felt a twinge of conscience.

"So I hear. Guess we got the house painted just in time."

"Yes." They fell silent a moment, then she rose from the table. "I better go and tend to my dinner," she said to Juanita, "and let you get yours."

"If you see Jimmy, tell him to come in, will you?"

"Sure." Jane rose from the table and as she passed Méndez she flashed her eyes into his gaze to seek recognition then bowed her head, blinking, and he noticed a spot of mottled pink on the side of her throat, like a blush. She smelled of soap and half-washed perfume. When he heard the front door fall to, he took her chair at the table, seething with indignation: over the past week it seemed that each time he had returned home Jane was here talking to Juanita. They had been shopping together frequently during the past few days, and Jane had demonstrated an auntly interest in Jimmy by buying him a few toys, gifts he and Juanita had argued about.

"You know," he said slowly, talking to her back while

she wrung out a dishcloth at the sink. "If I didn't come around now and then, she'd run all over you."

Juanita slapped the cloth onto the table and began mopping with large impatient motions like a surly waitress having to endure a lewd proposition.

"Lay off it, Raphael. Really—you're impossibly rude to her. She doesn't deserve it."

"That why you're going to cook for the nice white lady?"

She froze, leaning against the wadded cloth on the table. "Please, let's don't argue about my doing that for her. It won't hurt you. It was my choice, and I do feel I owe it to her."

"So does she."

Juanita tightened her lips, then strode to the sink.

"It's nice having somebody to talk to during the day," she said tightly. "I haven't had a girlfriend since we were at school."

"What do you talk about?" He tried to modulate the resentment from his voice to render the question harmless.

"Oh nothing much, really. Just silly stuff. Like I said before, she's lonely." She stopped to pass him a bitter look brimming with suspicion. "I can't see why *you* should mind."

He started to ignore the implication that he had designs on her, the latest in a serious of subterranean accusations which began the night of the dinner and had increased rapidly over the past two days. He decided to answer the hidden charge.

"If you're worried then discourage her from coming over. I do."

"Yes, oh sure! You stand around in the doorway posing like a conquistador. You think that doesn't excite her?"

"I don't intend for it to." He fell silent. "Anyway," he started up, as though their mutual disgression had been irrelevant, "Why should she be any more lonely than anyone else in the world?"

"I don't know, but she is. Maybe she and what's-his-name don't rub up against each other enough."

"So why come to you?"

"I don't really know. I've been trying to put my finger on what she thinks of me. I have something. She . . ." Juanita paused, furrowing her brow. "I don't know. She shifts pieces of me around like she was looking for something behind or underneath them. I don't know how to describe it exactly. She asked me how I learned to walk the way I walk. I thought she was kidding, so I just laughed, but she went on and on about it, about how natural my walk was and so I told her I just put one foot in front of the other."

"You didn't tell her you had a natural sense of rhythm?"

"You think she thinks that?"

He shrugged.

"I don't know," Juanita answered her own question. "She wants to learn something. Recipes, ethnic stuff— words, phrases, customs. I get tired of all that." She fell silent for a moment. "She sure has nice clothes. When we drove to Midland she bought a pair of boots for eighty-five dollars."

Méndez remained silent at the couch.

"She took Jimmy and me to lunch . . ."

"Oh Christ! Why'd you let her do that? Don't you have any pride?"

"I'm as good as she is," Juanita hissed. "And *that's* why she can buy my lunch."

"Can you buy her one?" He raised his voice. "Do you have as much money as she does?"

"Oh God! The woman is lonely, she wants a friend, she likes me, I like her—why does our relationship have to be political?" Juanita was almost shouting—it was uncharacteristic of her to defend herself so vehemently; Méndez sensed some change in her beneath the surface, as though she had arrived at some conclusion privately and had not told him yet.

"Your relationship is political whether you want it to be or not," he spat fiercely.

"Oh you don't understand anything about it. Why don't you leave us alone? Just let me be friends with her. You and I don't go anywhere or do anything and we don't have a TV and you spend your spare time scribbling in those goddamn notebooks—" she was shouting and when he looked into her flushed face he saw they had stepped off into a swamp of heretofore uncharted troubles. "So I don't see how a friend would hurt me. This may come as a shock to you, but she actually respects and admires me. I'm not used to people treating me that way—" she eyed him narrowly from across the room. "I'm not used to being treated as an equal."

"Quit feeling sorry for yourself."

"I'm not; I'm only saying she's nice to me."

"And that I'm not. But forget it. Go on."

"Like I said, she admires me."

"What does she admire about you?" he asked as though the answer, whatever it was, would be used as evidence against her.

"You think it's weird that someone would? I can tell you're going to make something insidious and complicated out of it, that you're not going to let her just admire me and me just like her back, you're going to turn it into an international incident."

"Look," he said wearily. "I just asked you what she

admired about you." He tried to make the question entirely innocent.

She looked at him uncertainly, faltering, then fell into his trap. "I told you before she likes the way I walk, she thinks I'm a good mother and a good wife—" she glanced meaningfully at him and he wondered what she had told the other woman—"and she likes . . . oh, maybe she summed it all up when she said she admired my personal grace."

"Is *that* what she said?"

"Those were her very words," Juanita said testily, daring him to make something out of them.He could, he saw, and he was about to, but he had to be careful, having pretended only a moment before that his question had been asked without an ulterior motive. He was happy to see that Jane's words had completely confirmed his suspicions.

"Personal grace, huh?" he drawled slowly. "What do you suppose she meant by that?"

"I'm sure that whatever I'd suppose would turn out to be wrong."

"I guess there are many things in this world to be admired for," he teased. "Intelligence, beauty, energy, sensitivity, humor, integrity, and personal grace."

"Oh go to hell," Juanita said morosely.

"Juanita," he chided, turning earnest. "Can't you see you're just a brown-skinned Earth Mother to her? She's completely out of touch with anything essential and doesn't even know it, but senses that she can get what she needs through you if only because you're married to *me.*"

The instant he uttered the idea, he knew he had gone too far—tears welled in her eyes and her cheeks quivered as she struggled to contain her anger.

"Oh you, you and your arrogant *machismo,*" she

said, shaking her head sadly from side to side. "You bastard. You mean you think the only thing she sees in me is that I sleep with you? Oh god*damn* you. I *knew* you wouldn't let me just have a simple friendship without making something weird out of it. You won't even let me be *me* without first being *you.*"

Clenching his teeth, he barged ahead. "Look, every time you talk about her, you always mention her money, her country club, her clothes, the shows she sees, the concerts she attends. You're living vicariously through her, you get status and respectability through her and you give her a chance to be real."

"You're going to do that once too often," Juanita snapped. "You think you're always running after truth and exposing it, but you only do it to other people. You don't even make any sense. You see something wrong with our admiring each other. Would you think it was healthier if we hated each other or were afraid of each other?"

"But it's mutual envy."

"You don't know that," she said fiercely. "And you know it. Envy is just admiration looked at by somebody like you."

"All right," he conceded.

"And what's wrong with wanting all those things?" she put in quickly on the tail of his concession, her voice rising. Ah hah! he thought. So *this* was what she'd been hiding.

"Oh, what's the use of wanting anything," she lemented when he didn't answer. "We'll never have anything anyway." She was silent a moment, deflated. "Raphael, I don't want much and I haven't asked for much in five years, have I? Have I been demanding?"

"No," he replied honestly. "Not until now."

"Am I demanding?"

"No, but you're about to."

"Let's don't argue any more. I want to talk to you about the way I feel about my life." She paused a moment. "My destiny, our destiny—" she halted, fumbling for something, and he remained quiet, thinking that it was odd of her to use such a heavy word. "It reminds me of a fat man trying to walk in quicksand. We're bogging down. Things aren't turning out right. I don't know for sure what I expected, but my mother and father worked hard to help me start school and I should have finished for them. I owe them something, and maybe by not becoming more than I am I've blocked something."

"How could you be more than you are?" he put in.

"I mean sometimes I wonder where I'd be right now if I hadn't gotten pregnant," she said bluntly. "Maybe I'd be teaching or something. They wanted me to break out of that cycle because nobody else in the history of our family had ever finished high school, you know that. I was *progress* to them. It makes me feel guilty that maybe I chose to stop the movement of that progress."

"That's silly. You have to be free to deny other people their preconceived notions about what your life should be, or else there's just no free will."

"Please don't argue with me about how I feel," she pleaded. She wanted him to let his guard down long enough to listen and absorb something of importance to her. Ashamed, he grew receptive.

"*Lo siento, querida.* Go ahead."

"Jane only magnifies all those strains on me. You came in dirty from work the other day and I remembered that my father was proud of his elevator operator's job because he wore clean uniforms and never got dirty. Don't object—I know all about how virtuous manual labor is. I'm trying to tell you how I feel, how I felt. Then, when I saw you, at that moment you and I and Jimmy were all better than what was happening to us, we deserved more and could get more out of life than what we had gotten to that moment. I know your mind—" she broke off, smiling weakly. "You want to know more *what*, don't you? More people, more places, more things, more ideas, more books, more paintings, more food, more music, more movies, more friends, more money, more conversation, more everything people amuse themselves with and grow because of. I want Jimmy to experience a wider range of things, but I won't hide behind what I want for him—I want it mainly for me." She sighed and let her forehead drop against the side of the windowframe. "When Jane came she brought it all out because it looked like that was her life."

She grew quiet. "Do you realize," she began a moment later, her eyelids closed, "that if she wanted to she could get on an airplane and go anywhere she wanted?"

"What would she do when she got there?" he blurted out despite his vow to remain receptive.

"Anything she wanted."

"Is that what it means to be more than you are now?"

She sighed, tired of struggling. "Of course not. That's the negative side. She's also free to become whatever she wishes to be or to find something useful and creative, to be *of service*."

"It's hard to be of service when you're getting on and off airplanes all the time."

"Oh," she whimpered, near tears. "Won't you ever

give up? Just let me *talk*, will you? It's not as though I'll ever get to *be* what I want to *be* so you don't need to argue me out of it."

"I'm sorry. I can't help myself."

"And neither can *I*—I know all the right objections and everything. I know there's no end to this 'more' business, that if you can't find satisfaction in one thing, a hundred more of them won't make any difference. . . . I'm not dumb, you know. But I can realize these things without having my realization affect my feelings. I can look at Jane and tell that she's not happy, that she wants what I have—a child and a simpler life. Jane's not happy being Jane, Juanita's not happy being Juanita."

The front door slammed; Jimmy came into the kitchen.

*"Mama, yo quiero ír a Costilla para—"* he began.

"Speak English!" Juanita snapped at him.

*"No!"* Méndez thundered, slapping the table with the flat of his hand. *"Let him speak Spanish!"* He glared at her. The outburst so startled them both that she and the boy crystallized in mute, expectant trembling as if they half-expected his shout to be followed by some equally violent act, but then Juanita regained her control. Her nostrils began to flare and her eyes narrowed and for that one small moment her hate for him vibrated outward from her tensed form like waves of heat radiating from the opened door of a furnace. It was an ancient argument, one of those unresolved questions of their relationship which arose from time to time to plague their peace.

"This again?" she said quietly, fiercely. "What? You want him to speak Spanish so he can wind up like some poor dumb peon chopping cotton? Or do—"

*"Es la lengua de la gente,"* he pronounced with

righteous malice. *"And those who do not know it are whores. Aguilar is right, he—"*

"Oh, Aguilar!" she shouted. "Is that letter what's eating you?" She flung her dishrag into the sink where it struck with a wet splat. "Some stupid dreamer with a head stuffed full of nonsense writes you a letter and now all of a sudden we're all whores because we're bilingual. You make me sick!"

At that moment, watching her posture at the sink with gnarled lips and stringy hair like some caricature of a harridan, he would have given his soul to the Devil to have been able to drive his fist into her face with force enough to crush her nose into a mangled lump of broken bones and ruptured tissue. He glared at her in a helpless fury; the boy turned and disappeared into the living room where he turned the radio on high and the rollicking laughter of a studio audience reverberated against the walls of the kitchen.

Juanita collapsed into a kitchen chair, sobbing, her elbows on the table, the heels of her hands pressed into the notches of her eye-sockets, but he wasn't having any of it—he rose from the table, yanked open the refrigerator door to extract a beer, then went out the front door in a huff. After he had sat perched on the top rail of the corral fence for a few minutes and had finished the beer, he had cooled down enough to lift his anger from her and search for some outlet for it, preferably into the channel from which it came—the Houstons. A week ago, he thought grimly, we were happy, safe and secure here. What was happening to them? Their argument had been utterly abrurd; neither one of them believed in Jimmy's learning any one language at the expense of another, yet they had discovered themselves polarized into dogmatic positions neither would have defended in a more sane moment. She had shortchanged Aguilar, though; his dream of a rediscovery of the roots of their heritage and of the restitution of the plunder and exploitation of that heritage which the Anglos had perpetrated for the past century was no more or less ethereal than her own vague yearnings for status, respect, and the illusory security of materialism—and at least Aguilar's plan had the merit of having its foundation be the *dignidad de la gente* rather than the further corruption of the already greedy. But even in his calmer state he could still hate her enough to see in her some base example of the primary danger of assimilation—in the mixture of cultures too often there was a mutual reinforcement of weakness rather than an exchange of strengths. Juanita was Exhibit A.

The following morning the Houstons left early to bring their plane-bound guests back to the ranch from Midland and returned about noon. Pulled up in the half-moon drive before the main house were Houston's Thunderbird and a dark, late-model Pontiac, from whose trunk two men dressed like golfers were removing luggage. Because he didn't want to meet them in any capacity, be it foreman or Tío Taco the house nigger, as soon as he and Bond had carried some sacks of mineral supplement out of the jeep and into the barn, he struck out for the far pastures as if in a hurry to attend to a chore, but spent most of the afternoon sitting in the shadow of the windmill on the far side of the mesa, listlessly pitching clods into the sandy water of the stock tank.

In the evening, he sat on his stoop, sodden in the twilight. Through the opening in the swaying curtains he could spy the Houstons' guests moving about in their living room, conversing, glasses in hands. Houston moved into view, his shoulders shaking with laughter, and Méndez felt crushed by the luck of their skins, by the unconcern of history. Jane appeared wearing a dark blue cocktail dress with a low neckline. Her hair had been built on top of itself in braided spirals and from her ears dangled long earrings of some lightweight metal. She played the gay hostess, seating herself in a straightback dining chair, perched on its edge, leaning forward, resting her forearm across the top of her crossed thigh, revealing her cleavage to the man who stood beside her. With her right leg crossed over her left, the hem of her dress rode far up her right thigh, and from where he sat Méndez could see the top of her stockings, the sheen of her leg glossy in the candlelight.

He caught his breath. Damnation! Juanita was right —he wanted the woman he saw through the window, yet it was no simple yearning to satisfy a lust. He wanted not so much to make love to her but to . . . violate her, and she had invited the response, provoked it rather, by treating him as though he were a lean black prizefighter and she a horny white empress. And what might have been a simple matter of desire became an ideological conflict—he wouldn't be satisfied with their coupling unless he could see it as the clash of science and poetry, the clank of gears versus the whir of bird wings: in short, for him to take Jane Houston would be a victory for oppressed peoples everywhere.

And he hated her at that moment with the intensity of a long-smouldering resentment; he hated Houston; he hated their guests, what they stood for, their freedom, their superficiality, their riches.

So the co-op, the commune, was born, the bastard product of the odd *menage à trois* of his beliefs, his hatreds, and the pressures put on him by others. While he watched them from his front stoop, he began to plan them out of existence. He went into the cottage and returned with a pencil and a spiral notebook, then sat listening with a mad and heady inspiration to the laughter and the music coming from the main house. Aguilar had spoken of the *chicanazgo*, of a nation with physical boundaries inhabited solely by *chicanos*. He was speaking as a harbinger—it was an idea far before its time, but in Denver talk was beginning to catch on about it. In his coldest eye the letter seemed perhaps too raving, too impassioned, but he could well anticipate Aguilar's refutation of that criticism. And it had implied that an accounting was necessary—in effect, he had asked for Méndez's reply to contain some credentials. Since they had not seen each other since college, Aguilar wanted to know *what he was doing.*

What was he doing? He smiled gleefully. Laying plans for the future, for *la raza.* For every blue line Houston had drawn in his plans to convert the ranch into a recreational facility for *los ricos*, Méndez drew another to convert it into an indigenous *kibbutz* for all his *chicano* brothers. They would have a communal dining hall. He and Manuelo and the Snake would all be busy, early on a bright morning, sawing, hammering, nailing, measuring, cutting. The women would bring coffee and tortillas and bean tacos. After the dining hall was built they would hold a fiesta in the flagstone patio with the fountain in the center. In the mornings before work, they would sit in the hall as the sun is just rising and exploding into the hall and slanting across the wooden tables with an orange light which vibrates in the steam pulsing from the coffee cups as they sit and plan the day's work, letting their belts out from breakfast, laughing.

For the next week it became his private obsession and when he was with Houston he was struck by the odd sensation that both their brains were whirring like gyroscopes with plans; Houston was hiring architects and engineers and lawyers to act his out, and Méndez had to be satisfied with filling three spiral notebooks with voluminous details regarding the structure of government, the construction of the dwellings (down to the selection of nails), the delegation of roles, managing the autonomous economy, placement of the truck garden, care of communal property, relationships with Anglo ranchers nearby, and so forth, inexhaustibly scribbled out more often than not while he sat on the toilet like some *chicano* version of Martin Luther setting forth the substance of his visionary schemes, and he was consoled again and again by the feeling that with every mark he made on paper Houston's hold on the property—his right to it—inched away like some quicksand victim disappearing and he was pleased to think that the earth, or at least this very small part of it, might be remade to support a better, more deserving, race of men.

# Four

Let the bastard wait. Something portentous in the message to report—command appearance—but Méndez refused to hurry. First he went into the yard, carefully shutting the shed door behind him, then began to unload the bags of mixed grain from the jeep and carted them into the horse stalls in the barn, then emptied one of the sacks into the feed barrel. After he finished, he dumped a bucketful into a trough for the one stud standing alone in the corral, then he washed his hands from a faucet inside the barn and leaned against the doorframe, smoking, letting the sun warm the front of his body. He stood there only a moment before he flipped the half-smoked butt into a puddle in the corral and strode toward the main house.

Jane let him into the kitchen.

"Somebody wanted to see me?"

"Bob's still in the shower. Go on into the den if you want."

Méndez let his mask slip a notch—the woman he had planned out of existence three days previous now looked a little less like a suburbanite and more like a bedraggled ranchwife—her reddish-blonde hair fell to just below her earlobes with all the artificial curl combed out, and she wore no makeup. Scuffed loafers. Pale-kneed blue jeans had replaced the ski pants she had arrived in; over her blouse she wore a man's sand-colored sweater on the right sleeve of which he could see a moth-hole the size of a dime.

"Party go all right?"

"Oh yes, fine." She looked away as she raised a coffee mug from the table to her lips; her hand trembled. She looked exhausted. "It's taken me three days to clean up the mess, though."

"Well if you could use some help I'm sure Juanita—" he said despite himself.

"Oh no!" she laughed. "It's *my* bed." Her eyes flicked out over the top of the mug and sent a signal, ambiguously playful yet bitter and ironic. "*I'll* lie in it."

He nodded, dumbly; they fell silent a moment.

"Coffee?"

He hesitated but when she made no move to secure another cup from the cabinet, he turned to go.

"No thanks—guess I better check in."

She shrugged with what he took to be an excess of indifference and moved back to the sink.

"He should be out soon," she said over her shoulder.

Off balance from his encounter with Jane, Méndez welcomed the opportunity to spend a few moments alone in the room. The den was a large rectangle whose eastern exposure consisted entirely of glass panes the size of chess boards; through the windows he could see down the length of the broad but shallow valley Houston planned to put under water. To the north and south rose undulant, mesquite-covered mounds, and at the base of the southern hills a knot of cattle gathered around a stock tank beneath a churning windmill.

Glancing about the room he was startled by the changes Houston had made in the past four to five days: the battered rolltop desk which had sat flush against the wall opposite the door was missing, as well as the creaky wooden swivel chair before it, and in their place he had put a metal office desk with a metal swivel chair upholstered in orange vinyl.

Lemuel's metal card table with its rusting corners was likewise gone. The man had a mania for repairing his own appliances and at any given time the table would contain the hulks and parts of, say, a toaster, a percolater, an alarm clock—items which would sit in disrepair for up to six months because he wrote directly to the factory for parts. After a time, Méndez understood that this habit was determined by neither penury nor parsimony—he simply considered a broken appliance to be in a temporary state of poor health, and he would not have thrown it away just because one part failed to function any more than he would have killed a cow merely because it had mastitis.

Absent from the wall was Lemuel's "hat rack," a mouldy buck's head with eight-point antlers; since it had hung in the same spot for twenty years, Méndez guessed that it had left an indelible scar on the wall, for someone—Jane, he presumed—had hung a Keene reproduction of a large-eyed nymph in its place.

Next to his desk Lemuel had nailed unpainted pine planks together to house his "library": a ten-year series of Reader's Digest condensed books, an old edition of the *Encyclopedia Britannica* with "St-To" missing, four Bibles, Law's *Farmer's Veterinary Advisor,* a row of thin-spined USDA monographs, and a gross of paperbacks bought at the drugstore whose contents ranged from murder mystery to popularized treatises on science, psychology, or finance. The entire collection had long outgrown the shelves so that in the past few years each time Méndez saw the bookcase it gave him the impression of something gorged, like a snake with a rabbit half-swallowed. And always dotted around the room were blocks of books to serve more pragmatic needs than reading pleasure—a door stop, a paper weight, a base to raise to desk lamp.

But now Méndez saw the books were packed in large cardboard cartons along the wall. The shelves had vanished.

Moving about the room, Méndez noticed the carpet now covering the oak flooring; annoyed, he belatedly checked the soles of his boots and traced his path back to the doorway, noting a few streaks of mud where he had walked. When Lemuel was here, he thought, the room always had the air of a kind of decompression chamber from the outside world to the inside of the house; it was alive with clutter—a pair of muddy boots dropped near a cane-bottom chair, a jacket and hat hanging on the antlers, newspapers and magazines in disarray on the desk, a pipe wrench lying on the floor, half the rifles unracked and leaning against the wall (he noted now that they were all racked and locked), the floor invariably dotted with small, irregular discs of mud from someone's boots. The room might have been an extension of the tool shed or the barn.

It had been a man's room; it had borne all the traces

of an elderly bachelor ranchman. At one time it contained some evidence of Frances's presence at the ranch, but after she left the room had carried only the smell of stale tobacco, gun oil, and aging newspapers, and occasionally the mildest whiff of after-shave just before he went on his quarterly trips to Dallas or Fort Worth, his monkish existence grown too cold to satisfy him. Méndez always wondered who she was, if there was a single "she." Somehow he could never picture Lemuel picking indiscriminately from the whores who frequented Fort Worth's beer-by-the-drink bars on the north side; on the contrary, he assumed that the man wasn't looking only for an orifice: most likely he needed the entire woman. No doubt he found living alone in the ranch house a lonely existence; at the end of a quarter when he spruced himself in pinstripe cowboy dress pants, boots the color of strong coffee, white dress shirt, and string bow tie, got in the pickup (which he'd have washed at the service station in town), and headed out for no one knew exactly where, he was heading toward a particular face and a particular body. Méndez couldn't imagine it any other way. Anything other than that would have made the old man less than he was. Maybe her name was Millie, and she was a widow or a divorcee some ten years younger than he, a "working girl," perhaps a realtor or the proprietress of a small dress shop. In short, a woman like himself in need of companionship thrice a year but no more—enough to keep the bones from turning brittle but not enough to change a life. Perhaps he had even asked her to marry him, to move to the ranch with him. And perhaps because she hadn't, the room, like the man, never underwent any fundamental change: it remained the expression of his frontier temperament.

It occurred to him suddenly that maybe there was unfinished business left—if there had been a woman, had she heard of his death? If he had one and she was still ignorant of it, a cruel irony was at play—the one real mourner of the old man's death, the one person who might mark his passing with the lament of an aged spouse and thereby prove his presence on earth might still be waiting his quarterly arrival.

But who was she? Who knew what the man did or had? It had been slightly less than two weeks since his death and already the sharp contours of his reality were blurred by memory. Unreal. Méndez felt as though he never really had a certain notion of the man's identity even when he was alive. The brief passing of time since the man's death had brought some sorry truth: he had not grieved, really, and had felt guilty that he hadn't grieved and had expected the grief to catch up to him, suddenly perhaps, or unawares, like stage fright delayed until one had already begun the speech. But as of yet it had not. He lamented the man's passing as an abstraction, as a part of the world gone, a piece broken off from the whole, but he felt little personal loss. And he also felt that the elder Houston deserved, like any man, to have his passing mourned, and so he had come to depend on the man's son to perform that duty and was struck to discover that the younger Houston didn't display any signs of loss, either. Méndez was careful in making reference to the elder Houston as they discussed the ranch's history, its habits, the rituals the man had performed as motions for keeping order on the ranch; he tried to allude to the man either by his first name or by the pronoun "he," taking care to avoid referring to him as the younger Houston's "father." Although no "God-rest-his-soul" was necessary, for a few days after the funeral Méndez abstained from any direct mention of the elder Houston in front of the younger but when it was absolutely unavoidable he tried to make the reference casual, as though to obscure the fact of his death. If the younger man was caused any pain by these references, he failed to show it in any way Méndez could see.

So there was a void of sorts. The man died, mourned neither by wife nor child nor friend. His relatives? They mourned the loss of kin, but how could any of them know who he was? They never came to visit, he never went to them. He shuddered. What difference had the old man's life made that no one noted his passing? Méndez owed him much, he knew. So why didn't he feel any debt? Perhaps because the man's attitude at bottom was that Méndez had been like some stray dog, to be fed and cared for only as it proved useful.

He was in debt to the man for his education, however interrupted it had been. But to think back on that was to be tangled up, lost somewhere, as though he had missed a turn and could not distinguish detour from thoroughfare, which he thought he could trace to his refusal to accept the Veteran's Forum and Samaritan's scholarship for the third year. *I can no longer in good conscience accept,* oh, he had written a very serious letter, a young gentleman's formal rage guiding the lines through an explanation that was more a denunciation of their ultimatum than a description of his feelings. Had he led a panty raid they might have simply clucked collective tongues, hiding smiles behind their hands, but they would allow no organizing of farm workers or even any open advocation of it: renounce or remit. And his response, he considered ruefully, was almost Pavlovian: you may take your scholarship and

shove it. Given the patterns of his high-school behavior
—the black leather jacket, ducktail, his *pachuco's*
cross, his minor brushes with the law—how Lemuel
had managed to get him the scholarship in the first
place was something of a mystery, though he could see
a certain logic to the selection. The Veteran's Forum
was a national organization of *chicano* veterans of
World War II—Gómez was a member—and it had
been their intention to give some deserving young
Mexican-American a full scholarship, but the Samaritans, a local service club of Anglo businessmen and
ranchers, had kicked in much of the money—and there
lay the rub. Méndez had probably been on probation
from the start and hadn't known it.

He wanted to reread Lemuel's letter, which he had
stored away in his notes but hadn't looked at in three
years; he settled for an imaginative reconstruction of it.
He had opened it while seated at a carrel in the library,
thinking matter-of-factly *a letter from old Lemuel,* but
a certain nervous, fastidious care which he found himself exercising in tearing the envelope so to leave the
letter intact caught him up: *it was, by God, a letter from
Lemuel*—the first he had ever received. Oddly enough,
he considered now, he hadn't even realized the nature
of its content until he had read it for the third time—
the first two readings emitted nothing but billowing
images of the old man's lean frame arced over the
battered desk whose rolltop was jammed forever open,
wizened shoulders jerking with the writing motions of
his hand, clutter of desktop: leaky fountain pens (he
hated ballpoints), empty Garret & Garret snuff cans, a
penknife, a bill spike skewering invoices and notes to
himself in an indistinct hand which generally concerned anything from a reminder to have the truck

serviced to the vagarious, philosophical musings of an unacademic mind: did birds have wings because they flew, or did they fly because they had wings?—Méndez remembered having seen the question scribbled on the inside of a matchbook cover impaled on the spike. And for the first time he had known what it felt to be homesick, or the closest approximation of that feeling it was possible for him in his circumstances to have felt. As the images dissolved he had grown aware of the quality of the old man's prose, and he lingered some moments over the labyrinthine rhythms, the commas and metaphors, before it finally occurred to him what the letter stated. Then, between the passing of initial shock and the onslaught of indignation, he had focused closer on the letter, struggling to discern what the old man *felt.* No harangues or tirades at his "behavior," not even the mildest "recommendation"—he was writing as the disinterested arbiter of a dispute, almost as though he had been asked to serve as a reciprocal spokesman. This persona of disengaged secretary severely disappointed Méndez, although he did not know what he had expected. Rereading still again, worrying the words until their individual and combined meanings split off, like capillary veins, into infinite branches of interpretation, he had thought he sensed jutting occasionally from beneath the Olympian detachment of the letter a kind of bemusement at the folly of human affairs directed more toward the pompous arrogance of the Samaritans' ultimatum than at Méndez's behavior. *Thought* he sensed, that is—the old man's feeling were always an enigma to him. He had folded the letter and slipped it into his breast pocket and sat motionless for a while, his eyes— charged with the quickened pulse of something important having just occurred—following the labial contortions of two sorority girls whispering some idiocy between themselves at a table near his carrel. Well, no question of how to respond to the Samaritans; he had been at a point in his life when each morning had brought a moment of meditation dedicated to studying ways he might bring his conduct more in line with his convictions, for only consistency could root out hypocrisy: there were food products on supermarket shelves to be shunned, newspapers to be not read, cafes to be not patronized, razor blades—Schick—to be not bought, and female companions to be discouraged from purchasing certain brands of underwear (Playtex bras and girdles—made in South Africa by black slave labor). It required a superhuman effort to stay abreast —one never knew how one contributed to injustice by using the myriad *things* of the world; a pencil grasped and worn to the nub, a match struck, a banana eaten —each little quirk and turn of human events revealed the pale underbelly of human exploitation. He tore a sheet from a legal tablet and began a letter to the Samaritans, but he burned his indignation out in the space of five rough drafts; from its ashes rose the probing, multicolored flame of several different, contradictory emotions. To begin with, they had one-upped him: he should have refused the scholarship long before they announced their ultimatum. So why hadn't he? He had been *playing* at aligning convictions with acts; the razor blades and grapes had been a piece of deception designed to balance out the grossest manifestation of hypocrisy. Why else try to hide it from his friends, and especially from Aguilar, with whom he had founded *La Voz? (I have a scholarship,* once or twice, never citing source.) Yet why feel *hurt* on being given the opportunity to part the final tie with inconsistent, hypocritical behavior? Despite their one-upmanship, hadn't they just handed him his final justification? The realization that he might be able to wear the squabble like a badge gave him the momentary comfort of the initiate who bears proud first wounds.

Yet why *hurt?* When the answer came, he groaned aloud, staring unconsciously at the girls, who looked up, offended. What a dupe, a goddamn, naive dupe he had been—no way of avoiding it now, one part of his development had been arrested by his faith in the system, his assumption that ultimately concept and reality were wed, and his hidden wish had been that the Samaritans as adult *Americans* could encompass diversity of opinion and in doing so might justify his highest notions concerning the democratic dialectic; hence he had been involved not in refuting the system but in solidifying it.

He included none of this in the letter to the Samaritans, which he finished on the sixth draft, and by the time he had hammered out the resounding rebuke on his roommate's typewriter his feelings had leveled out to a bitter pride over having learned an important lesson.

As the days passed and he ruminated on the hardening lump of his *destino* (the Spanish equivalent kept rising, a sweetish aftertaste), he could see this one act had unforeseen repercussions. For one, it meant he had to leave school: without the scholarship he couldn't attend until he had saved enough money to return. Although he had always thought he could act without regard to his own self-interest, he had not dreamed his convictions might demand he give up *this;* that is, he had never realized that he had so much interest in himself to sacrifice. That is, not the Education, but the education; in the sea of the intellect whose shore he had only recently discovered, he had plunged head first, wallowed and leapt in the waves, then struck out in a dory for the other side. The Voyage of the Burning Brain: Kierkegaard sighted at 9:30 A.M., Plato's *Republic* by eleven (part of the same archipelago?—Time out for synthesis, comparison, an anthropological excursion into the habits of the islanders). Then off for Hegel, Jonathan Swift, and the Deeper Implications of the Hard Rock Phenomena; by lunch he pulls aside Heisenberg's Uncertainty Principle, an island on which a towering mountain casts a shadow on the Literary Outpost of the Twentieth Century. By sundown exhaustion, supper over a twilight campfire, a hot dog shared with Martin Buber. The wireless brings a message: turn back stop cease coffee convs. w/others of like mind stop midnight sessions w/fellow poetesses stop records listened to w/ears like nerve ends stop girls in summer dresses reading Marx stop wine-and-weed discoveries of friendships in the dim hallways of unknown apartments stop exhorting minorities to shake off chains in outlaw newsletters stop smell of books in library stacks stop work on definitive term paper on WPA stop joy stop growth stop self or no more MONEY.

*Dear Lemuel* (would he object to that address?— well, no matter), *I hardly know what to say.* (No, know exactly what to say but not whether to say it. Dear Lemuel, I ache, someone cut into my chest and replaced my heart with a ten-pound stone: smooth, gray, the size of a classroom globe, it strains the bottom of its tissue-sack when I try to stand upright.) *It strikes me as odd that my sponsors should have such little faith in freedom that they should feel endangered by the very working of it, which is only to say that they have an upside-down notion of freedom—that t exists despite the exercising of it, rather than because it is exercised. I guess they were most disturbed by the article I wrote in an off-campus newspaper about the relationship between the power structure and Latin minorities in the U.S.* (Will you be able to read between the lines of this formal gobbledegook? he had wondered. I see you holding that wine goblet to the light, filled incongruously with Jack Daniels: you were trying to prepare me for college—do you remember giving me that beat-up copy of *Tom Jones* and telling me to come back after I had read it? We sat here, in your den, evening light hazing through the windows, sipping the whiskey you docked from my pay, and you asked me what I thought of this here Field-dang in that parody dirt-farmer voice. What did I think that there Field-dang was trying to say? I deliberately gave an incorrect reading, both because my interpretation gave me an image of myself as I was then and because I wanted to hear you correct me. Break out your Freud, Lemuel, I said, "I think he says that you can do anything you damn well please as long as you can get by with it," just to hear you correct me. We bantered awhile and you gave me *your* incorrect reading: what is more important than our opinions is how we feel about one another. In that exchange lay a microcosm of the history of epistemology, replete with myriad ironies of personalities, of things seen and unseen; thus it was a preparation, though not the one you intended.) As the letter grew longer, the tack of its appeal swung until it ran down the wind of a plea: would Lemuel stand behind him on principle even if he didn't subscribe to the content of the article? He never got around to mailing it; it sat on his desk, the unstamped envelope collecting rings from coffee cups, shavings from a pencil sharpener. If the old man had wanted to commit himself, he would have.

But the question contained in the unmailed letter received an answer of sorts: Méndez could, Lemuel told him over the phone after being informed of the letter to the Samaritans, return to the ranch as an employee whenever he wished. Exhange the nexus of Darwin-Freud-Marx for the mastitised teat, wine-and-poetry for hoof-and-mouth, and spend his days segregating cattle rather than integrating mankind, diverting well water but not history. (And so he did, but not until a year later.)

Lemuel had died without ever discussing the subject —no deathbed speeches—and Méndez's grief was subjunctive, nebulous, the projection of what might have been, although he was grateful he had been the recipient of the old man's charity.

Nothing remained of the man who had inhabited this room, and little remained of the leather-jacketed *pachuco* who began college as a result of what that man did except some lingering spirit of bitter rebelliousness long since ebbed away into a kind of permanent backwater of grumbling dispiritedness. Automatically he raised his hand to his face to look at his *pachuco*'s cross. It had signified his loyalty, his allegiance, his deliberate sacrifice of his own freedom to create an identity. It had meant that then, when he and Flea and the Snake were drunk in the Snake's Merc and had literally carved the crosses into their hands with a sewing needle dipped in India ink. Proudly he had given up the right to be himself in order to be not just the personification of an idea, but the ideafication of a person.

It made him uneasy for others to call attention to it.

Jane had asked what it meant; he had explained it to her in vague terms, making their group sound as benign as a high school fraternity, and Houston had piped up, using the word: "Oh come on, Jane. You know what a *pachuco* is." Something unpleasant passed through him on hearing the word in Houston's mouth, something which he saw on her features, too, and perhaps for that reason—that he was ashamed of his shame— he had left that small blue cross on his hand.

He heard laughter off in the kitchen, then a low mumble. In a moment footsteps sounded in the hall, then Houston appeared in the doorway, wiping his hands with a rag.

"Damn plumbing," he said. "You get cleaned up around here and you turn around and something else is busted." With the toe of one highly polished Wellington, he drew the bottom drawer of the desk open, chucked the rag into it, then shoved the drawer to with his foot.

"Sit down, sit down." He motioned to the room in general, then plopped heavily into the swivel chair behind the desk in a way that left no doubt as to who was in charge. He leaned back in the chair with his hands behind his head as Méndez searched for a chair and, finding none, settled himself on the edge of Houston's desk, aware that such a placement very subtly suggested a lack of respect.

"What's on your mind?" he asked bluntly but not antagonistically while Houston appeared to be locating the vocabulary to make an announcement. Houston looked away.

"Well, I've had to come to a decision of sorts." he began slowly. Méndez waited in silence for him to continue. He had been deathly afraid this was what awaited him here—Houston's half-apologetic manner didn't assure Méndez any that the decision might be to his favor.

"How many choices do you think I have?" he asked after a moment of silent consideration. Méndez couldn't tell if the question was rhetorical or not. He remained silent, waiting. "I can sell or I can keep—it's that simple, isn't it?" Houston spun in the chair, then rose to his feet and strode to the windows, his back to Méndez. Méndez watched the empty chair bob a moment, then settle. "Selling's simple. You probably know that wouldn't be any trouble at all."

"Pixley's been after some of it for years," Méndez put in to encourage Houston to get to the point.

"Right."

They lapsed into silence. Houston gazed out the windows while Méndez absently let his left foot knock against the empty swivel chair, turning it slowly on its axis.

"Far as I think now, selling's out of the question. My father worked too hard." Méndez smiled at the claim to family loyalty as a motive for keeping the ranch. "You know yourself how many years of his sweat and blood went into this land. But I just don't know. Everywhere I turn I'm faced with paradoxes about the whole business. Let me tell you something." Méndez heard his voice ricochet off the windows and arc across the room. "Selling it would mean failure to him."

"He's dead," Méndez blurted.

"True, but he haunts me. What he thought of himself haunts me. To sell would be to give up. You don't sell and leave unless you can't make it any more."

"What do you care if you're not like him?" Méndez said, while counseling himself to keep his mouth shut.

"I don't know. I don't even know why I'm bothering to tell you this." Méndez was supposed to consider hearing it a privilege. Don't do me any favors, he thought. His hands were sweating. Get to the point, damn you.

"Well, for whatever bad reason, I'm not going to sell at the moment. For a while, anyway. So the problem is what to do with this goddman albatross now that I have it. I've been thinking about a number of things. First of all was the dude ranch idea, the lake, the golf course, the pool, and so on."

"If you don't mind my saying so, this isn't the right region for it. There's nothing here but fresh air. There's not much water and the countryside takes some getting used to."

"I've thought of that," Houston said briskly, as though annoyed. "It's possible that those defects might be turned into virtues, given the right promotion. Also," he laughed suddenly, "I could put a losing business proposition to good use for a while, anyway. My father would turn over in his grave to hear me talk about making a failure out of the place to get some good out of it."

The idea made Méndez bridle, too. He understood how the ranch might be useful as a tax loss, but he couldn't bear to see it used that way, particularly since he had more meaningful plans for it in his spiral notebooks.

"Anyway, it turns out I can't get hold of the capital at the moment to do that." Houston turned and walked back around to the desk and into Méndez's view but did not look directly at him. "So the Rolling J will be a cattle ranch for a time yet."

"That doesn't make me unhappy."

"Good." Houston eyed him, then wandered out of sight again. "That brings us down to me and you." When he paused in hesitation at the end of the sentence, Méndez could feel the words "me and you" reverberate as if in an echo chamber somewhere in his skull. They both recognized that Houston had unintentionally expressed what the real problem amounted to, and Méndez wondered whether to comment on the other man's allusion to their lingering antagonism. He wondered how much of Houston's decision—whatever it was to be—was influenced by it.

"What to do about our jobs," he added weakly as if to dispel the truth his earlier phrase had revealed. "To be honest with you, I'd like the challenge of staying here and trying to make a go of it. If my father could do it, why not me?"

Méndez bit down hard on his tongue.

"On the other hand, I'd stand the chance of terrible failure that way. But I like the idea of a change. I could wax eloquent on the romantic notions I've stored in my mind about breaking away from sitting in an office hamstrung by regulations, shuffling forms back and forth through the mail and listening to people's petty complaints and coming down here with Jane and starting over." He laughed at himself, but to Méndez his self-mockery failed to disguise his persistent belief in the truth of those illusions. The insight frightened him. "I don't know if Jane could take it. Well, I don't really know if I could, to be honest, but I'll never know until I've tried, will I?" He leaned against the wall near the corner at the edge of the windows. "Out where the wind blows free and man's on his own to do or die— good God! What a lot of bullshit comes into my head just from looking out across the pasture there, but just as I think that I wonder if maybe there's some truth to it."

"Freedom is a difficult concept," Méndez put in stupidly. He had bitterly deduced that Houston was about to "resign" him and was apologizing for it before he did. He let his bootheels bounce against the previously spotless panels on the side of the desk.

Houston yawned, then stretched. "I've seen too many John Wayne movies," he announced, then sat down on the low sill beneath the glass wall. "What I really think is that I'll probably come to be just another absentee owner. It wouldn't be possible for me to change for another six months, anyway. These things take time."

The sudden extension of his fate gave Méndez a floating sensation. "You want me to stay on as foreman, then?" he asked, despite himself. Was Houston toying with him?

"Well. . . ." Houston let out, as if exhaling. "You know Crabtree, my father's lawyer?"

Méndez nodded.

"He suggested something that I thought interesting. He wondered if maybe I shouldn't make you a special partner in this place."

"What's that?"

"You'd share profits but put up no capital—your capital would be your know-how."

"Are you asking me?"

"I hate to bring these things up when they're so tentative, but at the same time I want you to know what's going on, what could happen."

"In other words, you're not asking me."

"Damn it, Méndez, I wish I could give you something definite on this, but I just can't until I've made up my own mind."

Méndez blew his breath out between his cheeks. "All right," he said, more calmly. "But what are the advantages?"

"For me they're obvious. If I kept the place and stayed away I'd be assured of it turning the same profit, if not more, and a partnership like that would give you the incentive to stay so I wouldn't have to be worrying all the time about how things were going."

"Huh!" Méndez exclaimed involuntarily. "And for me?"

"Salary plus commission, plus a guaranteed percentage of the sale price if eventually I did sell it. I estimate that careful management and upkeep would raise the price a good fifteen to twenty percent and therefore the man responsible would deserve to keep that, as a kind of fee." He shrugged modestly, as if to ignore any protests that he was being too generous.

"What salary?" Méndez heard himself ask, amazed at how he could still calculate.

"I'd expect you to take a cut—say twenty-five percent—but I'd give you, say, thirty percent of net gain yearly off the ranch."

"Are you serious?" Méndez asked, incredulous, his voice cracking slightly. His salary had risen, as of Houston's last utterance, to at least double its present figure. "Why would you do this?"

"I *haven't* done it yet, remember," Houston said, cocking an eye at him. "But I told you why. It relieves me of a lot of worry and makes money for me. I hold the deed to a ranch I can use for my own recreation and profit and I don't have to lift a finger." He smiled, almost apologetically.

"Son of a gun," Méndez whispered, rubbing his chin.

"I want to know if you'd be interested," Houston offered after a moment.

"Well *sure*," Méndez blurted out. "But why *me?* Why not somebody else?" There must be a catch somewhere. For almost two weeks he had seen himself on the brink of unemployment with absolutely no prospects, and now he stood what appeared to be a good chance of even bettering his present position, to say nothing of how this might bring the co-op one step closer to realization. He shook his head in disbelief.

"That should be obvious to you—you're more qualified than anyone else to do it. Look, I operate on merit and profit—these are my values: if I thought you weren't competent I'd find someone else who was, and if I thought you wouldn't make money for me, I'd get someone who would. Beyond that," Houston paused a moment in hesitation, "maybe I think you deserve it."

"As a person or as a Mexican-American?" Méndez heard himself ask.

"Both."

Uh-huh, Méndez thought. It was getting catchy, but precisely how he couldn't say.

"Look," Houston said, "we're talking about something that hasn't happened yet, and won't happen if at all for another six months. I'd still like a chance to think about making it do for myself, in the old way, by myself, with my hands." He turned his hands palm upward and looked from one to the other quickly, as though surprised to find some unpleasant substance had rubbed off on them. "But until then I'd like you to stick around."

Méndez returned to the cottage in a state of stunned

amazement. "Boy, he handed me a plum," he exclaimed to Juanita as he collapsed on the couch. He allowed himself to be excited about the prospect, explaining Houston's proposal, and interjecting at frequent intervals "a plum" until he had begun to sound obsessed to himself.

"That's wonderful," Juanita cried gleefully. She hugged him. "Oh God, that's great for us. For you. For everybody. I know you've been worried."

"Yeah. Won't it—*wouldn't* it—" he corrected himself and let the remainder hang in the air unspoken. It was too much to hope for and his hope made him anxious; a half hour later, having grown suspicious and pessimistic about the possibility, he felt much more at ease.

"Why?" he wondered out loud.

"Oh, Raphael!" Juanita breathed in exasperation. "Don't *do* that."

"Maybe it matters."

"Why worry about it?"

"Because it's cruel to hope for it if it doesn't turn out. Maybe he doesn't really mean to do it at all and he's just buying time. Maybe he thinks that's what he has to offer just to get me to stay long enough for him to come back. Maybe he thinks that if I thought he was coming back in six months to take over for good then I'd sabotage the place." He sighed. "I would, too."

"Oh God! You can give up on it if you want to, you can go right ahead and defeat yourself before it defeats you, but you're cheating *us*, you know that? You're not just cheating yourself by giving up before it's time to give up, you're robbing us, *me*, because you're afraid of what it might mean to succeed." She was almost in tears. He wished he hadn't told her; he could see that

_230_

she was counting on the possibility becoming a tangibility.

"What would it mean to you?" he asked wearily, suspecting that it would mean equality with Jane Houston and all that implied.

"I don't know."

"You mean you refuse to answer."

"I mean you weren't asking because you really want to know."

"What if I were?"

"Then I'd say that it would mean the satisfaction of seeing something happen to somebody which should have happened, the satisfaction of being that somebody. Being the beneficiary of justice, that's all. For once."

"Really?"

"You're surprised, aren't you? It isn't what you expected."

"If you knew what I expected, then it wouldn't be hard to lie, now would it?"

"Sometimes I wish I were a man so I could wipe that smirk off your face with my fist."

"Sometimes I wish you weren't so shallow."

"Oh God," she moaned. "Don't you see anything? Now you've made this partnership something only *I* want so you can resist and you won't have to face yourself."

"What do you mean?" he snarled, feeling her words pierce some layer of psychic defense.

"Nothing!" She fled the room.

He spent the remainder of the day gradually easing himself back into an optimism wary enough to allow him to enjoy musing about the possibility and still protect himself from failure.

It was nightfall before he made up to her and he did so then not because he felt he owed it to her but because it required too much energy and concentration to remain at odds with her—the house was too small. As they passed each other in the door shortly before supper, eyes averted, he reached over suddenly and pinched her cheek and she tried not to smile then gave in. The heaviness lifted; she went about preparing their meal with light gestures which moved things about as though for the pleasure in their noise. It occurred to him that this cycle of anger and reconciliation had happened much more frequently lately, but before he could worry about it he had already explained it to himself in ways that almost eased his mind—pressure of change, of uncertain employment, the sudden intrusion into their lives of other people whose influence, however minor, couldn't be disregarded. However minor—he could not bring himself to think the Houstons had such power over them, and yet he could not bring himself to make the obvious deduction from that premise: that the Houstons were only catalysts sparking the chemistry of some heretofore dormant virus into life.

Vaguely, he realizes that Bond has been steadily jabbing his shoulder for some time with the end of his shovel-handle and has apparently been asking a question. He shakes himself, turns back toward the pool which has soaked up the sand they've thrown into it. Bottomless, seemingly.

"What?"

"I said you know what you put me in mind of?"

"Did I answer?" Méndez asks glumly as he jabs his shovel into the earth. The sun has receded now and they both stand in the long, bellying shadow of the tanks.

"Hell, no. I swear you been losing your mind lately. All you do is sit around and moon. You put me in mind of what my Aunt Mildred used to do to Uncle Delbert—"

"Did you ever finish the story about the dogs?" Méndez breaks in, curious as to how long his mind has been wandering.

"No, but I'm getting to it. Be patient. When Delbert was a young feller he used to go out about once a week and tie one hell of a bender on. Mildred put up with it for about two years, then she got to where she'd just nag and nag and that wouldn't do no good, then somebody done told her a remedy that worked, well, sort of worked, at least he didn't get drunk quite so often, and when he did he didn't always come *home* to sober up because he was afraid to. What she did was one night when he come home dead drunk and passed out in the parlor before he could git his clothes off, why she went and got a bed sheet and while he was sleeping it off in the middle of the floor, she went and sewed him up in the sheet until he was locked in there just like a caterpillar in a cocoon. And the next morning when he woke up, he . . . well, you just think about that a minute, waking up that way."

Méndez shudders.

"Why do I put you in mind of that?"

Bond blinks, innocent. "Why, I don't rightly know. Maybe because you ain't been no more aware of where you are the past two days than old Delbert was when he was sleeping in the sheet. But to tell the honest-to-God truth about the matter, I was really thinking about how ever night after that drunk or sober old Delbert would have to lie awake for awhile thinking about being sewed up in a sheet after he went to sleep—I mean it would plumb *interfere* with yore peace of mind. And that's the way I was for a good three months after them dogs chased me back to the camp. I knew I was going to have nightmares about them. Sometimes their faces was big as basketballs and their fangs was like railroad spikes. Sometimes I'd be in a pit with them and couldn't get out. Sometimes they'd chase me through the woods and I'd wake up sweating like a mule. I knoed I had to figger out a way to get rid of them, but they's only so many ways to get rid of a fear. First thing is trying to ignore it. Sometimes that works. I knoed an old boy who was afraid of his own shadder. I mean it. Especially if it was laid out behind him where he couldn't see it. He always used to claim he could feel it creeping up on him. Now you might think that's pretty weird, but I tell you it gets to me somewheres deep. So most of the time he tried to pretend like it just wasn't there—he'd never look down unless it was high noon. Now some other old boys working with us on the same pipeline crew finely figgered this out, and they took to devilling this poor bastard about it: they never would *say* anything, but they'd do little things like say it'd be four o'clock and we'd be shoveling or pissanting pipe and he'd be casting a shadder ten foot long and one of these other old boys'd get on the *down-light* side of him, walk toward him, talking to him to get his attention, and when they'd get up a few feet from him they'd step *around* his shadder like it was real and they couldn't walk through it."

Méndez snorts, "You must think I'm an idiot."

"You haven't lived long enough to know what could happen," Bond says, laughing. "You got some surprises coming. Anyway, it didn't work nohow. You can't make yourself not dream something. You can finely train yourself not to think about the thing you're afraid of, but all you're doing is putting a cover over it. No matter how hard I tried to forget them damn dogs ever night when I went to sleep they'd show up in my dreams. It was like I was a criminal and I was on this here train and I knowed that when it stopped and I got off the law'd be waiting for me at the station. Sure enough there'd they be—big as hogs and sometimes horses, jaws wide and open like the mouths of caves leading straight down into hell. And they'd chase me —god-da-mity! I must of run ten thousand miles during that one month. Why I covered ever inch of territory I'd ever seen since I was just a baby, them dogs chased me back to places I'd even forgot about being to, and I'd wake up shivering or hollering and have to get up and fix me some hot tea with a whole lot of lemon in it or a hot toddy. Got to where I had to get dead drunk to go to sleep. Well, at the end of a month I knoed something had to be done—my eyes was starting to look like somebody'd been jabbing at them with the end of a broom handle and I'd done lost fifteen pounds and I wasn't what you'd call fat to begin with. So I knowed that *that* way to get shut of a fear wasn't gonna work. I just couldn't ignore it because it just wasn't possible. I figgered there was still a couple more things to try, and the next was to somehow convince them dogs that I didn't mean them no harm. I took to going over to my nephew's house two three times a week and I'd go out to the pen with him whenever he'd feed them—I figgered that if they saw me with him and he had a bucketful of food, well then after a while they'd get the idea that my smell meant food, that they'd wouldn't bite the hand that fed them. What turned out was that that was the very idea they got, but they got confused about what the food was and who was carrying it, and at the end of the week, he'd step into the pen and they'd smell me standing right outside trembling and they'd take to yapping—they wanted a bite a *me;* they was one that I thought was damn near desperate enough to crawl through one of them little squares in the hog wire to get to me. Nephew couldn't figure it out. 'Them dogs's been acting funny all week,' he said. And I'd look at them howling and snarling and trying to tear that damn fence down to get after me and I'd say, 'Well could be they sniff a coon or something.' But I knoed what it was. It was *me.*" Bond pauses to join Méndez in covering up the pool of glistening oil. "So I saw that wasn't going to work neither. There wasn't no use in me pretending that I could ignore them dogs in hopes that they'd think *I* wasn't there, because ever time I'd go up to that pen sure enough they'd recognize me. I think what I was trying to do was to get them outa my mind without having to have no truck with the actual thing. I was like a man who's locked up in a concentration camp trying to pretend its only a nightmare. So then I tried thuther way—tried dealing with the thing rather than the dream. I thought I'd pacify them some, so ever night for a week, I'd sneak up to the pen late at night, run up to the hog-wire fence and just when they'd bust into a godawful cater-waul I'd toss them a couple of my old dirty socks—they'd like to rip each other up to get one. Idea I had in mind was to just give them little pieces of myself so's that after a while they *might* just get their bellyfull of me and go on to something that smelled and tasted a little different. First night I give them the socks, the next night I tossed them a pair a old canvas tennis shoes I used to fish in, the night after that I chunked a pair of trousers in, then an old shirt that I did some house-painting in. But I got to feeling like I hadn't done right by just giving them my castoffs—I imagine that shirt wasn't too tasty, what with them paint spots and motor oil splotches and fish blood and whatever all over it—I mean I thought that if this was going to work it'd have to be a *sacrifice;* so one night I flung them sonsabitches the best damn hat I ever had in my life. This here hat had been through seven deer seasons—it was soft brown corduroy with a nice bill on her to keep the sun outa your eyes and it had fur-lined ear covers that folded up and tied on top the hat when you didn't need them, and when you *did,* why they come around your ears and down the back of your neck like warm oil. And did that hat fit! When you put her on it was like a woman's hands cupped around your head, holding you against her breasts. I stood outside that pen in the moonlight and I eased that hat off my head real slow. Them dogs was lined up on the inside of the fence growling and snapping, just waiting for their little meal of me, and when tears started coming to my eyes I turned away and slung it over my shoulder and I tell you when it hit the dirt on the inside of that pen them dogs come plumb unglued—you'd a thought I'd just give them a half a side of beef. Why, they was one that was so riled up by it, he just spun around and round in circles yapping and snapping at his own tail. Well, I went home and the next day I paid my nephew a visit because I didn't have nothing else to give them dogs and I wanted to see if I'd done any good. We was sitting in the kitchen drinking coffee and I said, like I had just thought of it and was just making small talk, 'How's them dogs of yours?' And he said, 'You know, it's the damndest thing. Looks to me like some poor bastard wandered into that pen and got hisself eat up.

Looks like they gobbled everything that was him and left whatever wasn't.' I felt real discouraged, because when he said that I knoed that they had gobbled everything that wasn't me and their real meal was still waiting for them. We went out back. There was my hat right in the middle of the pen with one of the earflaps tore off and right smack in the middle of the hat on the inside was a big brown turd. If I'd had any doubts before that about just how devilish and crafty they was, if I'd had any notions that all this here mess was only in my mind, why they was gone then—that dog that crapped inside that hat knoed *exactly* what he was doing. They was all off in one corner of the pen with their heads together in a huddle and when they looked up and saw who it was they grinned, I tell you they *grinned,* and then run over next to the fence and howled and yapped and growled—they was one put his nose through a hole in the hog wire so far I thought he was going to put his eyes out. My nephew said, 'You must of got some possum or coon on you—they're acting like you got something they want.' I said yep that was true, but they wasn't going to get it.

"So it got down to the only answer. I started saving my money, each week that come up I put a little back. I had done wrestled with the problem for three months and I'd done tried everything I could think of to solve it but *that,* so in the end that's what I was left with. Taught me a good lesson about solving problems. So I saved back a few dollars ever week from my pay until I finely had a little over forty dollars. I knoed that what I was going to do would piss my nephew off, but then I was desperate, you see, and a dog is a dog and a man is a man. So the first night after I saved up the money and there wasn't no moon, I lit out from the house and walked three miles to that dog pen and when they commenced to holler and lunge against the hog wire to get me, I pulled a shotgun out from under my coat and bloed them all to smithereens. I wrote a note to my nephew and sent the money in the mail."

# _El Perdido Se Va a Todo_

# One

To the north a faint orange light bellies against the underside of a cloudbank. *That must be it,* Méndez thinks. *It's true, he wasn't lying.* If he were closer he could see it flickering, could feel it press against his body. The boiling updraft surging to the sky sucks at things around its source like a mouth erupting in the earth. If he were standing near he could feel this suction tugging at his ankles like an undertow. He would hear the glass breaking, the large windows shattering inward, their fragments splintering and flying through the churning interior of the store. First the outer windows, and if he were standing within earshot the shattering of windows might call to mind the image of some maniac set loose inside to smash with libidinous abandon each buckling glass, like a berserk fireman wielding his axe.

But standing beside the corral at the fence on the ranch some three miles away, Méndez is aware of the pressure and motion and energy only as an abstraction.

Juanita comes out of the cottage and joins him by the corral.

"It *is* burning," she speaks after a moment of gazing at the flickering light on the northern horizon. She shivers; the crisp night air is chilly—the weather has begun to turn. "Oh Raphael—"

"Goddammit, why'd he have to do that, it wasn't . . . *necessary*," Méndez fumes. "He could have . . . well, I could have . . ." he trails off. *El perdido se va a todo,* he thinks. He who is lost tries anything. Juanita remains silent. "I guess I just didn't think it would come to that."

"Why did he call *you?*"

"I'm not sure."

"What did he say?" She sounded apprehensive.

"He said he got into the store and set fire to it. He got some money, too."

"But why did he call *you?*"

"Goddammit, I don't know," he snapped.

"But did he just say, 'Hello, I broke into the hardware store and robbed it and set fire to it,' then hang up, or what?"

"What?"

"You heard what I asked."

"I don't know. I don't know what he said. It's all a blur."

"But why . . ."

"Goddammit, Juanita," he cuts her off, almost shouting. "I said I didn't know. He probably wants help. Or something."

"What kind of help?"

"He probably wanted to know what to do."

"Raphael—" she hisses. "Did he ask for anything?"

"He might have—it's all a blur, I tell you." He tries to remember Manuelo's breathless, rapid-fire exposition in Spanish of what happened, what was yet to happen. "He said he was coming."

"Here?" she gasps.

"Ah . . . yes."

"Raphael, what will you do? What can we do?"

"I don't know." He gestures, helplessly, with one hand limp as Bond's white cotton glove.

"Oh Raphael, be careful. Just when things are going so well . . ." she blurts, then checks herself.

"I wouldn't do anything that would interfere with our self-interest. Don't worrry about *that*. You'll be with the jet set yet."

"I meant don't get *hurt*," she snaps, then spins on her heel and returns to the cottage.

When she vanishes, he feels some remorse for jumping on her so roughly. Her words usher him into a corner of his mind where Manuelo's violence has been ignored and not understood—something enigmatic in the man, some set of responses Méndez cannot himself assimilate, although he can conjure a rapport with their causes, the conditions leading to such an outburst. Hurt? He cannot see himself setting fire to things, although he can imagine himself arguing in favor of it.

But Manuelo did it. He thinks he can know what Manuelo thinks, can even duplicate the images which crowd his brain: bandsaws, hatchets, hammers, axes, wrenches, knives, and rifles; gougers, bullets, nails and spikes, rakes and spades—things to cut, chop, pound, split, wrench, gouge and hit and tear and scrape—all the hardware in the store must have lain before him like metaphors of his rage rising from his consciousness. Files and stones to make knives still sharper, wedges to force and rend, drills and bits and awls to pierce, to puncture.

But Méndez's attempt to reconstruct Manuelo's state of mind must by nature be limited—he cannot know that in the rear of the store, in the southwest corner, stored always in a dark, cool place in a bin with a padlock on it, lies dynamite.

Manuelo had come into the store one day for a pipe fitting and he quietly followed a clerk to the rear where the fittings were lined up on shelves or in separate bins. While Manuelo pored over the pieces, putting together some plumbing arrangement in his head, another clerk came through the door with a rancher who said he needed dynamite to dig a hole for a septic tank, and the other clerk opened the bin which held the dynamite and they all four—the two clerks, the rancher, and now Manuelo—looked into it as the clerk eased the lid open, slowly, as though a nest of rattlesnakes might be asleep inside, and then they seemed to check their breathing for a moment, looking at the stack of darkly burnished rods as though it were a dangerous treasure, a rare but poisonous species of viper. "Yep, we got her," the clerk said softly, pointing at the dynamite, proudly. The clerk dipped his hand into the bin and came out with a single stick of dynamite which he flipped once or twice in his hand, end over end, with bravura, then winked at Manuelo as though he expected him to dash away in fear, but Manuelo grinned back. The clerk closed and locked the bin, and he and the rancher returned to the front of the store. After Manuelo se-lected a new elbow from the pigeonholes along the walls, he stepped over to the bin and ran his fingers over the wooden lid, once, slowly, then returned to the front.

Beneath a bare bulb hanging on a wire from the ceiling, sitting squarely on the counter like a mechanical Buddha overseeing all the latent violence of the bristling hardware, was the cash register. Behind the register stood the clerk who led him to the back room. Manuelo asked for credit and as he stood before the counter with the fitting held up in one hand, the clerk smiled indulgently, apologetically: "Sorry friend," he said, "but this here's strictly a cash and carry operation." This he said immediately after nodding almost unconsciously as the rancher, striding out of the store with a bundle of dynamite, called back over his shoulder—"Just write me down on that." The clerk backed off slightly as Manuelo appeared to be making some motion preparatory to slinging the fitting at him, but then Manuelo simply held the fitting out to his side and dropped it to the floor with a violent curse.

Manuelo had actually expected credit, and it is this which Méndez would not be able to grasp. Méndez knows that even Anglos cannot walk into a store and automatically expect credit, especially poor Anglos, especially poor Anglos with a purchase of less than a dollar. Méndez knows this because he has the dubious gift of seeing as an Anglo, of being—to a point—an Anglo.

And what he could not understand about Manuelo's feelings was the other man's persistence in believing even after a lifetime of rejection and rebuff and discrimination that he was equal to any man, that somehow the accumulation of personal rejections he had suffered had not denied him his essential self. This subjectivity, this inviolate sense of self, is beyond

Méndez, who, like other members of society every-where, is perfectly capable of forgetting that he exists when society finds it convenient for him to cease existing. That Manuelo refuses to believe he is a second-class citizen, that he refuses to acknowledge even the expectation of discrimination to that point where each rebuff becomes as fresh as the original at age three or four—that he can forget this Méndez would label a mark of either hope for change or stupidity. Something distinctly childlike in his persistent refusal sets Manuelo apart from the other *chicanos* Méndez knows: most learn by age ten that they will never be treated as anything but *greasers*, but Manuelo, whether from an abysmally poor memory or a sense of his own independence that it cannot be dented, insists on receiving equal treatment as his due. Méndez would be forced to acknowledge that of such stuff are heroes made; were he to consider it long enough to find some comfortable place for the idea in his perspective Méndez would set that quality of Manuelo's alongside that same impetus which drove the leaders of all slave revolts throughout history—they contained something which could not for whatever reason be defeated, some voice within spoke: *I am a man among men, I am no slave.* In some less anxious and more romantic mood Méndez could warm to the notion of playing official biographer of the revolution: it might be his task, or so he might fantasize, to show how Manuelo or someone very much like him had said *I am a man;* how, born in a tar-paper hovel surrounded by mesquite and cotton, a man grew and simply failed to understand that he was less than a man. He led his people out of the wilderness. . . . He appeared from nowhere behind the barricades bareback on a stallion, waving a carbine clutched in his fist.

But Méndez is anxious; his hands tremble minutely as he hunkers by the corral fence, staring to the north where the glow of the burning hardware store nudges against the cloud bank. What will Manuelo ask of him? To the west, along the highway, headlights of cars wink and inch along, sluggishly.

He remembers another confrontation in which he had first imagined that all the injustices he and his fellow *chicanos* had suffered might accumulate and gather into a fury intense enough to start an insurrection, if not a war. He daydreamed about it, had machine-gunned in his head hundreds of adult Anglos by the time he was ten, but had never experienced anything which approximated that violence in reality. . . . Billy Teague and the Snake. . . . headlights and an arena. Like Elvis, the Snake didn't like to have his blue suede shoes stepped on. Méndez's *palomilla*—the Snake and Flea and Pete—called themselves *Los Diablos* and had painted the name in crude white letters across the backs of their black leather jackets. Taking a case of beer which Flea's older brother had purchased for them, they went to the drive-in to see *Rebel Without a Cause* with James Dean for the fourth time, but had to sit through a Doris Day movie during which they drank the beer and chain-smoked and jostled each other and made lewd, violent proposals to Doris Day or leered at stragglers who passed by the Snake's '51 Merc (on permanent loan to him from an older brother in the service) on their way to the concession stand.

During the intermission the Snake switched on his spotlight and played it on the screen, inviting a game of "chase me" with the drivers of other cars, drivers who would be anonymous to any adult not immersed in the ritual games of this subculture and who would recognize neither the identifying marks of each spotlight nor the pattern which characterized each man's play, but which were familiar to many in this audience composed largely of the same persons who were required to gather in Costilla High's weekly obligatory assembly (though of the four Diablos only Méndez and Gutiérrez still attended school): to them each light was distinctly individual. The Snake's spot could be identified by its double aura, something like an electric amoeba in the anaphase stage of mitosis, with two intense nuclei giving the impression of two pinched and squinting eyes—if you looked closely at the beam on the screen you could see a face in it, a face which did not really seem to leer as much as those watching imagined it to leer because it belonged to the Snake. The Snake played "chase-me" with a finesse which approached art: he had such control over the movement of his light that few could catch and pin it down with theirs on the screen; he was good enough to plant his light smack into the middle of the screen and never had to bracket or adjust it like an artillery piece—he simply aimed it, flicked the switch, and there it appeared in dead center. Generally his light was followed by a half dozen others, all amateurishly shifting and bobbing into position in an attempt to catch his in center-screen, but by the time they focused on the center, the Snake would be off and running, his beam darting up and across like a swivel-hipped halfback. Usually the novices would drop out one by one or bob clumsily around the periphery of the screen like young boys playing catch on the sidelines, leaving the field open to one or both of the Snake's chief adversaries, one of whom was L.D. Teague, Billy's older brother, a post-teen teenager who had left his father's farm after graduation and had adopted the lifestyle of a city slicker, living in Costilla's lone, two-story hotel and working behind the parts counter at the Ford agency.

Teague's light consisted of two concentric circles like two discs superimposed; the center disc was dim and the outer was bright, giving the beam the appearance of a circular band of light enclosing a vacuum. It was Teague's habit to try to slip his beam over the Snake's and catch it in the center of his own. On this particular night, no sooner had the Snake thrown down his gauntlet on the screen than Teague's light appeared almost instantly. The others dropped out to watch. Teague was quick this night and he caught the Snake's beam three times in succession after the ads came on and the Snake was artfully hiding in the lightest areas of the screen. The Snake had gotten cocky and had flitted into the groin of the celluloid man, a tall Anglo in a suit who was taking his family to the church of their choice. The man held the hand of his matronly but trim and meticulously groomed spouse who in turn held the hand of her pubescent, suited son who in turn was holding the hand of his young sister while they journeyed down the Walk of Life toward a stone church with a single steeple, smiling. The Snake landed on the man's crotch and Teague bagged him once there; the Snake feinted out to the far corner of the screen, where the clouds were sending forth a bright, Sunday-morning radiance, then flicked quickly to the left and rested on the woman's hat—Teague, who knew that the Snake's pattern was elusive but ultimately predictable—did not follow the feint but instead hesitated then zoomed in to catch the Snake for the second time on the woman's hat. The Snake made off for the bottom left-hand corner of the screen, beneath the Walk of Life, and Teague ducked into the radiant clouds to wait in ambush and bait the Snake to appear again. He must have known where the Snake would go because as soon as the Snake's double-auraed, squint-eyed beam violated the little girl's crotch, Teague came rushing out of the light and apprehended him, there in the loins of the golden-haired darling bedecked in frills and smiles.

Teague smugly flicked his light off, leaving the Snake to wander disconsolately in defeat about the field like a has-been gunman desperately challenging his inferior contenders. The Snake obstinately left his light on through the previews and into the credits of *Rebel Without a Cause*, until several blaring honks arose from the pit and he sourly flipped the switch of his spotlight with a low curse.

Had it been any other movie he might not have turned it out, but to distract the audience from *Rebel* would have been an act of sacrilege. This was their fourth viewing of the film, and the spirit of horseplay with which they had occupied themselves during the first feature dissipated almost instantly as *Rebel* began; they all slumped into the four separate corners of the Snake's Merc and grew cool, stolid, making occasional comments out of the corners of their lip-taut mouths and glaring at the passers-by. The movie always stirred them immensely. After it was over, they had always driven around in the Snake's '51 Merc (the same car which Dean drove in the movie) yearning for California and feeling a little displaced out on the *Llano Estacado*. The only part of the movie they didn't like was that Sal Mineo played the *chicano* too much like a suck-ass little *maricón*, but still they burned with indignation in the end when Dean and Natalie Wood are holed up in the old house and Plato (Mineo) has found them and they've befriended him and the cops come with their spotlights, floodlights, searchlights all converging on the front of the house—Plato comes running out of the house: "Don't shoot, don't shoot!" he yells and they kill him on the spot. James Dean and Natalie Wood come out of the house and Dean cradles Mineo's head in his lap. "Plato, Plato," he murmurs, then, not so much from anger as from incomprehension of the entire adult world of brutal hypocrisy and weakness: "Why'd you have to shoot him?"

Yeah! Yeah! Why did they have to do it? Sitting in the darkened car each burned with indignation; had Jim Backus been on hand to sign autographs he might have had his head caved in with a tire tool.

When the last scene faded from the screen, they all got out of the car, wordlessly, each feeling that peculiar comradeship, that sense of banding together against a world which fails to understand, and walked toward the concession stand, swaggering, each with a *frajo* pendant in the corner of his mouth, eyeing the knots of girls and postpubescent boys converging on the low, crackerbox building.

Inside the room lay an atmosphere of hush charged heavily with tension. They were mad. They were packed into an overheated capsule choked with catsup and mustard and popcorn machines and week-old hotdogs turning endlessly in the tin rotisserie with the grease-smeared window and the Dr. Pepper clocks and the ten-cent Cokes which cost a quarter and the thricemelted candy bars and the floor littered with crumpled napkins, the ends of hot-dog buns, cigarette butts, snapped straws, and dried hamburgers which tasted of an America gone forever into that hopeless and desperate state of mobility, the on-the-run America of drive-in movies, banks, cleaners, liquor stores, drug stores. Trapped inside this thing, they were all glaring at one another, a detail which escaped Méndez at the time, but which he begins to understand now: they were all Dean and everyone was against him, they all imagined themselves the hero of that movie. Then again, there was no target, no representative present of the world that shot Plato except for the owner of the drive-in—a scrawny, stick-necked, graying ghost of middle America, behind the counter now with white short-sleeved shirt, black bow tie, an apron around his waist, and a paper hat lined with a ring of rancid hair-oil pushed down on his forehead—but his obsequious bustle after small change made him not beneath their contempt, but beneath their active opposition. At the counter, he asked the Snake what he wanted in a peppy, step-right-up voice, and the Snake gave him an order for a hot-dog and a ten-cent Coke in a voice that suggested he was forced by circumstance to deal with a second-class enemy. Where was an adversary worthy of his attention?

Ah! Here—in the line just behind the Snake and Flea and Pete and Méndez, appearing through the mist of putrid vapors—were the Teague Bros. and their wrangler friend: three young men clad in Levis, Western shirts, boots, hats, and Levi jackets which identified them as members of another sort of club (just as the black leather jacket and the bicolored letter jackets identified their owners); embroidered on the back of each Levi jacket was a huge emblem of an eagle in gold together with the inscription "Future Farmers of

America" and the name of the town and state. Remembering this, Méndez is forced to pay grudging tribute to the power of the myth-maker to infuse his legend with such universal stuff that even in those years before youth became fully nationalized boys growing up on farms saw their destiny in the schizophrenic light of both tractor and California street-rod: they were never aware that their sense of a shared destiny with Dean implied a contradiction, a disparity between their lives as future sons of the soil and his as urban misfit. Perhaps there was no contradiction, perhaps the film itself expressed not contradiction to them but united the most disparate parts of their heritage and forged their future, perhaps the film best expressed for them the essence of what it meant to be born in America: a land where the sons of wetbacks who ape the lifestyle of a singing redneck truck driver from Memphis can find the same significance in a film as the sons of farmers who had never set foot in a real city but who had caught on in their own agrarian way, had sniffed the winds of change enough to adapt the urban games to their own rural setting—playing "chicken" on tractors in the middle of a field, buying records by black quartets singing songs which dripped with sexual innuendo and obscure allusions to living in the ghettos, reading hotrod magazines published by Jewish entrepreneurs who were born in New York and moved out West to become Rotarians and Seventh Day Adventists. . . . That both the Teagues and *Los Diablos* found themselves in the same celluloid fantasy in which a middle-class white boy in California thrashed his way through an industrialized, fragmented culture with a sidekick named Plato who was in reality a Puerto Rican rock-and-roll singer playing the part of a Mexican-American

with the name of a Greek philosopher, with this sidekick and a father whose role was played by a man
known mostly for his work with Disney Studios in the
role of Mr. Magoo—that Teague and *Los Diablos*
could seek and find alike in such a confusion of values
and traditions attested either to the power of art to
transcend the specific or to some mad yearning afoot
in the land. Yet that myth had miraculously coalesced
all those forces and had gathered them in this concession stand of a drive-in movie theater surrounded by
miles and miles of mesquite and tumbleweed, brought
them to bear on this single, ephemeral point in history,
plopped down among the week-old hot dogs and cigarette butts and Coca-Cola signs, myriad objects manufactured from a substançe created by a family of
French chemists, popsicle sticks, tubules of mustard
and catsup thinned to a watery gravy, tiny packets of
salt and sugar reminiscient of either a survival packet
or a box of C-rations (those men came back from the
war with some new notions on how to package things),
and amidst all this was a crowd of not less than thirty
persons pressing against the counter waiting to be fed,
hushed, angry, glaring at each other, Méndez remembers, united in their self-pity. With no target in sight
other than the man behind the counter and his wife
and children, whatever injustice they suffered must
have come from each other. They became victims
turned against themselves.

The Snake paid for his hot dog and stepped back out
of the line to eat it, distastefully peeling back the
grease-soaked wrapper and inspecting the blanched
pink dog buried in a stale bun.

"Shit!" he cursed loudly.

The Teagues stood just before him at the counter,
their backs turned to give their orders. They were wiry,

muscled boys, the cream of American youth, peach-fuzzed, freckled farm boys who had each lifted a calf every day from its birth to its maturity or at least until they could no longer get their arms around it: strong, white-toothed, open-faced milkers of cows and sloppers of hogs, darkly tanned from the waist up from summer days spent on tractors or in pickup beds, owners of electric guitars and skin magazines hidden in bureau drawers, with year-old prophylactics carried surreptitiously in their wallets and county-fair ribbons tacked to their bedroom walls; hopelessly innocent of themselves, they were the very stuff of which war heroes and lynch mobs are made.

"Hey Teague!" the Snake called out to the oldest one of the three standing at the counter. The muscles of Méndez's legs went taut and he poised slightly on the balls of his feet. Still smarting from three quick defeats at "chase me," the Snake was out for revenge.

The older Teague turned to look at the Snake, who arched his lips in a smile which seemed to say don't-sweat-it-man-I'm-*with*-you. Teague looked suspicious.

"Hey!" the Snake said loudly enough for the entire crowd to overhear. "You have to come all the way out here just to get something to slop your hogs with?"

A general tittering—the counterman frantically busied himself with pretending not to hear.

Teague brightened. "Yeah!" he cackled. "Them hogs really go for this shit."

Beside Méndez, Flea was swaying a bit from the half-dozen beers he had drunk.

"Hey, mahn," he drawled to Teague, "why doan you ask him for a hoggy bag?" There was general laughter in the room; the other Teague and their wrangler friend chimed in, snickering.

"So how is old Bess?" the Snake went on, alluding

suddenly to the school-owned sow with whom all members of the local FFA chapter were alleged to practice rites of sodomy. Teague momentarily flushed as if in indecision as to the Snake's intent.

"Yew want to take a little trip to Fist City?" he asked after a moment, apparently having decided to get right to the heart of the matter.

On the way to "Fist City," the caliche pit in which the teenage population settled its tribal conflicts, Flea kept repeating, "Go for his *cojones,* mahn, go for his pig-fucking nuts." Several considerations led him to urge this counsel to the Snake: first, the Teague who had extended this invitation to them was some twenty pounds heavier and two years older than the Snake; second, the Teagues were notorious for their farm-boy stamina, and last, Flea and Pete and the Snake and Méndez all knew that whatever constraints the Teagues might ordinarily feel against using "dirty" tactics would dissipate because of the nature of their adversaries; Méndez could imagine a dialogue between the Teagues—*them goddamn greasers'll go right for your nuts, so you'd best go for his before he hits yours.* Méndez pointed out the logic of this to the Snake when the latter appeared to balk at taking Flea's advice. "I don't know, mahn," he heard the Snake say as he drove the car onto the highway from the drive-in exit, "I doan't need no unfair advantage over that *gavacho.* Not right off."

Along the country road to the abandoned caliche pit the Snake stopped the car to let Flea and Pete out to piss; when they had stepped clear of the car, he turned to Méndez who was seated in the back. Méndez could see the skull-thin features of his face half-illuminated by the dash lights. "Hey mahn," he asked softly. "*Why*

*am I doing this? Why is it always me?"* His question
was not a reproach; no criticism of the other three lay
implicit in it—he wanted to know why he was the way
he was. Even then Méndez was known as the philosopher, the theoretician, and with four beers churning
hotly in his stomach in a solution of acid and adrenalin,
he redirected the question so that he was not being
asked to explain the nature of a man but rather to
exhort him to take up the banner of the just cause. He
evaded the real question and chose instead to coax the
troops up the last bloody hill. He answered as he imagined his father might have answered: "It's because they
are pig-fucking gringos and we are *la raza.*" This urgently, as if spat out, trying to suggest with it the
weight of inexorability, of fate, *destino:* God made us
better than them but they don't know it and we must
show them. The irrefutable and unanswerable illogic of
*macho.* (Was the Snake ever aware that he didn't answer the question?)

"Yeah," the Snake breathed to Méndez's reply.
"Damn right!" And took a long slug of beer as if to
prove it.

The quality of the moment was peculiar, Méndez
thinks in retrospect. The Snake had turned to him and
had momentarily removed the mask of cool and knowledgeable street fighter. It was as though he had blurted
out the question despite himself, as though a first question—"How come I'm doing *this?"*—had led before
he even realized it to "How come *I'm* doing this?" And
Méndez, in his indignation toward all things Anglo,
immersed in his fantasy of the tribe united against
some primordial enemy, had not wanted to face the
second question, had pretended it did not exist, but this
pretense only made the Snake realize that he had

stepped out of character and that Méndez was generously allowing him to resume his former role without loss of face.

"Yeah!" the Snake repeated, slinging his beer can out the window. "Damn right!"

Part of the audience who had enjoyed the preview to the fight in the concession stand had followed the Teagues to the caliche pit for the full feature. As they descended the rocky two-rut road down into the bottom of the pit, Méndez could see a half-dozen cars head-in on an open area half the size of a basketball court with their lights illuminating the open ground; some twenty Anglos stood around lounging on the fenders and hoods of the cars drinking beer. There were a few girls, their dates apparently having decided that watching Messkins take a licking was the proper way to end an evening with a young lady. Soulless bitches, Méndez thought.

They pulled into the circle and sat for a moment in silence.

"Damn right!" The Snake kept passing his hand across his nose as though it itched. "I'm going for his nuts."

"Hey greaser!" a shout drifted to them from across the open area. "Put down them tortillas and get your greasy ass out here!"

"Yeah," the Snake muttered. "Damn right."

On the other side of the clearing they could see the flash of metal—tire tools and bicycle chains, Méndez guessed—and thick sticks, like baseball bats.

"Shit, mahn," Pete said. "They got heavy stuff."

"They won't use it," Méndez said. "They just like to wave it around."

A delegation was sent to approach their car; Méndez

noted that it included both the Teagues and three other members of the FFA chapter. Scanning the faces that he could discern on the other side of the arena, he recognized at least a half dozen "jocks" and a clutch of hot-rodders—ordinarily these three factions of their high school subculture were suspicious of each other, but at this moment their alliance was unquestionable. The five approaching the car were swaggering and jostling each other, working at giving the impression of casual confidence, of joy at being granted an easy task. The younger Teague, however, kept tugging at the waistband of his beltless Levis and laughed much too loudly, revealing a boyish, snaggle-toothed mouth. The Snake lifted the door handle and let the door swing open an inch or two. The delegation surrounded the car, with the two Teagues standing just outside the driver's window.

"Hey there, Gutiérrez," the younger Teague called. "Somebody said one of you greasers called me a pig-fucker."

"Naw," the Snake said gently. He moved slightly away from the car door, then turned in the seat.

"Naw?" the younger Teague asked with an odd mixture of relief and disappointment.

"Somebody's lying to you."

"I told you he'd be chicken-shit," one of the other delegates called out from the rear of the car, then began jumping on the back bumper.

"I ain't a pig-fucker?" Prematurely assuming victory, Teague leaned over and put his head partially into the open window. "Well, it's a good thing yew didn't call me no pig-fucker because I'd shore stomp yore ass for *that*."

Méndez could see it coming: the Snake had eased his

leg up on the seat; he could see the smile flitting across his mouth.

"Naw," he said. "You're not a pig-fucker. You're a mother-fucker." And before Teague could collect his wits, the Snake slammed his foot into the partially opened door and sent him sprawling backwards; a split second later he was out of the car and was straddling Teague, pounding his face with his fists. Méndez and the others rushed out of the car, while across the arena the crowd of Anglos surged forward to get a closer look.

A sharp, deep concussion as though the heavens were clapped together startles Méndez out of his memory—to the north the flames which had only ebbed against the clouds now rushed skyward and the echoing waves of the explosion sweep by him as he turns his face toward the source of the sound. He hopes Manuelo and no one else was nearby when the store blew up—dynamite? Surely Manuelo didn't intentionally . . . He drops the thought. Even accidentally that would somehow make the charges against him more severe because there was something about an explosion in the psyche which would transform Manuelo's act, make it not merely robbery or arson but political sabotage, even if the explosives themselves were only part of the ordinary fixtures of the store.

He wants to think of something pleasant but knows he has no right to: he is morally obligated to turn his mind toward Manuelo's problem. He does not want to think of Manuelo's coming; he wants to remember his credentials.

He reconstructs: and what was the philosopher philosophizing? He was stunned, nervous, watching even from his lunar observatory. In the general scramble for positions after the Snake had flung Teague backwards with the door, all standing bodies converged on the two prone bodies struggling beyond the circle of light in the dust. From the moon, he might have seen with benefit of telescope two young men wrestling(?) making the beast with two backs(?). Hard to tell—too much dust, the circle of young men was drawn too tightly around them in the dim light, swaying, cheering—"Kick shit out of him Teague!!" From his lunar observatory the activity might have seemed unimportant.

Although part of him was taking notes from his vantage point on the moon, where the Snake's wounds and Teague's wounds were not connected to their nerve ends, another part of him was recording details from a position much nearer than the moon. Standing on the inside edge of the huddle around the Snake and Teague he saw across the circle a slender youth named Leroy McVey who played trumpet in the band and with whom he had had just that morning a bit of amiable banter about the fact that Méndez's name happened to be the same as that of another man who billed himself as "the world's fastest trumpet player," but now McVey stared across the huddle at him with piggish, hateful eyes which could not focus for long on Méndez's face, and Méndez returned the glare, think-ing—*you fucking hypocrite, you bollío sonofabitch when the time comes I'll rip your guts out!* He'd get them all, the idiot sons of farmers and businessmen and oilmen and merchants and realtors, all those who were united in vicarious power against *Los Diablos*, who held no power through their fathers, who held only that which they had decided upon themselves to take by their wits, their courage, and their energy, the creative energy of the involuntary criminal: he was sure the Snake would win, if only because the Snake's victory might affirm his most basic faith, that victory ultimately belonged to the rightful carrier of justice, of the true essence of humanity. Victories require victors and for Méndez that role had been assigned to a character not beset by any of the ordinary liabilities of character which plague normal humans. The Snake—he who transcends mortal limitations, the Tempter, the rebel against the manufactured and therefore false goodness of a world they awoke to, a world already fallen, and thus they had never been granted the choice of turning away from the good life because the good life was destined to be lived or not lived as the sons of businessmen, merchants, bankers, and oilmen chose to choose. The Snake—he who stirs fear, he who takes it upon himself to enclose, to swallow, to soak up, to infuse by osmosis, to take in all conscience, to absorb the world with the power of Cain: it was always him, Méndez thinks, because I and the others were afraid to do "evil" yet were born to nothing else because we awoke to a world of Christs with golden hair, and thus when we wished to maim, to strike back at that system, the Snake did it for us. He was our intermediary, our contact with forces beyond our own mortality; if our god was dark, if we felt unjustly and congenitally shunted out of the tribe of chosen people, at least the darkness was a god.

No, none of that. In truth there was only a young man named Jesse Gutiérrez, no Snake, no Deliverer, no Intermediary, only a young man driven by the same things that drove all of them, not really mature or intelligent enough to see that between himself and his *compadres*, between their desire to make a hero of him and his desire to be a hero they had forced him to wrestle, kick, wound, and otherwise try to hurt another young man almost precisely like himself and in almost precisely the same relationship to his tribe. We forced you, Méndez thinks, and you forced you and you did it, and whether or not there is courage in doing what one is forced to do is conjectural, but at least you know that others lacked even the initial courage to *become* forced to be what we made you, because our fear made us look ahead in anticipation of what such a role might require. You were an ordinary *pachuco* struggling extraordinarily with your condition, and when we play at heroes sometimes we become them. A hero is not forever, it is not a thing, a man, or an object, it is only a quality which appears in process, cropping up suddenly in an existential moment and perhaps disappearing forever. A man is never a hero; he is a man heroing for a moment, perhaps cowarding the next.

No, Méndez checks himself again: perhaps there was no heroing at all. Perhaps it took too much courage at that moment for him to not be what everyone else was requiring him to be. Surely that was it. On the ground pinned by the Teague boy in a scissor-lock which was turning his face into a knot of intense grimace like a surreal clock spring with an ache at the center of its coil was neither Snake nor hero nor anything but a child, a boy named Jesse Gutiérrez, age seventeen, girl-shy, afraid of loneliness, worried about his grades, highly suspicious of the feelings which overcame him at Mass, a worshipper of the Virgin Mother, secret possessor of the violet thrills encased in the loins of Marilyn Monroe, author of a poem buried deep beneath the boyish paraphernalia of his dresser drawer, a poem about spring which he was so ashamed of having written that he had only shown it once to Méndez and immediately after tried to disavow authorship of it, this

Jesse Gutiérrez who had turned to Méndez not fifteen minutes earlier and asked "Why is it always me?" It was only this vision of the Snake which can lead Méndez (or which Méndez imagines can lead) to an understanding of the business about the knife. Jesse Gutiérrez, the boy, the human boy, who also tied a cherry bomb with a rubber band to the belly of a horned toad, who pinned others to a clothesline by their tails then shot at them with a BB gun to watch them spin over and over like targets at a carnival shooting game, who fried ants with a magnifying glass, who led them (Méndez *et al.*) in a merry round of hog calling while they walked on the heels of a fat girl on the way home from school until the nape of her neck grew red and she burst into tears which sent the Gutiérrez boy into whoops of laughter.

Part of the event Méndez has recorded in one of his spiral notebooks:

"On a patch of earth on the surface of the Western Hemisphere, two young men for a brief span of time were closing their hands and placing them quickly on each other's bodies. One of the young men was not performing this as quickly as the other and was stepping backward with an awkward motion as the other advanced toward him. Still another human (the third) spoke to the slower one about a crude utensil the quicker one was alleged to have suddenly appear in his hand, and as he spoke he placed in the slower one's hand *another* crude utensil, part of a piece of primitive machinery, and counseled him (the second) to lay it upon parts of the quicker, or first's, body. At which point the quicker turned to still another, or fourth, human standing near him and asked him if he might not have possession of a primitively constructed and crude utensil that he was alleged to have but did not actually possess because he had handed it to this fourth human earlier so that he might not be tempted to shove it into the second, or slower, human's body, but now he desired to do such because the third human had told the second that he *already* had possession of that utensil and had (the third) given the second still another to lay upon, with force, the first, or quicker's, body, and was about to do so, the slower one was, because he feared the other already had possession of that which he, the quicker, was in fact only *asking* the fourth for. But he, the person who was standing near the first, claimed that he himself did not have possession of the utensil which the first had given him earlier for safe-keeping."

It happened so quickly he couldn't think: "But man!" he blurted out, "I haven't got it!" And before the Snake could argue, he saw Teague lunge forward, the Snake's own arm went up to ward off the blow, but too slowly, and Teague struck him across the head with the length of bicycle chain and knocked him to the ground. When the sons of teachers and merchants and ranchers and oilmen and realtors saw the blood gushing from Jesse Gutiérrez's head they scrambled away while Méndez and the Flea and Pete hovered over the Snake in the white dust billowing up from the wheels of the departing cars. After a few moments, they picked him up and sat him upright in the rear seat of his car, and while Flea and Pete were wiping away the blood from his head and struggling to stir him back to full consciousness, Méndez stepped to the rear of the car and flung the knife into a thicket of mesquite. While they drove to the hospital the Snake kept reviving in stages. *"Mi fila, mi fila,"* he moaned. Then later: *"Hey, man*

*—what happened to my knife?? I thought you had it. I didn't have a knife and that cabrón knew it. Where'd it go?"* Shocked and dazed, he kept repeating the question with a kind of wonder stripped of accusation, as though to say *Where in the world is there any justice?*

Méndez tried to explain. First he claimed that Gutiérrez had never given him the knife in the first place, then he claimed that if it had been given to him, it must have fallen from his jacket pocket, but then he stopped trying to explain, hearing in his voice a whine of self-justification. Gutiérrez did not pursue it, being too dazed even to register Méndez's words clearly.

A week later, however, he telephoned Méndez.

"All right, Méndez," he said flatly, quietly. "Where's my knife?"

Méndez swallowed. "I threw it away."

There was a long silence during which Méndez considered explaining why he had thrown the knife away but somehow he could not bring himself to say the words—it would take too many.

*"Adiós,"* the Snake finally said, for all time.

He should have said something, should have explained, he tells himself now, years later, particularly because he was right in doing what he did and the Snake was wrong in thinking of what he had done as a betrayal. Were he to explain, he would lay claim to his greater sense of humanity, to his feeling of community with all mankind, how both Teague and Gutiérrez were more worthy than the roles they were given at that moment to play. They were two young men playing roles at once too large and not large enough for them to play, roles which required that they do something which neither could really do, something which should not be done in the first place, or at least not done to another human.

He remembers certain sounds quite vividly—a kind of *shoo* when Jesse struck Billy across the nose, like the cry of pain given off by a small child on accidentally burning his finger on the stove. Or Jesse gasping for breath like an asthmatic child, his wind gulped in swallows forced between clenched teeth, like a boy exercising manly bravery while the doctor probed a broken arm for bone fragments—this while Billy enclosed his waist with a scissor-lock. That was why he threw away the knife, that was why he lied about having it when the other asked him for it—it was no betrayal, he thinks, it was an act of compassion for both of them: better only one be wounded than two. He simply wouldn't allow them to cut each other up, and he should have parted them before Billy's bicycle chain caught Jesse on the side of his head. He should have stepped in with an appeal not to reason or mercy or rationality or to legal consequences, but with an appeal to strike at the real roots of their hatred and alienation, exhorting them to turn to unite as *carnales*, brothers against the system. How could he have said it so they would understand it? Then again, if they were united as brothers, how could there be a system?

A flicker of light in the north engages his attention. When would Manuelo come? What is he doing? What is he up to? What does he want? Sadly enough, Méndez thinks, there's not a lot he can do for Manuelo short of giving him more cash and wishing him luck.

He feels a strong impulse to return inside out of the night air; he rises from his squat by the fence, stretches his legs to ease his cramped thighs, and hobbles toward his cottage. Overhead the sky hangs like a dark, rag-tag patchwork quilt of cloud and star. The humpbacked moon appears by fits as the low-slung clouds pass beneath it. As he walks toward the house he feels against his cheek the sting of sand lifted and pitched by the chilly, fitful breeze which gusts up, erratic harbinger of the new season.

"Did he come?" Juanita asks when he enters the kitchen.

"No."

He sits at the kitchen table, watching her as she finishes the dishes, her elbows revolving slowly. In a moment, she shakes the suds from her hands and retrieves a bottle of beer from the refrigerator.

"Thanks."

*"De nada."*

"What do you suppose he'll want?" she asks after a silence.

"I don't know, Juanita." He scans the headlines of a newspaper lying on the table: MAN, SON, DIE IN FIRE. So shall we all. LBJ WARNS REDS. TWO DIE IN TRUCK-TRAIN CRASH.

"You don't have any idea?"

"I just said I don't know, Juanita. Your guess is as good as mine—money, luck, good counsel—who knows?"

"I guess you have to help him, don't you?"

WIFE SHOOTS HUBBY IN SPAT. Light humor. Get him? Yeah, rightna spat. Ouch. Knows the man didn't die because he's a *hubby* in a *spat*. No need to read, Snead. Very familiar with that scene. WAR DEAD TOTALS LIGHT. Nice to know. Make up an all-time newspaper, a Superpaper, all headlines. TEN SMASH RED DEAD KILL MASH CRASH SLAIN KNIFE MAIM SHOOT BUTCHER DIE MURDER HACK RACK AND WHACK.

"I said I guess you have to help him, don't you?"

He looks up.

"Christ, Juanita, that's a weird question. Of course."

"No matter what he asks for?" She has turned to look at him, but his head dips down again to the paper. Unfinished thought about it. *A newspaper is nothing more than a bible of cops and robbers, complete with text and mythology.* A progress report on who's ahead in the game.

"No matter what he wants?"

He looks up. "Yes, I guess so." He gazes at her, helplessly.

"Oh, Raphael—" she whispers and turns back toward the dishpan in the sink.

"Oh, Raphael, what?" His voice grows tense, strained, daring her to finish her thought openly.

"Nothing."

"What do you mean, 'Nothing'? What were you going to say?"

She looks back over her shoulder at him.

"Can you listen for a moment?"

"Can I listen—"

"I mean without going into a rage. Can you face an idea squarely and look at it without rejecting it before you look at it?"

"That's a loaded question."

"I want you to consider something." She half-turns at the sink. "I'm serious, Raphael, I've never been so serious about anything. It's important for us, for all of *us* for you to consider something before you make a decision that affects all of us."

"All right." He folds his arms across his chest and leans back against the kitchen wall.

"No," she says, turning to face him. "You're not going to consider it, I can tell by looking at you. You're sitting there now just pretending as though you're going to consider what I'm about to say but you secretly think there's no real *need* to consider it, that it will turn out to be *beneath* your consideration."

"Jesus, Juanita, how can I win?"

"Oh Raphael—" Tears of exasperation well in her eyes. "There's no *contest.* Why does every moment of life have to be a struggle for you?"

"I don't know. You tell me."

She begins sobbing, quietly, but does not bury her face in her hands; she clenches her teeth, crying like a small boy, with anger.

"I can't go on like this, Raphael."

"Like *what?*"

"Fighting with you every moment of the day. You're impenetrable. Your walls are constant. Everyone is your enemy—I tell you I'm not built to take it."

"How have you stood it all these years?"

"It's only been this bad for the past year or so."

"Oh." His brow furrows.

"And it's been especially bad since Lemuel died."

"I guess," he conceded after a moment.

"I know that a lot of it is worry about what to do, where to go, who to be. . . ."

"Yes."

"But if you'd let me help you worry then maybe these walls wouldn't go up, if you'd let me help make decisions then whatever struggle was there would be in the open and not always subterranean."

He feels tired. The truth of what she says is evident. "Yes," he sighs. "You're right."

They remain silent for a few moments while she turns back to the dishes and listlessly dabs a plate with a dishrag.

"Okay," he ventures, calmly, after a moment. "What did you want me to consider?"

_272_

Juanita remains silent as if gathering her words together one by one.

"I want to know first of all why you feel you have no choice in helping Manuelo." Her back remains to him.

"No choice?"

"Yes, you don't seem to think of helping him as a matter of something you can decide."

"Yes, I guess so."

"So why?" Her voice remains soft, muted, gently persuasive.

"I don't know why," he answers after a moment of deliberation. "It didn't occur to me to ask."

"Well, would you agree that it *is* something which could be chosen from among other alternatives?"

"Yes."

"Couldn't it be possible to choose not to do it?"

"Sure, but how could you turn . . ."

"You're not considering again. Look, I'm not asking you to not help Manuelo. I'm only asking you to consider all the alternatives."

"You sound as though you have good reasons for not helping him."

She pauses to dry her hands on her apron, then opens the cupboard and retrieves a coffee mug which she fills from the pot on the stove then seats herself at the table across from him.

"I think so," she offers.

"And what are they?"

She falters, as though she hadn't been quite prepared to reveal her reasons, then plunges ahead, gesturing with her hands in vivid animation as she talks as if to forestall disagreement by sheer force of earnest intent. "I know what you'll say, but have you ever asked yourself what did Manuelo ever do for you? I don't mean that he *owed* you anything, I just mean he never went out of his way to do anything for you, so I don't see why you should worry about whether you owe him something or not."

"Two things," Méndez leaps in, "the first is that—"

"Oh Raphael!" she wails. "You're not even considering what I'm saying."

"Yes I am."

"No, you immediately jumped in to fight the idea in your head."

"Well—"

"Now, tell me truthfully. Did Manuelo ever do anything for you?"

He thinks a moment. "No, I guess not. But there's no reason why he should have—I've always been the one whose position was secure. He never had enough for his own family and himself, much less for me—why should he have worried about me? I didn't need his worry."

"I don't think we worry about people or help them because they need it—we do it because they deserve it."

"How do they *deserve* it?"

She dismisses his question with a wave of her hand, the ring on her finger flashing in the light. "We're not talking about the guiding principles of welfare programs and things, we're talking about you and Manuelo. I want you to consider something else, okay? Forget about whether or not Manuelo deserves your help, which he doesn't, and whether or not he ever did anything for you, which he didn't."

"God, Juanita, those are really cheap devices."

"Maybe, but it's the truth, isn't it? Something else —if Manuelo is in trouble with the law, and it sounds like he is, what good will it do *him* for you to help him?

Anything you might do to help him get away from the law might be bad for him in the long run. The best you might do is to talk him into turning himself in."

Méndez shudders. "I don't even like to hear you talk like this, Juanita. It doesn't sound like someone *I* married."

"Raphael," she hisses, "I'm *me*, I'm not you or even an extension of you and some day you're going to see that."

"I think I'm seeing it now. You mean you'd actually try to persuade me to turn him in?"

"Did I say that?"

"You said—"

"I said talk him into turning himself in."

"I mean you'd do that?"

"I'm not trying to talk you into anything. I'm asking you to consider all the possibilities."

"And one of them is talking Manuelo into betraying himself?"

"You should quit thinking of yourself and your precious integrity and think about Manuelo, if you really want to help him. How much better off will he be if he's killed by a posse or if he has to spend all his waking hours avoiding being caught? How well can he provide for his family then?"

"That's true," Méndez agrees sourly.

"Can you see how refusing to help him might be best for *him?*"

"Refusing to *help?*"

"In his terms. Refusing to aid and abet. But you'd really be helping by keeping him alive and well."

"I just don't like the idea."

"I know," Juanita answers. "But it deserves consideration. There's also something else to think of."

"What's that?"

Juanita smiles weakly. "You know, the trouble with telling you anything is that I already know what you'll think and you know I know it. I'm about to say that you could also consider us, the family, and what harm it might do us, all three of us, for you to help Manuelo."

"Why even bother to bring it up if you know my objections?"

"Because I don't think they're good enough. Look, I don't mind the idea of your doing something to jeopardize our security—my God, naturally I'm proud of you if you live according to what you think is right and to hell with the consequences. I can find jobs. And I agree with you that it's not just your duty as a husband and father to stock the larder; I know you feel a more meaningful responsibility of living up to your convictions for us," she rushes onward, more quickly now. "But I'm also selfish enough that I don't want to live without you, especially if it's because what you did had no effect and only turned out to be the wrong thing to do. I don't want to live alone while you're in jail for no good reason, especially when—"

"Especially when what?"

"Oh Raphael," she sighs. "Things have been going pretty well, haven't they? And now it looks like for the first time that we're moving ahead. I don't want to throw all that away on impulse. If you want to sacrifice it for good reason, that's understandable, even admirable, but to do it as a reflex—I'd find it hard to live with that."

"Is that a threat?"

"Oh God no, of course not. Please try to understand what I'm saying, try to see my side of it without being so . . . afraid it will swallow you up."

"Okay."

"And there's something else I wish you'd think about."

He looks up at her, surprised. "You've been thinking about this for a while, haven't you?"

"Well, I know you've been worried about Manuelo even though you didn't say much about it. I could tell. I sensed you've felt guilty and that made me afraid that you'd feel obligated to do something out of guilt instead of a better reason—because Manuelo either needed or deserved your help."

"True. I'm not sure guilt's not a good reason and I'm not sure my guilt isn't based on something real."

"Look, I know you're a have and he's always been a have-not—"

"So have most of our people, Juanita," he puts in heatedly. "And where we are damn sure isn't because we pulled ourselves up by our bootstraps. Chance, pure chance. Circumstance and luck."

"Should you feel guilty about that?"

"Shouldn't you try to equalize what chance made unequal?"

"Yes, but what if in trying to do that you make two have-nots?"

"I can't always act according to the outcome or I'd never do anything for fear the worst would come true."

"Yes, but to ignore the probable outcome would be stupid."

They lapse into silence for a moment, Méndez cupping his chin and jaw in his left palm, the index finger of his right hand blazing vague trails in the salt scattered on the table top. Juanita sips her coffee.

"All right," Méndez says after a moment. "What else was it you wanted me to consider?"

"The co-op."

"The co-op? How'd you know about that? Did I mention that to you?"

"No, I read it in one of your journals."

"What are you doing snooping in my journals?" he fumes.

"For you everything is private, Raphael. If I didn't snoop into your journals I'd never know what was on your mind. You don't invite us to participate in your fantasies much."

"This is really your night to kick me around, isn't it?"

"I'm not trying to do that. I'm only asking you to consider the co-op."

"What about it?"

"It's a good idea if you're serious about it. It might work. But so much of it depends on getting the land, on being free to put the plan into effect, on getting money, on being able to borrow money, and I guess I don't have to tell *you* that depends a lot on what other people think of you."

"Of course I've thought of that."

"It's cruel."

"How's that?"

"Well, that to help people like Manuelo and ourselves we may have to sacrifice him."

Méndez shakes his head, sadly. "I don't like that, Juanita."

She shrugs. "Those questions are always hard. Nobody ever said it was going to be easy, and if you wait for the perfect conditions you might as well forget about ever making anything real."

"That's what I like about you, Juanita—you're so *practical.*"

She bridles, rises from the table, and sets her empty mug on the drainboard. "You have no right to decide as though what you decided had nothing to do with me or Jimmy," she declares, her voice quivering. She turns her face away from him then vanishes from the room.

*The co-op,* he thinks. *El co-op* and *la raza.* Oh God, what to do—where did his loyalties lie? What were his responsibilities? Maybe what Juanita said was true—that in the end his responsibilities lay with all the Manuelos and not with one. The commune was the only answer there, the only way all of them—or many of them—would ever be safe and free, to band together and use the system to defeat the system. No more hassles after welfare checks and arguing with unemployment people and worrying about whether there's food in the cupboard—the pasture below the corral could hold a good-sized produce garden from which they could eat and sell off what they couldn't. The women could work that while the men took care of the cattle and the fences and whatnot. Maybe an oil lease or two, since they were already on the land: they'd keep that and use the royalties for the education of their sons. Using their profits for sabotage, using the system to destroy the system.

Juanita appears in the doorway to the bedroom clad in her housecoat, her face anxious.

"Raphael, I think I hear somebody outside. Maybe it's Manuelo."

He nods, she returns to the bedroom; he rises, then goes out the front door. Outside, the moon is momentarily hidden behind the clouds; lights are still on at Houston's house. Méndez waits a moment listening to the wind rattle the long, dry pods of mesquite beans beyond the corral, while his eyes grow adjusted to the dimness. A pebble bounces off the wall of the house next to his shoulder. Thrown by someone standing or crouching under the willow a few yards east of the corral. Méndez walks toward the willow, squinting into the cave-like shadows beneath the drooping limbs of the tree; he parts the branches, stoops, and enters the shelter formed by the limbs.

*"Qué has hecho?"*

Manuelo laughs, wearily. *"Mucho. Mucho, hombre."*

*"So you said."*

A silence falls. Méndez looks through the shadows as if to discern the nature of Manuelo's mission on his face, but his features are lost in the shifting blotches of darkness which pass across his face as the light, fitful breeze eases the willow's branches to and fro like a dressmaker lifting the arms of a sleepy child.

*"You did the fire?"*

*"Yeah."*

*"You heard the explosion?"*

*"Yeah."*

They remain mute a long moment, then Méndez turns his gaze toward Houston's house.

*"Someone, they could have been hurt."*

Hunkering now with his back pressed against the trunk of the willow for support, Manuelo shifts his weight from his left foot to his right. Méndez hears the creak of bone, a popping in the other man's ankle as he stretches out his left leg.

*"Maybe. The fire was an accident."*

"An accident?" Méndez remains standing above the hunkering figure. He feels like an indignant schoolmaster interrogating an errant schoolboy.

"I had a cigarette," Manuelo explains wearily, as though it couldn't really matter. "I was waiting in the back room until I thought it was safe—" he shrugs.

"But you didn't try to put it out?"

Manuelo looks up, surprised, then frowns as though suddenly understanding the linking piece of evidence in some private puzzle.

*"No,"* he returns firmly. *"Why should I?"*

*"I don't know. Did you get anything?"*

*"This."*

*"How much is there?"*

*"I don't know. Not much. Maybe fifty dollars. Some checks."* Manuelo groans with disgust at his own misfortune, than spits.

*"Anybody see you?"*

*"Quién sabe?"*

Méndez waits a moment to ask what is foremost in his mind, not wanting to seem overly anxious. They both gaze off toward the main ranch house where Jane Houtston passes back and forth before the dining-room windows, carrying armloads of clothing. Is she doing the wash? Méndez wonders idly while he waits for Manuelo to speak. He wants to know what Manuelo expects of him, but he cannot, will not, ask—Manuelo must request it himself without any prompting. Juanita was right—he owes the other man nothing. Manuelo deserves to be considered, but Méndez is not obliged to offer before it is necessary.

*"Anyone know you're here?"*

*"Tienes miedo?"* Manuelo's question darts across the space between them, a compact, well-aimed missile.

*"No, of course not, hombre."*

*"That's good."* Manuelo pauses a moment, then, matter-of-factly: *"I have much fear."*

Silence. Méndez senses Manuelo hasn't finished telling him the details.

*"I got this too,"* Manuelo continues, extending into

the darkened space between them some angular object.

Méndez takes it—cold, heavy metal.

*"Is it loaded?"*

*"No. I didn't have time to get shells for it. You have any?"*

"I think so. Well, I'm not sure. I had some in my desk but it seems to me maybe, I don't know—I gave some away I can't remember to who—"

"Forget it, mahn, forget it."

"I said I didn't know," Méndez urges testily. "What caliber is it?"

"I don't know, mahn. Whatever caliber you doan't got."

"We'll check it. You might be better off without it, you thought of that?"

"You wouldn't say that if it was you."

"I might."

*"I'm not going to be like a dog that rolls over on its back when something gets after it. I don't want to be at their mercy. I'm tired of them, I'm tired."*

"They can always outgun you, but you can win in court, sometimes," Méndez offers gently.

Manuelo laughs. "Who are you kidding?"

"It was only a suggestion, mahn."

"You got any more?"

"About the gun?"

"No, about what I oughta do now."

Méndez shakes his head slowly, sadly. "No. I just don't know. What are the choices? You can run and take a chance of either getting away or getting shot, or turn yourself in. I don't know."

*"Chingao!"*

Silence.

"What'll you do?"

Manuelo chuckles, bitterly. "I thought maybe you could tell me where I could hide for a while."

Méndez looks away.

"That's why you came?"

"*Sí.*"

"Well, I don't know. It doesn't sound very . . . smart."

"You're the *smart* one, Méndez, *you* tell me what's *smart* to do!" Manuelo spits out the words.

"*Mira, hombre,*" Méndez continues patiently, struggling to erase the impression that he is protecting his own interests. "*They'll look for you here.*"

"*In your house? A man like you—el jefe?*" His sarcasm worms its way into Méndez's ears like an insect.

"My house? Jesus, mahn, that's the *worst* place."

"*Sure.*" Manuelo giggles maniacally. "*How about under this house of yours?*"

Méndez sees that Manuelo's bitterness is turning against him.

"*In the attic, in the closet, or beneath the sink,*" Manuelo continues, mirthlessly giggling. "*They trust el jefe. They would not search in his garbage can. Chingao!*"

Méndez gestures helplessly. "They don't trust me. If I thought it would be the right thing to do, I'd hide you, mahn, I would."

Faintly, they hear the telephone in Houston's house ring in long, insistent spurts of urgency. Manuelo rises.

"*Ya me voy,*" Manuelo says.

"No, wait."

"*Por qué?*"

"There must be something . . ."

"*As you have said, I can only run or give up.*"

"What about that?"

*"That is for you. For you."* Manuelo stands weighing the pistol in his hand. *"Here."* He extends it into the space between them. *"Take this, un recuerdo."* Before Méndez can object, Manuelo pushes the pistol into his gut and releases it. Swiftly, with a motion which Méndez hears but does not see, Manuelo is at the edge of the protective skirt formed by the restless willow branches, then he turns and Méndez can make out, barely, in the dim shadows, the whites of his eyes forming half-moons beneath his pupils, burning through the dark in a cold, quasi-fluorescent light. Then he vanishes, leaving Méndez standing beneath the willow with the empty pistol in his hand.

# Two

"I must be out of my head!" Bond complains as he tucks his shirt into his faded Levis. "Who's he think he is to get me up in the middle of the night to go off on a wild goose chase after some poor pepper-belly who got hisself in trouble with the sheriff. God-da-mity!"

Méndez hovers by the doorway, jockeying his weight from foot to foot as he crunches the dried discs of mud on the floor of the bunkhouse with the butt of his rifle. Bond's levity angers him.

"Why are you going, then?"

"Hellfire, I don't know!"

"I guess yours is not to reason why."

Bond flushes slightly then turns to the wash basin, cocks a spigot open then dashes a palmful of cold water on his face with his good hand. When he finishes, he dries his face in the crook of his right arm.

"What about you?" He eyes Méndez narrowly, his voice tinged with reproach. "I ain't smellin no roses on you."

"They think it's Manuelo."

Bond whistles soft surprise. "Manwello!"

"Yeah." Méndez wonders whether to reveal Manuelo's visit. "Somebody in town saw him running down an alley after the fire broke out, then a pickup was stolen three blocks away from the fire and they found it about an hour ago out on the road to town about a mile from here."

"Whew! And they had the gall to ast you to hunt down yore own cousin!"

Méndez feels his cheeks burn. "Houston doesn't know that."

Bond squints at him earnestly. "Raphael, maybe you'd best not go. . . ."

*Don't go!* Juanita's words. *Raphael, there's nothing you can do!* He had paced before the window watching as the sheriff's pickup and a car bearing the six deputies pulled into the yard behind the main house; he had to check an urge to run screaming at them like a furious child windmilling with his fists—why didn't they leave Manuelo alone? He thought of sabotaging the pickup while it sat behind the house—ripping out the ignition cables, letting the air out of the tires. But when Houston knocked to give him instructions on catching up with the posse, he had retreated to the bedroom and let Juanita answer the door.

"How could I not go?" He finally answers with a plaintive note of desperation. "I owe it to Manuelo."

Bond's sparse brows are knitted with sudden curiosity.

"There may be a way to save him. I . . ." Méndez

hesitates, the words not gathering to be spoken. "I don't know yet what's going to happen. I'm not sure of what to do, but I won't have a chance to help while I'm sitting here."

"But what're you gonna do?"

"I don't know, goddamnit!" He hasn't thought more than one step at a time, hoping that he could work his way from moment to moment and that events would speak their need to him. He swallows to calm himself. "What do you think?"

Bond turns away to button up his Levis. "Don't go," he says seriously, over his shoulder. "Manuelo, he's . . ." he stammers. "Well, he's lost."

"You don't know that!"

"No, I don't, that's right," Bond huffs, then hobbles about the room in search of his hat. "I don't know about him, but I do know what might happen to you." He snatches his hat off the top of his bureau and jams it carelessly onto his head. "Naw, you're right. Why in the hell am I going on this *in*sane goose chase? What do I give a damn if yew or a hunnerd other idiots kill each other?" Furiously, he yanks the door to his closet open and jerks his ragged, fleece-lined herder's coat off a nail. "I'm just an old man without a home and just this piddly-assed job that any moron could do between me and starvation." He slams the door shut with the toe of his boot. "Let's go. Let's get on with it!"

"Go get your rifle."

While Bond disappears to the tack room, Méndez scurries to the jeep, starts it, and guns the engine in huge, leaping bursts of acceleration. Overhead, teeming with the season's first, premature, snow, thick banks of cloud skim across the sky in ragged chunks like ice floes crumbling against a breaker's bow; for seconds at a time the moonlight glasses against the obsidian surface of the night beyond the clouds, striking into fleeting relief the stark topography of the countryside between the house and the ridges. As he waits for Bond, the crisp wind sends tiny darts of ice and sand into his cheek. A blizzard could be on them soon—they have to hurry!

"Let's go!" Bond clambers over the side panel and flaps his glove in Méndez's face. "Go on, goddammit!"

"Where's your rifle?" he yells across to Bond as the jeep bounces out of the yard and onto the road leading to the highway to town, heading for the ridges where Houston told them to meet the rest of the posse.

"It wasn't there."

"Where—"

"I reckon somebody took it," Bond breaks in, cupping his hand beside his mouth. The wind threatens to whisk the words away before they reach Méndez, but he hears them, even above the whining of the gearbox as the jeep moves through the deep patches of sand in the two-rut road. The headlights jiggle up and across, splashing the mesquite thickets to both sides of the road with light.

"You think one of the deputies . . ."

"Nope, I shore don't."

Méndez doesn't either. Good Christ! If Manuelo now had a weapon, it would double his chances of getting shot—the posse'd have no qualms about firing at an armed fugitive. Goddamn! Too many things can happen! What to do? The alternatives string themselves out before him like so many half-buried mines in a field over which he is stumbling forward too fast to control his motion: he can try to help Manuelo escape, or he might try to draw their fire on himself as a decoy so Manuelo might get away . . . away to where? For how long? To another posse where no one would be present to protect him?

His eyes shoot ahead to the ridges which lie shrouded in the ghostly light—what is going on up there? He knows so little about the situation. If only he could locate everyone, learn their plans . . . how can he plan anything without knowing what the sheriff is up to?

"Hear anything?"

Bond wags his head.

Will Bond help? He wishes he knew. If not, what? Possibilities crawl before his mind with tantalizing sluggishness as the jeep races across the corner of a pasture. He could stay with the posse, allow them to capture Manuelo without killing him, and hope that his own presence as a witness would check them. Or if they don't want to kill him, it will surely be better not to help him escape, it will be better to help them bring him in where he can be protected. To Manuelo the hunt must seem the final episode in a saga of relentless pursuit which sprang up with his own conception; two hours earlier a bottomless lethargy in his slack limbs had conveyed to Méndez the extent of Manuelo's fatalistic despair, and when they parted Manuelo seemed bent on driving events toward a suicidal point of no return. Méndez has to argue that good reasons speak a need to stay alive (what are they??), to fight through a trial. Lawyers. He jumps ahead. The co-op. Solicitations for a defense fund. Whoa! What to do *now?* He tries to control his bewilderment by reminding himself that he can't act until he has surveyed the situation— he can only hope he isn't too late. As the jeep rushes toward the ridges, he yearns desperately for the leisure of a few hours to write the alternatives down in his notebook, to pore over them slowly, lovingly.

A shot!

"Yew hear that?"

Méndez nods, startled. His hands, oozing greasy sweat inside his gloves, grip the wheel as tightly as they can; he contracts the muscles in his legs, then yanks the gearshift down into second and races the engine.

"Hang on!"

The jeep ploughs along the sandy road sliding and heaving like a boat in choppy water; Méndez fights the wheel to keep the jeep from yawing off into the pasture. They dash on in silence; Méndez's eyes dart to and fro within the circle of light formed by the headlights, while Bond keeps himself upright in his seat by gripping the windshield brace.

"Keep listening!"

Bond leans out to project his head beyond the windshield; he cocks his ear toward the ridges to catch any sound riding on the stiff wind, and Méndez lifts his eyes from the snaking ribbons of sand to peer up into the ridges which ascend before and above them like dark, giant humps of ore. But he sees no movement, no light. He shudders. What if he's too late? He can do nothing, then. Goddammit, why hadn't he helped Manuelo when he had a chance? Better yet, why had Manuelo been so stupid? If he needed money, why hadn't he asked for it? Why hadn't he worked harder to get Manuelo a job? The co-op, the co-op. . . . He veers to miss a large yucca standing by the road; its long spines arch out to brush his shoulder as they pass.

What to do? His mind butts up against the problem with the blunt stupidity of a wasp buzzing against a window pane. *Drive! Drive!*

"Hey!" Bond points ahead—on the ridge a light flickers once, then vanishes.

Méndez plunges the jeep down into a ditch then drives it up the bank on the other side; turning, downshifting, he maneuvers up the road leading to the top of the ridge where they spotted the light; a moment later they have mounted the side of the ridge and ride into a clearing where the sheriff's pickup sits poised like a large metallic scorpion, its whip antenna quivering in the wind.

Méndez stops the jeep behind the tailgate of the pickup, and just as he unclips the ignition wires, the door to the truck cracks open, the dome light flashes on then off as a man climbs out of the cab, slamming the door behind him.

"What's going on? Who shot?"

"Dang if I know." The man hurries toward the jeep with his hands shoved deep into his trouser pockets and his shoulders hunched inward like stubby wings into his chest to ward off the cold—he is wearing only a light jacket of gray khaki twill with the frayed collar tugged up around the nape of his neck.

"Not much telling," he drawls. "Ain't much knowing what them crazy goons is up to." He shivers, then ducks his head toward the ridges. "They probably all drunk, anyway." His eyes flick into Méndez's face, then quickly away with recognition. "They ain't caught that poor old Messkin, anyway. Not yet, they ain't, I don't think."

"How do you know? You hear the shot?"

"They supposed to call me." The man tosses his chin upward toward the pickup with an odd gesture like a nervous tic. He chortles abruptly; the charge of air balls into vapor as it pops from his lips. "I been getting

_291_

Lou-ease-ee-aner. Shuh-reeve-port," he exaggerates half in mockery, then stamps his feet. "Getting cold—oooo boy!" Méndez can smell liquor on his breath when he turns his head.

"The shot—" Méndez climbs out of the jeep, nodding to Bond as he does. "You don't know who fired it? Where are the others?" He reaches into the back of the jeep for his rifle.

"No, couldn't say."

Méndez checks an urge to bash the man's head in with the rifle butt. He tugs savagely at the buckle on the sling to give slack to the loop, but his gloves make the job difficult.

"You're not one of Jentil's regulars, are you?" he asks, much too impatiently.

"Naw, hell no! Not me! I was *in* jail last week. Hell, he come downtha *ho*tel and got me outa bed. I guess he figgered I owed it to him."

"You know what direction the shot came from?"

The man faces the dim skyline and lets his head move from left to right, hesitating at points as though to test each potential location. Standing hunched over, huffing at his own breath as it swirls in the cold air, he looks pale, cold. The lines in his face loop about in contours like furrows in a field—from a distance his face would look like a giant thumbprint.

He slips his right hand out of his pocket and gestures uncertainly.

"I'd say up yonder somewheres." He looks at Méndez helplessly. "Wish I could help you out on that, but I just can't. Could of come from anywhere." His features adapt for their own purposes an expression of concern. Méndez recognizes in the man the elusive, unruffled amiability of the drifter, that slippery charm

_292_

of a man who survives from day to day by gulling strangers.

His sling loosened, Méndez swings the rifle onto his right shoulder and looks over to Bond, who kneels at the rear of the jeep to retie his bootlaces, performing the task with the ritual complications his handicap demands. Méndez longs to rush over and yank the laces from his sluggish fingers.

"Where are the others?" he snaps to the third man, then tries to vent off his agitation by kicking at the tires as he waits for Bond.

The man uses his right hand again to pantomime a signpost. The motion is precise, as though to compensate for the vagueness of his previous gesture.

"Up yonder a ways; I'd say couple hunnerd yards. They supposed to be in a clearing about one-third the way up the ridge. They's supposed to be some others come from over at that other ranch."

"How many?" Méndez tries to check the panic in his voice.

"Three, four. Ain't sure."

"What are you supposed to do down here?"

"Listen to the radio."

"What for?"

The man laughs nervously. "I guess because I didn't want to go with them."

"How come?" Bond queries suddenly, leaning on his right foot to check the tautness of his bootlace.

"I done a lot of things, but I ain't *shot* at nobody yet and I ain't been shot *at.*" He cranes his head to check their reaction, then grins. "I aim to stay that way. Sheriff says they's a pistol in the glove box but I ain't looked yet."

"Let's *go,*" Méndez urges Bond.

"You want some whiskey?" the man calls as they stride away from the jeep, but Méndez ignores him.

Bond follows as Méndez winds upward along the rock-strewn incline, his legs lurching dangerously near the needlepointed spines of Spanish dagger clumped in jagged profusion. He hurries, feeling his heart thud in the cavity of his breast. He can still hope to do something only if Manuelo is still alive.

"What fired that shot?" he throws over his shoulder.

"Don't know," Bond's voice bobbles, half-swamped in the rushing stream of his breath. "Shotgun maybe."

His heart plummets—that's what he feared! He forces his rubbery thighs to pump faster against the hillside. He scrambles upward without pause for a few moments, letting his eyes dart ahead to pick out a route then flick up still farther to catch any light or movement. He keeps his ear windward but hears nothing; aching, his muscles tell him that he is nearing the point where he can no longer hesitate or stop without running the risk of feeling the ragged impulse of his energy fall like the last spurt of blood from the jugular of a butchered hog. *Climb!* Some chance still holds that he can help either by giving Manuelo the posse's location or by drawing their fire—he winces and his hands leak sweat—or if escape is out he can reach Manuelo and keep the posse from shooting him. As he ascends the ridge, the moon appears to chop the hill in half, leaving the upper portion to fall away in the shadows of the shifting cloudbank. Where *is* Manuelo, goddammit!

"I hope he doesn't try to fight!"

When Bond doesn't answer, Méndez halts to glance backward: Bond is lifting himself slowly from rock to rock to catch up. Silently Méndez fumes over the delay; his own muscles are weakening but strain to send him off again. Below him Bond is edging closer, but then he stops to prop himself against a boulder, eyes shut, mouth agape to scoop up wind. As if by reflex, images of wheelchairs and lap robes flit through Méndez's mind. The old man's face is wan as powdered leather in the moonlight, the skin around his eyes gathered and bunched like an iguana's.

Méndez grits his teeth.

"Hurry up! Let's go, man!"

"Hold up a minute," Bond pants as he draws up with Méndez. "What do yew have in mind, anyway?"

Méndez poises on the balls of his feet. "I don't know." He regrips the rifle with vexation then tosses his gaze up the hill to reconnoiter. "Try to save him somehow."

Bond hawks a wad of phlegm downwind.

"Yew planning to help him get away?"

Conversation seems pointless; Bond isn't going to be much help. An impulse beneath his consciousness like a dormant but awakening spirochete twirling slowly in his bloodstream whispers an urgent message: *Move, save Manuelo.* Yet he hovers in indecision, rocking on his feet as though by Bond's orders he is transfixed in suspension like a pendulum.

"What if I am?"

Bond eyes him quizzically. "Yew go on," he sighs, the words trailing from his mouth in a thin ribbon of vapor. "Yew do what yew need to do. I can't help with that." He gestures painfully with his white glove. "But yew sure it's right?"

"Right!" Bond too? As he stares at Bond in disbelief, a vision unfolds of Manuelo suffocating inside a giant bell jar while spectators watch with mute indifference from outside, deaf to his pleas. He has denied Manuelo once, but not again! Not again! he promises, his head reeling with the sensation of slinging the words about in his skull as if to dash them to submission against those interior walls. His mouth drops open to speak, but he voices no words. A gust whips the tips of Bond's coat collar and stings Méndez's face with bits of grit and ice.

"Later," he growls, then jerks the rifle up hard against his shoulder blade, leans into the hill for balance, and moves up the hillside, his legs trembling. The wind pushes at his back to help him upward, and when he straightens after climbing a few dozen yards to run along level ground, he feels behind him the great round force of the air propelling him along the ridge with intermittent bursts of power. In a moment he pauses, winded, his chest ballooning and bellowing, and the cold air shocks his windpipe—the temperature is still falling. Just as he is about to push off again, he spots off to his left flank a tiny flicker of light. He dashes toward it.

After a few anxious minutes of scrambling across the rough terrain toward a parapet of rock which he knows encircles a clearing, he catches glimpses through the wind-tear haze over his pupils of three men gathered around a tiny fire—as he draws closer he sees that one stands upright, rocking on the balls of his feet, his face lighted for a brief instant as he dips his head forward. Beside him a smaller figure bounces on his haunches like an angry monkey; for a moment Méndez fears he is hallucinating—the upright man holds the end of a chain clamped about the neck of the smaller, wiry figure—but then the little man weaves away, and Méndez sees that he is waving a rifle. He bounces again; the light passes across his tiny spade of a face, alighting on his pointed chin to shadow his cheeks before he prances away. The third, a burly hump like a bear in an overcoat, jounces and waddles on his hunkers, moving his hands incessantly above the flame which appears to be generated through a fissure in the earth; around it all three figures revolve in separate rhythms, their motions fixed but complementary as if they perform a stylized ceremonial dance in which each part is subject to a larger design.

When Méndez vaults the parapet, the wiry man yelps, then swings his rifle on him.

"Hold it!" Méndez throws up his hands; the man falters, lowers the muzzle of the rifle.

"Goddamn! You could get shot doing that! You'd best stick with us and not go wandering around by yourself." The voice, nervous and rattled, belongs to Maggard, the sheriff's regular deputy.

"Who fired the shot?" Méndez demands as he steps toward them, fuming silently in dismay at how quickly Maggard had slipped the umbrella of his authority over him.

"You oughta yell," grunts the burly man. His long coat trails on the ground about him, giving Méndez the odd impression that like some demon he has poked his head and torso out of an underground lair. "That othern's a Messkin, too." He spits a stream of tobacco off into the darkness.

"Who fired the shot?" Méndez struggles to strip his voice of anxiety.

"Hellfire if we don't get out of here he'll be in Juarez lapping up tequila in nothing flat!" the little man whines to Maggard. When his hands flash through the light Méndez sees that an extra finger grows between the man's little and annular fingers on both hands;

dumbly he automatically records the fact that each extra finger impales a ring, his right a gold band, his left an Indian torquoise. He thought for an instant that he was to receive an answer to his question, but no one seems to have heard it; like something from dream, the three are enclosed in a bubble on which he pounds furiously but silently with his fists.

"Anyone seen him?" he asks Maggard.

The deputy jerks the lapel of his coat back to reveal a walkie-talkie hanging from a loop around his shoulder.

"Sheriff said to stay here," he pronounces hotly as if he expected Méndez to deny it, and Méndez understands at once that he has come onto the men in mid-argument.

The little man leaps into the air, then stomps his feet in a tiny circle.

"Getting cold, goddammit! If he don't call back soon, I'm leaving, you hear?" He wags his head toward the burly man. "How about you, Lloyd?"

The other man slowly unwinds from his hunkers, uncoiling his long, heavy legs, pushing his height upward foot by foot until at last he towers a good head above the others. He too smells of liquor. His weapon has been lying hidden by the folds of his coat, so that now as he looms just across from Méndez, the flame from the sterno heater lighting on the dough-lump contours of his face then glinting momentarily in his eyes, he produces the shotgun like a conjurer and holds it in both hands across his waist. Méndez feels dizzy; he searches in the sky for a stationary rest for his gaze, but his vision is knocked a glancing blow by the bank of clouds scudding overhead; the moon breaks through for a moment, but when he tugs his eyes from the clouds to rivet on the ragged crescent for an anchor, the earth upheaves slowly beneath his feet. He squeezes his eyes shut.

"All right, Maggard!" the big man charges. "You sure that thing works?"

"Look, Lloyd," Maggard pleads. "He said not to call. Now an order's an order." Méndez watches them glare at each other for a moment, then Maggard sends his gaze sweeping up the ridge as if some arrival were imminent from that direction. Méndez feels his legs quiver to break away and run, hears the dull throb of his blood coaxing him onward toward some goal whose vagueness coupled with the intensity of the impulse frightens him: it is as though his cells are locked together in a conspiracy of resolute determination to thrust him forward and have wrested control of his gravity-center.

"An order's an order," Maggard repeats weakly.

"Long as we're sitting here, he's running!" the little man pipes in.

"Where are we going?" Méndez blurts out. "What are we supposed to do?"

Glumly, Maggard rocks back on his heels. "We stay here until he tells us; then we're supposed to fan out along the bottom of the ridge."

"Where's the sheriff?"

"Up near the top of the ridge."

"Shit!" The big man lays the barrel of the shotgun upon his shoulder. "I'm going now. That bastard's going to get away." He turns to the little man. "You coming?"

"Yeah, I guess." The little man sends an appeal in a glance to Maggard as if to disclaim responsibility. "If you ain't calling."

"Ain't nobody *paying* us," the big man offers in disgust.

Over the deputy's protests, the two men readjust their clothing preparatory to leaving; Méndez grows tense, gathering his energy while he anxiously hopes to slip away in the exodus.

"All right, I'll call," Maggard announces in defeat, when it becomes obvious that the other two are on the verge of stepping off.

But no sooner has he opened his coat than two sharp reports like whip-cracks shock their hearing.

"What?!" Maggard cries.

"Get on the talkie!" the big man orders.

While Maggard makes contact with the sheriff, Méndez endures a giant surge of panic which threatens to hurl him into the darkness. Is Manuelo alive?

"Took a shot at the sheriff—" Maggard gobbles out of one corner of his mouth. "Got him spotted!"

He has to reach the sheriff! Frantically Méndez watches Maggard's face twist into desperate, frustrated impotence to see the other two men begin to sidle away from the flame paired like some absurdly sinister version of Mutt and Jeff while he is locked helplessly to the radio; Maggard beckons wildly with his right hand to stop them, but they pretend not to see and when they break into a run toward the base of the ridge, Méndez strikes out, racing away from the clearing—in a few seconds he hears Maggard shouting at them all in explosive curses, but he doesn't look back.

He climbs steadily for several minutes before stopping to roll his ear into the wind and to peer into the shadows on the ascent above. His lungs burn with the cold air sucked into them; the right knee of his Levis has torn and when he turns windward a long cold finger of air slips through the rent and coils about his thigh. Though he has long lost any sensation in his fingertips, his palms throb rawly beneath his gloves. Gasping for breath he shakes off a marrow-sucking weariness by refusing to acknowledge it, listening instead to the chant of his blood arising in the absorbent tissue of his brain: *Go, go,* it urges repeatedly.

In the final instant of his second listening pause a single crack like slow lightning echoes off the ridge. He sees no flash; a blur of motion on the skyline becomes a man leaping wildly across an open space then vaulting over a mound of earth and rock into an erosion ravine some fifty yards to Méndez's left and a good hundred up the hill. Another volley pursues the first, splitting the air then rolling away as though to peel back the surface of the heavens above them. Keeping his eye on the lip of the ravine, Méndez rushes up the hill. He is aware of himself as a target for the gunman on his left flank; he zig-zags off to the right of the ravine, feeling his thighs tremble and his lungs ache as he pushes himself as fast as he can without losing his footing. In a moment he finds himself running along a narrow clearing which sticks to the side of the hill like a furrow. He follows it until it comes dead-end into the mound forming the opposite lip of the ravine which had swallowed the leaping figure. He drops down against the side of the rim and waits, listening: as far as he knows the man still holds his position in the gulley, but nothing comes except the wind brushing and crackling like fire through a clump of dry buffalo grass near his head. After a pause he rolls over on his stomach and inches his body forward to see over the lip of the ravine.

Houston lies prone against the opposite bank, his back to Méndez. The sheriff is on his knees, bent over while he holds a walkie-talkie to his ear. He gestures with his free hand while he talks and when the wind shunts off to the side for a moment, Méndez can hear the sheriff cursing loudly. Méndez waits in frozen silence, then draws his rifle alongside his body, slowly, carefully, and eases the muzzle over the lip until the forestock rests on the ground. He aims the muzzle toward them, bringing it to rest at a point on the small of the sheriff's back.

"Hey!" he yells when the wind falters briefly. "It's me, Méndez!"

Startled, both figures whirl, the sheriff flings the radio down and claws frantically for the bolt on his rifle, but then Houston grabs the crook of his elbow. Méndez sees Houston's mouth moving, but he can't distinguish the words. He guesses Houston was explaining who he is, that he is . . . part of the team. He winces to imagine the other man's words. *Tío Taco!*

Houston is calling through cupped hands for him to join them. *Don't be too sure, cabrón!* He plunges down the bank of the ravine, feeling the raw, cold earth scrape against his hip. He hears a shot and a long, curving whine like a ricochet, and he sees with shock and horror that the sheriff still kneels with his rifle pointed at him as his body tumbles down the bank with an awesome inevitability toward the muzzle of the rifle.

But when his body comes to rest at the bottom of the ravine, he hears two more shots buzz overhead; he looks at the sheriff, who returns to walkie-talkie, cursing and waving his hand. Who shot?

Méndez crawls over to their position, trembling with fright and relief.

"Who shot?" he asks. "He still alive?"

"We're pinned down here, Harley," the sheriff is

saying. "If yew got your people spread out on top start them moving in." While he speaks his eyes turn like dull marbles into Méndez's face; a cataloguing process computes Méndez's identity in his brain, then his pupils shimmer minutely with recognition.

"I almost shot you, Méndez," he announces tightly, while he waits for a transmission. His voice quivers slightly, revealing his fright.

"Who shot? Is he dead yet?"

"He's out *there*," Houston says, peering out over the bony moonscape to keep watch.

"*Yew* got an education. Yew figger it out—that ain't no boogie man shooting at us."

"Where—" Méndez tries to ask, but the sheriff cuts him short with a gesture; they fall silent, the sheriff straining to hear the transmission he is receiving. Blood pounds in Méndez's veins, but now that he has come to a stop he has begun to shiver from the cold. Had he been shot at? For the first time the possibility that he could be killed creeps into his consciousness but he waves it away. Move out before you're used up! he commands himself. Get to Manuelo! Time is running short and he has no plan. The sheriff is like a turn-buckle on the loose ends of the dragnet—he speaks and the ends begin to gather toward the center to trap Manuelo.

A flurry of gunfire clatters abruptly up the hill from the base of the ridge.

"Maggard!" the sheriff yells into the mouthpiece. "Who fired! I told you to not let those people fire until I—" he cuts off to listen, fuming. "All right, now, you listen up," he orders, his voice shaking with frustration. "I'm sending Houston and his foreman down to link up between here and there."

Méndez panics, seeing that the sheriff is about to set a plan into motion which includes him. He tries to think but his brain seems ajar in its casing.

"Who shot?" he asks when the sheriff flicks the switch to the radio with a curse.

"We got yew *now,*" he spits vehemently, squinting out over the lip of the ravine. "I'll teach yore greasy ass to shoot at *me!*"

"Listen, what's the point of getting somebody killed?" Méndez feels the words rush out of his mouth like the reflex spasm of vomit. "I *know* him," he pleads. "He'll try to kill us all." He watches the sheriff eye him with suspicion; he is just on the verge of admitting kinship with Manuelo, when Houston breaks in.

"Yes, good Christ Almighty, Jentil—let's try to avoid that if we can—" Méndez sees that Houston's bored-but-bemused façade had vanished, leaving some earnest stranger.

"You know him?" the sheriff asked Méndez.

"Let me try to talk him into giving up." Time, he thinks. Just a little time. "If you could hold them off—" he nods toward the radio.

"You can trust him," Houston says.

Méndez rejoices to see the sheriff's features slip line by line into a gradual easing of hostility toward the idea and, finally, acceptance. They leave him no choice—he can't refuse without admitting he has done less than he could have to protect life. He sits a moment in silence. Suddenly he twists with abrupt animation from where he kneels and looks down the length of the ravine.

"Maggard's sending that old one-armed fella up this way—yew git on down yonder—" he points down the bottom of the gulley. "Leave about fifty yards between you and him. Try to stay where you can see me and I'll

_304_

give you the sign of when to tighten up." He falls close-lipped: he has no more instructions. Houston grabs his rifle, then climbs down into the bottom of the ravine and moves away. The sheriff studies his back until he is out of sight as though he doesn't quite trust him, then he slowly rotates his large head back toward Méndez to appraise him with glittering eyes.

"Git!" he hisses from between clenched teeth: his words are like an explosion blowing Méndez out of the ravine.

He has run as far as his lungs will allow without rest: he falls down the bank of an eroded gully which scars the ridge and collapses at its base, flinging himself down on his back; his internal gyroscope drives onward, spinning, tugging him up: *Run! Run!* Wind-whipped clouds roll by the mouth of the gully in long chains of dark gray balls like boats ripped loose from their moorings in a hurricane. To the east a configuration of cloud serrates the moon, giving the lighted quarter with its jagged edge the appearance of something torn from the whole, some part remaining after an explosion. He hears the wind begin to howl in long, hollow moans which rise and fall in orchestrated passages of sound and stillness; the cold needles into his clothes, invades his boots, numbing all but his insteps and heels.

Manuelo must be cold? Does he have a jacket?

*Go! Run!* his mind whips at his sagging body; he still feels the pull of the gyroscope inside his head.

*Run! Uncoil your legs and run!*

He leans up on one elbow—

*Faster!*

The wind tunnels down the gulley and blows against the back of his head; his vision of the clouds swims in a murky wash of vertigo: he squeezes his eyes shut a moment. *How good . . .*

*Run! You've got to run!*

But instead of rising he remains to rest a moment. Absurdly, a memory is unveiled. Manuelo swam in a stock tank in the dead of winter. The sun shone, the air was still, they broke the thin ice with sticks, then Manuelo crept in on a dare and emerged a moment later—the wind started up and seemed to sweep the sunlight away with it and his cheeks jittered and his lips turned gray-blue as the wind scraped across his wet skin which iced into the color and texture of a plucked fowl—

*Run! Save him!* He labors to his feet, forcing his legs to pump at kneebends beneath him to beat off the cold.

His arms and legs are impelled by a force he neither understands nor questions, a force like a great horse on which he is mounted, tied to the saddle, thrust through time. Rushing, wrenched, the motion dizzying, churning in a ball of nausea at the pit of his stomach, he tries to keep his footing on the side of the ridge, working to keep upright, in control, with gravity pulling forward and downward at its handle in the dead center of his body he is driven headlong downhill; long bars of snow in streaks of white outstrip him, flying by on the wind; he slips, popping his bones, then tumbles into a yucca and feels the prick of its limber spines, the stalk jutting like a revelation into his vision, a cobra jarred awake, then he pushes away with his palms and leaves the plant waving, its spines beating about in the wind like the tentacles of a creature anchored angry and helpless on the murky bottom of some night-pressed ocean.

Where is he?

The gibbous moon casts a pale, eerie light on the side of the ridge, illuminating the tops of boulders and sharp shoulders of rock jutting outward from the flanks of the hill like the cropped wings of a monolithic, earth-fleshed bird. Nothing. The clumps of mesquite and Spanish dagger form angular shadows beneath the light. He scans the top of the craggy skyline, but sees no movement. He waits a moment, struggling to hold his focus while his head revolves, then suddenly, a hundred yards or so to his front, a figure, dim, almost a negative flash of shadow more than something defi-nite, skirts along the top of the ridge from left to right, then disappears, obscured by the brush and rock. Méndez hitches up the rifle tighter on his shoulder and charges back up the hill, keeping the point of disap-pearance in sight, the soles of his boots slipping on the loose surface, then catching.

After a moment, he slides down a ladder of loose rock and onto a wide ledge beneath an outcrop; the sudden absence of wind almost causes him to tip back-wards; he rights himself and crouches, panting and moaning to catch his breath. *Save Manuelo,* the voice inside him screams to be released, and in the subter-ranean recesses of that cavern from which the voice issues a thought creeps forth that he does not under-stand, and his exhausted brain phrases it in dream language: *Save him, he is a wall to break through*—the words ghostly and cryptic and insistent.

Is that him?

Yes. Manuelo's head perches motionless while he surveys the field of fire farther down the hill; Méndez behind squats in the darkened leeward side of the rock. *He must be cold!* The wind gusts down among the rocks and flutters the sleeves of Manuelo's shirt. Méndez thrusts his foot forward to ease a quickening cramp and his rifle clanks against the wall of rock behind him. The wind betrays him: down the hill Manuelo raises his rifle, wheels, and vanishes beneath a rounded hump of stone. *It's me, Méndez!* Did he yell? Into the tunnel of wind? He springs away from the shelter of the outcrop, steeling his muscles against the force of the wind as he is pitched down the incline. Flecks of ice bite his forehead as he drops in long jolts, his feet clawing at the rock. Yell! Grab him! Tie him up and get Bond to help—are they headed toward Bond? Yes, maybe. They can't kill him if he's trussed like a pig on a spit, not even the most bloodthirsty posse. Betrayal? He'll think so, but if he really understands . . . Lungs pumping in spastic upheaval, he grabs at a passing rock to check his motion like someone tossed about in a cyclone and watches helplessly as Manuelo lopes away yard by yard, and the voice in his brain rips him loose from the rock and throws him upright and slings him toward Manuelo, forcing his legs to seesaw violently: *Go go go. He has to save Manuelo, he has to save* . . . His brain reels from the obsession of the vow he cannot control: like a gothic version of that rut in the cerebral flesh reserved for jingles and nonsense phrases it repeats its urgent message—*Save him! Save him!* His legs churn beneath him with the desperation of a short-winded swimmer in an underwater tunnel; his shoulder slams into an arm of rock protruding outward from a ledge; he staggers, then lurches forward again, closing in on Manuelo who has slowed to ascend the flange of rock around a pocket eroded into the side of the ridge like a sinkhole. *Hurry! Hurry!* And like some piece of machinery whose mechanism has been jostled he feels something sliding slowly inside him, some revolution like the awesome turning of a great, heavy-sided weight gradually but inexorably

as a ship listing from water in her hold will finally turn
—gradually, but inexorably, inevitably, with all the cer-
tainty of gravity—into that point of upward balance to
hang there suspended while some movement is still in
progress in the inmost molecules, pushing outward,
still, downward, and at the center of the motion, this
force, his sonar speaks its sounding: *Save him! Save
him!* he hears echoing in the watery tunnels of his
mind: *Runrunrunrunrun!* the words at last flowing like
a great cacaphony into a single, elongated moan.

Manuelo disappears over the lip of the flange, emp-
ty-handed. Méndez is heaved after him, wildly; he runs
along a ledge and tumbles into a thicket of yucca,
banging his forehead on a rock, stunning him for seconds before he feels himself lifted and pitched forward;
he topples over the lip and without looking flies into
space as though throwing himself off a precipice into
the yawning, shadowy mouth of a pit whose bottom is
unknown.

Manuelo is crouching in the bottom of the pocket,
head flung back, lungs heaving; he is sobbing, his hands
pressed against his face like the cold-shocked petals of
a blossom.

"Oh mahn, mahn," he explodes. "I thought I was
dead, I thought you . . ." he breaks off to shudder
violently. "And my gun—"

"They'll kill you," Méndez chokes out between
gasps. "I should've helped, I should've."

"I thought I was so, so dead . . ."

"I've got to save you all. If you run, you can't make
it! Give up!"

"I doan't want to die, mahn, I doan't!" Manuelo's
head snaps from side to side as though his words are
palms slapped against his cheeks.

"You've got to, they'll kill you!" Méndez screams into the stiff wind.

"What?!" Manuelo wails. "Is there anyone down there in the truck they came in? We could—"

"No, you won't stand a chance running!" Méndez grabs Manuelo by the elbow and begins pulling insistently on his sleeve as though Manuelo's limbs are tied in some difficult knot too tight for his fingers to undo. "Give up with me—I've got to save you!"

Manuelo rises and whirls, jerking away. "But they'll kill me! Please, mahn, please, let's go down there, let's get the truck. I doan't want to die!"

"But they'll kill you!" Méndez chants maniacally. "It's your only chance!" he roars, staring vacantly at the interior of Manuelo's open jaws before they close. He feels the backwash of momentum from his flight across the ridge, as though he has just stepped off a merry-go-round. He reaches for Manuelo, stumbling forward while Manuelo falls back with each step, bewildered, not understanding. Méndez thinks he hears a shout: his vision loops wildly upward where the clouds scuttle dizzily above him and he seems to turn topsy-turvy, to be looking down into the murky gray waters of a river when his sight swoops upward; bolting forward, half-falling, he regains his grasp on Manuelo, who struggles weakly.

"It's the only way," Méndez bawls. "I can't let them kill you!"

"Help!" Manuelo cries. "Help me, mahn, please, I'm asking, I doan't want to die!"

Like a target in a shooting gallery. Bond pops up atop the pocket, calling down, dream-like, something Méndez doesn't understand. He is too busy operating a titanic construction crane, his consciousness watching in awe from the cab of the crane while it extends its long, long arms in huge sweeping spasms of abandonment, disobeying his orders in a sudden wild flurry of revolt, the giant hands on the ends of the arms arching out to take Manuelo by the shoulders as he edges backwards, slipping away from Méndez's grip. Dimly he is aware that Manuelo is crying softly while he struggles with exhaustion against his hold: *"They will not let me come in alive, don't you see?"* he pleads, his face an open wound of misery. "They won't let me come in alive, please mahn," he weeps as though surrendering to a fact as incontrovertible as tides and lunar phases.

"Hey!" Bond yells. He has leapt down from the lip of the depression and stands off a way from them uncertainly. "Yew need some help?"

Manuelo curses and flails to free himself but Méndez jockeys behind him to enclose him in his arms like a vise, hearing the low, steady thrum of the voice beneath his consciousness spring up to shout into the resonating chambers of his brain: *Go! Run! Run!* and while his arms squeeze Manuelo's chest, that great weight inside him which has rotated to top dead center, to the upward point of balance now begins its gathering down-swing, plummeting its way through his very being, something fallen from a cliff they cannot stop now: *Manuelo would not deny him Manuelo shall be saved even against his will* and an odd rage overtakes him as he feels the other man's body resisting in his holding arms so he shakes like a dog with its catch in its jaws, this while watching from deep, deep within the cave of his mountainous body while a voice like a hurricane roars *Save him save him!!* With the insistent blindness of a prizefighter whipped into the ropes he locks his ice-taut grip while Manuelo squirms and twists, cursing him until he grows angry at this stranger in his arms who would stop him from *saving Manuelo* and he squeezes as hard as he can but feels the icy shock of a piercing crack along the top of his instep as the other man stamps on it with his heel; he staggers backward and Manuelo breaks free to claw desperately at the rifle still slung over Méndez's shoulder but Mendez is spurred by a hot surge of anger *Manuelo has no right to rob him of this chance!!* and he wrenches the rifle free then swings it around and jabs it into his face. They freeze; Méndez feels the wind rock him from side to side.

"*Cabrón!*" Manuelo spits, crying openly.

"You'll see!" he wails in return. "It's the only way!"

"Raphael—yew ain't gonna shoot him to keep him from being shot, are you?" Bond speaks as though to a child who has crawled onto a ledge.

"He can't deny me!" Méndez screeches. "We've got to save them—think of the co-op! If he runs, they'll kill him—GO GET THE SHERIFF!" he bellows; his gaze cuts over to engage Bond who hovers by bobbing and weaving in uncertainty, then Méndez hears a frantic clatter and when he looks back, Manuelo has just started to break away. *Save him save him save him!!* the voice hammers against his eardrums and he watches with horror as his giant arms crane madly up to raise and aim the rifle like eerie skeletal specters jolting in the moonlight.

"Raphael!" Bond screams.

Méndez yanks the trigger.

# _____Three_____

*How big's yore ordinary iceberg, anyway?*

Like a magician Bond conjures the question before
getting out of the pickup to go to the barn; into the
confused jumble of images already overcrowding Méndez's aching memory comes the picture of an iceberg
just as it had appeared in the encyclopedia at his ele-
mentary school: the color representation showing a line
of ice-green water below the surface of which the eight-
ninths of the iceberg came gradually to a point again,
just as the part above the water peaked, so that except
for the difference in sizes, the peak atop the water and
the point beneath it could have been mirror images of
each other. The point below was like the head of a great
rock-hammer poised above the ocean floor. *This could
have been the one which sank the Titanic*, the children
thought.

Bond is returning across the field. The toes of his boots send tiny sprays of drifted snow into the air. On the ground, the snow is thin and wind-whipped with spots of crust where it has thawed then refrozen. It is hardly visible from the road except where it shoulders up against clumps of buffalo grass like so many white-caps raised by a breeze across an open sea.

Bond is walking on the water. *Watch out for icebergs!* He leans against a stiff wind which flaps his pant cuffs and darts beneath his coat to belly out the back like a sail. His arm reaches up to weight his hat; the white glove flutters in the wind. Méndez, watching him approach, is weary of him. *But you have no right to be weary of anyone!* How can he have forgotten already if even for a moment? His own memories are the embodiment of a scourge used daily. Each memory is a vignette of moral instruction, an *exemplum* which he studies with the avid dedication of a monk doing penance through a daily ritual. Temptation to lapse has been great lately. There have been periods of up to an hour when he has managed to forget that Manuelo is dead, especially during the past two days as Houston's requested two-week moratorium on decisions has come to an end and he has begun to face the task of going out into the world. He can no longer be Houston's foreman, of course. It is out of the question. But why? Juanita and Bond both wonder. Because he does not deserve it. It offers too much security; he has sinned and must be cast out of the garden. The ironies which they've uncovered are cosmic jokes to him, leaving a flat, copperish taste in his mouth: make Manuelo's death have meaning by making the co-op come true— if Houston wanted to sell today Méndez would have little trouble getting a loan. But not just now. He cannot allow himself to stay on the ranch any longer, despite their other argument: if he remained the foreman he could use part of his salary to take on the responsibility of Manuelo's children—

"Ahhh," he moans softly as though stricken with sudden stomach cramps. The thought of Manuelo's children brings rushing into his memory a vivid replay of the girl bursting into tears, then leaping from the bed and flinging the iron through the screen. He lifts his eyes, as though seeking relief from Bond's nearing figure. He rehearses what his eyes tell him: Bond approaches, glove hand pressed to his hat, in his other a special tool which he had gone into the barn for the express purpose of retrieving—a tool like a large pair of pliers which they will use to tattoo the barless "j" of the ranch's brand on the ears of the calves for purposes of identification. Tattoo: like a reflex his eyes dart to the juncture of his left thumb and index finger. His *pachuco's* cross! His stomach plummets in a surge of nausea; he holds his breath in check and it passes in a moment but in its ebbing, images of the iceberg sway then drift away, supplanted by superimposed images of a beetle and a grasshopper: *he is in the head of the beetle; the eyes of the beetle probe the darkness as he sits behind the controls, moving the great beetle-body across the earth on which darkness lies like a stain; the beetle is rushing, the grasshopper waits, feeding, its head bowing to suck the hopper oil, feeling the oiled flesh of its metallic joints.* For days this feeling persisted . . . he had gotten in and out of the pick-up dozens of times in those thirty hours, so that in his memories doors appear like signposts to direct him, inward, like the pickup's door: *frost on the chromed handle in the purple predawn light, the button sticking down in the bottom*

_315_

*of its shaft in the congealed grease, but then later the side of the door was warm as the flanks of a cow as he pressed against it to let a car ease by while he was parked on the street in Odessa. The door to the cantina was tract-housing veneer with a small window the shape of a narrow diamond; it closed with a hollow chunk like the preparatory beat of a drum. He drank to avoid suspicion. He harangued the bartender: don't do it to your own! Not to your own people!*

He grimaces in disgust. How could he possibly have said that?

*Then he returned to Costilla . . . the dark, tile-red wood on the screen door at Fat Man's, the blob of dirty cotton bobby-pinned to the screen . . . and there is Gómez's fat face behind it, his woozy features expressing shock, concern, words rumbled off his tongue: They're looking for you! So he bolted, thinking in his paranoia that "they" meant either a chicano vigilante committee or the sheriff and his bunch, but when he returned later in the afternoon Gómez told him "they" were Bond and Juanita and Jimmy, his son. They were worried—*

He didn't deserve their concern. In the coldest, most objective light he could recognize the truth of that. The act of killing Manuelo was like a stone dropped in water; each successive ripple was a sorrow borne by someone else because of it, flowing into infinity. . . .

*Here, sit down and drink some tea, mahn, Gómez said. Yes, he thought. How did Gómez fit into the conspiracy to ensnare him? Were they all lying about Juanita and Bond and Jimmy? No, Gómez said, but he ran anyway, looking for Jesse Snake Gutiérrez to placate him and the rest of his old palomilla, not knowing what could be said to them because at that time he didn't know for certain what he had done except that he was being chased by some unidentifiable phantom he could almost feel breathing down his neck. . . . He ran to the poolhall in the* barrio, *and when he leapt up the wooden steps, the broad brown surface of the door fell away suddenly, sliding away to the left as though stepping out of the way for him, and when he tumbled over the threshold Gutiérrez was bearing down on him from across the room, cursing and crying, his upraised arms gripping the thin end of a pool cue, bringing the trim, compact length of the slender club arcing precisely down toward the middle of his skull—*

And still he didn't know why! He knew something was wrong, but he was shocked to see the depth of misunderstanding. He was in a pincer between the sheriff and *la raza* and no matter where he turned he was reviled. . . .

How conveniently he forgot that he had killed Manuelo.

*Let me explain! he screamed in Spanish. Explain what, he didn't know, or how. He thought that if he just kept going around to people then sooner or later he'd get to the bottom of the problem, but his pursuers were hot on his heels. He dashed out of the poolhall. Gutiérrez chased him, but not for long—he finally stopped and slung the cue at his back and Méndez was dimly aware of it lighting in the street just behind him, but he didn't look back. Later it was night and he was thinking: I'll go to Manuelo's—they'll never think to find me there because it's so obvious. But he couldn't have said why. He stayed outside in the street . . . stayed outside in the street. . . .*

It's very hard to force himself to remember this. His insides squirm: God! How could he have been so unaware of himself? How could he not have known what he had done? To kill Manuelo was one crime—to hide the fact from himself was still another. Icebergs! We are all icebergs! Or I am. Ripples of sorrow in the water. . . . So you stayed in the street, then what suffering did your innocence bring to bear?

*From under the shadows of the diseased elms he looked at the window on Manuelo's house, one lidded by a tattered and browning shade which glowed the color and translucency of moth wings; he couldn't know from the street the depth of their grief and lamentation, their grief, their—*

Yes? Don't hide behind abstractions. *You must name their grief, name their lamentation.* But he is slow to do so. Bond has almost reached the pickup. Gratefully, Méndez can put the memory away for the moment; it is like a great sore on his psyche which he cannot keep from rubbing even though he knows that will increase the itching.

Bond is back inside the truck now. He slams the door.

"Got it?"

Bond waves the tool as though brandishing it, then drops it on the seat between them.

"Another thing is," Bond begins thoughtfully as Méndez steers the pickup away from the far side of the field behind the corral and heads toward the mesa. "An iceberg ain't like a log floating in a river, that's for sure." Méndez is only half conscious of the strange undertones which Bond's stories have taken on during the past week, the half-mystical suggestions which arise mysteriously from the concrete objects within them with the tenuous but suggestive uncertainty of koans.

"A log floating in a river is a thing in the hands of

another thing which it isn't," he says, then turns to eye
Méndez. "If yew get my meaning. I mean that a log
ain't a river and a river ain't a log, but the log is taken
away by the river; the log is furreign to the river; that's
what I mean. If they be kin, they ain't close; they—"
he halts abruptly as if caught up in the motion of his
brain and is letting it spin itself out before he translates
the computations into understandable English. Kin:
the word is a contact point relaying Méndez down
another circuit of memory: *he knelt in the sandy street
outside Manuelo's house in the twilight; he tried to
choke back his tears. Inside the house . . . inside the
house were* los hijos de Manuelo, *their grief and suffering that he imagined from the street arousing his deepest
sorrow—they suffered, but he did not know why. Who
made them suffer? The twenty dollars was not enough
—he owed them much, much more. He rose and
stepped over the knee-high crumbling picket fence and
stole toward the window where the moth-winged shade
leaked ragged holes of light, like the radioactive radia-
tions of suffering from within pouring out the lighted
windows, uncheckable and unencompassable. At the
window he got down on his knees and placed his hands
in supplication upon the sill; he looked through a hole
the size of a grapefruit, the light blinding him momentarily, then as his eyes adjusted he saw it was the same
room where he had found Manuelo supine on the bed
only now it was Candelaria—*
   "Yew take all the little tiny cells in that log and
they's water in them all right, they gotta have it. And
. . . and . . ." Bond stutters with excitement as though
unable to keep up with his thoughts. He stares ahead
through the windshield, and when Méndez retreats
from the memory he cannot tell if Bond knows he has

been talking to himself. "Add to that the river and all the rivers of the earth like the veins of the earth pumping the earth-blood along its courses—that river must have the log cells under it for support and the log cells aside it for the banks; then it's got to be pulllled down by gravitations else it will fly out, and so the river is to that log like the bank is to the river—ah Gawd!" he breaks off to shake his head in amazement, then turns to Méndez abruptly as though he had forgotten him. "But that ain't quite the same case with an iceberg—an iceberg is another story. Yew could think of an iceberg as a place, not a thing. A place in the water where it froze up. It *is* the water, it ain't other *than* the water. . . ." he pauses, adrift. They ride a moment in silence, Méndez steering the truck up the steep incline to the top of the mesa where they will wait for Carlos and another hand hired for the occasion to arrive in the jeep with Houston.

"If you light fire to a train of powder," Bond interjects, "and you can see the flash moving toward the other end—that flash is the powder burning. Well—" Bond is almost shouting now. Perplexed, Méndez rotates his head slightly to the right to cast a sidelong glance at Bond. "THE ICEBERG IS THE WATER FREEZING LIKE THE FLASH IS THE POWDER BURNING!" His eyes are bulging, straining with the concentration of trying to convey something to Méndez, but Méndez is left bewildered—Bond's odd mannerisms and inflection give his words a peculiar intonation, like jeremiads thundered forth in advocation of the most primary laws of matter and motion. A glint behind his eyes is not identifiable—its nature obscured.

"Aw Gawd," he breathes heavily, turning away from Méndez. Rivulets of sweat trickle down his sideburns.

"An iceberg," he whispers slowly, "is water moving through itself. . . ."

Méndez brings the pickup into a clearing atop the mesa, heading out so that they see below them in the basin the nodding heads of the pumping units, black eruptions on a field of broken white.

He needs no lessons in icebergs. The greater part unknown; the surface is but a marker for the progress of the gross below the water line, the portion which responds to currents: *bowed before the window with his hands in supplication on the windowsill. Candelaria was . . . face-down on the bed, her shoulder-blades heaving violently with her sobs. He felt a savage rush of indignation—who did this to this child? Who makes her suffer? Goddamn them! As he watched, the girl's grief began to cycle as her sobs broke into an open, tearful howling which she cut short to suck up huge gasps of air like a floundering swimmer, then return, shoulders quivering with her emptying lungs, the loose strands of damp hair plastering themselves against her flushed cheeks. He moved to the other window, feeling the light full upon his face. Pobrecita! She was alone. Where was everyone—had they left her like they had left him? If they had, he vowed—Yes? You vowed what? What words did you use? Vowed to, to, to . . . Pronounce it! Vowed to save her, he the Savior, the new Messiah come to lead his people out of the wilderness, glory be to him! Had they left her like they left him? He would save her—Oh yes! Your salvation comes!—He broke and stumbled through the yard and into the alley behind the house, each desperate striking of his feet against the frozen earth sending a sharp needlepoint of pain up his shins.* Pity him! Pity his pain! He's leaving something out. Why? Because, because, because. Why did he run? *He vowed to save her. Then he ran. . . .* No. Then she saw him. *No, wait. Not at once. There were still a few moments of sweet blissful innocence still left for him, a few moments of reveling in that fury of indignation swollen with his vows to save her, his heart pounding with the sweet clean compassion of pity for the weak and hatred for the wicked, the sweet compassion of kinship, the clean protective anger hurtling out like a concrete cantilever from the structure of that anger to shelter her.* But then she saw him. *Saw somebody.* How could it have been anyone else? *No, he thought for a moment that she was looking at someone else, thought that she thought that . . . because her head was half-turned toward the window as she lay supine on the bed, but her gaze was directed downward, but then she . . .*

She what?

*She—*

"Green and white like glass like ice . . ." Bond shouts into his right ear. "Like mirrors, son, mirrors . . ." When he gazes over at Bond, Bond's eyes look through his own, beyond him as though his own eyes were windows leading into a world which Bond was seeing. "Don't you see? Don't you see?" Was he asking or chanting? His voice was a lure; Méndez flogs himself back into his memory: *she saw someone, him, and she was startled at first to see a face in the window looking in at her, and her features passed through a sequence like a series of stills which he has enlarged and slowed in his brain, controlling the projector of his memory in order to freeze each nuance of that progression so that he'll be forced to study it: amazement . . . click! . . . fearful curiousity : . . click! . . . then as she tried to discern whose face she was seeing outside the window, through the screen, the shade, as she—as she saw WHO IT WAS! But still he didn't think so, thinking she thought he was someone else. He thought of rushing in to reassure her and as he watched her features knot into a grimace of fear he wanted to smash through the wire screen and plunge his hands through the glass like plunging them into water and rescue her from drowing in her suffering, wanting her to see it was no stranger outside, it was Méndez and she needn't be afraid, then the girl's features looked in recognition, then tumbled into a monstrous anger: she leapt from the bed, her mouth wrenched downward by her cry and she snatched at the iron from the board by the bed and flung it backhand through the glass and into the screen where it shot out at him then jolted short like an angry dog leaping at the end of his chain. She knew who he was! He killed Manuelo!*

Frantically he cranks the window down a good six inches, lets his head fall back against the seat, pressing the nape of his neck. He's afraid he will vomit. He squeezes his eyes shut, breathing the cold air which rushes in through the opening. When he opens his eyes again he feels beads of sweat icing on his forehead.

*He collapsed against the side of the house, his cheek scraping against the abrasive edges of curling paint. He lay crumpled beneath the window for how long he didn't know, until he had collected enough courage to rise and look into the window again. An accident! he was going to plead. An accident! He would pay . . . he would pay. He rose and peered into the window again. The room was empty, all life had fled from it; an ominous judgment descended upon him as he gazed in shock on the interior of the room—the lifelessness there was the di- ect result of his glance! And then he ran—*

"CIRCLE OF LIGHT IN THE WATER!" Bond is shouting. "Right there. It shined and shimmered like the halo a mist around the moon except it was right there under my feet so I hollered PRAISE GOD! And fell down on all fours into the water and stuck my head into that circle of light. I took a drink—yew see?" A sudden inflection of urgency makes Méndez look at Bond, whose exhausted face is writhing in an intense grimace. Bond holds his gaze a moment, then turns away, closing his eyes. "In a minute I got up," he continues after a pause, wearily. "I got up. There was mud on my palms and my knees." Méndez waits a moment in silence, feeling his own head swimming in a fever of dizziness. He makes a feeble effort to tie Bond's fragmented speech together in his mind but fails.

"The whole, the whole, think of the whole *thang,* the whole that yore only just a little bitty part of, but yore just like it is, just the same and whatever yew think about it is what yew have to think about yew. It's all got to fit together like a puzzle because if it don't—" Bond shudders. "Then yew and I are a part of nothing. Yew can't damn yoreself without damning all life, and if all life is damned then let's just get it over with—"

"Iceberg," Méndez whispers. *I'm like an iceberg!*

Bond slumps in the corner of the cab, eyes closed, arms locked around his trunk for warmth or solace or both. He does not seem to have heard Méndez's confession. "Yew can't damn yoreself without damning all life," he repeats slowly. "The way yew think about yew is the way yew got to think about everbody, and if yew do that, then . . . I mean, yore all a piece of this world, ain't yew? Yew hate yoreself and yew hate all of us, and one of us has to be right, or yore right or we're all right, see? I mean . . ." Fuming and stammering Bond drops off. "Suppose . . ." he says but even though his jaw works up and down, his lips do not part. He seems to be entangled in his thoughts.

"I . . ." Méndez begins but falters, feeling the need to speak well up inside him like a great yearning, but the words must be peeled away from his brain like skin from flesh. "I want to know. . . ." Dizzy, he stops to close his eyes. "If I really hate myself because I killed Manuelo—" he swallows then wets his lips. "Or if I don't feel anything at all."

"Yew ain't getting nowhere like that," Bond says after a moment. "Yew got to think of something bigger, don't yew see? Something bigger than yore own misery."

They fall silent. Words! Mendez thinks. I'm sick to death of words. Stories, platitudes, examples, jokes, lectures, advice—all those words are like so many thin-skinned balloons bursting instantly on the pins of reality. He wants to scream because the words mean nothing to him; Bond is only babbling into the void.

"I have to pee again," Bond announces unceremoniously with disgust. "As long as yew hate life so much, I wish it was yore body that was wearing out and not mine—"

Bond climbs down out of the cab and shuts the door behind him. He stands beside the truck with his back to the door, his head bowed.

If I could wear it out, I would, old man! *He ran out of Manuelo's yard with the image of the girl crying aflame in his head only to be consumed and replaced by an image of Manuelo kneeling in the bottom of the pocket of the ridge, sobbing with relief. God! God! He was sorry! sorry! sorry!—a chant arose in his head in cadence with his footfalls and the pain in his shins and continued on when he reached the pickup. He drove blindly, overcome by bizarre states of altering heights and weights and sizes, driving the beetle down the beetle-road toward the metal grasshopper. Strangely, he had cleaved in two—one part his hatred of himself, the other the punishing judge of that hatred, one part the offender, the other the prosecuter. When he reached the pumping unit, he uncoiled a length of garden hose which was in the bed of the pickup underneath an overturned wheelbarrow, jammed one end in the tailpipe and the other through the window of the cab, but when he got back in the cab, he could not bring himself to turn the engine on. His cowardice sickened him like a virulent fever.*

And now he knows that he had never really been in danger of killing himself. It was mock payment, a signed I.O.U. on a piece of scrap paper, a demonstration of guilt and remorse, a simulation. He wanted to show himself what he could do to pay. But did not do. Would not. And he knew that at bottom he did not believe in his guilt, could not feel it—

"Iceberg!" he blurts out again. He rubs the tattoo on his left hand, the faded blue cross. Almost compulsively he reaches down into the seat with his right hand and holds up the tool they will use to mark the cattle. The jaws, like the jaws of heavy pliers, are open. In the roof of the open mouth is a block from which protrude six needlepoints forming the barless "J" of the ranch's brand—when the jaws are closed these points penetrate the flesh of the cow's ear.

*Pendejo!* he curses, then quickly, before he can even consider what he is doing, he takes the heavy pliers in his right hand and jams the mouth over the flesh between his thumb and index finger, then rising up with legs stiffened against the floorboard of the pickup he squeezes the handles of the tattooing tool as hard as he can, the needle-projections tearing into the flesh and gristle of his hand. His mouth opens in agony but the pain is mute; he grinds the pliers into the meat, pulling and jerking to let the needles penetrate deeper and deeper; the pain makes him gasp for breath.

In a moment, when the flesh is numb, he lets the spring on the handle retract the jaws with their teeth. He looks at his hand. Over the old tattoo of the faded blue cross he has six bleeding perforations forming the brand of the ranch.

Tears come. He balls his left hand into a fist and jams it into his jacket pocket, where, after a moment, the blood runs greasy between his fingers. Down in the basin below the mesa, the pumping units churn relentlessly; the sky is awash with the smoke from burning slushpits.